JIM & RACHEL BRITTS

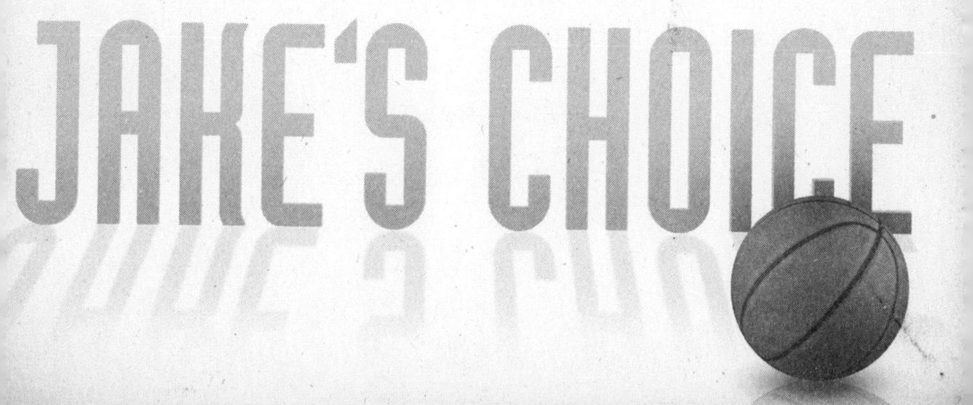

JIM & RACHEL BRITTS

JAKE'S CHOICE

Jake's Choice

Published by Outreach, Inc., in partnership with New Song Pictures.

Outreach, Inc., Vista, CA

ISBN: 978-1-9355-4115-8

Cover design: Tim Downs
Graphic design and layout: Alexia Wuerdeman
Editing: Marcia Ford and Toni Ridgaway

Printed in the United States of America

7:33pm | From: Amy | To: Jake
Just wanted to see if you made it safe to your dorm. Hugs and kisses

8:17pm | From: Amy | To: Jake
I can't wait to hear all about your new roommate. Love u <3

9:32pm | From: Amy | To: Jake
How did things go with your dad? Is he still there?

11:27pm | From: Amy | To: Jake
Are you alive?

1:01am | From: Amy | To: Jake
I've got an 8am class tomorrow please call. Very sleepy.

2:07am | From: Amy | To: Jake
Guess talking every night is NOT gonna happen zzzzzzzzzzzz

JAKE SCROLLED THROUGH AMY'S TEXTS as he finally stumbled into his dorm room around 3 a.m. Kentucky time… midnight Amy's time. How had he missed all these messages? And even worse, how had he forgotten to call her? Exhausted and irritated, he flopped onto his new bed without bothering to turn on the lights, cringing when he realized he had never covered the filthy mattress with clean sheets. At least he couldn't see the stains in the dark. Where had his first day of college gone?

Just ten hours earlier, Jake's stomach lurched under the seatbelt, his hands turning clammy on the steering wheel as he directed his truck into a parking space in front of Miller Hall—his new home. It wasn't the "Welcome to Kentucky" sign at the state border that had made the hairs on his arms stand at attention, nor the final merge onto Highway 64, nor even his first glimpse of the new downtown KFC Yum! Center. What finally set his nerves on edge were the few pockets of students scurrying along the icy sidewalks of the campus, knowing exactly where they were going and what they were doing...the classmates exchanging warm embraces as they hustled back into their routines...residents carrying only a duffel bag and maybe something they received for Christmas under their arm as they returned after the holiday break to their already-established dorm rooms.

Reality hit Jake like a too-firm chest pass: Ready or not, he was stepping into a world of peers who had already found their places and made their connections, and he was now the odd man out. The dorm floor initiations, fall fraternity pledges, and freshman orientations that started the bonding process for complete strangers to become lifelong friends were long over. There were no Resident Assistants waiting outside to help the new students like he'd seen in the movies—no banner across the dorm lobby welcoming Louisville's newest fresh meat. Those festivities had come and gone months earlier, while Jake had stayed behind on the other side of the country enduring a different sort of initiation: birthing classes. And he had nothing to show for those.

When Jake visited the university on a recruiting trip more than a year earlier, Coach had gone out of his way to make him feel like he would have friends awaiting his arrival. Today, there was no one ...except for his dad, who had immediately jumped out of the truck and gone to work loosening the bungee cords in the back to start the arduous unpacking process.

"You okay, bud?" Glen Taylor asked, snapping Jake out of his torrent of thoughts as he handed him a suitcase.

"Yeah, Dad," Jake grimaced. "I guess it's just starting to sink in." He exhaled a deep frosty breath that lingered in the frigid dusk air. He already missed the seventy-degree winter weather he'd been enjoying back home in San Diego. Wearing shoes other than flip-flops would be another thing he was going to have to get used to.

Glen passed Jake another piece of luggage, draped a stuffed duffel bag around his own neck, then hefted two boxes into his arms and headed toward the Miller Hall entrance. "Well, less thought, more action. I've got a plane to catch," he called back.

Jake slipped his computer bag over his shoulder and followed with the two suitcases his dad had already given him. *Why did I pack so much?* he groaned in his mind. His roommate had probably already filled the room with his own stuff and surely wouldn't want any of Jake's junk to intrude on his space. And how many trips were they going to have to make to unload everything? It was almost dark.

A blast of warm air struck Jake's face as his dad pried the Miller Hall door open while precariously balancing the boxes on his knee. Jake's stomach lurched again. While the frozen semi-ghost town outside had been daunting enough, the raucous gathering inside the heated lobby was overwhelming. Every eye turned to watch them struggle with their loads, but not a single person moved to help. Jake thought he could read amused ridicule and haughty scrutiny in those staring eyes, and he suddenly felt embarrassed about having his father with him. He stuck out like a whale in a bathtub. But what else could he do? *Pull yourself together, man!* he told himself as he tried to gather his thoughts.

Dozens of lively conversations competed with the background blare of classic rock. Looking for someone who might help him, Jake scanned the mix-and-match of red and black couches inhabited by a sprawling mix of guys and girls. Two brunettes caught his eye, and the one on the left wearing a black Louisville sweatshirt smiled at him. But before he could even respond with a head nod, she became absorbed again with the people around her.

Finally, Jake spotted a nondescript door in the corner with a sign labeled "Resident Assistant." But it was closed, as was the roll-up window next to it, and Jake figured that meant he was out of luck. Should he walk across the lobby to find out, or just pretend he knew what he was doing and head directly to his room? Since his dad was already headed toward the stairs, he chose the latter, trying to look as confident as he could. *Crap, I don't have a key,* he realized mid-stride. Unless his roommate just happened to be there, he was completely out of luck. But what were his other options? If nobody was going to reach out to the obvious newcomer, then he had to take matters into his own hands.

"Hey, do you know where room 317 is?" Jake heard his father's loud voice ask someone.

Jake looked up to see his father addressing at a couple deep in conversation on the bottom steps. Based on the death-look he received from the guy, you'd think Glen had just cursed them up and down.

"Ummm...why don't you try the third floor?" the guy replied, rolling his eyes and turning immediately back to the girl to make sure that this interruption would turn into nothing more.

Glen's face told Jake what he was really thinking, but fortunately he restrained himself. His bag, however, did not, and it "accidentally" banged the side of the jerk's head as Glen passed him.

"Watch where you put that!" the guy snapped.

Glen smiled back and gave him a little wink. "That's what she said," he responded, and kept right on trudging up the stairs.

Jake hurried by the guy, not waiting to see his response. "Dad," he scolded under his breath at the second-floor landing, "you're going to make me enemies before I even have a chance."

"Better an enemy than a friend who's a jerk, I've always said," Glen resounded not-so-quietly as the two rounded the final bend before the third floor. Upon arriving, Glen again rested the boxes on his knee and nudged open the door to let Jake enter the hallway.

If the lobby was intimidating, then the hall Jake stepped into was downright scary. There were college women everywhere. A couple girls outside of a nearby doorway sat painting their toenails, and the fumes of the polish singed Jake's nostrils. Hair dryers competed with music leaking out under different doors, but not enough to drown out the screeching of all the different female vocalists. *Is someone listening to Britney Spears?* Jake winced.

A girl wearing nothing but a towel nonchalantly walked by and smiled as if she wandered half-naked around guys all the time. Jake tried to divert his eyes like his youth pastor had taught him to do at the beach in California when the girls would pass by wearing those oh-so-distracting bikinis...but then another girl similarly dressed (or undressed!) walked out of the bathroom going the other direction. As he tried to find someplace safe to look, Jake caught his dad grinning and was immediately reminded that the two of them didn't quite share the same values anymore.

"Dad, I think we're in the wrong place." Jake moved quickly, backing into his dad until they were safe on the stairwell landing again and the door had clicked shut behind them.

Glen just chuckled. "Not a bad place to get stuck in, though, you gotta admit."

"Dad!"

"I'm just saying. You're in college now, son. You've got your whole life ahead of you. Loosen up a little and enjoy the scenery."

Of all the people Jake expected this kind of pressure from, his father was nowhere on the list. Pressure to do well in his classes and excel in basketball, sure. But pressure to loosen up? That was new in his father's repertoire. *He's changing more than I realized,* Jake figured, not sure that was a good thing. If his dad could cheat on his mom before, how would this new "looser" version of his father act now that they were separated? Jake didn't want to think about it. So instead, he moved toward the other side of the third-floor landing, where a door identical to the one they just fled from was waiting.

Jake looked at his dad and they both shrugged. How much worse could it be?

Upon opening this door, the sights, sounds, and smells that assaulted their senses assured them they were in the right place. Instead of half-naked girls, there were bare-chested men wandering the hall; instead of high-pitched female voices competing with the whirr of hair dryers, deep bass rhythms resonated off the walls; and instead of nail polish toxins wafting through the air, the distinct locker room aroma of sweaty socks greeted them. None of this was any more pleasant, but for Jake, at least it was more familiar, less threatening. He sighed a deep breath of relief as he scanned the doorways for room numbers.

"You must be the new guy," a burly voice echoed from behind, prompting Jake and his dad to spin around. The voice did not match the pale 6-foot-8 toothpick standing before them. His muscle-tank top, a few sizes too small, did little to hide his protruding bones and prolific tattoos. His lip ring and curly black hair—obviously dyed—further added to his spindly mystique. "I'm your roommate...Kyle Martin."

Jake was so startled by his appearance that he nearly missed the scrawny giant's extended paw. Catching himself, he quickly set down a suitcase and reached out his hand, which looked minuscule by comparison. "Jake Taylor," he smiled back at the first friendly face he'd encountered thus far.

"Dude, let me help you with your bags." Kyle grabbed the suitcase Jake had set down on the floor.

When it was clear that the heavy load would not cause his bony new friend to topple over, Jake followed him down the hallway. "Kyle, this is my dad."

Without breaking stride, Kyle called back, "I pity the foo'! What up, Mr. T?"

Glen gave a courtesy laugh. "Uh, you can call me Glen."

Kyle stopped at a room and banged his shoulder into the door to push it open. "Welcome to our home!" he gestured dramatically.

Jake had never prided himself on being a neat-freak, but if he was truly honest, the mere sight of a dirty shirt lying on the floor never sat well with him. So as he stepped toward the opening, Kyle's four inviting words did nothing to warn Jake of the disaster area that lay beyond.

Apart from the bare mattress that had obviously been used as a table—maybe even a trash can, judging by the many stains on it—the room was covered with errant clothes and empty snack wrappers. Posters that seemed to have nothing to do with each other plastered the walls, featuring punk and metal bands Jake was unfamiliar with, a few skateboarders, a snowboarder, Michael Jordan, a few movies, and numerous scantily clad women. A particularly voluptuous bikini model was pinned directly above Kyle's bed on the ceiling. And above Kyle's desk hung the Louisville basketball team photo, leaving Jake painfully aware of how much he had missed.

"I was in the process of cleaning when I heard you were here," the unfazed roommate chatted, throwing stuff from what was now Jake's side of the room onto his own. "I guess I'll have to get used to sharing a room."

Jake picked up a half-empty beer can from what was supposed to be his desk and dropped it into an overflowing trash pail by the door. *I think that makes two of us,* Jake wanted to say. He'd been warned that college roommates weren't known for being tidy, but he'd hoped someone talented enough to earn a full-ride scholarship to play basketball would at least know how to throw their dirty clothes into a hamper.

Glen wasn't quite as skilled in holding back judgment. "What died in here?" he thundered.

Jake shot his dad a nasty look, but it didn't matter. Kyle didn't seem to be easily offended.

"Ahh, you're hilarious, Mr. T! Just throw it all on my side. I'll take care of it."

After a couple of hours of shoving debris over to Kyle's side of the room, bringing the rest of Jake's stuff up from his truck, and finally finding an RA to give him a key, it was time for Jake's dad to head to the airport. Jake and Glen grabbed a quick bite to eat at a nearby McDonald's and then returned to campus to wait for the taxi. Jake had offered several times to give his dad a ride, but Glen insisted that Jake could better use the time turning his dorm room into something livable. So they hugged, which still felt a bit awkward after so many years without physical contact, and said their goodbyes.

Jake wasn't sure when it had happened, but sometime during their three-day road trip from California to Kentucky, he and his dad became okay again. As much as he'd grown to hate his father over the years, it felt good to get a lot of things off his chest, and even better to hear his dad actually apologize—repeatedly. So as the yellow taxi sped away with his father into the darkness, a peculiar sadness welled up in Jake's chest. If someone had told him a week ago that he'd miss his dad, Jake would have scoffed, but now his dad's departure reminded him of how much he was leaving behind in California—and how alone he now was.

With heavy steps, Jake walked back into the Miller Hall lobby, ignoring the dissipating crowd. The blast of hot air warmed his body, but his mood had caught a chill. He trudged back up the steps—this time making sure to stick to the men's side to the west—and headed to the only bedroom he'd ever had to share in his entire life. Somehow, this new living situation wasn't nearly as enticing as his childhood wish to escape from his parents' arguing by moving in with Roger, his one-time best friend. *At least Roger was clean,* Jake remembered wistfully.

Roger...his friend who had killed himself less than a year ago. While Jake still thought of him fairly often, he usually didn't feel as depressed as he did right now.

Jake had come a long way since that traumatic day last February when Roger, angry and alone, had walked onto their high school campus with a gun and fired a few random shots before taking his own life. That one horrible moment had rocked Jake's world and set him on a quest to figure out what his life was all about. But even though this past had shaped him, Jake knew that staying stuck in the past didn't help anyone, including Roger. He couldn't change what had happened by living in regret; he could only move forward and change the future. And for all he knew, this Kyle guy was someone whose story God wanted Jake to help rewrite for the better. Trying to ditch his gloom with this pep talk, Jake exhaled sharply and heaved open the door to his room. Kyle, who had been earnestly cleaning up his stuff as Jake was leaving earlier, had apparently gotten distracted and was now cooking up some Cup-o'-Noodles in a disgustingly dirty microwave.

"Dinner, huh?" Jake asked.

"Yeah, ya want some?"

"Nah, my dad and I just ate." Jake opened a box of socks, underwear, and toiletries, and began arranging them in drawers as Kyle slurped down his scant meal. Before Jake could unpack anything else, Kyle came over and plopped himself on the dirty mattress, noodle juice splashing onto the stained fabric.

"So, I heard you like to party," he smiled.

Apparently Jake's reputation had preceded him. Over a year ago on his recruiting trip to Louisville, several of the guys on the team had definitely shown him a good time. Pretty girls and an assortment of beer had both been freely on tap, and even though Jake knew it was all part of the recruitment game, he hadn't minded being the center of attention. The guys had actually been impressed by this seventeen-year-old's ability to handle his alcohol. And the girls...well, he'd been pretty good on his game there, too. He'd technically stayed faithful to Amy, but sometimes fish can nibble at the bait and not get caught—at least that was how Jake had rationalized it.

Fortunately, that was the old Jake Taylor: the Jake Taylor who hadn't yet witnessed his childhood best friend commit suicide a few feet in front of him; the Jake Taylor who hadn't yet become a father; the Jake Taylor who hadn't yet given up the party scene to follow God. But eleven months ago, that old Jake Taylor began the transformation into the new Jake Taylor. And while some of the changes that ensued had been difficult, the new Jake Taylor didn't regret them for one minute. His new faith had awakened him to a new life that was far more fulfilling than anything he'd ever experienced getting drunk with friends on a weekend night. But how could he explain all of that to his brand new roommate...who was currently his only connection to the rest of campus and the other guys on the team?

Jake searched for nothing in a duffel bag, trying to formulate an acceptable response. "Yeah, not so much anymore. Besides, I really need to get my stuff unpacked."

Kyle set his steaming Styrofoam cup on Jake's desk and leapt onto Jake's bed, his slender frame still eliciting creaks from the old springs as he jumped up and down. He kept his head tilted awkwardly to the side to avoid banging it on the ceiling. "Dude, you're in college now. Your mom's not here to make sure you cleaned your room. Tonight's party night!" He flew from the bed in a not-so-graceful dismount to the middle of the floor.

"Hey, what if we just jump on our own beds from now on?" Jake suggested with a smile.

Kyle grabbed his noodles and gulped them down like a Red Bull. Jake marveled that he could down so much of the hot, salty liquid without coming up for air. "I love this stuff!" he panted, crushing the now-empty cup and tossing it unsuccessfully toward the garbage can. "All the other guys on the team are going to be there. They're going to be pissed if you no-show."

Jake hoped Kyle's shots on the court were better than this last one, which lay untouched a foot away from its target. He opened up a suitcase and started hanging clothes in his closet as he deliberated the choice at hand.

As strong as his new convictions were, Jake's desire to fit in with the team was equally great. He knew Coach's exception to allow him to miss the fall semester did not mean the rest of his teammates were okay with it. While Jake was supporting Amy through her pregnancy, they had been bonding through hours of grueling strength and conditioning workouts and learning how they fit together into the playbook. Jake sure hadn't slacked—for the last six months he'd been up every morning before five to run and lift and shoot and drill and study those same plays alone. He was in the best shape of his life. Still, no matter how hard he worked, nothing could replace the team bonding he had missed, and he knew that it wouldn't be easy to become one of the guys.

But here was his chance. Couldn't he go to the party without compromising his values? *Why not?* he reasoned, committing to himself that if he had even the slightest craving for beer, he'd leave early.

"The party is in the hiz-ouse!" Kyle yelled, as he walked through the front door of the apartment without knocking.

They had heard the thumping music from down the street as they made the short trek from campus, but Jake had forgotten how loud these parties could get until the wall of sound escaped through the open door. Fortunately, the apartment complex seemed primarily inhabited by Louisville students, so none of the neighbors would probably complain.

Jake tentatively followed the long strides of his roommate into the living room, where about thirty people sat or stood around, most with drinks in their hands. The girls must have been hand-selected, because they were all gorgeous. Jake recognized most of the guys from the recruiting trip or from the pre-season program that he'd memorized from cover to cover. There, in the flesh, was Tony Anderson, the Louisville junior who was an expected NBA lottery pick. Jamal Hardaway, the sophomore starting shooting guard, stood a few feet away. In the corner, small forward Aaron Simon had adopted his D.J. alter-ego Nomis and was scratching out a funky beat. Jake grinned to watch him in action. His deft movements on the turntable were just as much in the zone as his sweet jumper from the left wing. Bojan Petrovic, the 6-foot-10 senior from Serbia, kept Nomis company, bobbing his head to the rhythm.

Along the other wall, Nate Williams, a freshman point guard who was already getting good playing time, sat on the couch, surrounded by a cuddling brunette and a caressing blonde. The Missouri native had adjusted well to the Louisville program, but he was no taller or stronger than Jake, and his outside shot wasn't nearly as consistent. Back home, Jake had secretly assumed it could have been him instead of Nate on the court, if Jake would have been with the team from the beginning. But suddenly, his confidence waned. Up until now, he could hardly wait to immerse himself in this college-ball life. Now, he felt completely out of his element and wondered if he'd made the right decision.

Unlike Jake's non-existent welcome to the dorm, every conversation halted the moment the two redshirt freshman entered, and every eye gave Jake the once-over. Apparently, they had been waiting for this arrival. Jake wasn't sure which was worse—being ignored or being inspected. He smiled to ease the tension. Kyle made the unnecessary introduction.

"Ahhhhh, yeah! Ladies and gentlemen, let me introduce you to Jake Taylor!"

Jake waved, unsure who to greet first.

"It's about time, freshman." Tony stepped forward, obviously the team leader and host of the party. "You got everything all squared away back home?" The sarcasm dripping from his words raised a low laugh out of most of the guys. Their eyes bore down on him like sniper rifles locked and loaded on their target.

"Uh, yeah," Jake responded, unsure if this was the routine razzing every new player received, or if his new teammates were genuinely upset at him for coming a semester late. How could he blame them? Basketball was a team sport, but Jake had chosen something other than his team.

Nate stood up and slowly walked over to a bar filled with an arrangement of beverage choices. As if asserting his dominance over Jake, he popped the top off a beer bottle and planted himself between Tony and Jamal.

Tony glanced at Nate sidelong, but addressed Jake. "You know what they say about guys who put hoes before bros?"

Jake scanned the crowd and weighed his options. Should he defend himself—and Amy—or just acknowledge his breach of the man-code with a grin? Suddenly, his mouth fired back without checking with his brain. "They must have a damn fine ho?" he shrugged.

Muffled *oh!*s encircled the room, and Jake caught a few smiles.

"This here bro thinks he's funny," Jamal smirked to Nate as he set his drink down. He walked closer to Jake, looking him squarely in the eye. "Nah," he breathed into Jake's face. "What they say about guys who put hoes before bros is that they're just big white-boy pussies who can't make the clutch shot." He looked over at Tony. "I'm not sure I want one of those on my team."

Tony remained stoic, while Nate sneered in agreement.

By this time, Kyle had disassociated himself from Jake and sat on the arm of the couch next to the brunette. Jake caught him smiling, his eyes following the action like an avid ping-pong fan. *He sure wilted quickly!* Jake wondered if this had all been a set-up—part of Kyle's plan from the beginning: Get even with the guy taking up his space by letting the team gang up on him.

Jake turned his attention back to his challengers. These were guys Jake had watched on ESPN, had admired, had looked forward to playing with. But the awe was gone, and Jake's natural instincts took over—he was never one to back down from a challenge. Ever since Jake was a little kid, there had always been some sort of switch in his brain that made it impossible for him to sidestep a dare. He was clearly being sized up by the rest of the team, and he felt his stance automatically shift to a confident swagger. Jake scanned the room again, his cocky smile he'd made famous at Pacific High growing wider with every second.

"So what do I need to do to prove I can hack it?" Jake calmly retorted.

The room came alive with low whoops and hollers of anticipation as Nomis scratched out a fresh background beat from the corner. Even the girls seemed intrigued by this new player in their midst.

Tony, Jamal, and Nate all glanced at each other, and Jamal took the lead. He walked over to the bar and poured two vodka shots, then walked back to Jake and handed him a glass. "How 'bout you start with this?"

All eyes were on Jake as he gingerly held the vodka, swirling it around in the glass. Ten minutes into his first college party, and he was already cornered. He hadn't had even a sip of alcohol since about nine months ago, when he'd walked out on a game of beer pong amidst angry and disapproving stares from all his friends. He'd realized then that the new church thing he was checking out didn't mix with his old activities, and so he'd bravely left and never looked back.

Now here he was again, but this pressure was even worse. It was all happening so quickly, and he just wanted to be accepted by the team so he could play ball. *One drink won't hurt,* he decided. It wasn't like he was slipping into that old lifestyle. He was just making a point.

He breathed deeply and downed the cheap liquor, trying to suppress the involuntary shudder that disfigured his face. He'd forgotten how nasty the stuff was. Jake hoped his old tolerance was as strong as it used to be.

Jamal smiled, but instead of pounding the shot in his own hand, he handed it to Jake. "Not done yet, Taylor."

Jake looked at him questioningly, wondering what the point of all this was and how many shots it would take to prove himself. But his inhibitions were already fading, and he swallowed the second shot before thinking. The alcohol tasted so foul, but Jake was starting to remember how loose and relaxed it made him feel. He smiled.

Nate brought Jamal another one, and Jamal traded Jake for the empty glass in his hand. "Third time's a charm, bro."

Jake downed it without hesitation.

"Now you're ready. Someone grab a ball."

While Jake thought it had been too cold that afternoon, it was like frozen-in-an-ice-cube cold that night. But there they all stood on a concrete basketball court in a park down the street. They lined the court wearing layers of clothing, their breath hanging in the air underneath the suspense. Tony carried the ball to center court and held it out to Jake, who quickly disrobed from the parka his mom had bought him as a going-away present. Dressed only in a sweatshirt and jeans, his body began to shiver in the cold air, as Tony handed him the ball at the top of the three-point line and walked back to the watching crowd.

"Clutch shot, freshman. Show us what you got," he mocked.

Jake's reputation hung in the balance of whether he could sink a single three-pointer with no warm-up, half-drunk, on a dark court barely lit by passing cars and a half-full moon, with all his new teammates watching impatiently. But this wasn't unfamiliar territory to Jake. He had logged hundreds of hours on a similar court back home. From there, he'd often transported himself in his mind to Madison Square Garden or Louisville's own Freedom Hall, where he would fire away from three-point-land with the seconds ticking down—usually to win the game.

Jake fingered the weathered Spalding and twirled it in his cold, stiff fingers. He bounced it one...two...three times as he scrutinized the old metal backboard with a slightly tilted rim, fringed by a sagging chain net. He closed his eyes, inhaled the frigid air deeply, and exhaled smoke like a nicotine addict.

Lord, please, please, please.

In one fluid motion, Jake locked his sights on the intended target, brought his arms up in perfect form, and released the ball without a care in the world, like he had done a million times before...

Swish.

Thank you, Jesus! Jake's confidence exploded as he finally dropped his arms and smiled over to the sidelines with his charming smirk. *And sorry about the drinking,* he quickly added.

"Awww dang! Taylor, you da man!" Kyle re-emerged as his buddy, clapping his gloves together in surprised celebration.

The girls smiled back, and the guys slowly got over their shock. Most of them joined with their own muffled claps, although Jake thought he saw a little disappointment on a lot of their faces, especially Nate's. Jake wondered if any of them had actually wanted him to succeed.

Tony stepped toward Jake and picked up his parka. "Welcome to the team, Taylor. You better get your priorities straight from here on. Now put your jacket on, it's like twenty degrees out here."

Jake quickly took his suggestion and followed the crowd back to the apartment. Conversations turned to other things, and Jake was able to sit the rest of the night on the sidelines nursing a single red cup—full of tap water. He entertained questions about California and heard all kinds of boasting about all kinds of play. Some of the girls tried to attract his attention, but he made it clear he wasn't interested, which was fine because there was always some other guy who was. He wished he could go back to his room but figured he was still on thin ice, so he stuck around until things started dying down a couple of hours later. Kyle and some others had disappeared into a back room, so Jake made the short walk back to their dorm alone.

✚ ✚ ✚

An hour later, Jake lay half-awake in his unfamiliar room. Suddenly the door flew open, and he bolted off the mattress trying to look busy unzipping the suitcase nearest to him on the floor. His new roommate barged in, and Jake suddenly realized how weird it must look for him to be working in the dark. He scolded himself for reacting so quickly. If he'd only stayed lying down, he could have at least avoided conversation by pretending to be asleep. Too late for that now. Jake just froze and prepared a lame excuse about not being able to find the light switch.

However, the excuse was never needed. Jake's roommate left the lights off and simply collapsed onto his own bed. A weak grunt escaped Kyle's lungs when his body hit the barely budging surface, and then he turned to the wall and started snoring within seconds.

What a day. Jake shook his head, which now ached with the promise of a hangover. His stomach was feeling a little queasy. He thought about going to the bathroom, but the long trek down the hall talked him out of it. While he was up, though, he figured he might as well find those sheets, so he started rifling through the boxes his mom had packed. Finding them in the dark proved to be more of a challenge than he felt up to, however, and after a few fruitless minutes, he surrendered to the nasty mattress once again. His roommate's snoring left little chance that he'd fall asleep any time soon, but Jake curled up on his side and burrowed his face into his pillow, longing for rest.

✚ ✚ ✚

Several hours later, Jake awoke from a lonely dream about Amy to sunlight streaming into his eyes. A dull ache pulsed through his brain as he frantically checked his phone for the time. 9:43. That was a record—he hadn't slept past nine in years. *Must be the time change.* He quickly counted back three hours and wondered if Amy was up yet. He couldn't wait to talk to her.

9:44am | From: Jake | To: Amy
Hey babe! Sooooo sorry about last night. I miss you soooooo much. Call me when you wake up.

6:45am | From: Jake | To: Amy
Did I mention how sorry I am? I'm sorry sorry sorry

6:46am | From: Jake | To: Amy
What did the vacuum say to his friend? You suck. I know I do, and I'm so sorry I broke my promise and didn't get to talk to you last night.

6:48am | From: Jake | To: Amy
Good morning good morning good morning it's time to rise and shine

6:50am | From: Jake | To: Amy
Are you up yet? Im dyyyyying to talk to you

WRAPPED IN A FLUFFY PINK TOWEL, her wet hair hanging down past her shoulders, Amy walked groggily into her bedroom and flipped on the light. She hadn't slept much last night, tossing and turning and tormented by bad dreams stemming from her frustration and concern over Jake never calling. Absorbed by grouchy thoughts and assumptions, she jumped when her cell phone vibrated loudly on the nightstand. She rushed over to pick it up. *Five missed texts?* She wasn't in the shower that long.

But just like that, all the annoyance and worry that had plagued her all night washed away like pollution in the rain. Her heart skipped a beat and a smile radiated across her freshly washed face when she saw that they were all from Jake. Suddenly she felt like a junior-higher with a crush. *It's just a text,* she grinned to herself. But those texts sent the storm clouds racing away, and as her grey-blue eyes scanned them, the forecast was clear and bright. Jake was safe and not lying in a ditch somewhere in nowhere-ville...*and* he wanted to talk to her and wasn't preoccupied with some college cutie he had just met. The relief warmed her as she flopped down on her bed to call him.

It had only been three days since he had last stood right in front of her in his driveway—three days since he'd made the promise to call her every night. Only three days since she'd gazed into those mesmerizing blue eyes of his...since she'd been held tight in those strong arms. Only three days since he'd waved goodbye. And yet, it felt like an eternity. Amy groaned at how much she missed him already. *How am I gonna make it a whole semester?*

The phone rang once.

"Amy!" Jake eagerly greeted her in his cute I-just-rolled-out-of-bed voice. "Look, before you say anything, I'm sooo, so sorry for not calling you last night. I met my roommate and then the guys on the team and just before I knew—"

"Jake, it's cool," Amy interrupted with 90-percent sincerity. "I just figured you got busy."

"No, it's not cool. I made you a promise, and I broke it. Just say that you forgive me."

Of course, just hearing his eager voice was enough already, but she couldn't help playing with him a little. "Or else what?"

"Or else I'll have to jump in my truck and drive 2,100 miles back so I can beg you in person," Jake pleaded on the other end of the line, then whispered slyly, "I know you can't resist me."

"Don't talk like that, or I'll have to call you on it," Amy flirted back.

Jake chuckled and they sank into silence.

"Don't tempt me," he said quietly, "or I might take you up on it."

Amy hadn't expected that hint of melancholy in his voice. He was finally living his dream, finally back on track after being willing to give it all up for her—and this is how he sounded? "Jake, what's wrong?" She rolled onto her side, her damp hair clinging to her bare back.

"Nothing. I'm fine," Jake assured her, but not convincingly.

"Jake," Amy coaxed.

"It's just...it's so good to hear your voice. I don't know. It's just not the same as how I'd always pictured," he relented. "And you're not here."

Amy wished she could reach through the phone and kiss him. She loved it when he dropped his manly macho mask and allowed his sensitive side to shine through a little. Since Jake had started getting into God this past year, he seemed to be growing more comfortable with this more "real" Jake. And while it had thrown her off at first, she had come to like it. Chris Vaughn, the youth pastor he was always hanging out with, was the same way in terms of not being afraid of vulnerability or sensitivity, and his openness was apparently rubbing off.

"So did you really just wake up?" Amy calculated the time change in her head, trying to lighten the mood. She was surprised that Jake had managed to sleep so long.

"Yup," Jake laughed softly. "I didn't get much sleep last night. But I couldn't wait to talk to you."

A thrill fluttered through her core. "Why couldn't you sleep?"

Jake sighed. "The guys had a party..."

He sounded reluctant and ashamed at first, which rekindled some of Amy's concerns, but as he began to explain, she just wanted to hug him. He slowly recounted the details of the previous evening, from the lousy vodka shots to his three-point shot to the snapshots of mindless conversations he'd endured for hours afterward. The more Amy listened, the more she wished she could have been there. That wish grew even stronger when he talked about the girls who had tried to flirt with him, but his tone assured Amy that there was nothing to worry about. She caught herself actually smiling a little as she heard how miserable he sounded, since that meant he'd be missing her more. Just as Jake started describing his new roommate, her eyes glanced at the clock on her dresser. *7:38.*

"Crap! Jake! I'm sorry to interrupt you, and I *really* want to hear about your roommate, but I have to leave in like two minutes, and I'm not even dressed yet!"

"You're not dressed, huh?" Amy could detect the smile in Jake's voice.

"Jake..."

"I love you, babe," Jake whispered.

"I love you, too."

"I'll call you tonight. Really."

"Jake. Is this really gonna work?" She hated the question the moment it left her lips. *Where did that come from?* It was hardly the kind of thing to bring up now, even more so since she was already running late for her first day of class. "What I meant was..."

"Yes." His answer was short, sweet, and absolutely perfect.

"Talk to you soon."

"Bye."

Amy ended the call and clutched her phone to her pounding heart for a few seconds. Her soaking hair and damp towel had left her with a chill, and she wished she could just curl up under the blankets and let the day go on without her. Instead, she pushed herself up and quickly pulled on a pair of jeans and a sweater. She pulled her hair up into a messy bun, slipped on the flip-flops waiting by the door, and rushed out to the living room, grabbing her backpack off the kitchen table. Who needed makeup? *It's not like there's anyone I'm trying to impress,* she lamented.

On the front door, her mom had left a sticky-note wishing her a good first day of school. *That's sweet,* she thought, as she stuffed it in her pocket and ran out to her mom's old minivan. But as much as she appreciated her mom's thoughtful gesture, it left her feeling kind of empty. Sure, a note was nice, but it had been weeks since they had sat down and shared a meal together, or even just a cup of coffee.

During Amy's pregnancy, their relationship had definitely improved, but it was still very much on her mom's terms—and Amy could never quite figure them out. When Amy had first worked up the nerve to tell her mom that she was pregnant, her mom was so mad that she wouldn't even speak to her. Amy figured she had deserved it for getting herself into that situation. After several weeks of the silent treatment, her mom had finally started talking to her again, and once Amy had decided to give the baby up for adoption, her mom even seemed to start going out of her way to be nice. In some ways, Amy felt like her mom would have preferred her to just get an abortion and never tell her about it. But apparently giving the baby away had served the same purpose—her mom just seemed relieved that Amy hadn't "ruined" her life by keeping it. Amy knew her mom had plenty of regrets from her own choice to have a baby at age 17—a choice that had left Amy feeling like a total burden growing up.

What Amy really could have used was someone who understood how hard the decision to give up her baby had been...someone who understood how she still struggled every day with the knowledge that a part of her was out there apart from her. A part of her she had felt kicking and hiccupping and moving around inside of her. A part of her with tiny fingers that curled around in precious fists... with a soft fuzzy forehead that smelled like heaven...with nearly translucent eyelids fringed by long, delicate lashes. A part of her who was also a part of Jake—an amazing miracle of love they had unintentionally brought to life. A part of her named Emily, who now lived across town with a wonderful couple named Frank and Jan, who loved Emily and could provide a life for her far better than Amy and Jake could have.

Amy longed for someone to share with, someone to cry with, someone to just hold her as sobs wracked her body, someone to comfort her as nightmares of loss woke her up every agonizing night. It would have been wonderful if her mother could have been that someone. But instead, her mom simply praised her for not ruining her life and kept speeding along, living her life as if she were trying to regain the years she had lost by having Amy.

Somehow, the last ten minutes from Amy's driveway to Rancho Del Oro Drive had escaped without notice. Amy looked up just in time to realize she had missed her turn. *Dang it!* She pulled into the left lane, ready to make a U-turn at the next intersection, and frantically brushed away the tears spilling over onto her cheeks. *At least there's no makeup to smudge.*

After a few more minutes, her car turned into Mira Costa Community College, barely slowing in time to avoid bottoming out on the huge speed bumps. She wound her way around the campus until she got to Lot 2. Apparently, early classes weren't so popular, judging by the vast selection of empty parking spaces. Before Amy was ready, her car was parked and the clock read 7:57. She needed to go—being late on the first day would *not* be a good idea—but she *so* didn't want to.

The first day of school used to be such a big deal back in grade school. Amy remembered how she would jump out of bed those mornings, dress in a new outfit, and boldly set out with her new lunch box in tow, eager to learn what the new year had to offer. Today, however, she felt only dread. *Maybe a new lunch box would help,* she sighed under her breath, as she reluctantly stepped out of her van.

The dingy, cracked asphalt contrasted so sharply with the glorious arrival to college that Amy had always pictured. Mira Costa Community College was a far cry from the prestigious Stanford campus she'd always dreamed of attending. For Amy, it felt like failure.

She'd worked so hard for so long to get the good grades and impressive list of activities that would get her into the university that could virtually guarantee her success in life. She'd planned out her entrance to Stanford since she was a little girl: how she would pledge alongside other girls just like her to be a cute sorority sister, and then meet a handsome scholar while studying in the library one day, and since he also was athletic and fun, they would dance through their four years of college together and finally become famous doctors or lawyers or politicians or something cool like that and live happily ever after. That beautiful dream had helped her through so many cold, lonely nights as a child.

Of course, once she'd started dating Jake in high school, Amy had started recalculating. Top-choice Stanford Cardinal gradually morphed into Jake's Louisville Cardinals, and the rest of her plans followed suit. But it didn't matter, she told herself, because she'd already met her handsome jock, and they still could do great things together, and most importantly, they would live happily ever after. The decision to join Jake at Louisville was a sacrifice she was glad to make...until the unexpected pregnancy. No amount of stretching and recalculating could fit a November baby into her first semester away at college—whether at Louisville or Stanford.

Amy winced, recalling the terrible hopelessness that had enveloped her as all her dreams started crashing hard. But then Jake—amazing, annoying, heroic Jake—had started picking up her pieces. He had sacrificed his own dreams to stay behind with her. How many guys would do that? And surprisingly, both of their goals were given a second chance. The coaching staff at Louisville had worked things out to allow Jake to "redshirt" and join the team a semester late. Meanwhile, the Stanford admissions director had persuaded Amy to defer her enrollment there for a year, promising that her hefty financial aid package would still be waiting upon her arrival. It had all seemed too good to be true.

But now the truth was sinking in like a heavy fog. She hadn't been ready to move on yet, and was taking an extra semester to figure out which dream to pursue. Jake was gone, and she was still here—alone.

That was probably the worst part about staying behind at community college—being alone. Amy hurried through the brisk morning air to the nearest cluster of classrooms. She wondered if she'd know anyone in her classes this semester. In high school, everyone had known who she was, and she'd thought she had friends everywhere. Of course, all that sort of changed when she ended up preggo during her senior year. Homecoming Queen, Cheer Captain, and all her other prestigious titles meant nothing after the rumors and sneers gained full circulation, and her popularity had pretty much evaporated. What hurt most was the loss of friends after her pregnancy was made public. Most of the guys and girls she had hung out with all through high school, not to mention those she'd known since elementary school, hadn't given her the time of day after that drama had exploded.

Amy entered her classroom and slid into an old plastic desk in the second row. She scanned the few faces scattered around the room, but as expected, she didn't recognize any of them. She checked the clock on her phone. 8:01. Where was everyone?

A few more unfamiliar people trickled in, joining the ranks of the sitting sleepers in the desks around her. To pass the time until *something* happened, Amy pulled out a spiral notebook and a pen, and before she knew it, she found herself doodling the Louisville bird mascot next to the ambiguous Stanford "tree." How ironic that both schools used a type of cardinal for their mascot. Which one did she want to be, though? Soon, a soft sketch of a baby's face took shape under her deft pen strokes, which she scribbled out as soon as she realized what she was doing. *Where is the professor?* Had she rushed off the phone with Jake for nothing?

The desks around Amy were filling up, and still there was no sign of the teacher. *Isn't there some kind of rule about this?* How long did they have to wait before class was cancelled? Amy watched the faces of people dashing into the room thinking they were late, only to relax with relief when they realized that nothing had started without them. She wondered if she would become friends with any of them before the semester was over. It would be nice to make a couple of new friends, but she really wasn't in the mood to be outgoing this morning.

Amy thought of Jake's group from church who had taken her in when she was floundering. They were a unique crowd—people Amy wouldn't have given the time of day before—but they were so loving and carefree and full of joy. Her favorite was Andrea—the chick she had formerly viewed as a rival! Amy loved Andrea's confident perspective on life and her ability to look beyond what others thought of her. But she was still only a junior in high school, and unless they were intentional, their paths just wouldn't cross. If Amy kept going to church, it might help, but she just wasn't ready to take that step. Sure, she was interested in the whole God thing, but how could God be interested in her...after all the mistakes she'd made?

A raspy voice startled Amy out of her thoughts, and she found herself staring at a balding mustachioed man. Suspenders held his brown corduroy slacks securely *above* his protruding waistline, which allowed his short plaid tie to meet them halfway down his chest. World Politics 252 had finally begun. At precisely 8:10 the professor, aptly named Mr. Borr, launched into his lecture—reading it word-for-word from the notebook on his podium in what Amy would vote the most monotonous voice she had ever heard. Amy struggled to take notes on his ramble, but even Mr. Borr seemed bored with his contrast of the United States' concept of *trias politica*—why couldn't he just call it what everyone else did, the separation of powers?—with the original versions of the Greeks and the Romans. Amy glanced around the sea of blank faces and realized that most were struggling just to stay awake. At 9:28, Mr. Borr closed his notebook and mumbled something about reading chapters 1 and 2 for homework, then slipped out of the classroom without another word. Half of the class rustled their comatose bodies into action, while the other half remained numbly seated. Amy joined the wave that was leaving, depressed by the thought of four more months of this.

Her next class was Psychology. She had signed up for it simply because it had fit her schedule, but five minutes in, she knew she had picked a winner. Professor Shane Sullivan was at least 65 years old, but he possessed the energy and enthusiasm of someone half his age.

"We're going to start class with a pop quiz," the jovial old man practically sang with a smile on his face as the class groaned in unison. The professor placed a survey on each desk, his little brown felt beret bouncing up and down the rows with excitement.

Amy started reading the questions and soon realized that this was a different kind of quiz. She pulled out a pen and went straight to work.

PERSONALITY ASSESSMENT

1. You naturally take responsibility.
   ❍ YES ❍ NO
2. After being around people for a prolonged time, you need to get away and be alone.
   ❍ YES ❍ NO
3. You feel involved when watching TV soaps.
   ❍ YES ❍ NO
4. You prefer life to be active and fast-paced.
   ❍ YES ❍ NO
5. When possible, you prefer to plan in advance.
   ❍ YES ❍ NO
6. You are consistent in your habits.
   ❍ YES ❍ NO
7. Your actions are often influenced by your emotions.
   ❍ YES ❍ NO
8. You enjoy having a wide circle of acquaintances.
   ❍ YES ❍ NO
9. You are rarely late.
   ❍ YES ❍ NO
10. You don't often get excited.
    ❍ YES ❍ NO

Continue onto next page →

After four pages of similar questions, Amy wondered what all this was about. But almost to the second that she marked her final answer, Mr. Sullivan placed another paper on her desk that gave instructions on how to tally up her score. Amy placed her results on the grid.

PERSONALITY ASSESSMENT

Check the box next to each number where you marked "Yes" on the assessment. Then total up the marks in each column at the bottom to see which categories are your strongest.

Choleric		Phlegmatic		Melancholy		Sanguine	
1	X	2		3	X	4	
5	X	6	X	7		8	X
9	X	10		11		12	
13	X	14		15		16	X
17		18		19	X	20	
21	X	22		23	X	24	
25	X	26		27		28	X
29		30	X	31		32	
33	X	34		35		36	
37	X	38		39		40	X
Totals:	8	2		3		4	

There was no denying it. Amy Briggs was most definitely a choleric...whatever that meant. She scanned back over her "Yes" answers, hoping to shed more light on this new label while everyone else finished. Finally, Mr. Sullivan directed the class to stand up and assemble at the four corners of the room based on their personality profile. All "Cholerics" were to meet in the front-right corner, so Amy merged with the flow of bodies and made her way toward her spot. Fourteen other students already stood huddled around a poster hanging on the wall, jostling each other to read the words listed under the title. A guy to Amy's left pushed his way to the front of the group, and a couple people behind her were crowding so close she could feel their breath on her bare neck. *Yikes,* she sighed, and craned her neck to see the chart without disturbing anyone.

CHOLERIC	
Ambitious	Knows the right answers
Impatient	Can see the whole picture
Self-sufficient	Quickly moves to action
Born leader	Competitive
Dynamic	Intellectual
Practical	Excels in emergencies
Energetic	High aspirations
Prideful	Hard worker
Unemotional	Motivator
Strong-willed	Long-term thinker
Independent	Hot-tempered
Optimistic	Cruel
Not discouraged easily	Impetuous
Confident	Organized
Goal-oriented	Effective communicator
Passionate	Stubborn
Insensitive	

Amy read the list quietly to herself over the other students' shoulders. She had to laugh at several of the descriptions that tagged her perfectly. Goal-oriented. *Yup.* Long-term thinker. *Ha! That's an understatement.* Self-sufficient. *Out of necessity!* But others were a little harder to swallow. Was she really insensitive? Or prideful? Stubborn, maybe. But cruel? *Yikes!* And unemotional? *Definitely not lately.* The others in Amy's new Choleric "support group" tittered and grunted and shook their heads alongside her, as they studied the best and worst parts about themselves.

"Pretty amazing that such a simple test could figure you out so thoroughly, huh?" the cheery professor asked, as he paraded around the room distributing large sheets of poster paper and packs of markers.

Amy followed his path and sized up the different groups. Hers was the smallest of the class, and she noted that it consisted predominantly of males—and slightly older ones at that. The Phlegmatics and Sanguines were larger and younger. She recognized a few former classmates from Pacific High in their ranks, but they never looked her way. The Melancholy group was larger than her own, but significantly smaller than the other two. She recognized a few more faces in that corner, but they were people she only knew as emo-weirdos in high school. She wondered what their names were. Maybe she'd introduce herself. But before she'd decided for sure, Mr. Sullivan was giving out more directions.

"Now, I'm sure you all found traits that you were eager to claim on your list, as well as a few that were less, well, positive. In your groups, I want you to quickly separate your list into two columns: Strengths and Weaknesses. Then, I want you to individually put a star next to the trait in each column that you most identify with. Talk amongst yourselves about how you see these traits at work in your day-to-day activities."

The buzz in the room was charged with energy as each group turned toward each other, and fifteen minutes quickly passed filled with focused chatter.

"There's so much we can learn from assessments and categories like these," Mr. Sullivan interrupted, standing on a chair in the middle of the room. He waved their four-page survey in the air as conversations died down and all attention focused back on him. "But now, here is what I want you to do." The instructor grabbed the survey with both hands and ripped it in two, crumpling each half into a ball for good measure. "Psychology is the study of the mind...and you can't put the mind into a simple box. Rip, rip, rip!" he exhorted, as the class hesitantly started following his directions.

Amy looked around uneasily and then stealthily slipped her questionnaire into her notebook. Maybe this simple survey couldn't give a definitive explanation for her mind and its workings, but it had piqued her curiosity and she wanted to study it further. She was also excited about sharing it with Jake, and she was already trying to figure out which category he fit into. Old Mr. Sullivan leaped stiffly from his chair and pranced to the front of the room, and Amy had to smile. Wherever this professor was taking them, she was along for the ride.

11:30am | From: Amy | To: Jake
Wow great psych class...cant wait to psychoanalyze you lol... call when you get the chance

2:47pm | From: Cari | To: Amy
Praying for you. Got time for coffee?

AARGH! THOUGHT AMY AS SHE READ THE TEXT. She had hoped it would be from Jake. Instead, it was from Chris Vaughn's wife, Cari. She had already invited her to hang out several times before, and this was getting awkward. Somehow Amy had always found a legitimate excuse not to meet with her. Now that Jake was gone, though, and her schedule was devoid of all human interaction besides classes, what could she say? It wasn't that Cari didn't seem nice, but she was the pastor's wife, for crying out loud, and meeting for coffee just sounded like such a commitment.

Amy let her phone slip from her fingers onto the library table, where she was trying to wade through that World Politics text. Mr. Borr had indicated that they needed to read through chapters 1 and 2 before the next class, but Amy had only made it through five pages in the last two hours, and there were 27 more to go. She buried her face in her hands and sighed. *What did I get myself into?* Suddenly, her phone buzzed again against the wood surface, and she snatched it up to see an unfamiliar number calling.

"Hello?" she answered quickly, a little louder than she had meant to. Was she even supposed to be talking in the library?

"Hi, this is Andrea!" the cheerful voice on the other end chimed. "I just wanted to see how you were doing, with Jake gone and all."

"Oh, hey Andrea," Amy responded without answering the question.

"So, how's it going?" Andrea prodded.

"Oh, y'know...it's going..."

"That bad, huh? Well, hey, I know you're probably busy and all, but I just decided to go out for the track team, and I figured I should start practicing ahead of time, and I've heard it's easier to get into shape if you train with a partner, so yeah...wanna be my running buddy?"

Amy was completely taken off-guard. "Well, ummmm..." What could she say? "When did you want to start?"

"I was thinking like...now."

"Oh."

"Please? I'd love the company."

Amy tried to come up with an excuse, but nothing came to mind. *Why not?* her brain suddenly considered impulsively. *It would be good for me.* And before she knew what she was doing, her voice responded, "Sure."

"Great!" Andrea cheered. "Meet me at the pier at, uh, 3:30, okay?"

The phone clicked before Amy could respond. What had she just got herself into?

✚ ✚ ✚

Thirty-nine minutes later, Amy self-consciously walked the block from her van to the beach, hoping no one would notice her in the too-snug black yoga pants and old cheerleading shoes she'd dug out of her closet. Fortunately, her baggy sweatshirt mostly covered up the pudge she was still all-too-aware-of from her pregnancy. Her entire life she had always been naturally thin, and cheerleading had provided just enough activity to keep her fit. But being pregnant had sure messed with that, and now she felt like a partially deflated blimp.

It had only been seven weeks since she had given birth, but it seemed like far too long already for the excess weight to linger. Of course, it didn't help that she had no baby to give credibility to her weight gain, and she hated the double-takes that people always did when she passed by—as if they were wondering if they should ask when she was due. *There's nothing in here, people!* she wanted to announce, just to get them to quit staring.

Jake had been so sweet, pretending that he hadn't noticed her "growth," but she had observed his furtive glances to her still-swollen belly and enlarged butt. And now that he was away at school, she knew it wouldn't be long before the college girls started competing for his attention. Who was she kidding? Did she really even stand a chance?

"Amy!" Andrea ran up behind her and gave her a big hug. True to form, Andrea's running outfit was an eclectic rainbow: knee-high socks bordered with green stripes, yellow basketball shorts, and a black tank top crowned by an '80s-style red headband and side ponytail.

Amy envied the cool confidence she exuded. If she could have even one tenth of it! "Hey! Where'd you get those socks?"

"I know, huh? Pretty awesome! I love the Goodwill store. So, what's the farthest you've ever run?"

"Uh, nothing." Unless freshman P.E. or a lap or two for cheer practice counted.

"Yeah, me too. So how 'bout we start slow and taper off, huh? It's probably like a mile or two down to the end of the road and back."

The two girls started jogging, and Andrea's chatter filled the air. She talked about her classes and what was going on at youth group, and how the lunch group was a lot smaller than last year but still going strong. She asked Amy genuine questions, but had no problem filling in the silent gaps with gab about the weather, the last movie she'd seen, or the latest deals she'd found at the thrift store.

"Seriously, Amy, you *totally* have to come shopping with me sometime," she said. "You'll love it. One man's trash is another man's treasure, y'know."

Amy appreciated Andrea's boundless energy and enthusiasm, especially since it allowed Amy to focus on her now-labored breathing. But even though she was tired, she found her mind was clearing, and she felt freer than she had in a long time. Before long, they had made it to the end of Beachfront Drive and were already on their way back; meanwhile, Andrea was running through who was currently dating who.

"Speaking of that, what's up with you and Jonny?" Amy piped in, vaguely remembering the story Jake had told about his funny friend's awkward first date with Andrea. After an attempted kiss, Jonny had dropped his bacon bits-covered ice cream cone on Andrea's lap, bringing their outing to an abrupt end. But the two had sure seemed to get along well all summer.

"Oh..."Andrea replied, and for the first time, her voice trailed off.

"I'm sorry! I didn't mean to—"

"No, no, it's nothing. Jonny's a great guy, and I really like him as a friend, y'know? He's funny, and *so* cute, and...I just think he likes me way more than I'm ready to like anyone right now, y'know, and I just don't want him to get hurt or anything."

Amy wasn't sure that she did know. Before dating Jake, she'd had a constant stream of boyfriends, and she'd never given a second thought about hurting them when she had been ready to move on. But it kind of made sense, now that she thought about it. *Maybe that personality test really was right about my weaknesses—maybe I am insensitive and cruel!* Amy shuddered and wondered if Jake had ever noticed that side of her.

"I'm just so busy right now, and I have so much life to look forward to..." Andrea was still talking, "...so I'm definitely not ready for a boyfriend. Unfortunately, it's hard to be *just friends* with someone who totally likes you, y'know, so Jonny and I haven't been talking much lately... especially now that Jake's gone."

Andrea's voice trailed off again, and Amy realized that she wasn't the only one who missed her boyfriend. That comment from Andrea would have made the jealous bug trample all over her six months ago, but today it felt nice to have someone who kind of understood.

"I've talked to Cari about Jonny," Andrea resumed, "and she recommended that I just give Jonny his space. Don't avoid him, but don't go out of the way to be friendly unless I want him to think I'm flirting."

"Cari, Chris' wife?" Amy asked.

"Yeah, she's so great. She's kind of my mentor, so we hang out like every other week. I don't know where I'd be without her."

Amy thought back to the earlier text from Cari that she'd never responded to. Maybe it wouldn't be a bad idea to take her up on her offer. *What's the worst that could happen?*

The two girls approached the pier and automatically slowed to a walk. Amy looked up at the seagulls soaring overhead, mesmerized by the way they drifted so effortlessly on the shifting breezes. If only she could learn to float along in life so easily. And then a whitish-yellowish poop-projectile spattered right at her feet, inches from bombing her head.

"Ewwww!" both girls shrieked in unison.

A disgruntled baby cried in a stroller to their right, and the mother picked the child up to comfort it. Amy's heart sank with longing, and she couldn't tear her eyes away. But then Andrea slipped an arm inside hers and gave it a little squeeze. They continued in silence toward the parking lot.

"So what made you go out for track?" Amy asked, breaking the awkwardness of the moment.

"I figured it was a good way to make friends."

"Well, thanks for calling me."

"You wanna do it again tomorrow?"

"Sure...Why not?" The grin she felt creeping onto her face warmed her.

4:54pm | From: Amy | To: Jake
You'll never believe where I just came back from

5:03pm | From: Amy | To: Cari
I've got class until noon tomorrow and then Im free til 330

AFTER ENDURING TWO NEW MORNING CLASSES the next day, Amy finally stood in line at Starbucks with Cari Vaughn and her adorable four-year-old, Caleb. Amy's heart was a tumble of emotions. She couldn't remember the last time she'd confided anything to an adult, and this felt weird. All through her Human Anatomy professor's introductory lecture this morning, she had been second-guessing this decision to meet Cari, wondering if there was some excuse she could come up with to get out of it at the last minute. But nothing had sounded plausible, and by the end of her Modern Dance class, she'd finally surrendered to the conclusion that maybe it would be good for her.

The line moved forward, and they were two people away from ordering. Then the small talk would have to end, and who knew what would come next. Amy's heart pounded. For some reason, she felt intimidated by Cari. Cari seemed to have it all together—perfect husband, perfect kid, perfect life...Amy almost didn't feel worthy. What would Cari think about her once she really knew what she was dealing with here? *I guess I won't have to worry about her bugging me to hang out again,* Amy reasoned. Yet, along with all of Amy's insecurities hid a flicker of hope that maybe Cari would have some answers.

They stepped up to the cashier, and Cari ordered a grande double chocolate chip Frappuccino for her and a child's hot chocolate for her son. She turned to Amy, who froze, suddenly realizing that Cari wanted to treat her.

"Uh, I'll just take a tall iced green tea," she stammered, taken off-guard.

"Are you sure that's all you want, sweetie?" Cari asked warmly. "Did you eat lunch yet?"

"Yeah, I'm fine," Amy assured her, hoping her stomach wouldn't betray her by growling. The truth was, she didn't think she could get much down, and even though she loved the fancy coffee drinks—that was one of the wonderful things she and Jake shared—she had given them up during her pregnancy, and now was trying to see how long she could last without caffeine. Besides, she definitely didn't need the extra calories.

Cari dropped Caleb's hand to pay for the drinks, and without hesitation his pudgy little fingers grabbed Amy's. He looked up at her and smiled, his beautiful caramel complexion glowing with complete contentment. He swung their arms gently back and forth in rhythm to the quiet tune he was humming, and it was all Amy could do to hold back startled tears. Her arms wanted to just scoop up this adorable kid and squeeze him, just the way she dreamed every night of holding her own daughter—her precious baby Emily, the child who wasn't really *hers* anymore. Emily was almost two months old and growing daily, and even though Frank and Jan had given her a standing invitation to come by as often as she wanted, Amy hadn't been able to muster up the courage for a visit since Jake had left. Did that make her a bad mother? *Mother.* Was that even the right word to describe someone who had given her child away?

The four-year-old holding her hand yanked it and announced excitedly, "I'm gonna get whipped cream up my nose!" His giggle was infectious.

"Wow, I hope that goes well for you, Caleb," Amy smiled back, hoping her tears were under control.

Cari smiled and explained, "Caleb loves to bury his whole face in the whipped cream on top, thus creating an amazing effect of whipped cream squirting everywhere, including up his nose. I think it's really the only reason he likes hot chocolate."

"Can I get bacon bits, too?" Caleb belted out.

Cari stealthily slipped her hand over her son's mouth as they grabbed their drinks and headed for the door. "Jonny babysat Caleb last week, and ever since then, our son wants to put them on everything he eats."

Amy chuckled, remembering Jake ribbing Jonny about his favorite ice cream topping. The three walked out the door and found a seat at a little bistro table on the patio. Even though it was early January, the sun was shining and it was pleasantly warm. Caleb looked angelic as he sat waiting for his drink with politely folded hands. But the moment he held the little cup crowned with the glorious creamy white mound, his face dove in and white flecks sprayed everywhere.

"Heeheehee!" Caleb looked up and grinned, his adorable face bearded like a mini Santa.

Cari tenderly rubbed her son's back and kissed the top of his curly little head. She handed him a napkin, but he just dropped it on his lap and let his mouth do the work. His little pink tongue emerged from the foam and cleared an oval path as the napkin sailed away on the breeze, landing in a nearby clump of bushes. Caleb scooted off the chair to chase after it and became distracted by the tantalizing loose dirt in the planter. Soon his hands were busy bulldozers, accompanied by the grunting and growling sound effects typical of little boys. New tears pricked at Amy's eyes as she watched him joyfully playing, and she quickly glanced away and sipped her tea, trying to focus on the refreshing liquid streaming through her straw. Her hands trembled. *What's wrong with me?!*

"So, how's Jake?" Cari asked, her dark eyes reflecting warm compassion.

"Ummm, I think he's good. We talk almost every night on the phone."

"Almost?" Cari picked up.

"Well," Amy hesitated, wincing at her slip. *Great, now she's going to think I'm a big whiner!* She hurried to explain. "He forgot to call two nights ago, but it was his first day moving into the dorm. And yesterday, by the time we both had a free minute, it was so late neither of us was very talkative...it's no big deal. He's got like a million things going on over there."

Still white-nosed, Caleb was busy shaping the rich dirt into a castle. Cari watched him for a few seconds, then turned back to Amy. "So, how is Amy doing?"

How are you? The infamous greeting spoken millions of times a day. Even when Jake asked about her day, Amy knew he was really only interested in the bullet-point summary, not the depth of her true feelings. But Cari's warmth somehow invited more. "I'm doing okay."

"That bad, huh?" Cari smiled back without flinching. Her deep motherly gaze invited elaboration, and Amy's inhibitions couldn't resist.

"Well, it sounds so stupid, but I guess I'm just feeling a little lonely and left out. My life has always been so planned…so figured out. But now I have no idea what I'm doing. I don't even know what I want anymore," Amy admitted, taking another long sip of tea to break eye-contact.

"Look! I made a moat!" Caleb yelled triumphantly, oblivious to the depth of the conversation occurring a few feet away from him.

Amy and Cari glanced over at a six-inch-deep hole filled with hot chocolate.

"Caleb, that drink cost a lot," Cari scolded.

"You don't like my moat?" the young architect questioned, with the saddest face a four-year-old could muster.

Cari sighed. "It's a great moat, honey, but next time maybe let's use water instead of hot chocolate, okay?" Undaunted, Caleb resumed his work digging to China as Cari turned back to Amy. "I don't think that sounds stupid," she said. "Actually, I think it would be strange if you didn't feel that way. All the plans you spent years working toward have veered off-course. Your boyfriend just left for six months, you don't have a close circle of friends anymore…and I'm guessing Emily is on your mind a lot."

Amy sat motionless as Cari deciphered her heavy heart. *How could Cari know all that?* Especially that last one. Could she know that, thanks to Emily being constantly on her mind, Amy hadn't slept a full night since a week after giving birth? It had taken that long for the weight of her actions to truly sink in, but once it did, it had become a weight she wasn't sure she could bear. Frank and Jan were wonderful people and would provide an amazing life for her daughter, and it would free Amy to pursue her dreams—whatever they were. So why did she still feel this emptiness in the pit of her gut? During the last few months of the pregnancy, she couldn't wait to get the baby out and move on with her life. But now she found herself missing those days.

Amy sighed and brushed away another runaway tear, and before she knew it, the confession just slipped out. "I'm sure the feelings will go away, but sometimes I regret giving her away."

The moment the words left her mouth, Amy wished she could take them back. Frank and Jan were family friends of the Vaughns. What if Cari told them Amy was having second thoughts?

"Amy," Cari touched her arm, "it's not wrong to have those feelings."

"It's not?" Amy was puzzled. *Who is this woman?*

"No. God created those feelings. It's called maternal instinct."

Amy just couldn't swallow that. "So is it wrong that I didn't have those feelings when I gave my daughter away?" she argued. "Where were my maternal instincts when I wanted to just get rid of her so that I could get on with my life? I was so focused on *my* plans...*my* body...*my* future...When did I ever think about *my* daughter?" With each point, her emotions swelled. "I was so selfish! And now look at me and my plans!" Now the tears were flowing freely, and soft sobs shivered through her body.

Cari grabbed Amy's hands and squeezed them warmly. "Honey, what you did was anything but selfish!" She dipped her head to look directly into Amy's lowered eyes. "You gave life to a miracle, and then unselfishly passed that gift along. You gave your daughter a stable future. That's not selfish. You gave Frank and Jan a child that they couldn't have on their own. That's not selfish!" Cari's firm insistence pressed hope into Amy. "And that's not to say you wouldn't have been a good mother. I'm confident that you would have done everything you could and made all the sacrifices necessary to give your daughter the best life you were able—kind of like your own mother. That's a fair choice you could've made. But in some ways..." she paused, as if trying to choose the right words. "In some ways, that would have been taking the easy way out...it's hard to surrender a part of you into someone else's hands. You chose the harder road. And that's not selfish."

Amy's head rested in her hands, elbows at the edge of the table, silent droplets running down her cheeks. She felt Cari's arm slip around her shoulders. Weary from not enough sleep and too much emotion bottled up for too long, a new torrent of tears seeped from her eyes. She buried her head in Cari's embrace and let it all out. All the frustrations and loneliness and jealousy and remorse came flowing out into Cari's tight hug.

"Mom, you made her cry!" Caleb's loud voice suddenly protested.

Amy looked up to see him pointing at her from his mounds of dirt. The sadness mirrored in his face was enough to bring a small smile to Amy's, and she quickly wiped her wet cheeks with the back of her sleeve. Caleb ran over and joined in the group hug, tracking dirt everywhere, including on Amy's new white hoodie. But how could she be bothered by that? Caleb's little arms squeezed Amy tight, and then he lifted his face to look her in the eyes.

"It's okay. Jesus loves you."

Amy reached out and tousled his curls, the unbearable weight she'd been carrying feeling somehow lighter.

Cari pointed her son back toward the makeshift sandbox. "That's right, sweetie. Thanks for sharing that with Miss Amy. How 'bout you go build another castle?"

"Okay." He turned, giving Amy one last charming smile. "Can I have your cups?" He pointed at the now-empty Starbucks cups on the table. Cari handed them to him, and he ran back to the dirt shouting with glee, "Oh baby!"

The girls chuckled, and Amy continued dabbing at her eyes.

"Please don't tell Jan," she whispered.

"Of course not. Your secret's safe with me. Remember, your feelings are only natural." There was a slight pause as both women watched Caleb form turrets and towers with his new molds. Then Cari leaned back and asked, "Can I share my own little secret?"

Amy nodded hesitantly, unsure what Cari could want to confide in her.

"Chris and I really haven't shared this with any of the students in the group, but just over a year ago, just before we met Jake, we had a miscarriage."

"Oh Cari, I'm sorr—"

"It's okay," Cari smiled sadly, but she wasn't finished. "Our baby was less than three months along, and we didn't even know if it was a boy or girl yet.... We never even got to meet it, but I understand those feelings of loss and loneliness, especially since we haven't been able to get pregnant since. And then, when we found out you guys were pregnant—Amy, can I be a little honest here? I was jealous of you."

"Jealous of me? Why?"

"Well, you had a baby you didn't want, and we lost a baby we did want...when Jake told Chris you were probably going to have an abortion, ooh girl, you know I prayed hard."

"Why didn't you guys try to adopt her, then?"

Cari thought for a moment and then answered, "Y'know, I think that would have just been a little too weird. It would have seemed like we had ulterior motives or something. And besides, Frank and Jan are amazing people who totally deserve a child. We already have Caleb. If God wants us to have another child, He'll make it happen. But that's not my point. I just wanted to show you that we all struggle with feelings that aren't quite right. Some days, it's all I can do to put on a happy face and pretend I'm okay. Some night's, I can hardly sleep because of dreams about the baby I don't have."

"Isn't Chris there for you?"

"Oh, yeah, my husband is great. But men just deal with stuff so differently." She chuckled. "It's like God gave them extra muscles to make up for their lack of emotion."

"I'm a human sand castle!" Caleb interrupted again, carefully lifting an inverted Starbucks cup from the top of his head. A tightly-packed sand tower remained, balanced precariously on his tight curls. Cari and Amy couldn't help but giggle, to Caleb's delight.

"Case in point." Cari gestured to her dirty son.

It was impossible for the four-year-old to remain perfectly still, and within seconds his tower collapsed into the chocolate moat. Cari turned back to Amy with genuine warmth. "You want to know what has really helped me through the tough times?"

Amy nodded, truly wanting in on this secret.

"It's knowing that God's in control. He wasn't surprised when we lost our baby. He had a plan for it before it was even growing in me. And He has a plan for our family in the future."

That sounded nice, but how could Cari trust so easily? "But don't you just want to ask God why?" Amy questioned.

"Heck, yeah! And I do ask Him, every day," Cari confessed. "But He doesn't owe me an answer. Instead, He gives me something so much better than that."

"What?"

"He gives me Himself. I don't even want to imagine what it would be like trying to move on without Him." Cari placed her hand on Amy's knee and squeezed it gently.

Amy had heard Jake talk about God in such personal terms, but it had always seemed odd to her. She totally got it that Jesus had made a huge impact in her boyfriend's life—the results were indisputable—but she had never experienced God like that before. Even if He could help her through some of the feelings she was struggling with, why would He want to? What did she have to offer Him? Except for the last few months of going to church with Jake, she had pretty much ignored Him her entire life. "I just don't think I can do it," Amy confessed, ashamed.

"You don't think you can do what?" Cari probed.

"I don't know, do everything God would want me to do."

Cari laughed. "Oh Amy, God's not asking you to be perfect."

Amy looked back, not understanding.

"He's simply asking you to surrender. To admit that you need His help."

"Would God really want to help me?"

A huge smile appeared on Cari's face as she leaned forward to hug her again. "Oh Amy, you have no idea."

2:57pm | From: Amy | To: Jake
Guess what?!?!?!?!

2:58pm | From: Amy | To: Andrea
I cant wait to share some good news on our run!!!!

5:57pm | From: Amy | To: Jake
Guess what?!?!?!?!?

JAKE READ THE CRYPTIC TEXT as he pulled his gym bag out of his new locker. He stuffed the phone into the front pocket of his jeans, figuring he'd call Amy on the walk back to his dorm. He wondered what her "big" news was. Chances are she just ran a couple of miles with Andrea again. *Maybe they ran it in under thirty minutes this time!* Jake scoffed silently. He was proud of Amy for her new exercise regimen, but was rather underwhelmed by her progress, especially in light of the last two strenuous days he'd had.

Throwing on his warm winter coat over a new Louisville sweatshirt, Jake hobbled through the University of Louisville Yum! Center's locker room toward the exit, feeling like a big aching blob. His entire body hurt. Jake thought he had trained hard on his own back home, but all his working out paled in comparison with the rigors he faced here. All-consuming pain was the consequence. But he knew he had to push through it, so after all the other guys finished practice, Jake spent an extra thirty minutes lifting, then went back to the gym to spend another thirty minutes working on his shots. Even though he wasn't technically even on the team yet, Jake knew what it would take to earn the guys' and Coach's respect.

Besides a quick pat on the back and an official introduction to the team, Coach hadn't given him the time of day so far. Not that Jake expected much different, but it was still quite an adjustment from high school, where he had been definitely the biggest fish in the pond. And after these last couple of practices, he wasn't sure he was even bait anymore. Nevertheless, it was fun just to swim in the same water as the rest of the guys—*if you can call torture "fun."* Jake grimaced as his shoulder bumped into a wall. But he still had to admit, he'd never been more excited about running wind sprints or retrieving balls or playing the opponent in a scrimmage. Here he was, finally at Louisville. And the team needed him.

The basketball season was nearly half over, and while an 11-4 record was nothing to be ashamed of, this was the University of Louisville, and anything less than perfection was seen as failure. The latest loss had come just four days earlier on national television, when the Cardinals fell in a nail-biter to West Virginia, one of their conference rivals. After the game, Coach had spent a good forty-five minutes dissecting all the things that had gone wrong during the final two minutes, when the Mountaineers ran off nine straight points to win by a bucket. Of course, Jake only learned about all this from his roommate—he'd still been on the road coming from California at game time. In order to achieve an NCAA tournament bid, the Cardinals would definitely have to step it up this season.

And stepping it up is exactly what Coach seemed to be "helping" the guys do in the practices since then. It hardly seemed fair to Jake that he had to do all the grueling punishments heaped on the guys for a loss that he wasn't even there for. But that was teamwork, and Jake was determined to be the hardest-working member-to-be on the team—even if it killed him! In high school, his quickness and hustle was what had separated him from the others, but here, everyone was fast and strong. Even lazy, sloppy Kyle-the-roommate knew how to get down and hustle when it mattered. By the time Coach finally broke the guys into half-court games of four-on-four, Jake's legs felt like jelly.

Jake was picked to guard Nate Williams, who was more than happy to show the rival freshman what Louisville basketball was all about. Jake had never been taken to school so badly in his life. Aside from an unguarded three-pointer that Nate practically dared Jake to take, there was no good news to write home about from this second practice. Nate sure hadn't looked that good on TV! Nate's new fire reminded Jake that he wasn't going to be able to just waltz in and take anyone's spot. He was going to have to fight hard to earn it.

Pushing through the front glass doors of the Yum! practice gym, Jake pulled out his phone and called Amy. He smiled as the phone rang, eager to hear his girlfriend's good news, even if it was about her casual jog through the park—anything to take his mind off the last five hours of torture and embarrassment.

"Jakey!" Amy responded before her phone even rang a second time. Although he would punch anyone else who called him that, he secretly liked the way it sounded coming from her.

"What's the good news?" Jake jumped straight to the point as he watched a breath of hot air escape his mouth and disappear slowly into the Kentucky evening. Man, he missed her! As he walked through campus passing a few other humans disguised as lumps of winter clothing, he imagined Amy wearing a little spaghetti-strap tank-top and denim skirt like those she had worn all summer. His mind's eye ran up and down her tan arms and legs, stopping to rest on a few other places along the way. He pictured their last lingering kiss and how he had held her soft, warm body close to his, her gorgeous eyes gazing right into him. In spite of the frigid air currently all around him, his body started heating up.

"Did you hear what I just said?" Amy asked, excitedly prompting a response.

Crap! "Yeah, babe. That's exciting!" Jake lied. *What did she just say?*

"Oh. I thought you would be, I don't know, a little more excited."

"I am!" Jake faked it again, hoping for some sort of clue. What had he missed?

"Okay. Well, after all our talks about God and stuff, I just wanted you to be the first to know—besides Cari, of course...umm, so how was your day?" Amy sounded disappointed.

Jake froze in his tracks as a smile exploded across his whole face. "Wait, did you become a Christian today?"

"Yeah." Amy sounded agitated. "That's what I just said."

"Woo hoo!" Jake exclaimed, leaping onto a cement bench a few feet away, the previous pain he felt from practice vanishing immediately. He raised his arms in triumph and shouted to anyone passing by, "My girl's amazing!" Hopping back down, he quickly brought the phone back to his grinning lips. "Did you hear that excitement?"

Amy laughed on the other end of the line. "Yeah, Jake, I heard it that time."

Jake shook his head in wonder. Who cared what anyone else thought? This was amazing. He'd tried so hard not to push Amy into anything, but it had been killing him that she didn't share his faith in God. She had attended church with him since the summer, but he knew she was just going for his sake. All of their conversations on the topic ended with her frustrated that it was so important to him. Chris had been clear that dating someone who didn't share the same beliefs would lead down a messy road, but the fact that Jake and Amy already had a child together kind of moved them beyond that point. So instead, Jake had prayed. And prayed and prayed. And tried to show her that God's love was better and deeper than any of the mushy feelings they had shared before. *I wonder what Cari said to her?* Jake puzzled, feeling a twinge of sadness that he hadn't been the one to finally get through. But that was stupid. How could he be bummed? His girlfriend was now a Christian! "Amy, I am so excited for you. For us!" Jake squawked. "You don't know how many times I've prayed for this. Tell me everything."

Amy started from the beginning, her voice sounding lighter and happier than it had in a long time. "I don't know why I was so afraid to meet with Cari Vaughn. She's like the nicest person I've ever met." Jake's mind got lost again in the allure of her voice until she suddenly exclaimed, "Oh my gosh, and she asked me to come check out the junior high youth group sometime!"

"Ooh! You got promoted to junior high, huh?" Jake chuckled.

"Seriously! Jake, what am I gonna do? I hated junior high!"

"You could always say no," Jake offered the obvious.

"How am I gonna do that? Tell her, 'Y'know, thanks for showing me how I can have eternal purpose, but see ya later'? Anyway, I'm thinking maybe it will be good for me."

Jake smiled, picturing his girlfriend surrounded by adoring middle-school girls. "You were Pacific High's cheerleading captain last year. That's just one step lower than Beyoncé to them."

"Are you saying that I have a big butt?" Amy questioned, her tone of voice suddenly serious.

What? "No, Amy. That's J-Lo, anyway. I just meant—"

"Gotcha!" Amy laughed playfully on the other end.

Sitting on that cement bench had left Jake's butt frozen, so he finally stood and continued the walk toward his dorm in awe of how giddy and full of life she sounded. "What did you do to my girlfriend? Are you sure you're not drunk?"

"Ha ha. You know I've been drunk before. This is sooooo much better."

✚ ✚ ✚

Two hours later, Jake finally said goodnight after talking with Amy about everything from God and faith to basketball and running. Jake hated to hang up, to lose the sound of her voice. Even though he couldn't see her, he pictured her beautiful face smiling and laughing, and he wished he could see it in person. He missed her so much!

One thing about being so far from each other, though, it was much easier to stay pure when it came to sex. When Jake had finally decided to fully follow God, one of the areas of his life he'd needed to change was his sex life. Chris had showed him a bunch of Bible verses and passages about how sex was God's idea in the first place, but that He had created it for a husband and wife to enjoy. Anything outside of that held negative consequences of varying degrees...as if Jake couldn't figure that one out on his own! Getting a girl pregnant while still in high school was definitely not his idea of a positive consequence.

At that time, Jake fully agreed and knew he wanted to wait until his wedding night to have sex again. Of course, at that time, he and Amy had broken up—which had made things a lot easier! Once they'd finally decided to start dating again during the summer, that commitment became a lot tougher, especially since Amy wasn't fully on board. She was already pregnant, she figured, so what did she have to lose? Sex had become such a habit in their relationship that they almost didn't know what to do without it.

So Chris had given Jake some great suggestions. He'd encouraged them to avoid situations that would leave them alone in private—like being alone in a room with the door closed, or at home when their parents weren't around. This forced them to try some new things and get involved in group activities, like Frisbee golf at the park or searching for the perfect gift at the dollar store. Hanging out at the beach or the mall with friends turned out to be a lot more fun than holing up in front of the TV by themselves. And watching little kids' T-ball games and passing out sandwiches to homeless people definitely helped them learn more about each other.

But even with all of these wholesome pursuits, there were many days when it was all Jake could do to rein in his racing hormones by going for a brisk walk. Fortunately, as the baby bump grew, Amy became more and more uncomfortable, and it became awkward even to get a good hug, which gave Jake the time and space to cool down and refocus on his goal of waiting until marriage. Until the week or so before he left for college, things had been going well. But as they both prepared themselves for the months they would spend apart, the temptations started coming on strong again.

So tonight, as much as Jake longed to be with Amy face-to-face, to hold her hand and see the light dance in her eyes when she smiled, he knew that moving away definitely had its benefits. There's no way he'd be able to hold a deep conversation with her if she was sitting right there next to him, her long legs perhaps dangled over his as her finger traced the muscles in his arm, her tempting lips distracting his mind from the words coming out of them.

Again catching his mind going where it shouldn't, Jake stood up quickly from his spot on the couch in the back corner of the lobby, the imprint of his butt remaining in the black microfiber. Jake carried his duffel bag past the same couple on the stairwell his dad had gotten the best of just a few days earlier. Their conversation seemed just as serious as before.

Jake's floor was nearly a ghost town. He jammed his key into the lock and opened the door to a dark room. He nonchalantly flipped on the light and immediately heard his roommate groan—a clear signal that he wanted the lights off. As Jake flipped the switch back off, feeling a little annoyed, he heard a second distinct voice from Kyle's side of the room.

"Is that your roommate?" A female's voice made him jump.

"It's okay, Jennifer. Don't leave."

"I told you, my name is Jessica," a now irritated voice whispered back, as if Jake couldn't hear every word they said.

Jake stumbled in the darkness over Kyle's mess, which was creeping back onto Jake's side. He and Kyle would need to agree on some ground rules soon. This was not okay. Jake knew he probably should go back out and wait in the hallway or the lobby, but he wanted to make a statement. He turned on a small reading lamp and looked down at his new University of Louisville basketball playbook. Maybe that could keep his mind occupied while his stupid roommate did who-knows-what with what's-her-name a few feet away.

"You told me you didn't have a roommate!" Jennifer or Jessica muttered, as she got out of bed and started to put her clothes back on. Jake quickly looked away, focusing every nerve on "3 Away" in the playbook in front of him.

"I guess I forgot," Kyle retorted weakly, without moving a muscle to stop her.

That sounds about right, Jake thought, as he loudly flipped the page as a reminder that he was there. He stared blurry-eyed at a new arrangement of Xs and Os. It was hard to concentrate with the elephant in the room. *How can a guy have sex with a girl and not even know her name? What an idiot!* How was that any different from hooking up with a prostitute? He shook his head at yet another reminder of the two very different places he and his roommate were coming from.

Finally, Jake heard their door open and close with an angry slam. Not a moment later, his roommate let out the loudest fart Jake had ever heard.

"Whew! 'Bout time she left! I was holding that thing in for twenty minutes," Kyle laughed out loud as he finally sat up in bed. "Thanks for finally getting home. That chick has no idea when she's worn out her welcome."

The room's new aroma wafted over to Jake's side like a thick, wet blanket. "Dude, that's nasty!" Jake protested, pulling his whole face into his shirt.

"Thanks."

Jake slammed his playbook shut and turned to face Kyle. The images of what probably had happened in their room over the past hour flitted unwelcomed into his head as he glanced at his roommate's naked body barely covered by a rumpled sheet.

"This isn't cool, man," Jake voiced, trying to hold back his temper.

"What do you want me to do? The Café was serving burritos."

"No, I'm talking about the girl!" Jake shook his head in disbelief.

"Who, Jennifer? What did she ever do to you?"

Was his roommate seriously this dense? "I don't care about *Jessica*, but I do care about walking into my own room with naked girls here." Jake stood up to face Kyle directly, and the smell of his roommate's odor struck him head on. Jake waved his hand in front of his face and then gestured at the pictures of girls all around the room, and finally at the one hanging over Kyle's bed. "Everywhere I look, I see boobs! And I'm sick of it. *This*—" Jake waved his arm toward the door, "just isn't working."

Kyle glanced up at his picture of the Playmate of the Month, and then his eyes darted back to Jake.

"Wait." Kyle's face looked horrified as a new realization seemed to dawn on him. "Oh man, I totally didn't see this coming." He paused, then asked, "Are you gay?"

"What?" Jake responded, totally not expecting that accusation.

Kyle mumbled on in shock. "You would think Coach would have warned me. I mean—"

"NO, I'M NOT GAY!" Jake interrupted a little too loudly, instantly wondering about the thickness of their walls and door. What was wrong with this guy? Didn't Kyle and the whole team know he'd missed the first half of the season to stay with his *girlfriend* during her pregnancy?

"Dude, then what is your problem with naked women?" Kyle puzzled.

"I just..." Words about his new faith and convictions and morals that had flown so freely from his mouth back at home now stalled at the edge of his tongue. Kyle stared at him unflinchingly, waiting for his explanation. Finally, Jake lamely muttered, "It's just...I have a girlfriend back home."

A smile of understanding slowly crept over Kyle's face. "I read ya." His mischievous grin worried Jake more than it comforted him. "You're afraid that your hot little California mama's gonna dump your sorry butt if she catches you cheating on her."

Jake hated the thought of his roommate thinking he was some wussy boy connected to a ball and chain hundreds of miles long. He wanted to tell him the real reason—that he'd lived that life before and was now determined to stay true to his relationship with Jesus.

But somehow, the words just wouldn't come out. "Uh, sure. That, and maybe I'm afraid my hot girlfriend could beat me up," Jake smiled.

"Good, 'cuz I don't want to spend the rest of the semester sleeping with a night light," Kyle chuckled, throwing a T-shirt advertising some brand of beer over his skeletal frame.

Ugh! Why was it so difficult for Jake to open up? He'd told tons of people about his new relationship with God and how it had saved his life. Why couldn't he do it now? With his heart beating uncontrollably, Jake blurted out, "Kyle, I'm a Christian."

His roommate poked his arms through his T-shirt and smiled nonchalantly back at Jake. "Yeah, so am I...Who isn't?"

Jake looked away just in time as Kyle threw off his scant covering and stood up. By the time Jake cautiously glanced back, he had pulled on a pair of jeans and a ball cap and was now headed for the door. "I'm gonna go grab a bite to eat. You want something?"

Jake shook his head. "Nah, I just ate."

"Okay, man." Kyle grabbed a wad of cash from the mess on top of his dresser and walked to the door. With one hand on the handle, he looked back at Jake with a grin. "You really had me freaking out with that whole gay thing."

"Yeah, well, to reiterate, I'm not."

Kyle walked out the door and shouted over his shoulder sarcastically, "I know—you're a Christian."

4:43pm | From: Chris | To: Jake
Grace fellowship church 9am 1392 pine ave check it out

JAKE GLANCED DOWN AT THE TEXT, then quickly slipped his phone back into his pocket. He'd forgotten that tomorrow was Sunday already. How did the week fly by so fast? *I'll look into it later,* he thought, realizing he had already neglected to return Chris's call from a few days ago. But right now, he was enjoying his first game courtside at the packed Downtown Arena, and it was awesome.

Jake had watched countless Louisville games on television, but the flat-screen just didn't do them justice. This afternoon, the Cardinals played host to last-place DePaul, and hospitality was certainly not on the menu. By halftime, it was a 27-point blowout, and things were getting progressively worse for the Blue Demons.

Coach's pounding all week had apparently worked, and the Cardinal team fought relentlessly, a new fire in their step. Tony Anderson was a stone wall on springs down in the paint, blocking shots and pulling down the boards ruthlessly. Jamal Hardaway was showing why he was one of the top three or four off-guards in the nation, carving up his defenders like a Thanksgiving turkey. And Nate Williams—that's the guy Jake was really watching, looking for chinks in his game. He was solid, but not unstoppable. As Jake studied the guy he needed to compete against for next year's squad, he was inspired. He couldn't wait to get his chance.

The other redshirts on the team surrounded Jake a few rows back from the bench, some intently focused on the unfolding action on the court, and others not so much. Kyle was one of the latter, sitting a few seats away and mostly concentrating on a couple of co-eds who were giving him their undivided attention. They laughed and smiled and flirted shamelessly, obviously stroking Kyle's ego as much as his non-existent muscles and unruly black hair. As he half-watched the game below, his running commentary informed the girls of all the things he would have and could have done differently had he been in the game.

Jake wondered what the ladies saw in him. Every time he turned around, Kyle was surrounded by new women—he was as bad as Jake's friend Doug had been in high school. Jake just didn't get it. But who was he to say anything? Ever since their awkward confrontation earlier in the week, he and Kyle had only exchanged a few words in passing. It was if his roommate had made the conscious decision that Jake was no longer a guy he wanted to get to know—probably because he was a religious weirdo who didn't like girls! *How ironic,* Jake thought wryly. But who cared? It wasn't like Jake was dying to be his friend anyway.

To Jake's right, however, sat Grant MacIntire, a redshirt from somewhere in South Texas whom Jake *was* hoping to get to know better. He was a tough guy to get a read on, very soft-spoken and reserved, but he was a dynamo on the court. He had an outside shot that was sweeter than candy, and his feet were lightning-quick down the court for long passes. He was even pretty good at scrapping his way into the mix for some sneaky rebounds. With an extra season to mature and get stronger, he would be a force to be reckoned with. Even though Jake had never actually had a full conversation with him, Grant seemed to be the most welcoming guy on the team, and the two had paired up for passing and rebound drills almost every day. While he never talked much, Grant was always the first to greet Jake with a smile and a nod.

Grant wasn't the only one Jake was getting to know. In front of him, a couple of other guys who had been relatively friendly at practice whooped and hollered and turned around to slap Jake on the knees after Jamal tossed an alley-oop to Tony, who pounded the dunk through the rim like a beast. Jake jumped to his feet with the others and cheered. As he was sitting back down, he took a quick sweeping glance around him and realized for the first time that he was actually starting to fit in. A glimmer of a grin played at the corners of his mouth, and he settled back into his seat feeling content.

With four minutes to go, Coach emptied the end of the bench, sending in all the reserves who rarely got any playing time. In the midst of Jake's state of satisfaction, an annoying thought flitted across his mind: If he'd attended the summer practices like the rest of the freshmen instead of serving Daddy-duty, he'd probably be on the court right now. A familiar stab of regret shot through his good mood, and he allowed himself to wallow in the irritation for a few minutes too long. This struggle had hounded him all summer, but rather than it growing weaker now that he was at Louisville—as he'd expected—it was actually growing more intense. He knew it took both of them to get Amy pregnant, but if she had only been stronger, they wouldn't have *both* had to derail their dreams. And even though he was now the one getting to resume his plans, he couldn't help but long for what could have been.

As he stewed in self-pity while watching the final minutes, one of the bench warmers fumbled a pass, and DePaul snatched it up and converted the steal into an easy layup. Seconds later, another Cardinal failed to read the defense and ran right into a lazy pick. The Louisville lead was still more than comfortable, but Jake found himself getting upset by these silly errors. The voice in his brain started sounding very similar to Kyle's bragging claims to the fawning flirts. Jake knew he needed to just get over it and move on, but sometimes it just felt good to be mad.

The game ended, and the crowd erupted in cheers. The guys all around Jake exchanged high-fives, waiting to follow the team to the locker room for the post-game debriefing. Jake found himself lagging a little behind, knowing it made no difference if he wasn't the first one in. His eyes tracked his shoelaces as he strolled out of the gym. Suddenly there was a shadow in front of him, and he looked up.

"You all right?" Grant asked.

"Yeah, yeah, I'm great," Jake put on a fake smile, surprised to hear Grant speak.

"Sitting out a season is no fun, huh?"

Jake snorted. "You got that right."

They walked side-by-side in silence until Grant piped up one more time in his light Texas drawl, "Next year, we're gonna show them a little sumthin' or other." He held out his fist.

Jake grinned as they knocked knuckles and continued down the tunnel toward the locker room.

✚ ✚ ✚

After grabbing a bite to eat and hanging out with Grant and a few of the other guys at a local burger joint, Jake walked into his dorm room a little before midnight. He emptied his pockets onto his desk, and his cell phone reminded him of Chris's unanswered text. *Crap!* Jake remembered that he had also not called Amy tonight. It was only 9:00 p.m. her time, but he just didn't feel like talking. *I wonder if I can get away with a text?*

While deciding on that one, he did a search for the church address that Chris had sent him. Turns out it was less than a mile from campus. Jake smiled. What a classic example of how cool Chris Vaughn was. Jake figured he'd probably spent a good half-hour researching different churches around the Louisville campus so that Jake wouldn't have to. Jake needed to give him a call. *Maybe after church tomorrow.* He brushed his teeth, read a quick chapter from the Bible, and sent Amy a short text about being tired and needing to get up early for church in the morning. He hoped that would appease her.

At 8:00 a.m., his alarm startled him awake, but his eyes refused to stay open. He hit the Off button and rolled over. Maybe he could check out the church next week. He started to doze off again, but Chris's advice to him before he left echoed through his brain: *Surround yourself with good friends. Don't get distracted by things that will bring you down. Stay in the Word. Find a good church.* How was he going to do any of that, let alone the last one, if he couldn't even get out of bed?

He rolled back over and forced himself to sit up, the chilly air raising goose bumps on his bare chest. He fought the urge to crawl back under the covers and finally stood up from bed. He threw on a pair of jeans and a clean T-shirt before grabbing his parka, which was getting far too much use this first week in Kentucky. He grabbed the pocket Bible that Chris had given him the first day he had checked out New Song almost a year ago, stuffed his wallet, phone, and keys into his pocket, and headed out the door. He glanced at the other side of the room where Kyle was out like a log. Half his body lay on top of the covers, and he was still wearing his clothes from the night before. Jake wondered how late he had been out.

The cold morning air hit Jake like a mallet to the head as he stepped outside onto a vacant campus. It was a beautiful day, but Jake brooded over how the same sun could have such minimal impact here compared to back home in California. He shivered toward his truck, wondering how long it would take the heater to warm up. The more he thought about it, he figured by the time his truck got comfortable, he could already be at church. *Might as well just take a walk,* he figured. The fresh air would do him some good. He headed west and couldn't help thinking about his first visit to New Song. That had turned out to be more than a three-mile walk—while he was still reeling from a raging hangover. Today was already off to a much better start.

Jake passed by a Dunkin' Donuts and debated stopping in for a quick cinnamon roll and cup of coffee. But a glance at the time revealed it was 8:53, which meant he needed to hurry up unless he wanted to walk in late. He hoped that Grace Fellowship shared New Song's tradition of a friendly donut-and-drink bar. He walked another hundred yards, turned the corner onto another busy street, and immediately spotted his destination.

Up ahead on the right stood a large brick building topped by a huge white steeple pointing straight up to heaven. The ample parking lot was gradually filling up as scattered individuals and huddling clusters waddled toward the front entrance. This was far different from New Song's converted warehouse, but Jake knew from TV and movies that this much more traditional-looking building was probably the norm around here. Out front was a large marquee with the message, "Always remember that hell is not cool." Jake laughed to himself, a frosty breath escaping toward the sky, and he looked around to see if anyone else noticed the humor. Apparently not. Everyone seemed intent on reaching the warmth of the church lobby. A few parents looked harried as they unloaded children from minivans crusted with dirty salt from the winter roads. Their children looked weary in their bloated winter garb. Senior citizens hobbled miserably across the bumpy black pavement. Jake didn't see a single person pause to greet anyone else.

He cut across the dead front lawn toward the entrance, where a gray-haired man in a brown suit stood passing out programs. Jake's smile was immediately met with a less-than-cordial glare.

"Son, the grass is still frozen, so please use the walkway next time." He pointed to a sidewalk filled with other people who obviously knew the rules.

"Oh, sorry." Jake extended his hand to take the program. "It's my first time here." He offered a smile to the man, who looked like he must have lost a bet to get assigned as the outside greeter.

"Welcome to Grace Fellowship," the man replied, his voice only slightly less gruff. He then turned abruptly to an older couple approaching—correctly—from the walkway.

Jake opened a heavy white door and entered a roomy foyer. Fortunately, the temperature as well as the crowd was significantly warmer inside. The crimson carpet was scattered with clusters of people engrossed in hushed conversations. On the wall directly ahead of Jake hung a giant map of the world with pictures of people pinned all over it. On the wall to the right, a sign for Sunday school was posted next to a bulletin board of various announcements. Jake glanced around optimistically for the donuts and coffee, but none were in sight.

Wandering through the lobby toward the auditorium doors, Jake had the unpleasant feeling that he was being watched. No one made eye-contact with him directly, but he caught more than a few abruptly averted stares. He suddenly realized that he stuck out like a monkey in a tutu. Not only was he the youngest person by far, but he was also the most casually dressed. As everyone else disrobed from their warm coats, Jake zipped his up even higher, hoping it would hide the stark contrast between his jeans and T-shirt and the dresses and suits that most people were wearing. He wished he would have listened to his urge to stop for coffee—not only would the caffeine be more than welcome, but it would have allowed him to sneak in without being noticed. *Too late now,* he chided himself, making a mental note to at least wear a collared shirt next time.

As he walked to the double doors, he tried to look purposeful with his stride, as if he knew what he was doing. Upon entering the auditorium, an even older man greeted Jake. In stark contrast to everyone else Jake had encountered so far, this one wore a smile as cheerful as the corsage pinned to his lapel.

"Welcome to Grace Fellowship," he beamed, thrusting his hand out to shake Jake's. The man had to be at least eighty, but his voice was energetic and his grip was firm. "I'm Jim, but my friends call me Buddy."

"Hi, I'm Jake. Umm...my pastor from back home told me to check your church out."

"You a student at the university, Jake?" Buddy asked, directing him away from the entrance by his elbow to let others pass by.

"Yeah, I'm on the basketball team."

"Oh wow, we got a celebrity here this morning!" Buddy patted him on the back and smiled.

"Well, I'm not really on the team yet," Jake admitted as a choir in red and gold robes entered the stage from a side door. His mind shot instantly to the movie *Sister Act*. As much as he would have loved to see Whoopi Goldberg waltz out in front to lead the choir in some lively show tunes, Jake was pretty sure that was not going to be part of this morning's repertoire.

Seeing Jake's attention distracted up front, Buddy grinned, "You better run and grab yourself a seat; our choir is doing a new number this morning."

Jake chuckled to himself, noticing the vast selection of empty pews he could choose from. Those that were filled were mostly occupied by people who were a good fifty years his senior. Jake helped himself to an empty pew near the back as the organist played the prelude to the choir's exciting new number.

What happened next Jake could only compare to a combination of all of the worst *American Idol* auditions he'd laughed at in his living room rolled up into one painful sound. "Oh the deep, deep love of Jesus..." the choir sang morosely. "Vast, unmeasured, boundless, free..." The dreary, sluggish tune of the song did not match the message of the lyrics at all, and the off-key performance only made it worse. But you wouldn't have known it by looking at the singers on stage. Most of them gray-haired seniors, each standing as tall as they could, looking like they were singing for the president. Some looked solemn, as if the significance of this performance rode on the gravity of their expressions, while others wore grins that lit up their whole face. All of them sounded horrible.

Jake looked around the room to make sure he wasn't the brunt of some major gag. But judging by the looks on everyone else's face, this kind of performance was not only tolerated, it was applauded. Jake fidgeted anxiously, wondering how much more of this he could take, when he felt a quick tap on his shoulder. He looked around to see Buddy sitting in the row behind him. Buddy leaned forward to whisper in his ear.

"The Bible says we're supposed to make a joyful 'noise'; that's what they're doing right now." He smiled and gave Jake a wink.

Another verse came and went, sounding pitifully the same, and Jake shifted in his seat, buckling down to endure it. Again, he heard a low voice behind him.

"See that foxy lady there in the second row? The one with the red flower in her hair? She's my wife." Buddy beamed proudly. "Been married sixty-two years last October, and she's purtier now than the day I first met her."

Sixty-two years! Jake marveled. He couldn't even imagine it, but it sure was cute. He wondered if he and Amy would even make it to a wedding, let alone six decades. How had Buddy and his "foxy lady" done it? Pretty amazing.

However unfriendly the rest of the church seemed to be, and however bad the choir was, Jake liked this guy. As the choir started their fourth verse—sounding as awful as the three before it—Jake found himself no longer cringing but actually watching the passionate fervor of the singers, especially Mrs. Foxy, with enjoyment. These people didn't need or want a recording contract. And most of them probably couldn't even hear each other without a hearing aid. But they were performing for God with all their hearts, and Jake was pretty confident that God was pleased.

The choir leader turned around after the song and instructed the rest of the congregation to stand up and turn to number 173 in their hymnals. Jake hadn't seen one of those since he'd visited his grandmother's church for occasional Christmas Eve and Easter services as a little boy. He found the page and smiled to himself as the rest of the room broke into the only hymn he remembered.

"Amazing Grace, how sweet the sound, that saved a wretch like me..." Jake mumbled the words on the page. How true that was. God's grace *was* pretty amazing when he took the time to think about it.

It was also pretty fortunate, for as Jake attempted to sing along, he realized just how much his own voice was lacking. When he had sung along at New Song, the band and the rest of the youth group had been so loud that he'd never really heard himself. But here in this sparsely populated room, where he could actually hear his own voice, reality checked in. He sucked.

Maybe I shouldn't have been so hard on the choir! he laughed to himself. But if the choir had the guts to get up there on stage…behind a mic…and belt the notes out with utter disregard for the tune, then what did Jake have to worry about? With new gusto, Jake sang out the last line, "…Was blind but now I seeeeee!"

Even though this was one of the weirdest places Jake had ever been, it actually felt good to praise God in his new hometown. After a couple more hymns that Jake had never heard before, the choir filed feebly off stage, and a gray-haired man looking to be only a few years younger than most of the congregation got up behind a large mahogany podium. Jake figured he must be the senior pastor.

He spoke with a laid-back Southern accent as he clutched the sides of the podium. He used nothing except his giant Bible as he spoke about Jesus' encounter with ten men who had leprosy. Jake leaned forward to try and pay attention, but the lilting drawl made every sentence seem like an eternity, and it was all Jake could do to keep his eyelids open. He was sure the pastor was saying something important, but Jake just couldn't get his mind to focus.

His thoughts began to wander to some of the messages he'd heard Chris give over the past several months. Chris had the unique ability to make him split his gut laughing in one moment and then be challenged to live differently the next. When Jake had groaned to Chris that he would never be able to find someone like him in Kentucky, Chris had humbly joked that guys like him were a dime a dozen. If Jake could stumble into New Song that easily, he was sure to find a replacement church at college. But after fifty-five minutes of this old preacher's droning, Jake wasn't sure how much more of the search he could handle.

Never in his life had he so looked forward to someone saying "Amen." The moment the word crept out of the pastor's mouth, Jake bolted toward the exit.

With one foot out the door, a familiar wrinkly, spotted hand grabbed his shoulder.

"It was a blessing meeting you today, Jake." Buddy threw out his other hand for a goodbye shake.

Jake felt a piece of paper between their hands and looked down to see a five-dollar bill in his palm.

"Wait a minute. What's this for?" Jake stammered.

"Young bucks like you can always use a little treat," the grandfatherly man squinted with delight.

"You don't have to do this," Jake awkwardly tried to hand the folded bill back to Buddy. He was pretty sure the old man needed it more than he did.

"I know, it's called grace. Weren't you listening to the sermon?" Buddy smiled and gave Jake a wink. "Just say thank you, go buy yourself an ice cream cone, and then pass some on to somebody else sometime."

"Thanks, uh, Buddy," Jake chuckled and shook his head.

Buddy slapped him lightly on the shoulder and then turned to greet some older members leaving the sanctuary. Jake stuffed the cash in his front pocket and walked out into the crisp air. The freezing weather certainly didn't whet his appetite for a frozen treat, but that coffee and donut still sounded good. Maybe it would be a good time to catch up with Chris...and Amy.

He walked back to Dunkin' Donuts, reflecting on the morning's experience. It had definitely been different from what he was expecting, and he doubted that he'd return there, but it was good to know he had a new "friend" in town, and he hoped to see Buddy again sometime. Jake ordered his much-craved caffeine and cinnamon roll, and then spontaneously decided to get one more to go. Buddy had said he should pass the favor on sometime, and what better opportunity than to try to sweeten up his roommate. It couldn't hurt...right?

10:37am | From: Jake | To: Chris
Any other suggestions?

2:06pm | From: 19565550832 | To: Jake
Dude come watch the super bowl

JAKE PUZZLED OVER THE TEXT from the unfamiliar number as he trekked back to his dorm. *Where's a 956 number from?* And who'd be inviting him to a Super Bowl party anyway? The team was traveling to tomorrow's game at Syracuse, and Jake couldn't think of anyone else who would have his number.

Jake texted back, "Who is this?" and waited for a reply.

He was walking back to campus from yet another church Chris had suggested—his third in the four weekends since he'd moved here. This one was yet another flop. Jake could understand why so many people gave up going to church if they were all like these: unfriendly, boring, and filled with people who looked half-dead. There were some highlights, like meeting Buddy, but none worth going back for. Even the donut table Jake had found today wasn't enough to drag a return visit out of him.

Part of the problem was none of them were like New Song. He tried not to compare, but either the sermon was different or the way people dressed up was different or the music was different or even the smell of the building was different. And, with the exception of Buddy, Jake had yet to meet someone who cared even a fraction as much as Chris. It seemed like most people sitting in the pews were just going through the motions. What was the use in that?

Chris had persuaded Jake to try one more church this morning, but the whole church-hunting thing was getting old. Last Sunday, Jake had just slept in.

Something was changing. Over the past month that he'd been away at college, Jake felt like he was fading into a bland existence. His classes were okay, but he was working far harder than he'd ever had to in high school to keep up with all the reading. And basketball was still fine, but all practice and no play sure took the fun out of it. Some of the guys were nice enough, but Jake sure seemed to get the brunt of Nate and Jamal's bad attitude—both on and off the court. And no one else really stepped out of their way to get to know him. Jake couldn't believe how different things were from high school.

The situation with his roommate was getting worse, too. Kyle rarely spoke to Jake anymore, and his mess had taken over Jake's desk and dresser and floor as if Jake wasn't even there. Meanwhile, Kyle's female visitors were more common than flies. Not wanting to deal with them nor the thick cloud of marijuana that Kyle often basked in, Jake retreated to the safety of the library for most of his studying. Jake had attempted several friendly gestures—like the cinnamon roll from several weeks back—but Kyle was rarely awake or alert enough to notice. He slept all day and stayed out all night, somehow fitting basketball practice in between. Jake wondered where he found time for classes and homework.

The crazy thing, though, was how vigorously Kyle performed on the court. In spite of his scrawny frame, he had a strong presence in the paint both on defense and offense. He could block shots with foul-free finesse and pull a rebound down and out of the tangle of larger grasping bodies before anyone even noticed. His shot underneath needed to get stronger, but his baseline jumper was money in the bank. Jake kind of enjoyed watching him push against Tony and some of the other big guys, and he tried to be encouraging, but Kyle didn't seem to notice.

At least Jake still had Amy. *I guess,* Jake sighed.

Amy really seemed to be doing great. She was still running with Andrea a couple of times a week, and the two had become really good friends. She sounded happier every time they talked, and her annoying nagging Jake had grown used to was surprisingly absent. She sounded more and more confident, talking with enthusiasm about what she was learning in her different classes, especially Psychology. On top of that, she was learning more about the Bible, thanks to her now-enthusiastic church attendance and weekly meetings with Cari. Almost daily, Amy flooded Jake with new questions about God and faith and what she was reading. Jake was really happy for her. But her increasing joy did nothing to help his increasing discontent.

So, here he was, meandering back to his room where books awaited him, enjoying the surprisingly "warm" weather. Funny that now he considered temperatures in the high fifties as warm—warm enough that he ditched his well-worn winter coat in exchange for a simple sweatshirt, warm enough to tease him into walking the mile and a half to church this morning rather than drive. On the way back, he stopped at a little park and called Amy from his perch on a swing. She had been asleep but sounded happy to talk with him. For the first time in a while, life actually felt good to Jake, and he smiled mindlessly as he approached campus.

Jake walked up the steps to Miller Hall, still with no answer from his mystery texter. Was someone messing with him? He knew he should just ignore it and go study, but he really wanted some plans for Super Bowl Sunday—so he gave in and dialed the number. Michael Bublé played in the background. *This must be a joke.* Jake winced.

"What up, Taylor?" a familiar but unidentifiable voice suddenly answered.

"Hey, man, why'd you have to pick up? I was diggin' the tune," Jake joked, hoping for a clue about who he was talking to.

The voice Jake knew he should know chuckled ambiguously. "What are you doing this afternoon?"

Nothing. This was the first time in his life he didn't have official plans to watch the big game, and even though he couldn't care less whether Carolina or New York won, he was a little bummed. "You tell me." Jake tried to sound cool.

"Party, clubroom of the Belfry. Come over anytime. Bring something to share," the voice instructed more than invited.

Jake nodded his head to no one. "Okay. But seriously, Michael Bublé?"

Click. Jake looked down at his dead phone. *Crap!* Jake cringed at the impeccable timing his battery had chosen to conk out. He still had no clue who he'd been talking to...but at least he now had plans. He had seen a liquor store on his walk back from church, so Jake turned back around to go grab his contribution to the party—a couple of bags of Doritos. He assumed "bring something to share" probably referred to something more of the liquid variety, but he hoped the chips would satisfy some cravings, too.

Once he finally got back to his room, he contemplated the pros and cons of heading directly to the festivities. East Coast time meant the game didn't start until after six, so he still had a few hours to kill somewhere. It would be fun to have an excuse to avoid studying and to actually hang out with some new friends, yet from years of his own celebratory gatherings, Jake knew that "hanging out" would probably simply consist of chugging down immense quantities of alcohol, and that was something he was still trying to avoid.

So instead, homework won out, and Jake settled down at his desk, trying to unpack Keats for his Brit Lit course. His eyes scanned the pages reluctantly, but his brain couldn't focus. Of course, the lingering dregs of Kyle's pot fumes mixed with the stale stench of his sweaty gym shorts didn't help. Jake kept finding himself staring out the window, his literature book never moving past page 433.

He was jolted back to reality by the ringing of his phone in its charger, and Jonny's face glowed on the screen. Jake smiled. He hadn't talked to his funny friend for a couple of weeks.

"Hey, buddy!" Jake answered, grateful for the rescue.

"Jake, dude! How are you?" Jonny replied.

They talked about the weather (it was eighty-five degrees back home and Jake was jealous), and school (Jonny was rocking pre-calculus), and that morning's church service (Jonny could only remember some illustration about Chris throwing a candy bar into a pool and pretending it was a turd) and the Super Bowl (Jonny had no idea who was even playing, but Andrea was hosting a party for the youth group at her super-nice ocean-view house, and Jonny was nervous).

"Dude, I can't figure out what shirt to wear. Do you think I should go with the yellow one with stripes, or my Manga heroes one?"

Jake was stumped. "Um, which one matches your eyes better?" he joked.

"Well, I don't have yellow eyes, so probably the Manga one." Jonny was serious.

"Then, yeah, go with that one."

"This is important, Jake, 'cuz I think I'm finally going to ask her out again tonight."

Poor guy. Months after their disastrous ice cream date, the boy still would not give up. Jake had to hand it to him for persistence. "What's your plan this time?"

"Well, what do you think? I just got my permit, so I was thinking maybe we could go to the movies or something."

"Bro, you still need an adult to drive with you. Don't you think it might be a little awkward with her mom sitting in the back seat the whole time?" Jake laughed, knowing Jonny's own mom was never home long enough to help.

"You're right," Jonny groaned. "Maybe just walking down to the beach for a picnic would work. I could set up a blanket ahead of time and candles and..."

Jake's mind drifted as Jonny's plans took shape. He thought back to his many picnic dates with Amy at their special spot by the cliffs, and different memories flickered through his brain. A bikini-clad Amy danced through his thoughts, and he felt her warm, sandy touch...

"Do y'think that'll work?" Jonny inquired.

"Sure, yeah," Jake stammered, hoping he didn't miss anything that could derail Jonny. "Just make sure you leave the bacon bits at home this time."

"Ha ha, very funny," Jonny laughed. "But seriously, I'm definitely not going to try to kiss her this time. I don't care if she tackles me."

Jonny asked him all about school and basketball and suggested he keep incense burning in the room to counteract all of Kyle's smells—and cut an onion in half to absorb all the germs. Jake smiled, entertained as usual by his quirky friend.

"Dude, I gotta go brush my teeth, but I'm praying for you," Jonny said abruptly. And like that, the conversation ended as unexpectedly as it had begun.

"Thanks, man. Tell the gang I said hi."

As Jake set his phone down on his desk, he felt a little something like homesickness creep in. He missed those guys. He missed Oceanside. He missed his old life.

If studying was hard before, it was nearly impossible now, so Jake decided to make some other phone calls. Chris was probably done with church by now, so he gave him a ring. He caught him and Caleb making their second round through the Sunday Costco samples. That guy really did love the place.

"What's Caleb got all over his face today?" Jake joked, remembering a few of the trips he'd taken with the Vaughn family to the happiest place in Oceanside.

"Why don't I let the man himself answer that one?" Chris offered.

"MEATBALLS!" Caleb's voice yelled enthusiastically into the other end of the phone. "Daddy, let's go again," the four-year-old ordered, already on to his next train of thought.

"I don't know where this kid gets it," Chris laughed. "Hey, did you check out the new church this morning?" he asked, his voice full of eagerness.

"Yep," Jake responded unsubtly.

"That bad?" Chris caught on right away.

"Let's just say that the only people that didn't have gray hair were bald," Jake complained. "And you never told me Christians in Kentucky were so grumpy."

"They aren't. At least, not all of them, I imagine. Maybe you should ask around on campus to see where other students attend. Caleb, put that down. You're not old enough for coffee."

Jake laughed at the thought of Caleb on caffeine. "It sounds like you're busy, man. I'll catch you later."

"Hang in there, Jake. I know God's got you at Louisville for a reason."

The mini pep-talk again reminded Jake of all he was missing back home, and he hung up with reluctance. He could use more of Chris' thoughtfully challenging guidance. Instead, he turned to his mom. He knew she was a prime candidate for the empty-nest syndrome, but he hadn't called her nearly as much as he'd planned. But there was no time like the present.

Pam had just come back from a "Spiritual Day Spa" event with other women at the church and was in good spirits. She had now been attending New Song for three months, and Jake still couldn't get over the changes in his mother. She was a different woman, so full of life and joy and confidence now.

"Your dad called me yesterday," Pam nonchalantly introduced the awkward topic halfway through the conversation. She chuckled lightly.

Unable to read what his mom was thinking, Jake could only respond, "Really? What for?"

"No reason. Just to say hi." She didn't sound overly excited or upset.

"Okay." Jake felt like the moments before a big game when the butterflies began to spread their wings and fly all over his insides. He waited for his mom to continue.

"Oh, and I ran into Jan and Emily at the grocery store last week," she moved on to the next subject. "That baby is soooo cute. She has your ears." Apparently his mom had nothing more to say on the last topic.

Jake was curious about his dad and what was going on between his parents, but he didn't press the issue. At the same time, he wasn't too excited to talk about his child. That whole situation just felt a little weird. Emily wasn't his anymore, so he might as well move on.

His mom must have taken the hint from his silence, because she changed the subject yet again to some new organic diet she was starting. From there they talked and laughed for another twenty minutes about things like the weather and his roommate and Pam's big plans to go shopping during the game today. This kind of conversation was something that had been lacking for the first 18 years of their relationship, and Jake wondered how things might have been different had they figured it out earlier. As Jake hung up the phone, for the first time in a long time, he was actually grateful for his parents, and he even missed them a little.

He was about to call his dad, but he glanced at the time and realized he should be heading to the party—he had spent the whole afternoon on the phone. *I'm turning into a chick!* Jake lamented. He threw on his Chargers jersey just to represent, grabbed a sweatshirt and the Doritos that had been begging to be opened all afternoon, and headed out the door for some solid guy time.

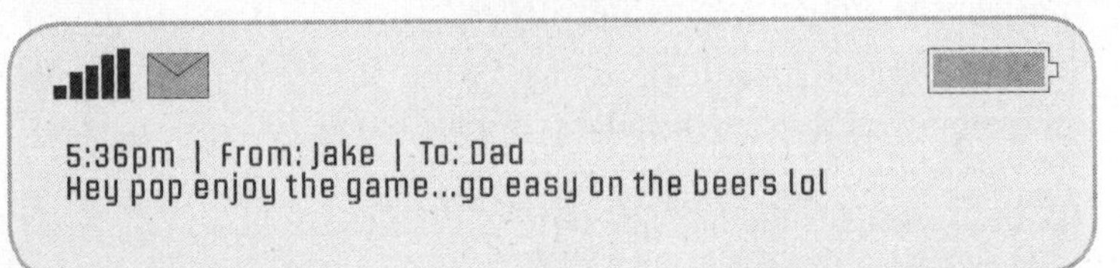

5:38pm | From: 19565550832 | To: Jake
Hey dude u comin or what

THE BELFRY WAS THE APARTMENT COMMUNITY where Jake had attended that nearly-traumatic party his first night on campus. Located about a mile away from the university, it was designed with students in mind, and its amenities boasted everything from flat-screen TVs to stand-up tanning beds.

Unable to find parking within the complex, Jake found a spot down the street and walked back to the action. Apartment doors were open, spilling out their muffled conversations, thumping music, and TV commentators. He passed clusters of loitering students in the parking lot, most holding glass bottles in varying shades of green and brown. Guys and girls were scattered everywhere, and Jake vaguely recognized quite a few faces from around campus. But he couldn't find anyone who would have invited him here.

His steps rapidly propelled him to nowhere, and he realized he needed to figure something out—quick. He didn't see anyone he knew well enough to strike up a conversation, and no one was going out of their way to greet him. His armpits started sweating profusely in spite of the chilling evening as he carried his puffy bags of chips through the mass of bodies, looking for someone or *something* to divert his attention. Suddenly this didn't seem like such a good idea.

In high school, Jake was always the one everyone knew, and the moment he arrived at a party, he was the center of attention. Tonight, no one even thought twice about his presence, and he felt totally alone. At this point, he would have even loved to tag along with Kyle. *I wonder if he's here,* the hopeful thought flitted across Jake's mind. Could he have been the one who texted Jake? No, that was definitely not his burly voice on the phone. *And he most definitely would not pick a Michael Bublé tune to greet his callers.* Unless, of course, this was all part of the joke.

Throngs spilled out of the propped-open double-glass doors of the clubroom up ahead, and Jake squeezed his way through the entry, hoping that whoever had texted him would see him quickly. *Not likely,* Jake grunted, as he wormed his way through the crowd.

Finally, he saw someone he recognized. Commentator Al Michaels looked back at him from the 60-inch flat-screen, inviting him into a conversation that everyone else seemed to be ignoring.

Jake glanced at his phone. Only minutes until kick-off. He could do this. While he contemplated plopping right down on one of the unoccupied sofas, his bulky bags of chips reminded him that he needed to unload his pathetic offering. Over to his right was a table piled high with a couple of kegs and countless cases of beer, so Jake walked over to try to inconspicuously stash it away. To his pleasant surprise, his Doritos weren't completely alone. He tossed his bags next to seven other unopened ones.

"Taylor, you made it!" the mystery caller's voice shouted from behind him.

Jake spun around to see Grant from the team walking toward him in a Cowboys jersey and a big smile on his face. They gave each other a man-hug and a high-five as the tension Jake had been carrying slipped away. Jake had read Grant to be a quiet guy who liked to keep to himself, but obviously there was another side to his practice partner—which was probably why Jake didn't recognize the more outgoing version of his voice on the phone earlier.

"You live here?" Jake questioned, as he opened a bag of chips with new confidence.

"Nah, man. I'm in Minardi. You want a beer?" Grant asked, grabbing a can for himself.

Minardi Hall was the mandatory residence for the entire basketball team. It also provided housing for some freshmen. Had Jake come in the fall as planned, it would have definitely been his home, too. He suddenly wondered why Kyle hadn't been placed there.

Grant waived a can at Jake, and even though the tiniest of cravings tickled his brain, Jake stayed strong. "No thanks, I'm good. You care who wins?"

Grant didn't pressure, but simply popped the top of his own and tossed back a generous gulp. "I always root for the underdog. So today, I guess that means Car—"

"Grant, who's your friend?" a petite blond wearing a close-fitting Jets jersey interrupted flirtatiously.

Her jersey must have been a size child's small, yet it was knotted in the back to make it even snugger, revealing a seductive inch or two of her sexily toned abs. The neckline was cut into a yawning V to give breathing room to her crowded chest. Some verses from Song of Solomon sprang to Jake's mind as he unintentionally admired her curves. She wrapped her arm cozily around Grant's waist but never took her eyes off Jake. Jake smiled back politely, exercising every ounce of self-discipline to keep his eyes from wandering down to the deep plunge.

"Nicole, this is Jake Taylor," Grant introduced, as a herd of guys rushed toward the big screen to watch the opening kickoff.

In the stampede, Jake was bumped forward, and his body brushed against Nicole's. An involuntary thrill raced through the pit of his stomach, and his hormones jumped to high alert. "It's nice to meet you," Jake grinned as nonchalantly as he could, trying not to send her any of the wrong signals.

Something about Nicole seemed very familiar, and Jake racked his brain for where he had seen her before. *Is she in one of my classes?* he puzzled. Or did she live in his dorm? Or maybe his brain was just playing tricks on him, grasping for something they had in common.

"You like football?" Nicole asked him, lightly touching his arm.

Jake's bicep flinched, which he tried to cover with a shrug. "Sure," he answered. "Do you?"

"Heck yeah! I grew up in New York, so we've been hoping for this game for awhile. C'mon, let's go grab a seat." She grabbed his hand and pulled him toward the couch without waiting for his response.

Startled, Jake stumbled forward and followed the assertive vixen before he knew what he was doing. He uneasily took a quick look back at Grant, who gave him a warning glance but didn't follow him. Nicole nestled her way into a seat on the leather sofa and pulled Jake down right next to her just as the Jets ran for a 13-yard first down.

"Woohoo!" Nicole squealed, jumping up from her seat. "That's what I'm talkin' about!"

Jake leaned back and smiled at her enthusiasm. He had to admit, he would have loved to see Amy get into sports like Nicole did. Amy dutifully watched all his games and easily followed what was going on. She even had a great memory for all his statistics, but when it came to professional athletics, she couldn't care less. While Jake and his dad had spent countless hours watching Lakers and Chargers games, Amy often resented what she felt was a waste of his time.

Nicole squeezed back into the narrow space next to Jake, and their bodies pressed together. "Do you have enough room?" she looked up and asked, her face mere inches from his.

Not sure how to respond, Jake simply nodded, trying to stay cool.

"So you're from California, huh?" Nicole probed, her attention focusing back on the screen.

"Yeah, born and raised," Jake replied, wondering how she knew that.

"I figured from your Chargers jersey." Her gaze remained fixed on the game.

Her subtle perfume entangled Jake's senses while her casual detachment drew him in. Who was this girl? And why was he so intrigued? Even with the game blaring through the surround-sound and the action jumping out from the gigantic HD screen in front of him, Jake found himself staring at the back of this girl who just floated into his life. As he sank into the allure, one last coherent thought shot into his mind: *Amy.*

Jake envisioned the look of horror and betrayal that would sweep across her beautiful face if she were to walk in the room and find this unquestionably attractive college girl practically sitting on his lap. He knew this was the one thing Amy truly feared about letting him go off to Louisville alone. More than once she had hinted that she had concerns about whether he would stay true to her.

It's not like you're doing anything wrong, man, something other than his brain objected. *You're just sitting here watching the game.* But if that were true, then why did he feel so guilty?

People smiled and laughed all around him, but Jake started to feel trapped. Part of him was enjoying every moment of being squeezed up against this extremely hot temptation, but the rest of him was growing all too aware of the bad feeling creeping over him.

"Shut up, shut up. It's the commercials!" Nicole's playful tone took control of the lively crowd.

Her hand rested casually on Jake's thigh, and Jake could feel his whole body begin to heat up. *Any nineteen-year-old guy's would in this situation, right?* He tried to concentrate on the baby Budweiser Clydesdales playing in a field, but the warmth radiating through his core left him utterly distracted. Then he realized that Nicole's hand had slid off his leg down to the couch cushion where his was resting, and they were now touching. It really wasn't that big a deal, but he knew he should probably move his hand.

He didn't. And neither did she.

The room erupted in laughter, but he missed the punch line.

Jake unconsciously squirmed in his seat. Nicole turned back toward him, the numbers on her jersey brushing tightly against his arm.

"You okay?" she smiled.

"Yeah, I just gotta go to the bathroom," Jake replied, mumbling the first excuse that raced to his mind.

"Okay, I'll save your seat," Nicole assured him nonchalantly, and her left eye blinked.

Was that a wink? Jake couldn't tell, but he knew he needed to get out of there. His palms were sweating worse than the first time he'd gone out with Amy. He had to pull himself together. He pushed through the wall of TV viewers into the still-crowded lounge area. *Crap!* He realized he had no clue where any bathroom was located. There had to be one somewhere.

"Bro, you know where there's a bathroom around here?" he found himself asking a guy grabbing a beer from the table.

The guy pointed to the corner, and Jake hurried in that general direction, finding an unoccupied bathroom at the end of a short hallway. Jake shut the door behind him and leaned back against it, breathing a sigh of relief as he felt his body temperature slowly head back toward normal. He walked over to the sink and splashed cold water on his face, looking at himself long and hard in the mirror. *What's going on here?* he asked himself. *What do you think you're doing?* He knew he needed to get out of this situation in a hurry, but what was he supposed to do? Why was he even feeling this way in the first place? What was wrong with him?

A knock on the door startled him out of his trance. "Jake?" Nicole's voice rang through the hollow wood.

"Uh, yeah?" Jake reached out to flush the toilet to make his story seem more believable.

"I gotta run. Just didn't want you to think I ditched you."

Jake ran the faucet while toweling off his damp face, took one more deep breath, and then opened the door. "Oh, okay." Jake tried to catch the surprise in his voice. "Nice meeting you."

"You too," Nicole smiled, reaching up to give Jake a goodbye hug.

Her jersey crept even higher, and Jake couldn't help but brush against her soft skin as he feebly returned the embrace.

"I'll give you a call sometime," she added, as she turned to go. Her fingertips waved goodbye over her shoulder, and with that she was gone, swallowed up into the crowd.

Jake felt his heartbeat speed up a little. A moment ago he was trying to figure out how to avoid the pretty little thing, but now that she was gone, he felt a twinge of disappointment. There was something mysterious about Nicole. *Like her last name,* Jake realized.

Jake retraced his steps back toward the TV, where he spotted Grant standing in the back trying to watch the game.

"What do you know about Nicole?" Jake asked his new friend as casually as possible after a few minutes of blindly staring at the TV.

"Oooh, I'd be careful if I was you," Grant warned, his eyebrows emphasizing a playful smirk. "Last I noticed, she was Nate's girl."

Jake suddenly realized where he recognized her from. At that first party, she was the blonde dripping from Nate's arm. She had been on the sideline during his little test. And since then, he'd seen her hanging out after practice a few times, presumably waiting for Nate. Well, that was one more reason to steer clear—as if Amy wasn't a good enough reason already.

So then why couldn't he get Nicole out of his mind?

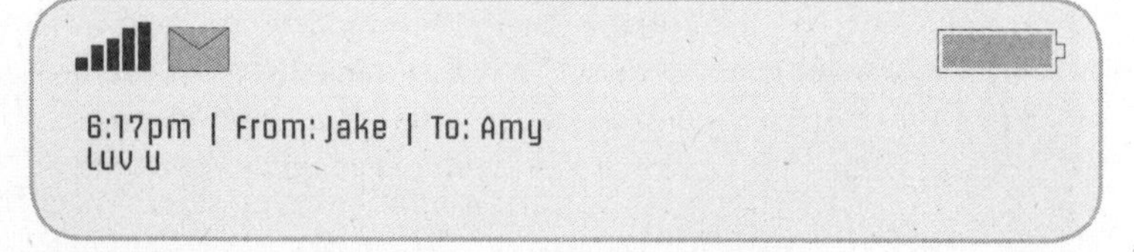

AMY SMILED AS SHE LOOKED DOWN at the text. Jake had sure stepped it up as a boyfriend over the past couple of days, calling and texting whenever he had an extra second. She didn't know what had gotten into him, but she wasn't complaining. *Maybe it was something he heard at church this weekend,* she figured. Whatever it was, it gave her hope that this long-distance relationship thing just might have a chance after all—something she hadn't been too sure of lately.

Jake had seemed to be changing, growing detached. Their nightly calls had grown routine and repetitive. And as excited as Amy was about all the new things she was learning at school and at church, Jake didn't seem to understand...or care. But then suddenly, yesterday morning, Jake called her on his way to his second class, just to wish her a happy Monday. In the middle of class, he had texted her that he was praying for her. And then at lunch, he texted her to say he was thinking of her. Little messages like that had continued throughout the day, and during their normal evening conversation he had sounded livelier and more interested than he'd been in weeks. Again this morning, he surprised her with a wake-up call and told her about a passage in the Bible that he had just read. Since then, they had exchanged well over a hundred texts, from funny ones to flirty ones to sweet ones. It was as if they were in high school again, unable to make it through an entire class without communicating. And Amy couldn't stop smiling.

During her fifteen-minute break between classes that morning, Amy had jumped on a computer at the library and found herself checking plane fares to Louisville. She found a couple of decent prices and started to daydream about surprising him with a trip east over spring break. She grinned just thinking about the look on his face when she showed up unannounced, especially now that she was looking so much better.

Last time Jake had seen Amy, the pudgy pregnancy cushion that was enveloping her body was leaving her feeling much less than beautiful. In the month since then, thanks to extensive hours spent with Cari and Andrea and some of the other girls at church, Amy had come a long way toward learning that true beauty came from the inside—and that the size of one's butt had nothing to do with the size of one's heart. For the first time in her life, Amy was starting to feel free from the pressure to always look her best and impress people. It felt good! At the same time, running with Andrea had given her a new love for exercise, and Amy enjoyed it every day now. Working out gave her a chance to process the thoughts and emotions that used to just run her ragged on the inside. She found herself far less stressed out and irritated, not to mention it had melted away all that excess baby weight she was oh-so-ready to leave behind. Amy couldn't wait for Jake to see this new and improved her...inside and out.

At the same time, she *totally* couldn't wait to see Jake. Talking on the phone was nice, but it didn't compare to seeing him face-to-face. And Jake couldn't hug her through the phone—and she *really* missed his hugs. His arms were so strong, and Amy loved the feeling of being swallowed up in his reassuring embrace. Cari and Andrea were definitely good huggers, but they weren't Jake.

As she drove, Amy calculated what she'd need to do to be able to afford the ticket. Her part-time job she'd started at the mall two weeks ago would help, but minimum wage wouldn't add up that quickly. Her mind tallied up her birthday and Christmas money, added it to her savings, and figured it had to be more than enough. *Maybe I'll buy it tomorrow,* she thought, giddy with anticipation.

But her happy thoughts were interrupted as she drove into New Song's parking lot, which was already filling with preteens gathering for the car rally. She'd successfully postponed taking Cari's suggestion to check out the middle school group at New Song for the last few weeks. But Amy had finally relented when Cari shared they were still a few drivers short for the huge event tonight. Amy drove her mom's old minivan, which could seat seven easily, so how could she say no?

Watching the crazy boys run around the cars and hearing the girls squawk around them made Amy wish she *had* said no. Just being around these squealing girls brought back a flood of uncomfortable memories. Amy recalled her own sixth-grade year, when her body started developing so much more quickly than the other girls' in her classes. She thought about how the other girls had teased and excluded her—and how the boys had stared. As the memories flooded back, they brought with them that lonely, rejected feeling, that desperation for a kind word or a loving touch from anyone...just a little acceptance from anyone at all. The feeling swelled sick in her stomach, and she automatically tucked her chin and folded her arms tightly over her chest—the way she'd spent most of that year walking through the hallways of her junior high.

Why am I here? she wondered, thinking that maybe it wasn't too late to drive back out of the parking lot and text Cari that something had come up.

"Paging Amy Briggs!" Amy heard her name coming from somewhere to her right. Chris Vaughn was shouting through a megaphone at her car from the lobby doorway. Behind him stood a huddle of adults holding loose papers.

Amy pasted on a smile and waved as she parked her car at the end of a row of other vans along the front curb. *Too late now,* she groaned as she slid out of the van and hustled toward the front door.

"Sorry I'm late," Amy nervously smiled and found a spot to stand next to Cari.

Her new mentor-friend locked elbows with Amy and whispered in her ear, "Thanks for coming."

Chris smiled warmly and continued his instructions to the group about the rules of the game. Amy tried to catch up as she received the same papers everyone else had.

"Now, does everybody have a camera?" Chris asked scanning the group.

Amy nodded, tapping her pocket to make sure she was packing her iPhone.

"You've got two hours to take as many of these pictures on this sheet as you can. Your group has to be in the shot."

Amy glanced at the sheet and let out an uncontrollable laugh as she read through the list.

CAMERA CAR RALLY

10-Point Pictures

Your team with a...

cop
teacher
ocean wave
cute dog
Wal-Mart Greeter
7-11 Slurpee
Porta-Potty
palm tree
marshmallow up nose
cheerleader
librarian
U.S. Marine
recently caught fish

25-Point Pictures

Your team with a...

snake
New Song Senior Pastor
school mascot
hundred-dollar bill
celebrity
city council member
baby less than 3 months old

50-Point Pictures

Your team with a...

local mayor
giraffe
person over 100 years old
man in Santa Claus suit
pilot and his plane
Lamborghini
hot-air balloon
cow

She poked Cari in the arm and pointed at the last one. "Where are we gonna find a cow?"

"Can't tell you; you're not on my team," Cari grinned.

Amy turned her attention back to Chris, who was finishing up the instructions.

"Finally, turn back to the 3 x 5 card stapled to the front of your packet. These are the students on your team. Just remember...the goal isn't winning a silly game; it's loving them." Chris' eyes gleamed with sincerity, and his voice turned soft as heads around the circle nodded in agreement.

No wonder Jake was so changed by him. Amy wondered how different her life might have been if she had known the Vaughns while she was struggling through junior high. She pulled out her 3 x 5 card with four girls' names written in Chris' chicken-scratch: Lindsey Calen, Melia Curren, Alyx Bogus, and Gabbi Lewis.

Cari peered over her shoulder to glance at her list. "I'll be praying for you," she laughed, and gave Amy a quick squeeze as she headed toward her car.

"What's that supposed to mean?" Amy called after her.

Cari responded over her shoulder, "You'll see."

A few feet away, Chris' siren blared obnoxiously, startling Amy out of her nervous stare. Apparently, someone else had prepped the students, because everyone in the parking lot started running to cars. At the end of the row, Amy's minivan now had a card with the number "5" posted on the windshield, and four impatient pre-teens stood looking at her. Amy gulped hesitantly, but the slamming of doors and the screech of tires peeling away from the church stirred a dormant competitive drive within her, and before she knew what was happening, she found herself running.

"Are you guys ready?" Amy shouted to her team, as she unlocked the passenger doors. Far from exuding the excitement she was expecting, the girls merely glanced at her and piled in. One skinny girl with frizzy red hair rolled her eyes. None of the girls grabbed shotgun, so Amy was left as a chauffeur. Trying to keep her confidence bolstered, she ran around to her door and jumped in the driver's seat, plunged her key into the ignition, and shifted into drive.

"Are you our driver?" the red-head questioned from the second row, her voice dripping with attitude.

"Uhh, yeah. My name's Amy...what's yours?" Amy smiled into the rear-view mirror as her minivan sped toward the exit. She was starting to see what Cari's comment meant.

"I'm Melia. Are you sure you're old enough to drive?"

The other girls chimed in laughter.

"Are you sure your car's not gonna break down on us?" another girl yapped from the back seat, as she noisily smacked a wad of gum in her mouth.

"How come I can't turn the radio on from back here?" a new annoyed voice spoke up directly behind Amy.

Thirty seconds in, and all of Amy's nightmares were already becoming reality. She gripped the steering wheel tightly, seriously considering an illegal U-turn back into the parking lot to drop off these spoiled brats. *Love them, love them, love them,* Amy reminded herself. *But was I this annoying when I was their age?* Amy glanced in her mirror just in time to see Melia climbing over the second row and falling onto two screaming friends in the back row.

"Hey! Put your seatbelt on!" Amy yelled.

"Stop tickling me!" Melia shrieked with laughter to the other girls.

"Get off of me!" a fourth voice now added to the pandemonium.

"You're gonna get me a ticket," Amy yelled again, but apparently her own ears were the only ones listening. A wild kick jolted her seat forward. "Ahhhhh!" Amy, exasperated, yanked the car to the side of the road and slammed the transmission into park. The mayhem suddenly ceased.

"Uh-oh. She's mad now," an unidentified girl piped up matter-of-factly. Amy thought it sounded like Melia.

"You know, girls, I've got a better idea." Amy's irritated voice reverberated through the minivan's now-silent interior as she turned around to face them. Four pairs of eyes focused on their team leader, and even though they were just crazy little seventh graders, Amy could feel that need for acceptance surfacing. She took a deep breath and tried to smile. "Let's start over. My name's Amy, and I don't know why, but I really want to win this silly game." A couple of the girls' mouths cautiously formed a smile. "What do the rest of you want to do?"

"We want to play," Melia announced for all of them after a brief pause, and the other girls nodded their heads in agreement.

"Okay, then," Amy grinned, "if we're a team, then we need to work together as a team. And it might help if I knew all your names. I know you're Melia, but—"

"I'm Lindsey," the pretty girl in the second row offered. Her soft brown hair framed her oval face in a cute little bob, and her brown eyes glowed with mischief.

So that's who kicked my chair! Amy guessed. "Nice to meet you, Lind—"

"I'm Alyx," an African-American girl with tight curls interrupted. "This is my friend Gabbi. She's shy." Gabbi also had a darker complexion, but her hair was tied back into a long ponytail. She waved, but said nothing.

"Well, it's nice to meet all of you girls," Amy said, pleased at the direction this was going. "Okay, now I really need someone to ride shotgun to help me figure out where we're going. Any takers?" She was kind of impressed that she was making this all up as she went.

For a moment, the four girls looked at each other in silence, apparently none willing to be the sacrificial lamb. Just as Amy was about to lose hope, Melia finally relented in a dramatic sigh that made it sound like she had just agreed to take a bullet for her teammates.

"I'll go."

She clumsily climbed back over the second row, nearly kicking Gabbi in the face, and wedged herself with a scowl into the front passenger seat.

"Thanks, Melia." Amy tried to sound cheerful. She handed the points list to the annoying red-head. "Now, since you're shotgun, you tell us where we are going first."

The new leader's eyes darted down the sheet, scanning the options.

"Let me see the sheet!" Lindsey belted from the second row as she reached out for it.

Melia knocked her hand away and spoke to the paper, "I'm the copilot!"

Amy skimmed the paper with her and offered, "I was a cheerleader last year. We could get out my old uniform."

Melia gripped the sides of the paper so that they crumpled a little. "Cheerleaders are stupid," she frowned, then looked at Amy. "But my neighbor owns a little snake." The corners of her mouth curled up into a devilish grin behind her unruly hair.

"Eeeeeeewwwwwwwwww!" the chorus of backseat analysts responded in unison.

Amy felt the same way, but she took a deep breath and looked to her navigator. "Okay, then. Where to, boss?"

It turned out the "little snake" was actually a colorful six-foot king snake that liked to slither slowly all over screaming girls. Hardly worth the 25 puny points that the picture brought them, in Amy's humble opinion. Melia's neighbor also had marshmallows, though, and the girls had way too much fun sticking them up each other's noses. Too bad that one was only worth 10. Next, they found a police officer on the side of the road writing up a ticket. Amy knew they should have waited for the cop to finish, but time was of the essence. So the girls put on their cutest faces to interrupt just long enough to grab a picture on the side of the busy road. Alyx's mom happened to be a secretary for the city planner, who reluctantly and anonymously leaked the home addresses of a city council member and the mayor. Both civil servants were surprisingly glad to pose for the pictures on their front doorsteps. The mayor even asked them to email him a copy.

With each stop, the backseat girls inched forward until the three of them sat double-buckled in the second row. "Luckily" Gabbi had brought her iPod, and Melia plugged it in to Amy's stereo before Amy could say no. Within seconds, they were squawking over which of the latest teen music sensations to start with. As they skipped from song to song, Amy wondered if her head could take much more of the ruckus. But then she heard a song she knew, so she took matters back into her own hands.

"Wait, wait, wait! Turn it up!" she screamed, and started singing along. "You'll be the prince and I'll be the princess. It's a love story—baby, just say yes!"

The girls split a gut laughing.

"What? I was good, wasn't I?" Amy defended herself with a smile.

"In the words of Randy, that was whacked, dawg," Melia retorted, throwing the girls into another giggle fest.

"Okay, okay," Amy conceded, as Taylor Swift's voice continued to blast through the speakers. "So where are we going next?"

"Where are we gonna find a giraffe?" Gabbi wondered aloud.

"Anybody got a really old great-grandma?" Lindsey asked.

"Or a baby sister?" Alyx shouted. "That's worth 25."

"My daught—I mean, I know a 3-month-old," Amy hollered back, hoping no one had caught her slip of the tongue.

"Did you start to say your *daughter*?" Melia looked at her inquisitively from the next seat as she turned down the volume.

Amy could sense six other ears had also caught her *faux pas* and were interested in an answer.

"Uhhhh, yeah." Amy felt her heartbeat speed up and her palms start to sweat.

"*You* have a daughter?" Melia asked with disbelief.

"Kind of. I mean, she doesn't live with me." Amy felt flustered.

"What do you mean, she doesn't live with you? Did someone take her?" Melia shot back.

"Uhhh, not exactly," Amy stammered, wondering how to explain this. *Me and my big mouth!* "I, uh, gave her up for adoption," she admitted, wishing they could all just get preoccupied with another song and turn off the inquisition. Amy had had enough of this Melia girl.

"I could never give my baby away," Melia said matter-of-factly.

The words stung like a thousand needles. Who was this girl, and why was she so intent on being so mean? But Amy refused to let her win and pasted on a forced smile.

"Okay, so never mind that one," Amy responded, pushing to speak in more than a whisper. "Anybody know where we can find a Lamborghini?"

The girls mercifully took the cue and started listing the wealthier neighborhoods around them. "Shadowridge has rich people," Lindsey piped up.

"That place is the ghetto compared to La Jolla," Alyx fired back.

Gabbi shook her head and spoke up in a rare outburst, "La Jolla is 45 minutes away, foo'!" Then she beamed, "My daddy's got one."

"Why didn't you say so in the first place?" Melia shouted from the front seat.

"What do you think I'm doing?" Gabbi yelled back, apparently fully emerged from her shy cocoon.

"No he doesn't!" Alyx exclaimed.

"Yes huh!" Gabbi howled.

"Nuh uh!"

"Yes huh!"

"Nuh uh!"

Everyone started hollering and squawking at each other in an unintelligible roar. Safe behind the wall of sound, Amy stealthily wiped away a few tears. She had gone almost a week without a baby meltdown, but here an annoying little girl named Melia had ripped the scab off her wounded heart without a second thought. *When will this ache go away?* Amy pleaded silently. But the lack of silence all around her gave her no respite, and she took a deep breath and plunged in.

HONK!

Amy pounded on the center of her steering wheel to get the girls attention. "Now, Gabbi, where do you live?"

"Tijuana."

The car groaned in unison with the girls as Gabbi giggled impishly. Soon everyone was laughing, and Amy felt the steely grip around her heart loosen its hold a little.

"I think El Capitan High School might have a cow in its Ag department," she offered.

"Oh yeah!" Lindsey remembered. "My brother told me about it. Her name is Bob."

The girls erupted in giggles yet again, then swooned when a song came on by some young heartthrob Amy hadn't heard of. While they enthusiastically sang along, Amy's own heart throbbed quietly in her chest. *Maybe Jake will understand.*

10:22pm | From: Amy | To: Jake
These girls r driving me CRAZY!!!

11:03pm | From: Amy | To: Jake
Knowing every word to Taylor Swift finally came in handy lol

11:37pm | From: Amy | To: Jake
We need to talk!

11:42pm | From: 15185559340 | To: Jake
Wanna grab coffee tomorrow

HEARING THE BUZZ OF AN INCOMING MESSAGE yet again, an exhausted Jake finally closed his Spanish III book and reached into his backpack to find his phone. Holed away at a back corner table in the library, he had stuffed the phone in there to keep from getting distracted during his last three hours of conjugating verbs, memorizing vocabulary, and writing an essay in Spanish about his favorite holiday. Since he couldn't remember half of the words he wanted to use to describe Christmas, he ended up writing about the Fourth of July, focusing primarily on the food. Who knew he could write so much about *frijoles y hamburguesas y limonada*? *¡Ay caramba!*

His advisor in high school had encouraged him not to drop Spanish his senior year, but the possibility of getting out of school at lunch every day seemed too good to refuse, even if it meant needing to take an additional class in college. Now he kicked himself for that short-sighted decision. A week into the class, Jake's Spanish professor had already put him on probation, thanks to a pop quiz on the third day that revealed how *mucho* in trouble Jake was: He got a thirteen out of one hundred. So Señora Perez had made him sign a contract where he committed to studying at least an hour a day until his grade moved up to a B, or else he'd be forced to drop down to Spanish II. Who would have thought, after growing up in San Diego, it would take moving to Kentucky to learn Spanish?

Jake packed up his books and walked out of the hushed library into the brisk night air. He scrolled through the missed texts and laughed, picturing Amy driving around town belting out a Taylor Swift song at the top of her lungs with a bunch of middle-schoolers. The third text, however, left Jake scratching his head. He'd heard those exact four words—"we need to talk"—from Amy countless times before, and they usually meant he had done something to screw up. Most times, he had a pretty good idea what he'd done or not done to warrant the "Jake, we need to talk!" But he was seriously clueless today. He thought he'd been doing great since Sunday, going overboard to mask the feelings that had surprised him upon meeting Nicole. Did Amy guess what was really going on? *How could she?* Jake reasoned. He wracked his brain for other things he could have done to warrant the "we need to talk" line as he scanned down to the final text.

His heart froze, as if he were watching a cheesy horror flick. While he had no idea whose number was connected to the invitation to grab coffee, his fear—and hope—was that it was Nicole's. Since their cozy conversation at the Super Bowl party, he'd bumped into the blonde knockout just once, yesterday before practice, but she'd said she was in a hurry to get to class, so their encounter didn't involve anything more than a quick hug and hello. But that hug had taken Jake half of practice to get over. A few jarring screens from Nate sure helped. *But how would she get my phone number?* Jake tried to bring himself back to reality.

Feeling like he clutched a weapon behind his back that could betray his closest ally with one swing, Jake inhaled the frosty air and dialed Amy.

"Hi Jake," Amy answered on the first ring.

Jake couldn't tell if her voice sounded upset or just tired.

"¡Hola, señorita bonita!" Jake tried to lighten the mood. "Sounds like you had an interesting night."

"I don't think I've ever had so many voices vying for my attention for two hours straight," Amy laughed exhaustedly. "Jake, my head feels like it's been pounded by a jackhammer all night."

Jake chuckled, realizing that maybe for the first time "we need to talk" didn't mean he was in trouble. "That just means they liked you. I told you they would."

"I'm not sure about that, Jake, but that's not the problem," Amy's voice cut short.

Uh-oh. Jake immediately shifted into alert mode. "Okay...so, what *is* the problem?" he asked as tenderly as he could.

On the other end of the phone, he heard what sounded at first like quiet sniffling, but soon broke into full-on sobbing.

"I miss Emileeeeeeeeeeeeeeey," Amy sputtered out, her voice a high-pitched moan.

Jake stopped in his tracks about a hundred yards outside of the library. Had he space-cadeted again and totally missed part of their conversation? His mind searched for clues but came up with blanks.

"Amy?" Jake answered back softly and hesitantly. "I think I missed something," he confessed.

More sobs.

"Tonight one of the girls—who was absolutely annoying and mean, by the way—her name was Melia. How ironic is that, Jake? She practically has her name!"

Again, Amy burst into sobs.

"Oh?" Jake tried to comfort her, but knew he was failing miserably.

"I let it slip that I had a daughter," Amy's voice quivered, "and Melia just wouldn't let it go. She said she could never give up *her* daughter. She was so nasty, Jake, but maybe she was right. I gave my little girl away, Jake. Am I the worst mother ever?" Her voice broke into despondent tears.

Truth be told, while Jake sometimes felt a tiny pang of loss when he thought about the baby they gave up, for the most part, he felt relief. Out-of-sight meant out-of-mind, and giving their child to Frank and Jan had given him a fresh start to his life. He knew Amy felt the loss a little more than he did, especially since she had chosen to stay behind in the same town for an extra semester. But that was her choice, and he didn't know how to help her from where he was.

"The girl's in seventh grade." Jake shook his head, trying to sound sympathetic "What do you care what she thinks, anyway?"

"It's not even what *she* thinks; it's what I think of myself. I suck!" Amy sighed as her sobs began returning to just sniffles.

"Amy, you don't suck, and you're not the worst mother ever," Jake reasoned.

"But don't you ever wonder what would have happened if we had just kept her? If you had stayed here, and we both got jobs and went to school part-time and tried to make our little family work?" Amy pleaded.

What could Jake say to that? Was it selfish to say that he was glad they didn't? Was it insensitive to remind her that they had made their choice, and there was no use in living in the past?

"Amy," Jake pleaded softly. "I don't know. We probably could have made it work. But it would have been tough, really tough. And don't you think Emily is in a better place? I mean, you've seen how much Frank and Jan love her. They're going to be able to give her so much more than we ever could have."

"I know," Amy sighed, not sounding entirely convinced. "It just sounds so selfish sometimes...do you ever miss her?"

Jake exhaled, watching his breath linger on the cold air. "Sure," he answered vaguely. "Sometimes." Suddenly a double-beep alerted him to another incoming call, rescuing him from this awkward response. He glanced down at the screen and recognized the number from the earlier text. *Nicole?* Jake knew in his gut this was definitely a call he should ignore, but he couldn't resist the allure of this mystery woman.

"Is someone on the other line?" Amy's question broke into Jake's private thoughts. She must have heard the clicking. "Who's calling this late?"

If she only knew. "Uhhh, I dunno," Jake answered with a half-truth. "Can you give me a sec?" He tried to sound nonchalant.

"Sure," Amy replied stoically.

Jake waited an extra beat for Amy to elaborate, but there was now only silence.

"Okay, one sec." Jake quickly switched over to the incoming caller before she changed her mind. "Hello?" he answered nervously. *Why was his heart beating so fast?*

"Hi Jake, it's Nicole."

Even though Jake had half-expected her voice, it still sent a shiver down his spine. "Hey, Nicole! It's Jake...I mean you know that...Er, how's it going?" *Stupid, stupid, stupid.*

She giggled. "Sorry to call so late. I don't know if you got my text, but I wanted to see if you'd like to get coffee tomorrow morning?" Nicole sounded so innocent.

Jake knew the obvious answer should be a resounding no. He had a girlfriend, a rival on the team, a borderline F in Spanish, and, oh yeah, a girlfriend.

"I must have missed your text," Jake lied as a stalling tactic.

"No worries. What do you think?" She stuck with the full-court press.

"Uh, I've got class at nine," Jake stammered.

"So you're free before then?"

This girl's relentless! "Uh, yeah," Jake's mouth responded before his brain stopped him. He cringed. On the other line his girlfriend waited, oblivious to what he was doing. What *was* he doing? "Nicole, I've got someone waiting on the other line," Jake exhaled.

"Oh, sorry! How 'bout 8 a.m. at Common Grounds, then?"

"Uh, sure," Jake agreed, simply trying to get her off the phone, he rationalized. Besides, coffee was just coffee and nothing more, right?

"Okay, good night!" Nicole shot back, hanging up on him before he could say another word.

She's always leaving first, Jake noticed. Something about that was so attractive. Jake hesitantly clicked back to Amy.

"Amy, I'm so sorry," Jake attempted to re-enter the conversation.

Silence greeted him.

"Amy?"

The phone clicked, and suddenly Amy's voice came through. "Sorry, Jake! Cari called while you were on the other line, so I just told her I'd call her right back. So who was calling you?" she asked, without the scent of interrogation.

"Uh, just a friend," Jake magnificently downplayed. "Soooo, were Chris and Cari there tonight?"

"Yeah, Jake, it's kind of their job," she laughed quietly. "Hey, sorry about freaking out a second ago with the whole baby thing. I think I'm just missing you a ton right now."

Less than thirty seconds ago, Jake was making plans to hang out with a hot college co-ed in the morning, and here was Amy apologizing to him? Her kindness felt like a sponge wringing out guilt on top of his head. Part of him wanted to confess it all, and then pluck out his eyeballs so that he'd never look at another woman again. "I miss you a ton, too," he responded almost inaudibly.

"Jake, do you think I'm insensitive or cruel?"

Where did these questions come from?

"Absolutely not." *Compared to me!* "Do I even need to know why you're asking?"

"No, I'm glad you answered correctly," Amy giggled.

Jake tried to picture her lying on the floor in her bedroom, her pink cell phone glued to her ear. Yet he could only see Nicole's bare midriff and bulging chest peeking out from that gloriously snug jersey.

7:59am | From: Jake | To: Grant
Did you give my number to Nicole?

8:03am | From: Grant | To: Jake
ur welcome

8:03am | From: Jake | To: Grant
Dude I don't need u setting me up

8:04am | From: Grant | To: Jake
Dont u like hot chicks? Lol She said she had a hw question

JAKE THREW HIS SWEATS on over his weightlifting clothes, bypassing the showers until he got back to his dorm. After lying awake for several hours last night, he had woken up still uneasy this morning. He'd decided to work off the tension in the weight room before meeting Nicole for coffee. The extra workout helped Jake to work out his plan to tell her the whole truth about Amy, Emily, and his zero interest in anything more than friendship. Not to mention, Jake hoped that maybe if he showed up all smelly and nasty, his scent would do the work for him. With his gym bag slung over his right shoulder, Jake made his way to the university's popular coffee shop and arrived five minutes late—intentionally.

His mind flashed back to the countless mochas Amy had picked up for him on her way to school as a gesture of her love. All of a sudden, the rich smell of coffee beans revolted him. *What am I doing here?!* Apprehensively, Jake glanced around at each of the occupied tables, but Nicole was nowhere to be found. And she wasn't one to just blend into a crowd. His plan to make her wait had played out much simpler in his mind...but maybe this was his chance to escape.

"Jake!" He heard her spirited voice from across the room.

The short but athletically built nymph glided toward him. She too was wearing sweats; the only difference was, where his were baggy, hers fit to show off every gorgeous curve of her body. Jake noticed the stares from a few other guys sitting around and, whether he liked it or not, his possessive instinct kicked in. He hurried toward her.

"Sorry I'm late. I had a Pilates class, and I guess I got carried away." She smiled as she approached, reaching up to give her traditional welcome hug.

I'm sure she greets everyone this way, Jake reasoned to himself, ignoring the tight embrace.

"Looks like you've been working out, too," Nicole grinned, playfully tugging his sweatshirt zipper up and down.

Apparently his B.O. wasn't doing its job. Her intoxicating fragrance was, however, and Jake inhaled. For someone who had just worked out, Nicole looked stunning. Her makeup was flawless, and her hair was pulled up into a bouncy little ponytail. Standing just inches from her, Jake felt his body once again start to heat up. Reacting quickly, he turned toward the menu board.

"Do you know what you want to order?" Jake asked coolly, reminding himself that he was still very much in control. He hadn't done anything wrong, nor was he going to. He loved Amy...and Nicole was just a friend. That's all she was.

"Yeah, I'm getting a double chocolate chip mocha Frap, but put your wallet away, pal. It's my treat," she laughed, nudging her way in front of Jake in order to hand a crisp twenty-dollar bill to the freckled girl behind the counter.

"I'm not gonna let you pay for me." Jake pulled out a few crumpled bills from his pocket and placed them on the counter.

"Men! You're all so proud. Remember, who asked who on the date?" Nicole brushed the bills off the counter onto the ground. As Jake bent over to pick them up, Nicole ordered for both of them. "Two grande chocolate chip mocha Fraps." She smiled victoriously as Jake stood up and reluctantly wadded his cash back into his pocket.

So much for being in control. He hated chocolate chips ground up in a drink. *Wait, did she just call this a date?* "Uh Nicole, really—"

"I know, but you better remember who hooked you up when you get drafted in the first round a couple years from now," she interrupted with a sly smile. "Why don't you grab us a table, and I'll wait for the drinks."

Jake found himself doing as he was told, finding an open table in the back corner next to some kind of abstract art. He sunk into a comfy old chair and stared at the splatter of seemingly random colors on the wall. His mind raced with conflicting emotions. What guy wouldn't feel at least some sense of exhilaration to find himself in this situation? He should be more concerned if his stomach did *not* feel like it was going to leap out of his body. *I mean, this girl is drop-dead gorgeous in workout sweats, for crying out loud!* And it felt good to be pursued. At the same time, what if Nate Williams walked in right now? Regardless of whether Nicole was Nate's girl, Jake was pretty sure he wouldn't be happy to see Jake with her. Jake glanced nervously at the entrance of the coffee shop. Then another mortifying thought crossed his mind: *What if Amy walked in?*

"So, I've got one question for you." Nicole startled him out of his guilt. She plopped into the other chair and slid his least-favorite drink across the table like an experienced bartender. "Who *is* Jake Taylor?" She leaned forward, never taking her eyes off him as her perfectly parted lips enclosed around an innocent straw.

A million different ways of answering her question flashed to the forefront of his brain, but the winning shot that flew out of his mouth was, "Well, I've got a girlfriend back home, and a baby named Emily." A mixture of regret and relief flooded over Jake, knowing his words were probably not the ones his "date" was hoping to hear.

But if Nicole was disappointed by his more-than-direct response, her face definitely didn't show it. "Oh! That's so cute!" she beamed back. "How long have you guys been going out?" She reached her hand across the table and tapped his wrist. "Let me see a picture of her," she ordered.

The tranquility Jake expected after his confession was less gratifying than he'd anticipated. "We've dated almost four years," Jake answered cautiously. If he were honest, their relationship had recently enjoyed more ups and downs than a rollercoaster, but Nicole didn't need to know that. "I don't have any pictures here."

"Four years and you don't carry a picture? What's up with that, Jake?" Nicole playfully reprimanded him and then laughed flirtatiously. "I'll bet she's worried sick that you're gonna find a replacement while you're away at school."

Jake leaned forward in his chair, the bit of calm he'd briefly enjoyed suddenly surging to high alert. "No, no, it's not like that. I just don't carry my wallet when I work out," Jake explained, desperate to make Nicole understand. "Besides, I'm the one who should be worried."

Nicole raised her eyebrows and smirked. "Oh?" Her lips regained contact with the straw, and she looked at Jake inquisitively.

How was he supposed to describe Amy's surpassing beauty to a girl who was equally attractive? "She's going to join me here next year anyway," Jake said, although that wasn't necessarily the truth. In fact, he and Amy hadn't talked about next year for awhile. He made a mental note to bring that up the next time they talked. Having Amy here would sure make situations like this easier! "She just couldn't come now, with the baby and all."

Nicole's big brown eyes silently invited him to continue. And against his better judgment, he did. He told her about their breakup, and then their unexpected pregnancy. He explained how he gave up his college dreams to keep Amy from getting an abortion, and then how they had decided to give their baby up for adoption, which had given him the chance to come to Louisville after all.

The more Jake rambled, the more intrigued and sympathetic Nicole seemed, and while Jake sensed that his words weren't having the desired effect of turning her off, at the same time he enjoyed the undivided attention she was giving him. Whenever he mentioned a sacrifice he had made or an inconvenience he had experienced, she stroked his arm compassionately, and she made comments and asked questions that made Jake feel like he was really the hero of it all.

Suddenly he realized, *Crap! She's not giving up!* Well, if his workout stench hadn't worked, and the blatant truth hadn't worked, maybe talking about God would. So then Jake started talking about Roger's suicide, Chris Vaughn, and all about his new relationship with God. Jake told her about New Song, the youth group, and his recent quest to find a church in Louisville. And somewhere in the middle of all this, he stopped seeing her as a beautiful temptress, but instead as a girl he could possibly share his faith with. He knew he was messing it all up, but Nicole seemed to be really interested, asking lots of insightful questions.

"You guys gonna order anything else?" an annoyed voice interrupted.

Jake looked up to see a heavily built server standing at their table, looking like he belonged in a mechanic's garage instead of a coffee shop. Jake glanced down at his watch. *10:30!* They had been sitting at the table for over two hours, while he was supposed to be taking notes, not only Stats but now in World Civ...on the other side of campus.

"Crap! I missed my class!" Jake jumped up in alarm. *Where did the time go?*

The server got the clue and slipped away.

Nicole laughed, grabbing Jake's arm. "Jake. It's college. You don't have to go to *every* class."

Although he'd promised his mom just the opposite, Nicole's reminder helped.

"If it makes you feel better, I'm missing a class, too," she added.

"Thanks," Jake smiled.

"Thank *you.*" Nicole stood up and took Jake's hand. Her warmth transferred to him and radiated throughout his whole body.

"For what? Babbling on for like an eternity?" he grinned.

"Could I go with you on Sunday?" Nicole asked out of the blue.

Jake's grin faded into a blank stare. "Where?" he stammered.

"Church, silly." Nicole swatted at Jake's shoulder. "I've always wanted to go."

Strike three. Apparently the God-talk didn't drive her off either. So now what was he supposed to say? As if he could deny someone who was interested in God. Jake flung his duffel bag over his right shoulder. "Sure...that would be great."

Nicole reached out to give him a big hug goodbye. "Great! Then it's a date." Nicole beamed as she turned to walk away.

She gave her trademark little fingertip wave, but Jake's stare fixated on her retreating backside, his eyes drawn to her toned glutes that flexed perkily with every stride. *It's a date?* he wondered. But was it really that bad if they were just going to church?

2:13am | From: Jake | To: Grant
Dude I need u 2 do me a HUGE favor.

JAKE TOSSED AND TURNED, wondering if Grant was still awake to get his message. Probably not. Jake knew he shouldn't be either, but he couldn't help stressing out about Nicole's request to go to church with him. He had managed to push it out of his mind at first by continuing his frequent contact with Amy. But then tonight, Nicole had texted him wondering how she should dress for the service, and Jake just couldn't ignore his predicament anymore. Sure, he was only taking her to church, but it just didn't feel right. So as he lay sleepless in bed, Grant's name popped into his head, and he figured it was time to phone in a favor. And who knew? Maybe it would open up an opportunity for Jake to talk to Grant about God, too. Jake had been elated as he pressed the Send button, hoping and praying that Grant would come through.

Just then, the door swung open, and a tall, skinny silhouette was framed against the bright hallway lights. A loud belch informed Jake that his roommate was home from another late night of partying. Just as Jake was about to turn over toward the wall, a second smaller figure appeared next to Kyle's lanky frame, and they both stumbled toward Kyle's bed.

"Don't even think about it!" Jake spoke sternly into the darkness.

Visibly startled by the voice coming from the person he clearly had assumed was asleep, Kyle groaned. "Dude, you're such a buzz kill! Just give us ten minutes, bro." And then he threw in a bonus: "I'll clean up the room."

Kyle's ever-expanding pig sty was wearing thin on Jake, as was the constant disapproval he tried to stifle toward Kyle's activities. So, the meager offer—one that should have been the norm of their living arrangement—was enough to get Jake to cave in and take the bait. Unwilling to lie there listening to his roommate's quick romp in the sheets, Jake reluctantly grabbed his pillow and comforter and staggered through the darkness to the hallway outside. As he passed the couple, the stench of alcohol was thick, and the girl's glazed eyes and goofy giggle made it clear that she wasn't going to remember much of this inconvenient event.

"Ten minutes!" Jake growled as the door shut behind him.

Jake flopped to the hallway floor and lay down, staring up at the speckled ceiling tiles, his mind wandering back to his impending second "date" with Nicole. He had wanted to tell Amy so much about this opportunity God was giving him, but he feared that the moment she found out that it was another girl—and an extremely attractive girl, at that—she would flip...which is why Grant coming along would be such a problem-solver. If it was another guy *and* girl, then Amy wouldn't think twice, *plus* having Grant there would hopefully send Nicole a pretty clear signal, as well. The weight Jake had been carrying started to slip off his shoulders as he processed through this solution. He snuggled down into his comforter to wait out the ten minutes until he could go back to his own bed.

Five hours later, the alarm from his phone startled him awake, and he stiffly stood up from the hard hallway floor. "Hmph!" Jake grumbled, wondering if the girl was still in their room. He stumbled into the room where he *should* have been sleeping, and sure enough, there were Kyle and his "friend" passed out in the heap of dirty laundry that he called a bed. *That's so gross!* Jake scowled, grabbing his shower stuff and staggering back out the door to start his day.

A few hours later, Jake met up with Grant outside of the English Composition class they had together, and Grant was eager to help out...until he found out that the favor entailed accompanying

Jake and Nicole to church. Jake wasn't sure what Grant was more opposed to—hanging out with Nicole or going to church. But Jake begged and pleaded and explained all the reasons why this would be a good idea, until Grant reluctantly relented, and Jake promised to buy him a donut afterward.

✚ ✚ ✚

On Saturday night, while most of his floor was out partying, Jake figured he should brush up on his Bible-reading—something he'd neglected far too much in his first month and a half at Louisville. He flipped through the pages randomly and read something about a dude named Samson who lost his superhero powers after shacking up with a prostitute. Weird story. Jake made a note to ask Chris about superpowers later. He also made a note to beware of Nicole—not that she was a prostitute or anything, but there were definitely some striking similarities with Delilah's persuasiveness.

After writing a quick entry in his prayer journal (and realizing with chagrin that the last one was from over two weeks ago), Jake realized he should probably investigate a different church, since taking his guests back to any of the old, stuffy ones he'd already visited would leave them all with cold feet. He searched online and found a choice that seemed like it could work. Based on the attractive Web site, West Park Baptist seemed like a friendly church that was pretty modern—and it had pictures of young people on the home page! Jake mapped out the directions and settled into bed, hoping his nervousness would allow him to sleep. He said a quick prayer, asking God to make everything work out okay tomorrow, and slipped into dreamland before he had a chance to start worrying about it.

✚ ✚ ✚

Sunday morning, Jake woke up bright and early, his nerves tingling with excitement and anxiety. He tried not to get ready too quickly, then tried not to drive too quickly over to Grant's dorm. But he still ended up knocking on Grant's door at 8:51, nine minutes earlier than their proposed meeting time.

Complete silence greeted Jake's knocking, as did his subsequent pounding, as did his ensuing phone calls. Jake started to panic as he visualized his brilliant plan unraveling. As much as he hated to admit it, he was actually kind of looking forward to hanging out with Nicole this morning. But he definitely didn't want to do it alone! His mind started racing through all the potential reasons why Grant wasn't answering. Was this his way of getting out of the favor? Maybe he never came home from a late night of partying. Or what if he'd been abducted? An irrational shock of fear set Jake to pounding on the door again.

"Dude, I know you're in there!" he yelled, not caring if he woke up the whole floor. Finally, after what seemed like hours, the door creaked open, and Grant stood there in a pair of purple briefs. He rubbed his eyes sleepily.

"Give me five minutes," he uttered robotically, leaving the door open for Jake to walk in as Grant shuffled to the bathroom.

"Nicole's waiting," Jake grumbled aloud while inwardly sighing with relief that he wasn't going to have to face this morning alone. He sank onto the couch next to the door and shot one of the pillows in a sweet arc across the room. If it had been a basketball, it would have been a perfect swish.

Grant's room was everything Jake and Kyle's room was not. It was immaculate, except for the couch pillow Jake had just tossed on the floor. Grant shared the room with some guy on the cross-country team who lived in the area. But apparently he went home every weekend to wash his clothes, and the two of them never really talked.

"What church are we going to?" Grant asked from the bathroom.

"It's called West Park Baptist. I've never been there, but the Web site looked cool." Jake glanced down at his phone and saw that they were now officially late. Trying to be patient, he checked his Facebook page, where Amy had posted "Enjoy your time at church tomorrow!" *If only she knew,* Jake winced. He commented back to her, then left notes for Jonny, Andrea, and Chris. He realized he'd never heard back from Jonny after last weekend, and he wondered how his plan to ask out Andrea had fared. Jake assumed Jonny hadn't even come close, but he made a mental note to call him later.

"Let's do this thing," Grant yawned, emerging from the bathroom in a layered baby blue polo and dark jeans. His khaki loafers and carefully sculpted hair finished off the ensemble that made him look like a model stepping out of a Ralph Lauren catalog. His musky cologne added an extra zest.

The tiniest surge of jealousy shot through Jake's brain as he absorbed the sense of style that Grant was able to exude with mere minutes of preparation. What if Nicole found Grant more appealing? Then Jake reminded himself that was exactly the kind of thing he should hope for, but a lingering shadow of disappointment clouded his mind. He figured he should give Nicole a little heads-up, so he texted her: "We're on our way."

"What time did you go to sleep last night?" Jake laughed, as he and Grant left the dorm and headed toward Nicole's.

"Don't ask," Grant groaned, refraining from spilling the details.

Sleepy silence filled the brief walk to where Nicole sat on a bench waiting. Even from a distance, she was stunning. Her striking sheer blue dress wasn't particularly inappropriate, but she filled it in such a way that it got Jake's full attention. And then there were the long leather boots. Amy had a pair just like them, and for some reason they always drove Jake wild. Paired with meticulously curled blonde hair, dramatically shadowed eyes, and perfectly glossed lips, she was enough to elicit a second look from anyone with eyes and hormones. From Jake, she received a simple unbroken stare.

Grant whistled under his breath as they waved hello, then mumbled, "Nate Williams know you're taking his girl to church this morning?"

"I told you, she's not his girl," Jake corrected for at least the third time, his gaze still unbroken.

"Riiiiiiiiiiight," Grant assented sarcastically. "Just remember who warned you. You're playin' with fire, dude," he whispered, a forced smile plastered to his face.

Nicole stood up, apparently unbothered that she'd had to wait an extra ten minutes and unfazed that it was no longer just she and Jake.

"Didn't know you were the church type," she smirked, as Grant bent down to give her a hug.

"Jake told me you were going, so I begged to tag along," Grant smiled. "By the way, you look fine, girl."

"Thanks," Nicole flirted back. "I just threw this old thing on."

She turned to give Jake his warm welcome hug, and his body heated up involuntarily. At the same time, he couldn't help but get a little irritated at Grant's teasing. What was going on here?

"Well, I didn't get all dressed up for nothing," Nicole grinned.

"Did she just quote *Braveheart*?" Jake asked Grant in mock disbelief.

"I believe she just did," he confirmed, reaching out to knock knuckles with the girl who never ceased to amaze.

She winked at both of them and smiled. "I've got three brothers. Chick-flicks weren't allowed in our house." Her subtle step forward brought her arm in contact with Jake's.

Grant not-so-subtly wrapped his arm around Jake's shoulder and pulled him away from Nicole. "Where's your truck, Taylor? I don't want to miss a single hymn," he mocked.

"Ahhh, yeah, it's in the lot just around the corner," Jake spoke through his thoughts, which had been drawn wayward by Nicole's tempting body.

"I call middle." Nicole smiled coquettishly.

Jake continued to battle his hormonal contemplations throughout the drive to church, and he was only too relieved to pull into the packed West Park parking lot. It instantly reminded him of New Song—casual, lively, and cheerful. Even though they were running about five minutes late, so were a couple dozen others, judging by their scurrying toward the row of glass doors. Jake grabbed his pocket Bible from the glove compartment and led the group of three toward the unknown.

They passed a young and very frustrated couple dragging their screeching toddler in the opposite direction. Just one glance made it clear that their smiles were only a millimeter deep as they tried to weather the tantrum.

"I wanna go back to the damn church!" the boy shrieked at the top of his lungs.

Jake and his friends couldn't help but laugh.

"This place must be awesome!" Grant joked under his breath.

The group approached the entrance, each of the three looking for a door without a greeter. As they veered to the vacant one on the far left, a smiling woman in her mid-forties intercepted them.

"Welcome to West Park!" she greeted warmly, opening her arms to hug them like they were old friends.

Jake and Grant quickly ducked behind Nicole, trying to sneak past as she reluctantly received the woman's embrace. But on the other side, a cavalier middle-aged man whose shirt was open almost as low as Nicole's was ready and waiting to pump their arms with a firm handshake. His grey chest hairs tangled with a gold chain as they poofed out from his neckline.

"Creeeepy!" Nicole mumbled as she joined the guys, and Grant shuddered.

They walked together into the packed auditorium, which was designed more like an amphitheater than a church. Stadium bleachers wrapped around the back facing the gigantic stage up front, where a worship band of at least 15 people played a song Jake recognized from back home. The band was led by a spiky-haired guy in skinny jeans playing guitar. He looked like he was in his twenties. Spotlights twirled and spun patterns on the wall while the lyrics were posted over close-up video shots of the band on gigantic screens all over the room. People of all ages stood clapping, dancing, and singing along.

Jake had grown to enjoy the singing at New Song but found himself a little overwhelmed by all of this. It felt more like a rock concert than a church service. But the energy was contagious, and even as they walked Jake found himself clapping along. He stole a glance at his two guests; they appeared to be awestruck.

"Pretty awesome, huh?" Jake shouted over the music.

Grant and Nicole looked at each other and nodded hesitantly in unison. They were clearly not too impressed.

A younger guy in jeans and a pink polo motioned for the group to follow him. His "Hello! I'm a Greeter" sticker lent him enough credibility that they trailed behind him to the upper bleachers, where he found them three available seats together. Jake half-expected to see someone selling peanuts and sodas.

Jake was the first to squeeze into the row, and Grant had followed close enough behind him to make sure he got the middle seat, which left Nicole on the end. Even just a single seat away, Jake was less distracted by Nicole, and it made a world of difference. But at the same time, Jake felt that weird tinge of jealousy again toward Grant. He was starting to wonder if Grant's "huge favor" really wasn't all that inconvenient.

As the band broke into another upbeat song, Jake tried to get a read on his two friends. Neither of them seemed too into the experience. Jake prayed a quick silent prayer for both of them and focused his attention on the words on the screen.

The band ended their set with a bang, to the roar of the audience, as a man about Jake's dad's age got up to address the congregation. His deep voice reverberated through the large auditorium. "God is good..."

The mass of people in attendance shouted back in unison, "All the time!"

"And all the time..." the pastor retorted without skipping a beat.

"God is good!" the mass of people responded on cue before breaking into spontaneous applause.

While Jake tried to play it cool at first, the energy was infectious, and he secretly hoped that the whole interchange would be repeated, because he was ready now. Instead, the pastor introduced the sermon.

"My name is Pastor Randall, and this morning we're in week two of a ten-part series through the book of Genesis. So grab your Bibles and turn to page two."

Jake scolded himself for just grabbing the pocket New Testament but found a Bible in the seatback in front of him and opened it up. He sneaked another sidelong glance at Grant and Nicole. A minute into the sermon and Grant's eyes were already fluttering with sleepiness. Jake wanted to nudge him but settled for the wish that God would somehow help him learn through osmosis. Nicole, however, at least appeared to be listening. *Maybe this will work out after all,* Jake hoped.

"Remember last week, we talked about how God created the universe," the pastor summarized. "Call it the Big Bang if you want, because God spoke, and 'BANG,' there it was."

Chuckles resounded around the room. Jake liked this guy. He wasn't Chris, but he seemed personable and funny, and his deep voice was comforting to listen to.

"Today, we're gonna study the first married couple in the Bible. We'll learn here why so many men's projects never get completed. Adam was busy doing his job naming all the animals when all of a sudden...naked woman! He had a hard time focusing after that."

The room erupted with laughter. Jake glanced over at Nicole, who chuckled lightly. But Grant...out for the count. Jake debated elbowing his friend, but concluded that whether he liked it or not, Grant was fulfilling his mission of making this a non-date with Nicole. So he settled back and tried to enjoy the sermon.

"And notice that God created them Adam and *Eve*, not Adam and Steve," Randall quipped, to the accompaniment of quiet sniggers. "He took a rib from Adam's side and knocked him out, and then created His greatest masterpiece yet: woman! Observe that He did not take the bone from Adam's head, which could give woman the idea that she is above man. Nor did He take it from Adam's foot, to give man the idea that he was above woman. Oh no! Where did he take that bone from?" the pastor called out with growing fervor.

"His side!" the congregation called out all around.

"That's right," Randall affirmed. "He took the rib from Adam's side, to remind us that we are equals, created to help and support each other, to love and embrace each other, to cherish and protect each other."

Pastor Randall continued on, masterfully mixing humor and heart, and Jake found himself really enjoying the sermon. He didn't take down nearly as many notes as he normally did with Chris, but there was no doubt that this preacher was entertaining. After a closing prayer, the praise band appeared back on stage, their lively music startling Grant out of his cat nap.

"Why they gotta play their music so loud?" Grant complained, standing up to join the several thousand other people singing in unison. He half-heartedly clapped along for a few moments before giving up and stuffing his hands in his pockets.

After another song, the offering passed by, and then there was a solo by a blonde chick who sounded like Celine Dion. Her glittering tunic and substantial jewels sparkled under the copious spotlights. Finally, Pastor Randall jumped back on stage, thanked everyone for coming, and dismissed them with a dramatic benediction. The masses started moving toward the exits, carrying Jake and his gang along with them.

Jake turned to his friend, still waking up from his nap. "Dude, next time maybe you should get some sleep the night before."

"Next time?" Grant looked over at Nicole and smiled back at Jake. "Next time, you on your own, bro."

Jake smiled back, but a thousand thoughts raced through his mind. Did Grant hate the service that much? Or did he just assume there wouldn't be a next time? What did he have against church? He sure hadn't seemed to mind hanging out with Nicole. Was this a total flop? But what if Nicole still wanted to join him next week? He felt a hint of delight at not having to compete with Grant's advances. But he had a girlfriend! And he'd have to tell Amy sometime.

"You drool when you sleep," Nicole punched Grant playfully on the arm.

"I wasn't sleeping. I was meditating."

"Right." Nicole turned to Jake with a smile. "Thanks for letting me tag along, Jake. I really enjoyed it." She squeezed his arm, sending a chill up his spine. "I definitely wanna go back to the damn church!"

The three laughed together, but Jake's stomach felt anything but jovial.

7:42pm | From: 17605552938 | To: Amy
Stuck at the mall can u plzzzzzzzzz pick me up

AMY STARED AT THE TEXT with the mystery number for a good two minutes, racking her brain as to who would want a ride from the mall. Finally, she gave up and texted back, "Who is this?"

She was already finding it incredibly difficult to read her drier-than-burnt-toast *West and the World* textbook. The last thing she needed was a fifteen-minute drive to the mall for someone who obviously thought they were closer friends than they actually were. Besides that, she was tired from her run with Andrea that afternoon. They were up to five miles three times a week now, and while their pace probably couldn't be considered fast, Amy was pretty proud of herself. Not to mention, she'd been doing some kick-butt exercise videos on the days in between running, and she was still sore from a rockin' core workout she'd barely made it through yesterday. Her abs, buns, and thighs lived up to the instructor's promise—they were protesting every movement today!

Amy's phone vibrated, and she grimaced as she stretched over to pick it up.

7:46pm | From: 17605552938 | To: Amy
Melia...duh!

Amy's heart sunk. *Melia.* It had been almost two weeks since the scavenger hunt, and Amy still couldn't get Melia's words out of her head: *"I could never give away my baby."* What did she know? She was only a seventh grader. But her little twitty response wouldn't leave Amy alone.

7:48pm | From: Amy | To: 17605552938
Why dont u ask your parents

This wasn't her responsibility. When she'd agreed to drive for the scavenger hunt, she was doing Cari a personal favor and just checking out the whole middle school youth group thing. But Melia had done a pretty good job of ruining that. Maybe if it were one of the other girls she'd have picked her up, but definitely not Melia.

7:49pm | From: 17605552938 | To: Amy
Theyre gone...c'mon!

Ugh! Amy thought to herself, looking down at the twenty pages of reading she still had to do tonight. What was this girl doing at the mall by herself this time of day, anyway? And on a school night! Amy's thumb rested on the Reply button, not certain what she would write. She glanced back at her textbook. It definitely wasn't going anywhere. And a break from studying would be nice...but Melia? Amy turned off her desk light and grabbed her keys. *What am I doing?*

Twenty minutes later, she pulled her minivan alongside the red curb in front of The Zone, where her new young "friend" was waiting. The night of the scavenger hunt, with all the girls vying for her attention and all, Amy had never really looked closely at Melia. She was just the annoying red-head. But tonight, Amy did a full analysis as her car made its slow approach.

Melia was tall and skinny, and her faded jeans reached a little too short on her long, gangly legs. Her baggy pink t-shirt was stretched out and clashed with her unruly red hair. But behind that untamed mane hid a relatively cute face, and while Amy still harbored annoyance toward this crazy girl, her imagination ran ahead and pictured how she could fix her up. With a little style update, make-up, and hair care, she could be the talk of the junior high boys' locker room.

"Aren't you freezing?" Amy asked, trying to snap the image of a junior high boys' locker room out of her mind as Melia opened the passenger door.

Melia smiled brightly and shook her head as she tossed her backpack onto the floor of the front seat and jumped in. "Nah, it's not that bad."

The goose bumps covering her arms spoke otherwise, and Amy nonchalantly turned the heater up two notches as she drove away toward the mall exit.

"Thanks for picking me up," Melia spoke softly as she stared out the window.

"Sure, no problem," Amy responded without the full truth, taken slightly aback by this new quiet persona of the brazen seventh grader. "But I'm curious. Where did you get my number?"

Melia giggled to herself, her gaze still averted. They pulled up behind a line of cars waiting at a red light at the exit of the mall parking lot.

"Don't go anywhere!" Melia fished in her backpack and grabbed a brown paper bag, then jumped out of the car.

"Melia, what are you do—"

But she was already gone. Amy watched her zigzag through a couple of idle cars to a man holding a cardboard sign on the median. Melia handed the surprised man her lunch bag and shook his hand. Up ahead, the light turned green, and cars began to pull forward.

"Crap! Melia," Amy groaned under her breath. This girl was nothing but trouble! She inched the minivan forward, rolling down her window to get the little Good Samaritan's attention. "MELIA!" Amy shouted over the sounds of traffic. She was pretty sure several of the blaring horns were directed at her.

Melia raced back to the van and jumped in just before Amy pulled into the intersection. Amy glanced at the toothless man standing at the corner, who now gave both of them a wide smile and wave goodbye.

"Melia, you can't just jump out of cars in the middle of the street!" Amy scolded, realizing that her high-pitched voice sounded a lot like her mom's horrible angry whine.

"Sorry! He just looked so sad," Melia sulked.

How do you get mad at a girl for being nice to a homeless man? An uncomfortable silence settled on the van.

"I dialed my number from your phone when you weren't looking." Melia's abrupt confession came with eyes focused unflinchingly on the cars ahead.

"You what?" Amy asked, confused.

"At the scavenger hunt. You left your phone on your seat at one of the stops, so I called my number really quick and hung up."

"Why'd you do that?"

Melia finally looked over at Amy, a guilty smile tugging at her face. "Uhhh..."

Amy glanced over at the semi-contrite countenance beside her and shook her head. "For the next time you needed a ride, huh?" Her annoyance was mixed with admiration at the pre-teen's foresight. "How often you pull that move?"

Melia's smile grew wider. "You were my first. Take a right on Ocean Boulevard."

Quiet descended once again. Last week, the girls had yapped enough to make Amy's head spin, but now Amy didn't have a clue as to how to fill the awkward silence. *What do you talk about with a seventh grader?* Several conversation starters bounced through her mind, but they all sounded pretty cheesy. But desperation can't be picky, and what she finally heard pop out of her mouth was, "So, was the mall fun?"

The short reply: "Yeah…sort of."

"Well, did you buy anything?" Amy prodded.

"No." Yes or no questions obviously weren't getting Amy anywhere.

"Didn't see anything that was cute, huh?"

"Didn't see anything that was free."

"Sucks to be broke," Amy offered, unsure how to respond. "I know how that is."

Melia tapped her fingers awkwardly on the armrest.

"Soooooo, were you hanging out there with friends?" Amy grasped for something to keep their struggling conversation breathing. Anything was better than the awkward silence.

"No. Take a left at Rancho Del Oro."

Amy put her left blinker on and turned to look at Melia. "Wait, so what were you doing there?"

"Just hanging out."

"Oh." Amy was rendered speechless. She couldn't figure out this girl. And how did she get to the mall in the first place? *What a great question!* "How did you get to the mall in the first place?"

"I walked."

"From where?"

"School."

The green light ahead turned yellow, but Amy was so focused on the dying conversation that by the time it registered in her brain she had to stomp on the brakes, and they landed halfway into the crosswalk. "You walked by yourself from school?" Amy exclaimed incredulously, as their heads whipped back into the headrests. She didn't mean to sound so surprised, but Melia's middle school was all the way across town. "How long a walk is that?"

"I dunno. My dad said it's about five miles," Melia replied, as if it was something every seventh-grade girl did by herself after school.

Amy had thought she was tired from running five miles with Andrea at the beach earlier in the day. But Melia? By herself, with a backpack, over all these hills? This girl was a stud! "Isn't there somewhere a bit closer to school you could hang out?" Amy questioned.

"Sometimes, I get invited to a friend's. Sometimes, I go to the library." Melia shrugged. "I'm not allowed to be home 'til after eight."

The light turned green, and Amy pulled into the upper-middle-class neighborhood. "You mean your curfew is eight," Amy corrected, glancing at the radio clock and realizing she was thirty minutes late.

"No," Melia reiterated calmly. "My parents don't let me come home until eight."

"What?" Amy probed, taking a right at the first turn where Melia was pointing. "Aren't they worried about you being out so late?"

"They want a few hours after work where it's just the two of them," Melia continued, as if this was how all healthy families operated. "My house is the one with the blue Suburban on the left."

Amy looked at the nice home with the manicured front lawn and several inviting lights on inside. "Melia, I don't get it. You're really not *allowed* in your house until after eight every night?" Amy's family was screwy, but this just didn't seem believable. What kind of parents would lock their daughter out?

Melia opened her door and put one foot on the sidewalk. "Shhhh. You're gonna get me in trouble." Melia glanced at her house a little nervously. "I'm not supposed to tell anybody, 'kay? Promise you won't tell anyone else." Melia's face turned serious, looking Amy squarely in the eyes. "Promise!"

"Okay, I promise. I just—"

"I gotta go," Melia interrupted, her sweet smile re-emerging. "Thanks for the ride!"

"You're welcome..."

The slamming car door cut Amy off, and she watched Melia run a few steps toward her house. But then she abruptly turned back around and opened the front passenger door again.

"You should really become our small group leader at church. Stacie, our old leader, is moving," Melia's words fired like a machine gun. Before Amy could even answer, Melia shut the door again and made a mad dash for the front door.

Amy watched her knock several times before the door was finally opened and Melia went inside. No one took a step out to see who the stranger was that had given their daughter a ride home. But was Melia really telling the truth? Did her parents really not care? Amy didn't know what to think, but she was pretty sure that this wasn't the last time she'd hear from the girl. She drove away and said a quick prayer for Melia.

8:36pm | From: Amy | To: Cari
I need your advice

8:37pm | From: Amy | To: Jake
R u awake? Plz call me. Luv u

5:42am | From: Jake | To: Amy
Sorry babe, Ill call this afternoon

JAKE TEXTED HIS APOLOGY on his way to an optional morning weight workout, picturing Amy cuddled up asleep right now on the other side of the country. *It must be nice,* Jake groaned, wishing he was in the comfort of his own bed, too. He had stayed up far too late last night... chatting with Nicole. And this morning (could it even be considered morning, yet?) he was paying the consequences. But Nicole had questions about God and stuff, so what was he supposed to do? Of course, when he had received Amy's text last night—being still very much awake—he had chosen to ignore it rather than explain his guilty truth. He seemed to be doing that a lot more lately, especially since Sunday. Nicole just wasn't letting up, and he didn't want to squander an opportunity to show her God. At least, that's what he kept telling himself.

But it was getting harder to keep juggling this balancing act. Life was exhausting enough as it was, but adding women into the equation exponentially increased the difficulty. It wasn't like he was out partying all night and sleeping all day, like Kyle. Or even that he was sitting around all day listening to music and updating his Facebook page, like some of the other guys on his floor. Basketball alone absorbed at least four hours a day, sometimes more after a loss. Add to that 12 units and an all-you-can-eat buffet in the dining hall, and Jake was always doing something. He was trying to keep his grades up, his body healthy, and his basketball skills competitive, and something had to give. So far, those somethings had become God and Amy. And Jake hated that. They should be at the top of his priorities. But since they weren't clamoring for his attention as much as the rest of his life, they were easier to let slip aside.

Jake wondered what Amy wanted to talk about last night. *I should've answered,* he scolded himself, wishing he could do it over again. He walked into the empty weight room and threw his bag on the ground next to the dumbbells, early as usual to make up for his semester of lost time. He took his frustrations out on the helpless 45-pound weights he curled up and down with each arm. *Seriously, what are you thinking, dude?* he fumed. He hustled from curls to rows to lat pull downs to sit-ups and back again to curls.

"Don't take it out on the weights, bro." Nate Williams patted him on the shoulder, startling Jake out of his inward rant.

In Jake's nearly two months with the team, the freshman guard had said very few words to Jake, and it had been pretty clear that he wasn't interested in more. So the unsolicited advice took Jake by surprise.

Jake smiled and put the weights down to face the guy he hoped to one day replace. Nate continued with a condescending tone.

"You gotta learn to control that anger, son, or it will control you…I think I learned that one in church."

Busted. Had he found out? Surely Nicole wouldn't have told him. Or would she? "Good tip," Jake answered back, noncommittally.

Nate was still smiling, so maybe he didn't know. Or maybe he didn't care?

"You need me to spot you?" Jake offered, looking down at the empty bench-press where Nate was stretching.

Suddenly, Nate's smile turned more sinister. "Nah, I lift the big-boy weights. No offense, y'know." He patted Jake patronizingly on the back and walked back toward the entrance, where other teammates were just starting to show up. He yelled out to them, "Church-boy here thinks he can spot me! Ha ha!"

Jake heard the taunting laughter and felt his muscles tense up underneath his sweatshirt. He'd been busting his butt for almost two months and still got zero respect. If this was about Nicole, fine—they could talk about it. But for Nate to deride his work ethic...that just wasn't cool. "Dude, your midrange jumper sucks," Jake fired back before his brain could stop him.

Nate stopped in his tracks about ten feet away and shook his head. By this time, most of the teammates had congregated around the free weights and now stopped their stretching and warm-up routines to watch. Jake had a sinking feeling in his gut. Why did he have to open his big mouth?

"Did that pansy just say something to me?" Nate asked Tony, Jamal, Bojan, and the other curious observers.

The 6-foot-10 Serbian obviously missed the rhetorical nature of the question and answered him with a thick accent. "He said your midrange jumper sucks, Nate."

The other guys cracked up to hear the insult repeated, which infuriated Nate even more. He spun around and walked directly back to his accuser, jabbing his finger inches from Jake's face.

"Y'know, I'm starting to get sick and tired of you. You're like a fly that just won't go away," he snarled.

Jake could feel his heart pounding with adrenaline, and his fingers clenched into a fist. What would he do if Nate swung? The last fight Jake had been in was in the weight room back at home, with his best friend Doug. That one had been over a girl, too, and Jake hadn't fared too well. He could only imagine how much worse the consequences would be here. "Chill out, man," Jake said under his breath. "It's not worth it."

"Just stay away from my girl," Nate hissed, his right arm shooting up at Jake's face.

It stopped a few inches short of connecting, but Jake still flinched back, causing him to trip over his own dumbbells to the ground. The team erupted in laughter as Nate lifted his hands in mock peace.

"If that wasn't the sorriest fight I've ever seen," Nate jeered with a cocky smile. As he turned to walk away, he gave Jake a condescending wink. "Trust me...you can't handle her."

From the ground, Jake watched the rest of the team mock him and return to their workout routines. Up until now, Jake had resented how little attention the other players had paid him, but how swiftly all that had changed. Jake slowly stood and picked up his stupid dumbbells and returned to his curls. What a morning.

✚ ✚ ✚

Jake was relieved to see Grant waiting for him outside their English Comp class a couple of hours later. His best friend on the team had missed the optional workout that morning but had obviously already heard all about it.

"Hey, Twinkle Toes," Grant ribbed with a grin.

"So aren't you, like, ashamed to be seen with me?" Jake only half-joked as they knocked knuckles.

"Nate is an ass, and his midrange jumper does suck. Coach tells him that at least once a week," Grant replied under his breath. "Not sure I would have said that to his face, but..."

"He was actually walking away," Jake corrected with a smile.

"Dude, you got some serious huevos," Grant kidded, opening the door for the both of them. "But I told you to watch out for her. She ain't worth it."

"I know," Jake groaned, berating himself once again for letting her get him into this mess.

"All I gotta say is, you better practice your jumpers," Grant elbowed Jake in the side. "Talk is cheap if you can't back it up."

Jake smiled at his friend and slapped him on the back as they entered class for an hour and a half of writing practice.

✚ ✚ ✚

Two hours later, on his way to Spanish, Jake gave Amy a call. Her peppy voicemail greeted him on the fourth ring.

"This is Amy. You know..."

"Hey, Amy, I'm blanking on your schedule again, but I'm on my way to Spanish. Then I've got afternoon practice. Hopefully we can talk tonight. Love you."

Jake didn't really mind that Amy wasn't there to pick up the phone. Whatever she needed to talk to him about was probably another heavy load, and he was already carrying plenty this morning. She'd been struggling so much lately with giving up Emily, and he just couldn't relate. It felt like she wanted him to feel the same way, but the truth was, he didn't. Jan and Frank were great people and fully capable of taking care of *their* child. Why couldn't Amy just accept that and move on? That baby was the reason Jake showed up to Louisville a semester late—and why he was now on the outside looking in on the rest of his teammates. If it hadn't been for the baby, would this morning's embarrassing conflict ever have happened? Obviously he couldn't tell Amy all that, but he just was tired of talking about it.

Just then, Jake's phone buzzed. He sighed and quickly pulled it out of his pocket to greet Amy. "Hey, babe," Jake answered, trying to sound upbeat.

"Babe, huh? That's a little fast don't you think?" Nicole's voice answered playfully on the other end of the line.

Jake's face turned bright red as he turned the corner to the foreign language building on campus.

"Oh! Uhhhh, I thought you were somebody else," Jake back-pedaled, his armpits suddenly damp with sweat. *Stay cool, man. Just say no.*

"Sure, babe, whatever you say," Nicole joked back. "Hey, I'd love to stop and flirt, but I checked out a Bible from the library and I have some questions. Any chance we could get together tonight for a little while?"

"You checked out a Bible from the library?" Jake stalled, trying to unpack her request to "get together." *Say no, man, say no. Remember this morning!*

"Yeah, yeah, this thing is a huge sucker. It takes up most of my backpack. I just really need to talk to someone," Nicole continued, now almost in a begging voice.

"Yeah, I don't think your boyfriend would be too thrilled about us hanging out," Jake retorted. There, he'd done it. He'd said no.

"Jake. How many times do I have to tell you? Nate's not my *boyfriend,*" Nicole responded flippantly and then turned on the sultry charm. "C'mon. Are you going to be a good Christian and tell me about Jesus or not?"

Ugh! Jake struggled. Who was he to reject someone who had spiritual questions? And what if God had brought Nicole into his life for this reason? And then his mind started to picture her alluring curves, and he wondered what kind of tantalizing outfit she might wear to meet him. His body craved one of her tight welcome hugs, and then his pride kicked in. He considered how sweet it would be to avenge Nate's insult by throwing his warning right back in his face. Jake wasn't scared of him. Screw that cocky Nate Williams. "Okay, I'll give you thirty minutes," Jake compromised.

"Great! Come by my room—817—around eight. Gotta go, see ya, babe."

She hung up before Jake could debate the meeting location. He took a deep breath before walking into class. If he gave Amy a phone call right after dinner, that would leave them at least an hour and a half to talk through whatever she needed to discuss. And reading the Bible with Nicole would kill two birds with one stone. Maybe this balancing act wasn't so impossible after all.

✚ ✚ ✚

Every practice was grueling, but this afternoon felt like three hours of torment. After putting the team through thirty minutes of suicides and other conditioning drills, the coaching staff broke the team into skill rotations, then defensive drills, then offensive run-throughs, and finally two half-court scrimmages. Pretty normal routine. But as luck would have it, Jake and Nate were pitted against each other for the better part of the afternoon. Although the freshman star didn't do too much trash-talking, his smug swagger made it clear who had dominated earlier that day. Basketball was a team sport, but every basket, assist, rebound, and steal felt like a personal victory or defeat. Jake was holding his own, but just barely, and every play felt like he was battling against the disapproval of the entire floor. By the end of practice, he was exhausted.

With minutes to go, Nate held the rock at the top of the key, and Jake guarded his adversary up tight. He crouched down low in defensive stance, his right arm perched high, prepared to block any pass. His legs were burning and his arms felt like lead, but every muscle was taut, ready to spring in an instant. With sweat dripping down his nose, he fought to stay focused on Nate's every move.

Nate whispered to him with an arrogant smile, "Don't trip on this one."

Jake winked back. "Still waiting for you to sink a jumper."

Nate's face transformed into a scowl and he faked left, then elevated into the air a few feet in from the three-point line. But Jake hadn't been sitting on the sidelines watching him all season for nothing. He outjumped the taller guard and swatted the ball back in his face. It bounced off the top of Nate's head, where Jake's outstretched left hand palmed it down. He took a step over the three-point line to backcourt and then suddenly threw up his own jumper right in front of a dazed Nate.

Swish.

"Oooooooooh!" the rest of the guys on the court responded in unison, as Jake relished the rare praise. Out of the corner of his eye, Jake caught Coach watching from the sidelines.

"Tell your girlfriend to stop calling me," Jake smirked, as a whistle blew to end practice.

Jake's in-depth description of his dazzling play really didn't do it justice as he recounted it to Amy later that evening, but she didn't seem to mind. Of course, he neglected the whole girlfriend part, but what she didn't know couldn't hurt her.

"So have they retired your number yet?" Amy joked.

"Babe, I don't even have a number," Jake confessed.

"Well, you're number one to me."

Jake chuckled, basking in the warmth of her encouraging voice. He missed her. But he couldn't escape a nagging sense of guilt. Leaning back in his desk chair with his feet perched on his bed, Jake eyed his bedside clock as it slowly inched toward eight.

"Remind me again why he doesn't like you," Amy questioned.

"Ohhhhh, I don't know," Jake side-stepped. "I think he's just worried about next year." Which was partially true. Jake glanced at his clock again: it read 7:45. *Crap!* He'd never gotten around to asking Amy about what was bothering her last night. "So, uh, what did you want to talk to me about yesterday?" *Am I really hurrying my conversation with Amy to hang out with Nicole?*

"Oh, it's not as big a deal now. One of the girls I drove around for the junior high car rally called me up asking for a ride from the mall."

"I knew they would love you. How'd she get your number?"

"Long story. But the part that bothered me so much was when I was dropping her off at home. She said she wasn't allowed to go home 'til eight."

Jake listened as he quietly grabbed his shoes to get ready to go.

"You mean her curfew is eight."

"That's what I said. But no, she's not *allowed* to go home until then. Jake, that's crazy...she's in seventh grade."

"That's weird." Jake tried to sound concerned. "What did you do?"

"I texted Cari and asked for her advice. She promised to call the girl and take care of it. I don't know. I kinda feel guilty, though."

Jake slipped his arms through his jacket with the phone still attached to his right ear. "Why? You didn't do anything wrong," he reassured.

"Well, I promised her not to tell anyone. She's probably gonna hate me now."

The clock now read 7:55 and it was at least a ten-minute walk to Nicole's dorm. It felt deceitful to be talking to Amy while en route to another girl's dorm, but what choice did he have? *I'm just a spiritual mentor,* Jake reminded himself. He grabbed his own Bible, quietly locked his door and continued on in the conversation. "So you're worried that a seventh grader might not like you anymore?" Jake half-joked.

"Ugh. Jake, you don't understand," Amy groaned. "What if I get her in trouble or something?"

Jake made his way down the stairs into the dorm lobby. There were people everywhere. "One sec, Amy." Jake hurried through the noisy room and hit a brick of cold air as he pushed through the front door. "Sorry about that. I'm on my way to a...uh...study group." *That's the truth, right?*

"Oh, I didn't know you had plans. I'll let you go then. Just please pray for the girl. Her name is Melia."

"Meli-a? That's a lot like Emily." Jake wished he hadn't voiced the connection the second it released from his mouth.

"Helloooo! I already told you that last time. Why do you think I'm having such a hard time with it?!" Amy snapped, then sighed. "I'm sorry. I don't mean to take it out on you. I'm just worried about her." Her voice sounded frail. "I love you, Jake Taylor."

Jake walked briskly though the cold air toward Nicole's dorm room. "I love you, too."

✦ ✦ ✦

Jake hadn't walked on an all-girls floor since his accidental visit the first day when he was moving in, but today he was prepared. Nicole Martin lived on the eighth floor in Unitas Tower, and Jake used the climb to work off some of his nervous jitters. Halfway up the first floor, his legs reminded him of the day's grueling practice, but it wasn't like he could back down now. *God, please use me today to answer her questions,* Jake found himself praying as he lumbered up the stairs.

He opened the door to the eighth floor and wandered down the hall, hoping he'd catch his breath before finding Nicole's room. A few girls and guys roamed around him, but thankfully he didn't recognize any of them. *811...813...815...*Jake could hear the sound of reggae music from inside the next room down. Jake pulled his pocket Bible from his back pocket and held it at his side. He gulped down some air and reached for the door. Suddenly his cell phone vibrated in his pocket. *Uh-oh.*

8:04pm | From: Nicole | To: Jake
Look whoz bhind u

JAKE LOOKED AT THE TEXT, puzzled but relieved the moment he saw it was only from Nicole. Suddenly, he felt a body close behind him, and two hands reached around to cover his eyes.

"Guess who?" Nicole's unmistakable voice rang mischievously from behind.

"Ummmm, give me a hint," Jake played along. *This isn't flirting. You're just being friendly.*

"Sometimes, you call me 'babe'," Nicole laughed, her hands still covering his eyes.

Jake could feel certain parts of Nicole's body leaning into him as she reached up from her tiptoes, and a tingling thrill raced through him. *This isn't cool, Jake,* he admitted to himself. "Uh, I give up," he laughed nervously and spun around to remove Nicole's hands from his face. Now he was mere inches from her luscious lips, and her big blue eyes were staring straight up into his. *Don't even think about it,* Jake warned himself, but his body remained frozen.

Nicole's arms rested on his shoulders, then pulled him into the warm hug he'd looked forward to earlier. Maybe it was just his imagination, but this one seemed to linger a bit longer than usual.

"I'm so glad you're here, Jake," she greeted him genially, as she pulled away. She wore a completely innocent black T-shirt over some tight jeans, but Jake's eyes still feasted on the scenery. Nicole brushed past him, opening her door to an empty room.

Jake surveyed the relatively clean arrangement with bunk beds in one corner and a couch in the other.

"Sorry to scare you! I was studying in my friend's room," she giggled.

"You didn't scare me," Jake chuckled, pausing two feet inside the doorway, his Bible clutched tightly.

"Sure, tough guy!" Nicole kidded, grabbing his arm to lead him further into the room. "I made us some coffee."

Jake glanced over to a coffee-maker in the corner steaming with a fresh brew. He had to admit, it did smell pretty good. "Uh, great. Thank you."

Nicole poured the hot liquid into two white mugs. "I kinda stole these from Denny's," she laughed, carrying the steaming drinks directly over to the couch.

"You can't just steal stuff like that," he frowned, shocked by her frank confession. Who does something like that?

"That's why you're here," she grinned. "To set me straight." Nicole patted the cushion next to her, as if to remind him where he belonged.

Jake stood motionless. In his four years of dating Amy, sitting alone on a couch had never led to just talking. Once again, he found his game plan fizzling away.

"Come on...I don't bite," Nicole prodded, as she picked up her behemoth Bible sitting on the floor next to her feet. "I've got a ton of questions and only 25 minutes left with you." She held up his coffee so he had to come and get it.

You're just here to talk about the Bible. That's a good thing. You're strong. You can do this. Jake pepped himself up and walked confidently over to the couch, grabbing his coffee and sitting down a good foot and a half from Nicole. "OK, then, let's get to it...what do you want to know?"

"Okay, let me see," Nicole turned to a page marked with a yellow post-it note. "So what's the difference between Jesus and God....Are they like the same or not?" Nicole looked at him with inquisitive eyes.

Jake was immediately impressed with the depth of her question, and a calm washed over him. Maybe all she really did want was to talk about the Bible. What was wrong with his sicko mind to expect anything more? Ironically, though, her seemingly pure interests made her more attractive than ever. "Ahhh, well, Jesus is God's son, but he's also God," Jake started, trying to remember how Chris had answered that same question at a Q & A night at Souled Out.

He took a sip of his coffee and glanced into Nicole's eyes for a moment. She nodded along like what he was saying made perfect sense.

"It's like my dad is my dad, but he's also a son and used to be a husband," Jake continued, knowing he was probably making it worse with every syllable that left his mouth.

"Hm. Okay, I think that makes more sense." Nicole smiled sincerely.

"It does?" Jake asked, incredulous.

"Sure, more or less. So, why are there all these different, like, chapters all named after people with weird names? Like Malachi, and I don't even know how to pronounce this one: H-a-g-g-a-i. And then there are big numbers, and then there are little numbers. I don't get it."

Jake smiled, remembering his own confusion when he had first read the Bible Chris had given him. He had just been relieved there was a table of contents! "Well, the Bible is organized into 66 books, usually named after the person who wrote it—"

"I thought God wrote the Bible," Nicole interrupted.

"He did. Er, at least He wrote it through humans who recorded His words, and—"

"You mean, like, God talked to them?"

"Yeah, I guess."

"Like in an audible voice, as if they were his secretary or something?"

"Sure, maybe—"

"Has God ever spoken to you that way?"

"Uh, no, not exactly, but that's kind of what the Bible is for nowadays."

"Why do you think God doesn't speak to people like that anymore?"

"Well, he does sometimes, but he also uses things like his Bible, and other people, and..."

"Like how you're speaking to me now?" Nicole smiled, her hand reaching over to rub Jake's back.

"Uh, yeah, sure." The questions had started coming so quickly that Jake wasn't even sure what he was saying anymore, and the light touch of her fingertips along his neck sure didn't help. He loved it when Amy would caress the back of his head and run her fingers through his hair, and for the moment, he kind of forgot who it was that was currently stroking him. He dropped his head forward and stretched his neck back and forth, lost in the tickle of her touch.

"Ooh, Jake, you're really tense," Nicole noticed.

Immediately, Jake's muscles tightened in response. *Jake, dude, what are you doing?* his intellect questioned. But as Nicole's gentle scratching turned into a shoulder massage, he did nothing to stop her.

"Here, scoot forward," she nudged him, and he willingly obeyed. Her knees straddled his back as her fingers kneaded his worries away. Her small hands were extremely strong, and Jake's resolve loosened right along with his tight muscles. Nicole continued like nothing was going on. "You said your dad *used* to be a husband?" she asked.

"Yeah. My parents separated this past year."

"Oh, that's too bad," Nicole sympathized. "My parents are still together, but they totally hate each other."

"That's how mine were. They thought they were actually fooling me," Jake laughed weakly, as Nicole dug her hands into his back. The feel of her body pressing firmly into his dissolved any negative feelings remaining, and he chuckled softly again.

"What are you laughing at?" Nicole teased, running her hands down to his lower back. She rested her chin on his shoulder, and her breath tickled his ear. "I don't know, even if it's just a façade....it's comforting in a weird way," she mused, her hands continuing to work their magic.

Those hands felt so good. Jake completely melted. Whoever thought a Bible study could be so enjoyable? "So, any other questions about the Bible?" he mumbled.

Nicole sat up quickly, as if startled by his question, and her hands lightened up. "Um, oh, yeah. Why do the people in my Bible keep saying 'thee' and 'thou'? Is that just how they talked back then?" she asked, without missing another beat.

Jake laughed out loud, and Nicole playfully punched him in the arm.

"Don't you dare laugh at me," Nicole warned with a playful glare. "I'm tougher than you think."

"Oh, I believe you!" Jake conceded, throwing his arms up in surrender. Nicole poked him in the side, causing him to flinch. "You're just reading an old version. My Bible uses normal words." Jake opened up his pocket Bible and held it up for her to read.

Nicole peered over his shoulder, her body leaning snugly against his once again, and read to herself through a couple of random lines from the book of Acts.

"This is way easier to understand!" Nicole looked over at him excitedly. "Any chance I could borrow yours?"

"Yeah, yeah, I've got another one in my room. Keep it as long as you want," Jake offered, turned on even more by her enthusiasm for the Bible.

"That's so awesome! Thanks so much," she chirped excitedly. Her fingers poked at the ticklish spot in his side again.

"Whoa! Wait a minute," Jake protested, reaching around to return the favor. Nicole lunged out of the way, but not in time to keep Jake's fingers away from her torso, and she collapsed onto the seat cushion with breathless giggles as Jake followed in hot pursuit. The tickling escalated until Jake found himself laying on top of her, staring into her mesmerizing eyes.

"Jake, I've got one last Bible question," Nicole whispered, her hands resting on his bare skin underneath his sweatshirt.

"Yeah?" Jake replied weakly, his eyes focused on the movement of her mouth.

"I was reading my Bible yesterday," she murmured, "and it said, 'Greet ye one another with a holy kiss.'" Her lips parted in a delicious oval. "What does that mean?"

Before his mind could even deliberate on what he was doing, Jake leaned forward and tenderly planted his lips on Nicole's. They felt soft and full as he closed his eyes and enjoyed the nervous feeling of a hundred butterflies crashing into one another all over his body. One thing led to another until he pulled away and gazed deep into those beautiful entrancing blue eyes. Blue like the sky...like the ocean... like Amy's.

"CRAP! I gotta go!" Jake blurted, jumping up from the couch and knocking his half-full mug of coffee all over the floor.

Nicole looked at him coyly, as if willing him to stay. He knew he owed her an explanation, but not here, not now. He strode to the door without looking back, when suddenly his phone vibrated. He whipped it out of his pocket, terrified of who it might be. *Chris Vaughn.* He cringed. *Absolutely not!* Jake shoved the phone back in his pocket and slammed the door shut behind him. He ran down all eight flights of stairs and rushed into the freezing night, gasping for air to clear his mind. *What have I done?*

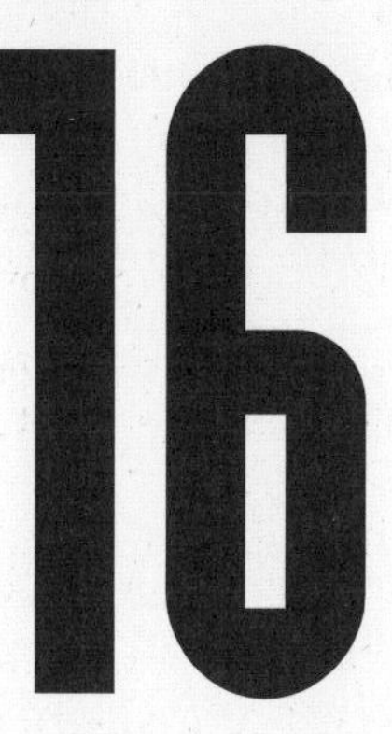

16

6:34pm | From: Chris | To: Jake
What does it take to get a phone call back?

FROM HIS USUAL TABLE at the back of the library, Jake read the text over and over again. This was the fifth time his mentor and friend had tried reaching him in the past three weeks, but Jake could never work up the nerve to call him back. He knew the questions Chris would ask—questions Jake didn't really have the right answers to anymore. No, he hadn't been to church in a while. No, he hadn't been reading his Bible. No, he hadn't been doing any of the things he knew he should be, not for the last three weeks anyway. He could already hear the disappointment in Chris's voice. But he couldn't help it. Things had changed. Jake had changed—a lot—all since the night of the kiss.

That one stupid night.

In the three weeks since, the snow and subfreezing temperatures had melted away. Jake had exchanged his parka and gloves for sweatshirts and even occasional flip-flops. He no longer saw his breath in the late afternoon air. And leaves and flowers were starting to bud everywhere. But, in spite of the springtime thaw, Jake's heart felt colder than ever.

Over those three weeks, midterms had come and gone. Jake's grades had survived for the most part. He was struggling in some classes, but he was determined to earn all As and Bs—which would still require a minor miracle in Spanish. But even though he was passing, Jake still felt like a failure.

The basketball season had wound down to a less-than-stellar close. Tony Anderson had gone down with a sprained ankle during the final week, pretty much dashing Louisville's already tenuous hopes of qualifying for a NCAA tournament berth. They were invited to the NIT, but as the opposing team's fans had chanted in the final game, who cared about the "Nobody's Interested Tournament"? It was a subpar consolation prize for a team accustomed to national championships.

But while the rest of the team was bummed, Jake wasn't sure he minded so much. He would never admit it out loud, but for the last three weeks, Jake had been looking forward to the end of basketball season. During the last three weeks of practice, he had merely eked it out. He didn't know if Nate knew about his evening with Nicole, but it didn't matter. Nate had been right—she was too much for Jake to handle. He had strayed too close to the fire and was definitely feeling scorched. Ironically, Nate seemed to play with less intensity, too. Maybe Nicole was like that chick Delilah that Jake had read about—she knew just how to suck the power out of a man.

Nicole! Since that horrible, thrilling, tempting, elating, embarrassing, breathtaking, awkward, guilty evening three weeks ago, she had pretty much faded out of the picture. Jake still daydreamed about her tight hugs and her enticing body, and he woke up many nights reliving that one passionate kiss, but their direct contact had dropped to virtually nothing. She would still smile and wave when he saw her around campus—or while she waited for Nate after practice—but that was it. She didn't even try to talk to him. Jake knew he should be relieved, but it kind of irked him. How could they share something that intense and she not even want to *talk* to him? Wasn't it the *guy* who was supposed to just hit-and-run? Was he just a game to her? Then again, he must have looked like an idiot to Nicole that night—freaking out about a single kiss, running out the door like a sissy. She obviously thought he couldn't deliver. *So why would she want to waste her time on me?* Jake cringed.

Of course, none of this should have mattered to him, because he had an amazing girlfriend back at home. But unfortunately, ever since that disappointing mistake of a night, things had changed there, too. Oh, Amy was just as good as ever, but Jake just couldn't help but feel awkward when talking to her. He never even came close to telling her about the incident with Nicole, but he carried it around like a dirty little secret that threatened to jump out and expose him at any second. And while he could tell that Amy was doing everything she could to keep their relationship going, Jake was having a hard time reciprocating. They were still chatting most nights, but Jake found less and less he felt like talking about.

The hardest part with Amy was that it seemed like everything was going perfectly for her. She was getting straight As, just as she had all throughout high school. She loved the small group of seventh grade girls she led at New Song. She claimed they were teaching her far more than she could possibly be teaching them, and he could feel the joy she was exuding. She was still running with Andrea a couple times a week and had a standing coffee date with Cari on Friday afternoons. Her life was great. Jake liked hearing the enthusiasm and passion in his girlfriend's voice, but he found himself mildly jealous of her. He was the one supposed to be living it up at his dream school, but she seemed to be the truly happy one.

Last week, Amy had spilled the beans that she was "surprising" him with a visit during her spring break, and Jake hoped that spending that week together would push their relationship right back on track. If nothing else, it would be a good way to get Nicole out of his mind for a while.

As he kept thinking about the changes that had occurred over the last three weeks, Jake realized that he just felt alone. He was surrounded by tons of people every day, but everyone seemed so detached from him. Sure, Grant was still a friend, and Jake had been trying to get out more. But the parties and the socializing left him feeling empty. No matter how many people he chatted it up with, he rarely felt as if he could be himself, and he still ended up alone in his dorm at the end of the night—lately, with a hangover of regrets.

He and Kyle definitely weren't getting along any better, and Jake had even heard secondhand that Kyle had requested a roommate change for next year. It was no big surprise, and Jake was going to do the same thing anyway, but it sure didn't help his loneliness. Things just weren't what they used to be in high school. Jake missed the old New Song gang. But he wasn't sure he'd still fit in there, even if he tried.

Jake looked down at Chris's text again. He glanced at his watch: It was 4:47 p.m. California time, almost time for Chris to be home for dinner with Cari and Caleb. *That should keep the conversation short,* he figured. He reminisced about the beginning of their friendship over a year ago, when a drunken Jake had interrupted Chris' family time to ask him for a ride home after a party.

"Ah, what the hell," Jake muttered under his breath to an unconcerned library. He collected his books and made his way toward the exit.

On the second ring, Chris's familiar, animated voice answered. "Jake! What's shakin', my man?"

Jake could easily envision him smiling ear-to-ear with his goofy grin, sporting his usual collared shirt, pair of jeans, and haphazardly spiked hair. Just the thought of Chris brought a smile to Jake's face.

"Sorry I've been so slow in calling back," Jake apologized.

"No worries, man. I know you're busy...You're never gonna guess who's sitting next to me right now," Chris added.

"Give me a clue."

"He likes bacon bits, and he—"

"Turn your speaker phone on!" Jake interrupted. He waited two seconds and then shouted into his end of the line, "Jonny Boy!"

"How's it going, Jake?" his friend replied with a less-than-enthusiastic greeting.

Jake and Jonny had spoken a few times in the first two months Jake had been away and had made good use of Facebook in between, but the last few weeks Jake had pulled away from Jonny, too. He suddenly felt bad about how his silence affected others. "Jonny, look, I'm sorry for being a lame friend and not talk—"

"Jake, don't worry about it. It's not you...I'm having a rough day," Jonny sighed.

"Oh. What's up?" Jake questioned, realizing how much he missed his buddy. Jonny was evidence of Jake at his best—looking out for the lonely, helping the hopeless. In the aftermath of Roger's shooting, Jonny was Jake's redemption from a life of failure as a friend. Unfortunately, Jake wasn't really doing much good for him right now, on the other side of the country.

"My mom got stationed in Okinawa. I'm moving there at the end of the month."

Jake could almost see his friend's hopeless face as he sat shotgun in Chris' car in front of Jonny's mobile home.

"I'm gonna be there for my whole senior year...I don't even speak Okinawan," Jonny complained.

Jake stifled a mild laugh and looked out at the dark, empty quad in front of him. A group of students strolled by without even looking his way. "Oh, man. That really sucks, Jonny," Jake responded lamely, unsure of what he could say to offer encouragement. "But I have heard that the girls there like tall dudes," he attempted.

"Really?" Jonny's voice perked up for the first time.

"All righty, Jake! How about I call you back in fifteen minutes?" Chris interjected, obviously trying to steer the conversation in a different direction.

"Jonny boy, I'll call you soon," Jake promised. And he meant it.

"Do you think I'm tall enough for—"

Chris piped in again. "Really gotta go, Jake. Talk to you in a few."

Jake chuckled, thinking about Chris trying to veer away from that tangent. *Oops,* Jake thought, wondering what else he should have said.

There was no way he was heading back into the library to kill fifteen minutes, so Jake stuck the phone back in his pocket and headed toward his dorm, mulling over Jonny's predicament. This would be at least the fifth time Jonny had been forced to move since sixth grade. No wonder he had no friends when Jake reached out to him almost a year ago. But now that Jonny had finally found a group of friends where he fit in, he was forced to move again. It seemed so unfair. And it sure put Jake's loneliness in a totally different light. *God,* Jake prayed for the first time in nearly three weeks, *please help Jonny through this transition. I hope he doesn't go back to the way he used to be.*

Just as Jake entered the mostly vacant dorm lobby, his phone rang again. After confirming it was Chris, Jake answered. "How's Jonny?"

"You know, honestly, I think he'll be okay." Jake could hear the engine of Chris's green Toyota Corolla turn over. "What I want to know is, how's Jake?"

Jake rolled his eyes, finding a step halfway up the first floor to camp out on. "Busy...but not like high-school busy. I never knew how much free time I used to waste."

"Like revisiting the sample tables over and over again at Costco?" Chris laughed.

"How many times this week?" Jake questioned.

"Counting tomorrow, twice. But I'm serious, man...I'm gonna quit one of these days."

Jake knew that wasn't true. Taking students through the sample lines and then sitting with them over a hot dog and soda to talk about God would be—and should be—a part of Chris Vaughn's life until he was old and gray...or until he ran Costco out of business.

"How's the youth group?" Jake asked, avoiding any more talk about himself. Although he had not made church a priority here in Louisville, he missed the Souled Out services back home.

"You know, it's going just okay," Chris spoke calmly. "It's not like we're doing anything differently than last year, but only about half as many students are coming. I've got to keep reminding myself that God loves me no matter what size the group is."

It was those kinds of answers that had drawn Jake to Chris in the first place. In a world where everybody was *always* doing great, Jake appreciated that his youth pastor always called it like it was.

"Okay, I'll be praying for that." That was the first time Jake had told someone that in a long time. He felt phony just sounding spiritual.

"I'd appreciate that. So, back to you. How you doin'?" he asked in a bad Joey Tribbiani impersonation.

Jake's seat on the stairwell immediately become uncomfortable. "I don't know; life's just okay, I guess." Jake copied Chris's answer. A herd of girls raced past him up the stairwell, almost stampeding him. Realizing the danger in this spot, Jake stood up and began to slowly march up the stairs to the third level.

"Chris, I wanna shoot straight with you." Jake took a deep breath. "I haven't been reading my Bible, I haven't been to church in about a month, and I'm just not feeling God here...I'm sorry." Chris was the last person he wanted to let down, but Jake at least owed him the truth.

"Okay."

"Okay what?" Jake waited for one of Chris's pep talks that had challenged him so many times before.

"Okay, I understand that college life is tough."

That's it? No wonder the youth group had shrunk in half. Chris had really lost his game.

"Let me just ask you one more question, Jake." Chris' voice sounded weary.

Jake leaned against the wall just outside the door to his floor. "What?"

"Are you truly happy?"

Chris' penetrating question made Jake drop his backpack to his feet. "No, not really," Jake responded honestly, looking at himself in the reflection of a window.

"Then figure out what you were doing when you last were...I'm confident you'll find Jesus there."

He didn't sound angry or disappointed, the way Jake had anticipated. And his challenge wasn't anything radical. It was the simple truth—the thing that had gotten to Jake in the first place.

"Thanks, Chris."

"Call me anytime." Jake knew that Chris meant it, too.

Still pondering Chris's words, Jake practically walked right into Kyle, who was carrying a cardboard box out the door.

"Whoa! What the—?" Jake dodged his angry roommate, who sped down the hall in gargantuan strides.

Realizing Kyle wasn't turning around to provide an answer, Jake entered their room to find half of his roommate's stuff already packed in an assortment of garbage bags and boxes. Five minutes later, Kyle reappeared, looking madder than the last time.

"Kyle, what's going on?"

His roommate glared at Jake angrily as he bent down to pick up another box. "Coach took away my scholarship," Kyle snapped.

"What? Why?"

Kyle dropped the box and sat down on his bed. He covered his head with his hands and growled. "They found some cocaine in my locker." He pounded his fist hard on the bed. "I could kill myself right now!"

Jake had never seen this side of him before. "I'm really sorry, man," Jake uttered helplessly.

"I'm so stupid; my dad is *so* pissed."

Although they had been far from friendly lately, Jake found himself awkwardly walking over to his roommate's disgusting bed and sitting down next to him. "Do you really have to leave school immediately?"

"I'm failing all my classes; what's the point?" Kyle looked up, and for the first time, Jake detected a scared and vulnerable kid hiding behind all those tough tattoos and piercings. "I thought you'd be happy to see me leave," Kyle added.

Jake would have expected that as well, but for some reason, he hurt for his roommate. "I know we haven't been the best of friends," Jake smiled at that understatement of the century. "I just know how much you love playing basketball here...this really sucks."

Kyle chuckled quietly, and then the two sat in silence for a few awkward moments.

"Your dad ever pressure you to be somebody you're not?" Kyle mumbled sullenly.

If Kyle only knew. Jake's entire childhood could have been summarized in that simple statement. Jake remembered how his best was never good enough according to his dad's standards. No matter how well Jake did, his father always expected more. "Yeah," Jake answered softly.

Kyle stood up from his bed and kicked his Louisville gym bag across the room. "I never wanted to be a basketball player," he laughed cynically. "I wanted to be a musician. But my dad couldn't imagine having a 6-foot-10 son who didn't play hoops. It was his idea I go to Louisville." He paused. "Now I might get to spend some time in the slammer." Kyle turned and looked down to face Jake. "I'm sorry I made fun of you with the guys."

Two months earlier, Jake had wanted to strangle him for making his life so miserable, but tonight, he just shrugged. "It's cool, man."

"I better get my stuff down to the curb; my dad's gonna be here in twenty minutes." Kyle picked his duffel bag back up and headed for the door.

Jake picked up a poorly packed cardboard box and followed Kyle. "I'll give you a hand."

For the first time in their three months of being roommates, they had something like a real conversation as they carried down box after box of Kyle's junk to the curb out front. Kyle's dad drove up in a shiny new Suburban, and the former roommates hugged goodbye. Jake wondered if they'd ever talk again and felt bad that it had taken Kyle's departure for them to get to this point.

Later that night, after his first decent conversation with Amy in weeks, Jake lay awake in bed brooding over the last few hours. He felt as if he held pieces from several different puzzles in his hands, but no matter how hard he tried, he just couldn't make them fit together.

10:11am | From: Jan | To: Amy
Any chance we could take you up on your offer to babysit tonight?

AMY DISCREETLY RESPONDED TO THE TEXT, using her purse to shield her cell phone from her favorite professor. "Sure, what time?"

The moment she sent it, a lump of hesitation settled in her throat. While part of her was excited to see her baby, the slower, more rational part of her brain reminded her how painful these visits always were. Besides the inevitable bump-intos at church, lately Amy had tried to steer clear of the couple she had given her daughter away to almost four months ago. Amy could already see Jake's eyes and chin on this little miracle, and it killed her to know that Emily would grow up calling someone else "Mom." *Why do I keep offering to babysit*? Amy berated herself, huffing under her breath.

Mr. Sullivan must have heard the sigh, because he looked right at her. Amy quickly dropped her phone into her purse and snapped to attention with an eager head nod and a smile. In other classes she wouldn't have cared, but this one was different. She loved old Mr. Sullivan, and she lived for Mondays and Wednesdays from 10 to 11:30 when she learned all about the basics of psychology. After only a few of these classes, Amy had been inspired to check out her options for majoring in it. Most schools—including Louisville—offered extensive programs in psychology. But she still had that scholarship package waiting at Stanford, and the more she looked into their top-rated counseling program, the more she wanted to go there.

Unfortunately, she hadn't managed to bring any of this up with Jake yet. Going to Stanford would be such a huge change in their plans, and she wasn't sure if that's even what she really wanted. But wasn't that why she had stayed behind this semester...to find out what *she* really wanted? And if Stanford was what she decided was best for her, Jake would certainly be supportive, right?

Her confidence in that answer was waning. He'd been drifting away again lately, no matter how hard she tried to be positive and encouraging. She didn't know what to do. She hoped her visit in a few days would spark something, because she feared she was losing him. *Would going to Stanford be worth losing Jake?* she agonized, and her heart echoed back with *No!...I don't think so...or would it?*

Chuckles all around Amy brought her back to reality again, and she promptly refocused her drifting thoughts back on the lively bald man in front of her.

Today's topic was the psychology of persuasion in today's culture. Mr. Sullivan shared about a researcher who sent out Christmas cards to a bunch of perfect strangers. Although he expected *some* reaction, the response he received blew him away. Christmas cards from people he'd never met came pouring back from all over the country. The amazing part was that most people never even asked who he was. They just added him to their mailing lists and sent back their own holiday greetings. Professor Sullivan called this phenomenon "reciprocity" and explained how the depth of its power in our society was nearly impossible to resist. This led to a discussion of how every person in the room was somehow controlled by reciprocity's influence, and from there they dove into a dialogue on how to harness the rule of reciprocity to one's benefit. The key was to give people something they considered valuable enough to make them feel indebted to you.

The whole concept was intriguing. Amy had never scribbled so many notes in a single class before. By the end of the lecture, her hand was throbbing, and her mind was overflowing with concepts that she knew would take her the rest of the day to process.

Since Andrea couldn't run on school days anymore, thanks to official track practice, after several hours of laboring through homework in the library, Amy headed to the beach. *My whole life has been about reciprocating favors!* she thought as she pounded the pavement along the Strand. She reflected on how she would scrub the whole house spotless or hurry to make dinner for her mother because she felt guilty that her mom had to work so hard to support her. She was always the obedient child, not wanting to be more of a burden than she already was. But it never seemed to work...or maybe that was precisely the problem. Mr. Sullivan had explained that often reciprocity can become a vicious cycle that leaves the reciprocator feeling permanently indebted. Amy loved her mom, but she had grown up with constant reminders of how much she had sacrificed to have her, and Amy could never make that up to her.

As Amy jogged in place at a stoplight, her thoughts wandered to her dad. He had stayed with her mother when he got her pregnant in high school, but he'd been completely out of the picture since he ditched them when Amy was in kindergarten. *Too bad reciprocation didn't work on him!* Suddenly, her mind wandered to the drawer full of letters he had faithfully sent every Christmas and birthday since then. They all sat unopened at the bottom of her desk, begging to reveal their contents. *No!* she protested, unwilling to let her thoughts go there. As the light turned green, she raced ahead, eager to outrun the memories. *He doesn't deserve to have me read them,* she justified, but then she thought, *Is that why I don't open them up—because then I would have to owe him something...like forgiveness?* This reciprocation thing was crazy.

Eager to stop thinking about her father, Amy skipped ahead to a happier subject: Jake. Yeah, reciprocation was alive and well in that relationship. From the beginning, Jake had been different from any of her other "boyfriends"—if that's what two-week junior high relationships could be called. She had earned a reputation in middle school, so she had lived up to it with each subsequent boy who had wanted to go out with her. She had craved the attention and affection, so she had done what they wanted and pretended she liked it.

But then Jake had come along—kind of shy and more interested in basketball than anything else. He had liked her for who she was, and they had a ton of fun together. But she wasn't used to a relationship that was just based on friendship, and she worried that maybe something was wrong with her when he didn't push her to go all the way. *Was that why I was so eager to get him to have sex with me?* She knew if she gave him that, then he would owe her. And it had seemed to work pretty well...for a while.

But there had always been that nagging fear that someday Jake would grow tired of her, that someday he would just move on, like everyone else. So she had worked herself dizzy keeping up with the spiral of reciprocation, always trying to find new ways of keeping Jake happy. When she found out she was pregnant, the cycle spun out of control...until Jake broke the pattern and gave up everything for her.

But in fact, it had simply reversed it—now she was the one indebted to him, feeling guilty for taking away his dreams. And as hard as she tried, she just couldn't seem to make it up to him. Even though Jake had been able to accept his full ride at Louisville after all, Amy knew this semester hadn't been easy on him. And even though he never said it, she was pretty sure he thought it was her fault.

Ahhhhhhhh! her mind screamed as tears pricked at her eyes. Maybe it *was* her fault. That was the price of reciprocation. In desperation, Amy pushed her pace faster, and her breaths came in ragged gasps as they forced themselves past the gigantic lump in her throat.

If it really was all her fault, then how could she even think about going to Stanford after everything that Jake had given up for her? How could she be so selfish? The Louisville undergrad psychology program would probably be just fine. It was the Stanford post-grad program that she was really excited about, anyway. And if she upped her hours at work and took out some loans, she could probably scrape together enough to cover the tuition at Louisville. Or she could enroll in a community college around there for another year to establish residency and save on the tuition. Did it really matter *where* she was taking her classes, as long as she and Jake were together? The more she planned it out, the more excited she felt. It all made so much more sense when she looked at it that way.

Amy sprinted to the end of her run, relishing the power she felt in her stride. The wind whipped past her face and filled her lungs with life. She felt good! Hands on her hips, she walked toward the stairs away from the beach, sucking in the salty air. A glance at her stopwatch thrilled her even more: She had run almost six minutes quicker than normal for the five-mile loop. *Wow!* Settling all of her thoughts took a load off her shoulders, and it felt good.

But deep down inside, something still didn't feel satisfied.

Amy walked to her van and stretched a little as she checked her phone. No new messages from Jake. Her heart sank a little. *He's busy,*

Amy! What do you expect? she chided herself and proceeded to send him an "I love you! Can't wait to see your sexy self in only 3 days!" She smiled to think of being with him again.

There was a message from Andrea, just saying she was praying for her. Andrea was always so sweet like that. Amy made a mental note to call her back later to tell her about her speedy run. Then she had a message from Jan, clarifying that the time they needed her tonight was six to eight. Jan concluded the message with "I'll make you dinner."

Ha! thought Amy. *That's totally reciprocation!* She smiled, appreciating the gesture nevertheless. She shivered as a breeze chilled her sweaty skin, and she slipped on a hoodie. As she zipped it up, another chill caught her from the inside. *Wait a minute.* An idea sprang to life. *That's why I can't stay away from them!* Amy realized that, if she was truly honest with herself, the deep-down reason why she kept offering to help out with Emily was that she felt as if she owed her daughter. She had given her away, and now babysitting her, thinking about her, holding her at church—these were her feeble attempts to make it up to her.

Fresh emotions threatened to drown Amy again. She sat in the driver's seat fighting back the tears until she couldn't hold back any longer. A torrent of salty drops ran down her cheeks and fell to her lap as she hid her face behind the steering wheel. She clutched it with white knuckles, relying on its stability to keep her from fading away. Would she ever be free from the torment of her decision to give her baby up?

Amy sat back and stared out at the waves in the distance. They never stopped crashing in, did they? Is that how she was doomed to live—forever beaten down by the relentless fury of regret? Discouraged, she turned the ignition and backed out of the parking space.

As she pulled onto the street, Amy turned the music up loud to drown out any emotional outbursts still waiting to happen. The radio belted out some country song she wasn't in the mood for, so she pressed preset number one. Nothing. Number two. She just wasn't feeling the hip-hop groove. Number three. Back to the country song that didn't make the cut. Number four. She had been surprised to discover that she liked most of the songs on the new Christian music station Cari and Andrea had both recommended, but right now, it wasn't doing it for her. Number five...Perfect!

Amy tapped into her loudest, gruffest voice as she sang along passionately with Blondie, not caring who might see her going a little crazy behind the wheel. It felt so good to belt out the angry lyrics! Amy was pounding the top of her steering wheel to the rhythm of the synthetic organ interlude when she caught a glimpse of a familiar figure trudging alone down the sidewalk in the other direction. Her bulging pink backpack and curly red hair were unmistakable. Without a second thought, Amy flipped on her left blinker and cut into the far-left lane in order to bust a U-turn and pick up her young friend.

While Amy was pretty certain she wasn't supposed to have favorites in her small group of seventh grade girls, it was too late for that. Melia had snagged a tender spot in Amy's heart, and she just couldn't resist that crazy girl in spite of their rough start. Amy was learning what a special person Melia was as she exposed more and more fascinating facets of her personality. Like last week: Right in the middle of group, Melia announced that she was going to try out for *America's Next Top Model*, and she would appreciate prayer as she tried to learn how to walk in heels. Amy laughed to herself, recalling the seriousness on Melia's face. The week before that, after visiting her grandmother in a convalescent home, Melia had shared how she wanted to learn to be a masseuse, so she could make sick old people more comfortable.

Amy still wasn't sure what the story was behind Melia's family, though. After the first weird time Amy had given her a ride home, Cari had followed up with Melia's parents, who gave a completely different story. They assured Cari that their daughter was welcome to walk in the door anytime after school; it was her choice to stay out until after 8 p.m. That hadn't sat well with Amy, but she didn't know what else to do about it—especially since Melia had gotten mad at Amy for telling someone else about it.

The green arrow appeared on the signal light ahead, and Amy cranked the steering wheel into a tight turn. Melia was several hundred yards down the road; Amy drove until she passed her and then steered the minivan into the bike lane a couple of feet in front of her.

"Melia!" Amy yelled, punching her blaring radio off as her nearly-broken automatic window slowly descended on the passenger side.

Melia jumped in fright. "Amy, are you stalking me?" she squealed, resting her hands on her knees for a moment to catch her breath. Melia's long-sleeved top looked uncomfortably hot on one of Oceanside's warmer spring days.

"Yeah, I'm pretty scary-looking, you know. Need a lift?" Amy asked, reaching over to unlock the passenger door.

Without hesitation, Melia threw her backpack in the now-familiar shotgun seat and jumped in.

"Where are we going?" Melia asked, immediately turning the radio back on.

"I was gonna ask you that," Amy laughed, yelling over the music. She watched out the side mirror for an opportunity to merge back into traffic. "You want a ride home?"

"What about Borders?" Melia evaded the offer. "I'm almost done with a book I'm reading there."

A short break between cars opened up, and Amy stomped on the accelerator to make the opening.

"You go, Danica!" Melia yelled. Her reference to the race-car driver wasn't lost on Amy, who let up on the accelerator just a bit.

Once her feeble van reached the speed of the surrounding cars, Amy exhaled and turned the radio down. "Wait, you don't buy the books you read in the store?" she questioned. It was rush hour, and as soon as Amy made it up to full speed, a sea of red brake lights greeted her over the crest of a hill. She stomped on her brakes this time, glancing enviously at the nearly empty lane of cars heading in the opposite direction.

"Don't worry. I'm really careful with the pages," Melia replied, spontaneously breaking into a duet with the male voice on the radio.

Amy decided the whole book issue wasn't worth pursuing; she had done far worse when she was that age. Amy glanced down at the clock on the radio: It was almost 5:00 p.m. Her original plan was to stop by home for forty-five minutes to shower and change before heading over to Jan and Frank's. That plan was obviously out the window now, but a new one was forming in her head.

"What time you gotta be home?" Amy shouted over Melia's version of Bon Jovi.

Melia answered without breaking from her *American Idol* practice. "I told you before—8:00," she sang loudly and slightly off-key to the tune of the song on the radio.

Amy was pretty certain Jan and Frank wouldn't mind. They had always seemed like chill people and knew Melia from church anyway. "You want to help me babysit for two hours?" Amy asked, turning down the music for a second.

"Who are we babysitting?" Melia asked, turning the music off and staring at Amy.

Amy took a deep breath, remembering Melia's unintentionally painful words the last time they had broached this topic. "Uh, we're gonna babysit my daughter."

Melia gave a wide grin. "Cool." With that, she turned the radio back on, switched to the hip-hop station, and adjusted the bass control so high that Amy was confident her little minivan was bouncing up and down.

After a brief stop at the library—where Amy got Melia to check out the book she was reading—and sending a warning text to Jan, the girls arrived at the Merrill residence at two minutes before six to report for duty. The Merrills lived in a two-story townhouse that was part of a new development on the city line that separated Oceanside and Carlsbad. Frank and Jan hadn't left Emily alone with a sitter since they'd brought her home from the hospital, so they were a little edgy as they walked through the myriad of things Amy needed to remember in case an emergency arose. They were grateful for Amy's willingness to help out, though, and were looking forward to leaving for two hours to go out to dinner like normal people.

Jan had just fed Emily, who was drifting off to sleep in her adorable pink and green nursery, which made everything pretty simple. After Frank and Jan finally left, Amy and Melia devoured their plates of lasagna as they watched an episode of *Who Wants to Be a Millionaire?* Every time one of them answered a question right, they did a silent high-five and quiet victory dance so they wouldn't wake up the baby.

Ralph, a sailor from North Carolina, was halfway to winning his million when the crying started. The quiet whimper over the baby monitor soon morphed into an ear-piercing shriek. Amy and Melia both jumped up and ran to Emily to try to calm her down.

"Oh, Emily, it's okay," Amy crooned, as she rushed into the room. The little girl who had spent nine months growing and kicking inside of her now lay on her back, kicking and punching unhappily at the air. Amy reached into the exquisite crib and gently scooped Emily into her arms. "It's okay, sweetie. I got ya," Amy whispered tenderly into her ear, rocking her softly back and forth. Within a matter of seconds, the screaming stopped, as Emily reached out and grabbed Amy's lip. Amy kissed her delicate fingers and pressed her daughter to her chest.

"You're really good at that," Melia commented from just inside the nursery doorway.

Amy started, having forgotten that she wasn't alone. As she continued to sway back and forth, she explained to Melia, "She just wanted to know that she wasn't alone."

Melia took a few steps forward and looked carefully at Emily for a few moments. With hesitation, she placed her pinkie finger in reach of Emily's tiny grasp, and the baby latched on.

"She's got my finger!" Melia chirped, her face brightening into an excited smile.

"That means she likes you," Amy affirmed, kissing the fuzzy top of her child's head.

Melia's eyes grew wide. "Can I hold her…just for a second?"

Deep down, Amy didn't want to let her go, but she knew she couldn't hold her forever. "Okay, but you've got to sit down." Amy nodded in the direction of a cushy, crisp white glider on the other side of the room.

Melia immediately planted herself in it and looked up with eager eyes. Amy gave her baby one last kiss on the forehead and slowly lowered her into Melia's arms.

"Now make sure to keep one hand behind her head," Amy instructed as she propped a pillow underneath Melia's elbow. As if Amy was the expert on any of this.

The seventh grader's face lit up as the infant reached her tiny hands up toward the new stranger's face.

"If you're okay, I'm going to go make her a bottle," Amy asked, squatting to Melia's level to make sure her baby was safe.

"We're doing fine," Melia responded confidently as she smiled down on the four-month-old.

Amy quietly got up and grabbed the bottle Jan had pre-mixed and left in the fridge. She placed it in the bottle warmer and pushed the button exactly as she'd been told. As she waited for the light to indicate it was ready, Emily's cry started up again.

"I'll be there in one sec," Amy hollered from the kitchen as she waited impatiently for the warmer to finish its job. Emily's yowling became more frantic. "C'mon, hurry up!" Amy muttered under her breath. The cries became shrieks, and Amy couldn't take it any longer. She grabbed the lukewarm formula and hurried back into Emily's room.

"Shut up, you stupid baby!" Melia was scowling, shaking little Emily's body forcefully to get her to be quiet.

"Melia! What are you doing?" Amy shouted, dropping the bottle of milk and racing toward them. She scooped the baby out of Melia's clenched hands and held her tightly to her chest. "It's okay, baby. I'm not going to hurt you," Amy whispered soothingly into Emily's tiny ear as she frowned at her young friend.

Melia glared and ran out of the room.

The baby's wails stayed strong, and Amy surveyed her whole body to make sure she was okay. Had Melia hurt her? Slowly the screams subsided to whimpering sobs. The sobs eventually turned into hiccups, and it appeared that she was fine. *But what if I had come thirty seconds later?* Amy worried. She couldn't have lived with herself if anything had happened to Emily on her watch. She held the perfect little human in her arms, gently patting Emily's back until the hiccups disappeared and she was able to take the bottle. Once Emily had her fill, Amy raised her to her shoulder and nuzzled her face in the baby's soft skin. A flood of words surged from her heart without warning.

"Emily," she said, "I'm so, so sorry. I'm sorry that I didn't want you. I'm sorry I chose to abandon you before you were ever born. That I was afraid that you'd wreck my life. That I wasn't responsible enough to take care of you or give you absolutely everything that you deserve. I'm sorry that I gave you away..." What started as a few lonely tears soon became an unstoppable flow down Amy's face as she held her daughter tightly in her arms. "But I want you to know, beautiful Emily, that your mommy loves you with all her heart, and she will always love you. Frank and Jan do too, and I know they will take care of you better than I ever could, but you need to know from the bottom of my heart that I'm sorry." Amy's voice broke, and she couldn't go on. She cradled her daughter in her arms and prepared herself to let her go.

God, she spoke silently, *Emily is Your child more than mine...or even Jan and Frank's. Please take care of her. And I don't know if I even deserve it, but could You please help her to grow up knowing how much I love her?*

Ten minutes turned to twenty and then to thirty, and while her pain did not completely disappear, Amy could feel the guilt she had been carrying slowly float away as she quietly made amends with her daughter.

Emily had fallen back asleep long ago, but finally Amy was ready. She laid her back down in her crib, stroked her fuzzy head one last time, and quietly walked back to the family room.

Melia sat stoically watching Alex Trebek fire off questions to three eager contestants. It was obvious from Melia's red eyes that Amy had not been the only one crying. Amy grabbed a seat next to her friend and placed her hand softly on Melia's shoulder.

"I'm not mad at you, Melia," Amy sighed, trying to look into her eyes.

Melia didn't move a muscle but stared straight ahead, as if what was happening on TV was the most important thing in the world at the moment.

"Can we talk about what happened?" Amy prodded.

Melia shrugged, nudging Amy's hand off her.

"Melia." Amy was starting to lose patience. "Why did you get so mad at Emily?"

"She wouldn't stop crying," Melia muttered under her breath. "She deserved it."

Amy swallowed back her shock and shook her head calmly. "No, Melia, she's just a baby. Shaking her like that could have caused serious brain damage. She needs to be loved and cared for."

Melia crossed her arms, her gaze fixed straight ahead, and snorted with disdain. But a single tear slid from the corner of her eye down her cheek. Amy reached out with her thumb and wiped it away.

"Why do you think that's what she deserved?" Amy questioned softly.

Melia slowly turned her head to face Amy. "When you're bad, you get punished. It's just the way it is."

"How do you get punished when you're bad?" Amy asked hesitantly.

Melia's head snapped back to look at the TV. She sat on her hands and fidgeted. "My parents love me. They tell me they do."

But the fearful tone of her voice made Amy wonder what that "love" really looked like. Suddenly an image from her past—one that she'd dared not think about for years—flitted to the forefront of her brain.

Five-year-old Amy sits playing with her dolls on the floor. Raucous laughter echoes through the doorway. Her parents and other relatives are all celebrating something, and they all had too much to drink hours ago.

Her creaking door slowly opens, and her uncle bumbles in. Amy is terrified and tries to back away from him.

"Where ya goin', baby girl?" he slurs. "Ya know I love ya, don't ya?" She starts to cry, and he walks closer, putting a finger over his mouth to instruct her to be quiet.

Amy snapped out of that horrific memory just in time and tentatively reached out to give Melia a hug. Melia flinched.

"Love isn't supposed to be hurtful, you know," Amy urged.

Fresh tears formed in Melia's eyes. "It's not that bad anymore."

"But if someone is hurting you, then we need to do whatever it takes to protect you."

"I'm okay, I promise."

"Melia—"

"I'm fine!"

Amy leaned back. Chris had taken her through a thirty-minute training before she started working with the middle-school group, and reporting child abuse was one of the issues that had come up, but what was she supposed to do with this?

"Okay," Amy sighed. "But you have to promise me that if *anything* happens, you will tell me immediately," she said, resolving to keep an eye out for anything else that looked fishy.

"Sure," Melia mumbled.

Amy wasn't sure if "sure" was good enough.

8:37pm | From: Amy | To: Cari
I need some advice

9:57pm | From: Amy | To: Jake
Plane just landed

AMY FELT GIDDY WITH EXCITEMENT as she hit "Send." She was moments away from seeing Jake! It had been less than three months since they had said their goodbyes, but for her, it might as well have been an eternity. So much had changed in her life since then, and she could only imagine how much had changed for Jake.

On top of all her excitement to see her boyfriend, so much had transpired in the past five days back at home that it felt great to get away from Oceanside for the week. Work had been stressful; school was demanding. Remnants of Professor Sullivan's eye-opening lecture still rattled around in her head, and thoughts of what might be happening to Melia were keeping her awake at night.

Amy still didn't know what to do about her young friend. When Cari had immediately called Amy back after her plea for advice on Wednesday night, Amy had panicked. Instead of asking about what to do with her concerns for Melia, she lamely retreated to her two go-to issues—sadness at seeing Emily and nerves about visiting Jake. Her mouth refused to voice the possibility that Melia was being abused. After all, Melia had merely said she was punished, and she had emphasized that her parents loved her. Maybe Amy was simply reading her own traumatic past into Melia's evasive responses. Amy didn't want to overreact. But disturbing images from her childhood were beginning to resurface after being dormant for over a decade, and she kept waking up in a cold sweat from nightmares of her uncle's heavy body pressing her into silence.

Amy slipped her purse over her shoulder and shuddered, wishing the passengers in the front of the plane would disembark a little more quickly. She was on spring break, and she was here to spend six glorious days with her boyfriend. And nothing was going to bring her down!

My boyfriend! Amy sighed with a grin. Besides his hugs, and of course his cute face and irresistible charm, Amy looked forward to just reconnecting with Jake in person...observing his passion for the ways he saw God at work, watching him look out for the hurting and the lonely around him. These were things she had thought were a little weird before he had left for college. But now that Amy shared his faith in God, she remembered all those quirks with new admiration. Jake was a guy who had truly lived out what he believed, and Amy was so ready to see that side of him again.

She was also excited to meet all his new friends, get a glimpse of his daily routines, and form a better picture in her mind of his life in Louisville. Sure, he'd shared some details in their conversations on the phone, but something was definitely lost in translation that way. Jake was a guy, she reasoned, so of course he didn't enjoy talking as much. Which is why Amy was so eager to experience it all directly.

She twirled her phone in her hands, wondering why Jake hadn't texted her back. Her plane was a few minutes early...maybe Jake was still driving? *Oh, I hope he isn't late!* She grimaced inwardly, trying to still her trembling fingers by sitting on them.

People started moving into the aisles a few seats ahead of her, so Amy stood up and grabbed her carry-on from the overhead compartment. A new wave of nervousness washed over her. *What if Jake isn't attracted to me anymore?* Amy brushed her growing bangs away from her eyes and pressed her freshly glossed lips together. *What if his friends don't like me?* She fiddled with the wide bangle bracelets around her wrist. *What if I just don't fit in here?* She straightened her top around her waist.

Amy had agonized for days over what to wear for this new "first" impression. She didn't want to look as if she was trying too hard, but she obviously wanted Jake to like what he saw. She finally settled on a fitted but flowing grey tunic with flowery sheer layers over a lace-ribbed black tank top and black leggings. She figured Jake would appreciate the high black boots, since he always liked it when she was a couple of inches taller, but now she wondered if they were too much. *Maybe I just should have stuck with jeans and a sweatshirt.* She wriggled her nose, surveying the casually dressed passengers all around her.

Well, it was too late for a wardrobe change now! The person in front of her finally moved, and Amy took a deep breath and stepped forward. *Here's to Louisville!* she exhaled and walked toward the exit.

She stepped into the small, nearly empty terminal, not really expecting Jake to be waiting, but her heart sank just a little at his absence nonetheless. They had arranged that he would pick her up by the curb outside of the baggage claim in order to save a few bucks on the rip-off airport parking. But the hopeless romantic in her couldn't help wishing for a scene straight out of the movies, bouquet of roses and all.

Oh well, she sighed, wondering if Jake was even as excited about this visit as she was. After those few days last month when he had called and texted with delightful devotion, he had drifted back to sporadic, detached phone calls. Lately, it was all she could do to keep the conversation going for longer than five minutes. She had brought up his seeming disinterest once, but he'd just gotten upset at her, and she didn't want to come across as an overly possessive nag. She knew he was stressed about midterms, so after he'd finished his final project last week, she'd sprang the news of her surprise visit on him. It was hard to tell whether he was just tired or what, but she'd definitely shed a few tears after that disappointing conversation. But she had already bought the plane ticket, and here she was. *God, help me make this work,* she prayed, still wondering why he hadn't yet returned her text.

Following the signs to the baggage claim area, Amy stepped onto a half-filled escalator to go down a level. Murmurs and chuckles all around her drew her eyes down to a spectacle at the foot of the stairs. Waiting with a big black sign that read "I ♥ AMY BRIGGS!" in glittery red print, Jake stood with a goofy smile on his face and a gorgeous bouquet of lush red roses wedged under his arm.

Before Amy even had time to fully comprehend it all, Jake spotted her and yelled unapologetically at the top of his lungs, "THERE SHE IS!"

Immediately, fifty-some sets of eyes turned their heads to catch a glimpse of the lucky lady, and a chorus of feminine "ahhhh's" sighed all around. Amy's flushed red face and glowing smile made her easy to pick out.

"That's so cute," a woman's voice from a few steps down floated up.

Amy smiled, dabbing at her now-moist eyes as the escalator brought her closer and closer to the man who had once again outdone her dreams.

Before she could even step off the revolving track, Jake grabbed her into his arms and recklessly spun her around.

"Welcome to Louisville!" he whispered into her tingling ears as he held her tight.

She turned her face, and his mouth met hers with a luscious kiss for everyone to see. Amy's heart swooned, and her body relaxed in the firm grip of his strong arms.

"Whoa!" Amy grinned, finally taking a step back to retrieve her luggage, which had been temporarily forgotten at the base of the escalator.

"Why don't you ever greet me like that?" a woman in her late thirties said to her husband, as they walked around the passionate couple.

"Give me just a few days to myself, and I will," he replied, inciting his wife to clobber him on the back with her oversized purse.

Amy wrapped her arms back around her man and squeezed him tight. "I love you so much, Jake Taylor."

Jake kissed her on the forehead and grabbed the handle of her pink suitcase to pull along behind them as they walked hand-in-hand toward his truck.

"Wait! What about the sign?" Amy looked back at the sparkly poster board Jake had left leaning against an airport trashcan.

"What are you possibly gonna do with that thing?" Jake shook his head as Amy ran back for his discarded artwork.

Amy grinned, rolling it up like a scroll. "Scrapbook."

✚ ✚ ✚

Jake had to admit that when Amy had dropped the bombshell that she was coming to visit him on her spring break, he was a little bothered. It wasn't that he didn't appreciate her making the effort or even that he didn't want to see her. He was just a little worried about how it would go. It was one thing to hide his uneasiness from a distance, but once she was here—face-to-face—it was a whole different ball game...a game he'd rather not play.

But even so, he knew he needed to make her visit special. So he'd made the poster—it was Grant's idea to add the glitter—and planned a picnic. Pretty soon, he was actually looking forward to her visit. On the way to the airport, Jake had picked up a dozen roses—another of Grant's brilliant ideas—and before he knew it, he was waiting at the bottom of the escalator, wondering if he'd have to fake his feelings when Amy walked out looking as pudgy as she did when he'd left. Nicole's toned body kept creeping into his mind, and it was all he could do to remember all of Amy's other great qualities.

But nothing could prepare him for what he saw floating down the escalator. He knew it looked like Amy, but his mind was filled with disbelief. His eyes traced up her sleek boots—*oh, those boots!*—over her slender body up to her long, silky hair, and they nearly popped out of his head in surprise. Far from the plump post-preggo girlfriend he had left behind, Amy descended toward him in brilliant beauty. Her waist was tiny, her legs long and lean. Her entire body was shaped with slender feminine muscles, and Jake was rendered speechless at how hot his girlfriend looked. She wore less makeup than she used to—far less than Nicole!—but an inner glow warmed her cheeks and radiated from her eyes. Amy was gorgeous!

The thrill of attraction raced through Jake's insides, while a twinge of shame reminded him what Amy could never know about Nicole.

After teasing, flirting, and kissing the entire drive back from the airport, Jake had only one thing on his mind when he showed Amy up to his dorm room. Sure, he knew they had boundaries, but it had been so long since he'd been close to her that his hormones were definitely speaking louder than his convictions. Before he'd left for Louisville, he'd been the one who'd enforced the limits on their physical relationship, but tonight he wasn't feeling so strong. He knew they shouldn't have sex. But would it be that bad to play around a little?

As the door shut to his empty room, Jake was happier than ever that Kyle was gone. He leaned back against the door and pulled Amy into him. He wrapped his arms around her oh-so-sexy body and let his kisses cover her hair, her forehead, her eyes, her cheeks, her chin...His hands wandered down from her delicate waist to the small of her back to her rear, where he eagerly let them rest. Amy pulled back in hesitation, but with just a little pressure she was pliable in his embrace once again.

Chris had once joked that you should "never touch anything you don't have," but there was a lot of Amy that Jake could enjoy without ever crossing that line. Chris had also advised Jake that he and Amy should never lie down together, but again, Jake rationalized that they were definitely in the clear on that one...for now.

"So! Show me your room!" Amy pushed back once again as his kisses grew more passionate. She turned around abruptly and took in her surroundings.

Jake didn't mind if she played a little hard-to-get, and he definitely didn't mind the view she left him with. He watched her hungrily as she walked around the room, trailing her fingers along his furniture, bending over to inspect the pictures of the two of them on his nightstand, examining the books on his shelf. She circled around one more time and stopped to stare out the window.

"So..." she started again, but her voice trailed off.

Jake knew he should contribute something to the conversation, but he was so mesmerized by her presence that he could only stand and stare dumbfounded. After a few breathless moments, Jake walked over and encircled her waist once again with his hands. Her abdominal muscles flinched under his touch.

"So, what are your plans for this week?" Amy asked softly, her head falling back and resting on Jake's shoulder.

"Well...," Jake stammered, still having difficulty putting coherent thoughts together. He grabbed her hand and pulled her over to his bed.

"Jake, maybe we shouldn't," she choked out quietly.

"Let's just sit down and talk," Jake cajoled with a nonchalant grin.

He sat back against the wall and patted the space next to him. Amy pulled off her boots and timidly joined him. He wrapped his arm around her shoulder. She curled up and rested her head on his chest.

"I have class until almost noon tomorrow," Jake took the lead, "but then I was thinking we could grab a bite to eat, and I could give you a tour of the campus. I'll have to do a little homework each day, but there's a great park nearby we could hang out in. Maybe catch a baseball game or something..."

"I'd love to meet your friends..."

"Totally! I'll introduce you to Grant tomorrow. And some of the guys from the team are hosting a party on Friday night."

"Oh," Amy said, her voice sounding a little disappointed.

"And maybe we could look around at some of the dorms to see where you might want to live next year. You could maybe sit in on some sociology classes."

"Psychology?"

"That's what I meant," Jake quickly recovered, kicking himself for the slip.

"Yeah, about that," Amy hesitated.

"Or you could just come to class with me," Jake hastily added, wondering if he had said something else wrong. "And hey, runner girl, what if we went jogging together sometime?" Jake patted her thigh.

"Do you think you can keep up?" Amy taunted.

"Oh! Is this a little trash-talking I'm detecting?"

"I'm just saying..."

Jake poked at Amy's ticklish spot, and she squealed.

"What? What's the matter?" He tickled some more.

She twisted out of his reach. He pounced after her, both of them giggling wildly. They playfully wrestled, arms and legs flailing, until Jake took control and pinned her with his body. He found himself staring into her blue-gray eyes, and suddenly the image of Nicole in a similar alluring position flashed to the front of his mind.

Eager to relive that moment while eliminating Nicole's face from the memory, Jake plunged in for the kiss and didn't let up.

✚ ✚ ✚

"Jake, I think we should stop," Amy whispered almost an hour later, after their longest kiss yet.

"Come on, babe, I've really missed you," Jake argued playfully, rubbing his thumbs on her waist as he held her. He dipped his head for another kiss.

A rather large part of Amy desperately wanted to give in like she had done so many times before, when they were in high school. But annoying as it was, she just could not get Cari's face out of her mind. Surprisingly, the faces of her seventh grade girls also flitted across her brain as she contemplated how to respond. *How can I honestly tell them to wait if I'm not willing to myself?*

"Jake!" Amy cried, as his lips caressed hers and his fingers traced a path down her thigh. Her voice came out stronger than she intended, but the surprise force was just what she needed. She pushed Jake away from her and leaped off of his bed, pulling down her tank-top from where it had begun to creep dangerously high.

She surveyed with shame the damage from their past hour or so of making out. Her gray top lay strewn on the floor; Jake's shirt dangled from his desk chair. There, on his rumpled bedding, Jake leaned on one elbow, looking up at her with stunned puppy-dog eyes. His chest muscles flexed as he shifted his weight. Amy couldn't help but think she was looking at one of those bare-chested guys in the Hollister advertisements in the mall. Working out had done Jake good, she had to confess.

"Babe," he pleaded, stretching out his muscular arm toward her. His chiseled abs rippled.

"Jake," she sighed, sitting against the edge of his desk.

As thrilled as she was to finally be with Jake again, she was disappointed to have to be the one who repeatedly had to tell him to settle down. They both knew firsthand the outcome of what could happen when they let their desires run loose. So why didn't Jake care more about staying true to his original boundary lines? More than that, this was their first time together as Christians, so why wasn't this struggle any easier?

In her own casual but direct way, Cari had warned Amy of the extreme sexual temptations they would face after being away from each other for so long. But Amy had never anticipated that it would be this hard! Cari had also emphasized that sharing a room was not an option—no matter how harmless it seemed. That one had seemed like a no-brainer to Amy, and she had just assumed Jake would be on the same page there. Now, standing in the middle of Jake's roommate-less room at one in the morning, she realized that maybe she had made an unsafe assumption. With new understanding, she realized that the bed on the other side had been neatly made up for a visitor. She also realized that finding a place for her to stay should have been one of their *pre*-trip conversations.

Amy faked a yawn and looked over at Jake's clock. "It's getting late. And you have class tomorrow," she hinted, walking over to her suitcase and fiddling with the handle. She hoped that he would catch the discomfort on her face, but he just groaned and heaved himself up from his bed. He turned to set his alarm clock. Amy hated being such a prude and knew the reality of finding another room for her to sleep in at this hour would be awkward at best, but she at least had to give it a try.

"Um, Jake?" she started. "Did you by any chance find a girl I could stay with this week?"

"Why would I do that?" he continued, concentrating on his clock. "Now that Kyle's gone, I have an extra bed here, so it's perfect."

"Yeah, but isn't that against the dorm rules?" Amy pressed.

"Don't worry about it. Guys do it all the time."

"Yeah, but it's not exactly appropriate," she prodded, shocked by Jake's nonchalance.

"What? It's not like we're gonna sleep in the same bed." Jake sounded annoyed.

"Jake, I really don't think I should—"

"Ughhhhh!" Jake clenched his fingers in exasperation. "Why do you have to be this way?"

"*This* way, Jake?" Amy flinched. "Since when has trying to do the right thing been a problem for you?"

"Amy, you only have a few days here. Can't we just *try* to have a good time and not argue over little things?"

"Little things?" Amy questioned, stifling the threat of tears.

What was going on here? She inhaled deeply and walked over to the other side of the room where Jake had made up the extra bed, picking up her shirt and boots on the way. She folded the tunic and slowly placed it on top of her suitcase, deliberating her options. It was 1 a.m. What else could she do? They could talk about the sleeping arrangements for the rest of the week in the morning.

"Fine, Jake," she sighed, as she sat at the edge of the bed.

"I'll stand guard at the bathroom if you need to use it before you go to sleep," Jake offered casually.

As much as she hated to take him up on his unappealing offer, she knew she would only be miserable later if she refused. So she quickly fished her toothbrush and face-wash out of her bag, watched as Jake made sure the coast was clear, and then raced through her bedtime routine before anyone could catch her. Back in the safety of Jake's room, Amy slipped under the blankets of the spare-bed fully dressed. She turned her face to the wall and pulled the sheet up all the way under her neck.

"Good night. I love you," Jake offered, with a hint of apology.

Amy remained silent.

7:59am | From: Jake | To: Amy
Working out then class. Be back at 1145.

SHE MUST HAVE SLEPT THROUGH JAKE'S ALARM,

because when Amy finally woke up after 9 a.m., she was alone. When she checked the time on her cell phone, she saw the text from Jake.

With almost three hours to kill, she relished the opportunity to just relax in bed awhile, unrushed. She was still tired from a night of fitful sleep and knew she needed to figure out another option for the rest of her stay. Her thoughts turned to God, and she prayed in her favorite position—lying down, her face turned toward heaven.

God, what should I do here? she pleaded. *I really need some ideas! Could You please make Jake see how important this is? I don't know what's going on with him, but we really need Your help to stay sexually pure. You know I want to do things the right way, but I can only stay just so strong, especially if Jake keeps pushing.*

Suddenly, she had an idea: If nothing else, she could sleep in Jake's truck. Obviously, that wasn't the best-case scenario, but it would sure feel better than sleeping in Jake's room. With a sense of relief washing over her mind, she turned her prayers to other things. She prayed for Jake in his morning classes, as well as for his life in general here in Louisville. She talked to God about Melia and her concerns there.

She prayed for her other seventh-grade girls, and Cari and Chris, and Andrea, and her mom.

As she enjoyed the peaceful calm of chatting with God, Amy suddenly realized another sensation screaming loudly through her whole body. She really had to go to the bathroom! Not wanting to walk in on some half-naked guys taking a whiz, nor for anybody to know she had spent the night, Amy quickly stuffed a change of clothes, her toiletries, her Bible, her psych book, and her purse into her backpack and cracked open the door to scope out the hallway. With no one in sight and no sounds of stirring, Amy breathed deeply and tiptoed as quickly as she could toward the exit. *Please God, please God, please God,* she breathed, hating the thought of what a guy would assume if he saw her. Just as she reached the hallway door, another door creaked open several yards behind her. She lunged into the crash bar and never looked back as she slowed down in search of the nearest ladies' floor.

Luckily, at that exact moment, a girl walked up the stairs and into a door on the far side. Hoping she'd be able to just blend in without any questions, Amy followed at a distance, relieved to find an empty bathroom—without urinals.

After getting ready, Amy wandered downstairs and was about to make herself comfortable on one of the lobby couches when she looked outside and saw what a pretty day it was. She strolled outside and down the sidewalk, taking in the sights of the campus that she could call home next year. It was nice, but it wasn't Stanford, and her heart didn't swell with excitement. *God, is this where I should be?* she wondered.

She made a lap around some old buildings and headed back toward Jake's dorm before she could lose track of where she was going. A bench stood in a pleasant sunny spot, and Amy figured it would be a great place to wait for Jake to return.

She pulled out her Bible and journal, and eagerly finished reading the last two chapters of Galatians. Her thoughts and observations took up nearly two pages of notes, and there was so much she couldn't wait to discuss with Jake—in person. She grinned just thinking about it. Finally, they could discuss the Bible together, face-to-face.

Jake would certainly understand her concerns from last night when she showed him verses like "For the sinful nature desires what is contrary to the Spirit, and the Spirit what is contrary to the sinful nature. They are in conflict with each other, so that you do not do what you want." Or "But the fruit of the Spirit is love, joy, peace, patience, kindness, goodness, faithfulness, gentleness and self-control." Or "Those who belong to Christ Jesus have crucified the sinful nature with its passions and desires." They both belonged to Jesus now, so maintaining their self-control when they were together shouldn't be a problem. *Right?*

Filled with hope, Amy shut her eyes and basked in the warmth of the sun on her face. When she looked up, she saw Jake coming toward her, head down and hands in his pockets. Even dressed in his workout sweats, he looked so cute.

"Going my way, sailor?" Amy flirted as he was about to walk by, unaware of her presence.

Startled, Jake jumped. "You know, I could get used to surprises like this when you move here next semester," he grinned and took a seat on her lap.

"Ewwww, gross, Jake! You're all sweaty!" Amy pushed him off, and Jake exaggerated his fall, collapsing onto the bench next to her. Amy wiped the invisible perspiration off her jeans and leaned over to give Jake a kiss. "You, my friend, need a shower."

Jake grabbed her hand and flirted back, "Wanna join me?"

Amy's whole countenance changed, and she leaned away and crossed her arms. "Okay, what is that about?"

"What?" he feigned innocence.

"How are we supposed to stay pure when you make comments like that?" Amy leaned forward and whispered. "Or with you being all over me like last night?"

Jake smiled and patted her hand. "Come on, babe, I was just playing around."

"Jake, we've played around before...I'm pretty sure we don't want to be going down that road again." She paused before hitting on the biggest issue. "And I don't think we should be sleeping in the same room, either."

Jake groaned in frustration. "Are you serious?" he complained. "Come on, nothing's gonna happen."

"Regardless, it doesn't feel right, and anyway, I promised Cari we wouldn't. So you are just going to have to find me a girl I can stay with, or else I'm sleeping in your truck."

Jake slouched against the back of the bench and let out a loud sigh.

"C'mon, babe," Amy prodded gently, scooting closer and winging her leg over Jake's knee. "It's not that bad. Think about how much fun we can have if we're not constantly being tempted to...you know." She swung her leg back and forth and hooked her arm through Jake's elbow. "Let me show you what I read in Galatians just now," she added.

"It's cool," Jake interrupted before she could read him the verses. "I just don't know any girls on campus." A playful grin played at the corners of his mouth.

"You don't know *any* girls, huh?" she teased, leaning forward to give him an Eskimo kiss with her nose.

Jake wiggled his head back. "You're already more woman than I can handle." He dropped his nose and moved in for a soft, slow kiss.

✚ ✚ ✚

After a solo shower and a change into clean clothes, Jake brought Amy over to his favorite lunch spot on campus, where Grant stood waiting for them just outside the entrance. A strange, strained look covered his face.

Jake approached him with a firm handshake and one-armed hug. "Everything okay?" he whispered in his ear, out of range from the trailing Amy.

"You'll see," Grant whispered back before turning to Amy. "And you must be Amy!" he erupted with a huge smile and an embrace usually reserved for longtime friends.

"Yeah, yeah," Amy hugged back, a little taken aback. "I'm hoping you're Grant."

Grant winked playfully. "Of course! Jake told me so much about you, but when he boasted how hot you were, I just assumed he was exaggerating. What's a girl like you doing with a bonehead like him?"

"Well, y'know..." Amy grinned.

As Grant and Amy bantered back and forth, Jake's mind searched for an answer to Grant's cryptic warning. What lurking drama could make his friend so uneasy?

Suddenly, a familiar voice behind them immediately made everything clear. The hairs on the back of Jake's neck stood up at attention.

"Is this who I think it is?" Nicole approached innocently, sporting a black tank top that left little to the imagination. She nudged her way into the group of three, staring right at Amy.

"Amy, this is Nicole," Jake croaked out through ever-tightening vocal cords.

Amy extended a friendly hand to her. "Nice to meet you."

Nicole patted Jake on the shoulder but never turned her attention from Amy. "Jake has told me *so* much about you."

"Really? Jake, you told me you didn't know any girls," Amy teased with a smile.

Jake forced a chuckle, trying to hide his awkwardness. Would Nicole spill the beans on him?

Grant came through like a pro, knocking knuckles with Nicole and placing his baseball cap on her head. "That's right, you are a girl!" he bopped the rim of her hat. "We always think of her as just one of the guys."

Nicole twisted the hat sideways and threw up her hands in some gang-like sign, but Jake couldn't get a good read on what she was thinking. Suddenly, she pulled her phone out of her pocket.

"Oh my gosh! I gotta run. But Amy, we should totally hang out while you're here. Where are you staying?"

Jake's heart accelerated far beyond what was healthy as Amy glanced over at him. *Please don't, please don't, please don't,* he cringed.

"Funny you should ask..." Amy grinned.

Jake didn't have to hear anymore. He knew his worst nightmare had just become a reality.

Sitting on opposite sides of the couch in Nicole's dorm room, Amy found herself spilling her guts to her new girlfriend, oblivious to what else had transpired on that cozy piece of furniture less than a month ago. Nicole's warm, deep eyes drew her in, and before long Amy was confiding her struggle of whether or not she wanted to actually come to Louisville for college.

For the past few days, tension had been escalating between her and Jake, and she still hadn't managed to bring up her indecision to him.

He'd more than hinted a ton of times at how great it would be when she joined him here. But it seemed like every time she got close to sharing her thoughts about Stanford with him, they either started arguing or kissing again. She didn't want to ruin the rest of their time together, but she really needed him to hear her out on this. She just wanted to weigh the pros and cons together.

Unfortunately, Jake just seemed to want to make out. Every day, he'd been pushing her farther and farther, and as good as it felt to be with him, she knew they needed to stop. She'd tried to divert him with going for a daily jog, a romantic picnic in a nearby park, an afternoon of miniature golf and the batting cages, and a night at the movies, but every time, they just ended up in his room afterward getting a little too close.

All of Amy's hopes for the trip were being dismally shattered. The boyfriend she had been so eager to reconnect with on a deeper level had sunk back down to the Jake she had known in high school. And while that Jake wasn't a bad person, it wasn't the best he could be.

Tonight, after the movie, Amy had found herself once again in a compromising position on Jake's bed, with no end in sight. She felt herself wavering in her new stand for purity, caught between her desire to stay true to her convictions and the even stronger urge to show Jake how much she loved him. She toyed with his belt, passions clashing within her. She was so tired of fighting. Maybe if she gave him this, he would finally be open to talking with her. She unclasped the buckle and slid the button through its hole. Jake responded with new eagerness.

Suddenly, one word flashed through her mind. *Reciprocation!* Mr. Sullivan's cheery voice echoed through her head. She stopped cold, and her hands dropped to her sides. *What am I doing?* she moaned. Her previously caressing hands now pushed against Jake's strong chest, straining to get him off her. When he relented, she sat up and started sobbing into her hands.

"Not again," Jake groaned under his breath, lightly touching her bare shoulder.

She shrugged to knock his hand off, and he didn't resist. Feeling stifled and unable to breathe, she quickly stood up and put her clothes back on, surprised and ashamed at how much had ended up on the floor. Jake just sat there and watched silently.

"I love you, Jake Taylor, but I can't do this." She gently grabbed his face and kissed the top of his head, tears streaming down her cheeks.

"I gotta go."

Jake didn't stop her.

Unable to go far in her heels, she took them off outside of Jake's dorm and walked around the darkened campus for the next thirty minutes, trying to sort out her thoughts. But the night was cold, and she had left her jacket in Jake's room, and soon she had a chill. With nowhere else to turn, she went up to Nicole's room, hoping her new friend was either out or asleep.

But Nicole was waiting with a warm hug and a listening ear. Ironically, sharing the whole mess with Nicole was surprisingly easy. Amy listed the pros and the cons of coming to Louisville—leaving out her struggle to stay sexually pure—and as much as she tried to convince herself that there would be countless perks to living in the same city with Jake, and as much as she argued that it could be good for their struggling relationship, she just kept coming back to the same conclusion: Her heart definitely lay elsewhere.

"I don't think that sounds crazy at all," Nicole reassured soothingly.

"I just feel so selfish. Louisville has a counseling program. I could make it work," Amy gushed.

"But Stanford is your *dream*. If you don't do this, then you will resent Jake for the rest of your life," Nicole sympathized.

"But what if I lose him?" Amy vacillated. "I mean, what if our relationship can't handle being apart for so long?"

Nicole reached across the couch and placed her hand delicately on Amy's knee. "Amy, what you guys have is special," she said. "Anyway, if you can't take a few months apart, then you'll know it was never meant to be."

Amy's head had repeatedly assured her of the same things Nicole was saying. But something in her heart just didn't feel quite right. *Is our relationship really strong enough to endure three more years of being apart?* Amy agonized. Based on the last three months, she was pretty sure it wasn't. Based on the last three days, she wasn't even sure if they could make it being together at all. She loved Jake. But was their precarious relationship worth giving up her dreams for?

6:33pm | From: Nicole | To: Amy
Wanna get ready for the party together?

AMY GLANCED NUMBLY AT HER PHONE, startled by its urgent buzzing. For the past four hours, she had watched Jake and Grant battle it out in some shoot-'em-down-blow-'em-up warfare video game, and she didn't know how much more she could take. She hadn't planned on doing much to "get ready," but she was only too eager for an excuse to escape.

What a disappointing final day here! After her abrupt departure last night, Jake hadn't returned her texts or calls until after 10:00 this morning. When she had suggested they go for their daily jog, he had excused himself, claiming that he needed to work out with some of the guys. Amy had decided to take that opportunity to go for an extra long run on her own, which had been nice, but by the time she got back, Jake was at some study group. When he finally came back from that, they went out to lunch, but something had changed. They both seemed to be making an effort at conversation, but there didn't seem to be much else to talk about. The yawning distance Amy had been feeling on the phone lately was just as bad as ever.

After sitting by a fountain for a while, quietly eating ice cream cones, Jake suggested that they stop by Grant's and see what he was up to. Amy really wanted to talk about her Stanford dilemma—and

Nicole's advice from last night—but she chickened out at the last minute and agreed to hang out with Jake's friend.

And so, here they all were, the boys mindlessly wreaking havoc on each other while Amy helplessly watched.

"Hey, Jake?" Amy timidly interjected, hesitant to interrupt the boys' intense play.

"Yeah?" Jake called back as he took one of Grant's planes down in an explosion that rocked the surround-sound. "Ohhhhh!" he yelled, celebrating at Grant's expense.

"Nicole just invited me to come over and get ready for the party with her."

"Yeah, sure, do whatever you want," Jake encouraged, clicking his controller violently with his thumbs.

Grant looked over at him with a curious squint, giving Jake the opportunity to knock out another of his vehicles.

"Boo-yah!" Jake shouted triumphantly.

"Okay. Then I guess I'll see you in a bit." Amy slowly got up to go.

"Yeah, yeah, we'll stop by and pick you guys up in like an hour," Jake agreed, his eyes never leaving the screen.

Amy came over and kissed the top of his head.

Jake squeezed her leg. "I love ya, babe," he grinned. "Make sure you wear something hot...I definitely wanna show you off before you leave."

Great! Amy groaned as she walked down the stairs. She had never minded being paraded around as Jake's trophy-girlfriend before, but this just wasn't the setup she wanted for the important talk they needed to have. Besides, there was no way she wanted to be connected with the groupies that followed the university's sports stars around, ready to appease their every appetite.

Amy hadn't done much partying since her pregnancy, and she was sure this wasn't the scene she wanted to end her visit with Jake in. Hopefully, Jake was still just as passionate about his sobriety as he'd been when he'd left, but based on the changes she'd seen in him this past week, she had her doubts.

Well, at least she was finally going to get the chance to meet the rest of his teammates. They had been playing all week at the NIT, but after a second-round loss, they had come home yesterday, and tonight was their night to celebrate the end of the disappointing season.

She walked into Nicole's room, ready to just spruce up her make-up and slip on a cuter top to pair with her jeans. But when she saw the outfit Nicole was rocking, Jake's suggestion started to sound a little more appealing. Even Amy was stunned by the confident beauty Nicole radiated in her short dress, high heels, and dramatic makeup. She was just taking out the final curlers from the front of her head, and she tossed her hair around as if she was in a shampoo commercial.

"Hi!" she beamed, flipping her hair once more with fervor.

"Wow, you look great, Nicole." Amy smiled.

"Really? You think so?" Nicole asked flippantly, pouting her lips to cover them with lipstick. She did a full turn in front of her full-length mirror and posed with her hands on her hips. "I guess it'll have to do," she shrugged, a smile of satisfaction evident on her perfect mouth.

Amy rifled through her suitcase, suddenly relieved she had decided to pack a few more "daring" outfits.

"I'm sorry I can't hang around to get ready with you." Nicole sat on the edge of her bed, scoping out Amy's choices. "But Nate just called and said he was on his way to come pick me up. Can't keep him waiting too long, if you know what I mean." She winked.

Her phone rang, and she informed the caller she'd be right down.

"Okay, gotta go," she said airily, and like that, she was gone.

Newly inspired—with a tinge of competitive daring—Amy set to work on fixing herself up before her date came by.

✚ ✚ ✚

"Damn, Taylor!" Jamal belted out from across the apartment as Jake and Amy strolled into the small party hand-in-hand.

Jake had to grin. He knew he had the hottest date of the night, hands down. He watched appreciatively as the other guys surveyed his girl.

Jamal walked over and stuck his hand out to Amy. "My name is Jamal. How would you like to spend the rest of the evening with someone actually on the team," he flirted, giving Amy a wink.

"Sorry, I prefer blondes." Amy winked back, wrapping her arm snugly around Jake.

"Lucky me," Jake shrugged with an edge of arrogance.

The room echoed with a chorus of "oohs" from the other teammates and their entourage.

Nate stepped up and draped his arm around Jamal's shoulder. "Do ya think Taylor would mind if I took a shot, then?" he joined in, giving Jake a piercing glance.

Unwilling to step into that minefield, Jake grimaced guiltily. Amy tightened her grasp around his waist, which made him only too happy, and she wrinkled her nose playfully. "I think I'll stick with this one here, but thanks for the offer," she bantered.

Nicole walked up and wrapped her bare arms around Nate's body, obviously not wanting to be left out. She locked eyes with Jake in a challenging stare.

"Well, look who's the big winner." Jamal broke the subtle tension with a smile and a soft uppercut to Jake's shoulder. He reached for two beers on the counter behind him and handed them to his guests.

Although she'd drank almost as much alcohol as water during most of her high school career, Amy hadn't tasted a beer since the day she'd found out she was pregnant, and she had no interest in trying it again. She waited apprehensively to see Jake's response and was disappointed by his eager acceptance.

"Thanks, man." Jake smiled, flipping the top and chugging down a few gulps immediately.

Apparently he'd forgotten about that commitment, too. On the same night he'd told her about his new plan to save sex for marriage and the boundaries that commitment would entail, he'd also vowed to give up drinking until he was at least 21. Amy had thought it was silly at the time, but tonight she wished she could get that Jake back. She put her unopened can back on the counter, figuring that at least *she* would stick to the good idea.

After taking Amy around to meet the other guys and spending time hearing all about the consolation tournament, Jake found himself bored at the fringe of some other trivial conversation. Amy was holding her own, chatting it up with the various guys who came over to presumably hit on her under the guise of friendly banter. But Jake knew that this was probably not the way she wanted to spend their last night together.

What else can we do? he thought, his brain a little soggy from the six beers he'd already had. Obviously, going back to his room was out of the question, not that he'd be opposed to it. The outfit Amy was wearing tonight sure didn't help him in that area! Amy just wanted to talk, it seemed, but every time he gave her a chance, she was always challenging him to a standard of living he just didn't feel like stepping up to anymore. Maybe all that stuff Chris had taught him was good while he was in high school, but things were different here. And some of those convictions just didn't make as much sense now.

Jake caught Amy giving him the eye, and he leaned over to whisper in her ear. "Do you want to go outside for a while?"

"Yeah." She smiled gratefully.

Jake slid his hand to the small of her back and guided her through the bodies toward the balcony.

At that moment, Grant walked in from another room. He rested his hands heavily on Amy's shoulders and whispered in her ear loud enough for anyone nearby to hear, "If you weren't my boy's girl, then... look, pretzels!" He stumbled a few steps over to the bowl to take a large handful.

Amy smiled sadly. "You think you should keep your friend from drinking any more?" she whispered to Jake, as Grant went for another beer.

Jake shrugged, unwilling to get involved. "He'll be your friend too, when you move out here next semester," Jake smiled, taking another sip from his beer.

Amy froze. "Let's go outside," she prodded, and Jake led her out the sliding glass door. She leaned against the iron railing. "Uhhh, I don't know how to say this but..."

"You're not coming to Louisville next year," Jake finished her sentence.

Amy couldn't tell whether he was mad or indifferent. "No...or yeah...or, I mean...I don't know," she sighed. "How did you guess?"

"The tenth time you gave me a weird look after I mentioned the idea kind of clued me in." Jake leaned against her, and they both stared down at the busy street five floors below them.

Amy rested her chin on his strong bicep. "Jake, you know I want to be together—"

"Do you?" Jake shot back, a strange edge in his voice.

"Yes," Amy replied, taken aback by his sharp response. "Of course I do. But remember that day at your house as you were leaving to come here? You told me to figure out my dream. I've been fighting it for a while now, but Jake, I think I figured it out."

"Amy, they have a psychology program at Louisville." Jake's voice sounded irritated.

"I know, but it's nowhere near as prestigious. And Stanford offered me a scholarship. Do you know how big a deal that is?" Amy snapped with impatience. *How could Jake not understand this?* She turned around. Their faces were centimeters apart.

Jake stared down at her, a strange mixture of anger and affection flashing in his eyes. His hands moved from the railing to her barely clad waist, and she could tell he was going in for the kiss. She quickly turned her face toward the wall.

"Jake, not now," she groaned. "I'm trying to have a serious conversation here."

"Amy, what do you want from me?" Jake fired back, throwing his arms up in the air and walking a step away.

"I want you to support me, to encourage me, to release me to pursue my dreams."

"Me, me, me! Do you even hear yourself? I never knew you were so selfish," Jake mumbled.

Like a punch to the gut, Jake's words made her take a step back. "Selfish?" Amy repeated, breathless. All of Nicole's words came flooding back into her mind, and she found herself getting angry. "Jake, if you were so unselfish, then you would be happy for me right now! You are such a hypocrite!" In exasperation, Amy slammed the mostly empty beer can out of Jake's hands onto the wooden balcony.

Jake shook his head in anger. "How dare you call me that!" he seethed. "As if you have any idea of the pressure I'm under!"

"Oh, that's right, I forgot. Because my life has been a piece of cake the last few months."

"There you go again, always making it about you," Jake fired a second arrow straight into her heart. "Well, have you ever thought that maybe it's all *your* fault? *You're* the one who can't stop moping about the baby. *You're* the one who can't stop living with past regrets. When are you going to just move on?" he yelled.

"Move on! Did you ever think that maybe that's what I'm trying to do now?" Amy shouted back, then growled under her breath. "Move on? Maybe what I really need is just to move on from *you*! I've spent the last four years of my life trying to help you live out your dreams. *You're* the one who chose to stay home. *I* had it covered. I never asked for your help!"

"Oh! So after all I gave up for you, this is the thanks I get?" Jake exploded, sounding a lot like his father. "You know, I should have never interfered. I should have just let you keep your stupid appointment and get rid of your stupid pregnancy, and then I could've come to Louisville as planned, and my whole life would be so much better right now!"

Amy doubled over, the pain of his words stabbing her like a knife. "You're a jerk, you know that?" she stared with a wounded glare at his now turned back. "No wonder Roger killed himself," she mumbled into the dark air beyond his head.

Smack!

Amy never saw Jake's hand until it whizzed by her face and connected with the stucco wall behind her head. He clutched his hand and seethed in silence, while Amy wondered if the sting of his blow hurt his fist as much as it did her heart. She gasped, but neither of them said a word, and a heavy darkness surrounded them.

As tears trickled down her flushed face, Amy finally turned to Jake, a calmness seeping over her. "Jake, I don't think this is going to work out...I guess it's time to move on."

Jake met her cool gaze with steely eyes and a spiteful smirk. "Good luck at Stanford, Amy." He cradled his bleeding knuckles. "I hope your dreams come true." With that, he turned around and strode through the sliding glass door back into the party, never looking back.

Amy stood motionless, the cool Kentucky air sending shivers through her too-exposed body. A single tear quickly gave way into hundreds. She attempted to wipe them away with the palm of her hand, but now they were coming too quickly. Black mascara smudges streaked her arms. God, please make him come back out here, Amy prayed desperately under her breath. Her phone vibrated in her pocket, and she looked down to see a new text from Jake.

11:42pm | From: Jake | To: Amy
Thanks for a great night

21

12:02pm | From: Cari | To: Amy
How was your trip?

2:23pm | From: Amy | To: Cari
We broke up

2:24pm | From: Cari | To: Amy
Want to come over?

2:24pm | From: Amy | To: Cari
Already on my way

WITH ONLY AN HOUR AND A HALF before she needed to report to work, Amy was in desperate need of some Cari time. She drove her car right past her own exit and straight on toward the Vaughn neighborhood, arriving in the driveway within ten minutes.

Before Amy could even knock on the dark blue front door, Cari flung it open and just embraced her. No words were spoken—Cari simply held her in the doorway, giving her a safe place to finally let it all out. After Amy had regained her composure out on the balcony the night before, she'd done a pretty good job holding in the tears at Nicole's and during her miserable flight home. But now they would not...could not...stop. Sobs shook her body until there was nothing left to wring out, and Cari just held her tightly, stroking her hair, rubbing her back, infusing her with comfort.

Finally, Amy looked up, a weak sigh rattling from her constricted throat.

"Oh, sweetie," Cari rubbed her hand comfortingly. "I'm so sorry."

Behind Cari's now wet right shoulder, Amy spotted Caleb standing a few feet away. He carried his blue blankie and stared up at Amy with sad curiosity. When he caught Amy's eye, he rushed over to her and hugged her leg.

"Hi, Caleb," Amy greeted the cuddly five-year-old as she wiped off her wet cheeks.

Caleb reached up with his prized blanket. "Want to borrow my blankie?" he offered.

"Aw, thanks, buddy." Amy grinned, hugging the gift in her arms.

"Mommy lets me have cookies when I'm sad. Are you sad?"

"Well..." Amy hesitated.

Cari closed the front door. "Peanut butter or chocolate chip?"

"What do you think, Caleb?" Amy asked, crouching down to get to her favorite five-year-old's eye level.

"Bofe!" Caleb whispered loudly.

Amy smiled back at Cari, who was already on her way to the pantry.

"Caleb, I'll give you one cookie now and another one in thirty minutes if you go play alone quietly in your room," his mother bargained.

Like a cute but serious little man, Caleb stroked his chin as he thought over the proposition. "Can I play with G.I. Joe?"

Cari nodded as if she was giving him the deal of a lifetime and handed him a chocolate chip cookie on his way up to his bedroom. She held out the package of fresh bakery cookies to Amy and led her over to the couch.

"So what happened?" she asked, handing Amy a box of Kleenex.

Amy sighed, unsure where to begin. "I don't know. Things were going pretty good, I guess...but everything just seemed a little off. I kept trying to bring up my decision about where to go to school next year, but every time we'd end up getting in some kind of argument." Amy rubbed her forehead, wondering what she could have done differently. "The whole time he was just kind of different, more like the old Jake, the one I knew all through high school...You know, before God." Amy shook her head. "So then last night, it was my last chance to talk to him, but we had to go to some party that his teammates were throwing, and things just escalated. We both said some pretty mean things to each other, and before I knew it, I called it quits, and he just stormed out…And that was the last time I saw him."

Fresh tears cascaded down her face. Cari rubbed her back.

"Wait a minute," Cari clarified softly. "How did you get back to the airport then?"

"Ugh!" Amy groaned, reliving the nightmare of the previous twelve hours. "I took a taxi."

"Oh, honey!"

"Cari, it was horrible!" Amy gushed and started to spill the details.

She recalled how alone she felt on that cold balcony, wondering if Jake would ever come back for her. Part of her wanted to text him, call him, do whatever it took to plead with him to come back. But pride wouldn't let her. He was the man. He was the one who walked away. He was the one who had almost hit her. Why should she go groveling to him?

"Wait a minute—he almost hit you?" Cari interjected, her mother lion instincts raring up.

"Well…yeah. I mean no. I mean…" Amy hesitated. She hadn't planned on telling anyone that part. "He punched a wall…but only after I said something really, really terrible."

"What did you say?"

"I called him a jerk and then told him it was no wonder Roger killed himself." Amy winced in shame.

"Ohhhhh," Cari sighed, resuming her rubbing of Amy's back. "Well, yeah, that was pretty harsh," she agreed. "But let me tell you something: No man ever has a right to hurt you. Do you hear me on this? Never."

Amy said nothing as a replay from when she was six flashed through her brain. She squinted to stop the memory and tapped her forehead with her fist. "Please don't tell Chris," she pleaded.

"Well, I can't promise you that…but I'll think about it. So what happened after that?"

Amy recounted the events of the night before. After waiting for what seemed like an hour, Amy finally pulled herself together and strode back through the party and out the front door. A few people looked at her with mixed expressions, but she didn't give them a second glance—although what seemed to be a haughty smirk on Nicole's fabulous face did burn an imprint on her mind.

Once Amy escaped from the party, her troubles had only just begun: She didn't have a clue how to get from the apartment back to the university. Fortunately, a map at the entrance to the complex pointed her in the right direction, and she began the chilly two-mile walk with grim determination. She shuddered now to think that she must have looked like a streetwalker, all dressed up in her far-too-hoochie party garb.

"Served me right for dressing like that," she cringed.

"Girl, you are writing the textbook for what *not* to do in college." Cari patted her hand. "But I think God was looking out for you, huh?"

"Yeah, in spite of my stupidity!"

"Hey, if God didn't help out stupid people, He might just get bored up there. So was Nicole there when you made it back? There's something about her that doesn't seem quite right."

"No, no, she was really sweet," Amy assured Cari. "I don't know what I would've done without her. But no, I don't know how late she got in from the party." That was a good thing, because although Nicole was a good listener, Amy was in no state of mind to rehash all the heartbreaking details of her fight with Jake to her.

"And that was about it," Amy concluded. "Fortunately, my flight left early this morning, so I called a taxi and left the university without any human contact or a single look back." Tears were starting to well up again, but Amy tried to stop them by focusing on the positive. "I'm so glad my boss wouldn't let me take off tonight's shift. Otherwise, I would have still been there for two more days...I don't know what I would have done!"

As the reality of what had happened started to sink in, silent tears started seeping uncontrollably from Amy's eyes again. Then came an irrepressible lip quiver, which turned into an unstoppable whimper, which turned into a desperate weeping, and that's when Amy collapsed once again into Cari's comforting arms.

Was it really true...were they really done? Was there anything she could do to take back those horrible words?

Cari rubbed her back in silence, letting her grieve in peace. A few minutes after the worst of the storm had passed, Cari spoke up. "It sounds like Louisville was a pretty rough experience for you."

Amy sniffled, smiling at the grand understatement.

"And it sounds like it's been pretty rough for Jake, too—in a different way. You said he's changed? In what ways?"

"Well..." Amy grabbed a pillow and clutched it to her chest. "I guess he just wasn't excited about the same things anymore. Any time I tried to talk about God or what I had read in the Bible or...or...anything, we'd just get distracted."

"Distracted, huh?" Cari looked at Amy closely. "You mean, with the physical stuff?" she shot straight.

Amy could feel her face turning red. "Yeah," she confessed, avoiding eye contact. "Looking back, that was the first red flag. Cari, from the first night, he was all over me."

Cari didn't seem shocked by anything. "Did you...?"

Amy shook her head violently. "No, no. We got close a couple of times, but we never had sex," Amy affirmed emphatically. "Actually, that seemed to be a big part of the problem—I think Jake was just frustrated that I kept stifling him and holding him to these boundaries that he doesn't care about anymore." She sighed, thinking about how much tougher this conversation would have been if she'd given in. "Cari, I can't lie. I almost didn't make it. We did some things I'm not proud of. But I kept thinking about you and my girls, and deep down I knew it wasn't worth it."

Cari smiled, obviously relieved. "Amy, I am so proud of you. I know that must have been hard."

Amy turned and looked at the window, watching the sunlight dance through the leaves as they fluttered in the breeze. She wished the peacefulness out there would seep into her aching heart. "Jake said I was selfish," she spoke distantly, her voice cracking a little. "But is that really such a bad thing? Being selfish with my body, selfish with my dreams?"

Cari reached over and placed her hand on Amy's shoulder. "Jake's statement said a lot more about himself than anything else."

Amy looked at her, confused.

"My husband is far from perfect, but one of the things that I love most about him is that I know he's my biggest fan." Without even shifting her head, Cari called up to her son, "Caleb, ten more minutes, honey."

"Awww, man!" Caleb's voice whined.

Amy glanced over to see Caleb sitting on the top of the steps. Head down, he slowly marched back to his room and closed the door.

"You deserve a man who doesn't just want you to support him, but who will passionately cheer you on to live out your dreams, too. Amy, if Jake can't be happy for you receiving a full scholarship to one of the most prestigious universities in the country, then I'm sorry, but he's not the right guy. He doesn't deserve you." Cari pulled the pillow out of Amy's grasp and lightly bopped her on the head. "If he doesn't respect your commitment to purity, if he doesn't share in your enthusiasm for God, if he even *thinks* about touching you in an inappropriate or hurtful way...then he's got another thing coming. I don't know what got into him, but there is *no* way I'm going to let him treat my sistah like that!"

Amy blushed. She'd never had anyone like Cari in her life before, and it was nice to feel someone being protective of her.

"I know it's going to be rough for a while," Cari continued. "But let Jake go. Give your heart time to heal. And then watch out. Because if God allows someone like Jake to leave you, that can only mean He's got an even better guy waiting in the dugout."

For the past twelve hours Amy had been thinking about all the ways she could get Jake back, no matter what it took. But now she caught a glimpse of a wider perspective. *Could there be life after Jake Taylor?* Amy grinned to herself. As much as her heart still hurt, she knew she had to give it a shot.

"You haven't been single much, have you?" Cari broke into her thoughts, tossing the pillow back to Amy.

"No. What's 'single'?" Amy shook her head, smiling.

"Maybe it's time you went through a season without a guy," Cari suggested. "Let Jesus be the only man in your life for a while."

Amy didn't quite understand what that meant, but she liked the sound of it.

"Well," Cari glanced upstairs and warned, "I think our thirty minutes are just about up."

"BOMBS AWAY!!!" Caleb shouted from the top of the stairway, launching his G.I. Joe action figure into the living room. He had twisted his blankie around the arms of the plastic figurine in order to get it to function as a parachute, and now it sailed slowly down to the feet of the women below.

"Brilliant kid," Amy grinned.

"Me want cookie!" Caleb yelled in his best Cookie Monster voice as he stormed down the stairs.

"Okay, Cookie Monster." Cari tousled his hair and stood up to place a cookie on a napkin at the kitchen counter.

"And I've gotta go get ready for work," Amy grimaced. She got up and gave Caleb a high-five and Cari one last hug. Just inside the door, she turned around. "Can you still have Chris call Jake? I'm really worried about him."

"He's already a step ahead of you," Cari reassured her. "Just left a message this time, but he'll keep trying."

"Thanks...for everything."

5:29pm | From: Chris | To: Jake
Dude, I just heard the news. Give me a call.

7:03pm | From: Chris | To: Jake
I promise, I won't take sides

8:42pm | From: Chris | To: Jake
Seriously, are you ok bro?

SERIOUSLY, JAKE DIDN'T WANT TO TALK TO CHRIS.

Which is why he kept deleting each text message and sending each phone call straight to voicemail. What was there to talk about? It was over. By this time, Chris had obviously heard the whole story from Amy's perspective anyway, which means Jake was in for a lecture on so many levels. And he was pretty sure he didn't want any of those.

At least this means Amy got home safely, Jake realized with a tiny sense of relief as he fingered his scuffed-up knuckles. All day, a nagging sense of guilt had mingled with the throbbing pain, plaguing him over his rash reaction and his failure to make sure she got to the airport okay...or even home safely from the party last night. *What kind of guy doesn't at least make sure a girl has a ride home?* he derided himself. *Even if it is his ex!*

He still had no clue how she'd managed, but it wasn't his concern anymore. Besides, she could have called him. She was the one who said she wanted to move on. Well then, fine, he'd given her what she'd asked for.

After he'd walked away last night, he had planned on going straight back to his room to nurse his wounds and brood in private, but Grant had intercepted him, babbling about the good stuff in the back room. While Jake had always avoided the back room activities of some of the other players, last night he figured he deserved a break. Amy had been hounding him all week, and it felt good to just let loose. It wasn't as if he did any of the really bad stuff—just a joint or two to take the edge off. But whatever he had really knocked him out, and he woke up this morning with a painfully swollen hand, surrounded by a bunch of other passed-out drunks.

He drove back to campus feeling sulky and depressed. *What's wrong with her?* Why couldn't she just accept him for who he was? She was always trying to change him, make him live the way she wanted. Well, what if he wanted something different? And what if he wanted the freedom to be able to change what he wanted?

Coming to Louisville had really opened his eyes to the reality that life held a ton of options. And now he felt like checking some of them out. For the past several months, he'd been trying to live life with one foot back in Oceanside...and straddling a fence is never comfortable! Amy had been the only daily reminder of his life before Kentucky. Now that she was gone, there was nothing holding him back. He could finally fully move on into the next season of his life. *Maybe this is a blessing in disguise,* he shrugged, gingerly opening his second bag of chips.

Knock, knock, knock!

Jake's door rattled, and he jumped. Not surprised that Grant would come by to check on him, Jake swung the door open carelessly.

"Hey, come on in," he mumbled through a mouth full of Cheetos as he moped back to his desk chair.

"Thanks!" a distinctively higher-pitched voice giggled.

Jake spun around, and there was Nicole standing cheerfully in the doorway, holding two Starbucks cups.

"Oh, wow," he stammered, quickly gulping down what he'd been chewing. "Hi! What's up?"

"I just heard the news," Nicole put on a sad, pouty face, "and I wanted to check on you. Oh, and I thought a coffee might cheer you up." She offered the drink to Jake and tenderly inspected his wounds. "So, how are you doing?" she prodded sympathetically, pulling Kyle's old desk chair up to Jake's desk.

"Well...I guess I've been better," Jake started, pausing to sip the hot beverage. *Yuck!* he stifled a grimace. It was some sweet peppermint-y mocha mix. So far Nicole was 0 for 2 when it came to ordering for him, and Jake couldn't help but remember how Amy had always guessed right—even from the first time she'd surprised him.

Nevertheless, it was a nice gesture, and it was nice to have company. And although Nicole was probably the most inappropriate person with whom to share his pain, Jake found himself quickly pouring out his frustrations to her.

"She's a really nice girl, Jake, but she doesn't deserve you," Nicole consoled him after he'd ranted for awhile. She reached her hand across the desk to gently rub his bruises. "You were willing to give up so much for her, and if she doesn't appreciate that, there's something wrong with her."

That's exactly what Jake had been saying! He didn't know why Amy couldn't see it, but it was nice to have *someone* understand.

"You're a great guy, Jake, but girls like her are everywhere." Nicole batted her empathetic eyes. "Don't waste your time...Besides, long-distance relationships never work out."

They continued to talk for nearly an hour, and Jake was already feeling a lot better. And the longer they talked, the more he was beginning to see some of the advantages to being single again. Somehow, over the course of the last sixty-plus minutes, their chairs had steadily rolled closer together, and Nicole's hands had crept higher and higher up Jake's leg in soothing consolation. Now, in one final brazen move, she stood up and straddled Jake in his chair.

"Let me show you how you deserve to be loved, Jake Taylor," she whispered, cupping his face in her soft hands.

She pulled his lips toward hers, and unlike their last moment of passion, none of the familiar guilt plagued him. He was single. He didn't owe Amy anything.

All the tension that had been bottled up within him now released with fury, and he surrendered to it with reckless abandon. Whereas Amy had been the one to keep reining his passions in all week, Nicole had no such plans, and so even though Jake didn't intend for the kisses to lead all the way to sex, before he knew it, their clothes were flying, and they had collapsed in a sweaty, lustful heap on his bed.

The moment passed, and Jake rolled over and stared up at the blank white ceiling. What had he just done? Not only was this the first time he'd had sex in over a year, but it was also the first time he'd *ever* done it with someone other than Amy. He wasn't sure what he thought about that. And his hand was throbbing.

Nicole tried to cuddle with him, but she appeared to get the hint pretty quickly that Jake was done for the night. She got up and got dressed, then came back over and sat on the edge of Jake's bed.

"Nate is going to be out of town next weekend, so call me if you want to hang out again." She smiled, tracing Jake's stomach muscles with the tip of her finger.

Jake forced a smile and watched her go, then continued to lie staring at the ceiling for the next forty-five minutes. Finally, his head dropped to the side, and he saw the bed Amy had slept in just a few days ago. It was perfectly made, so unlike the way Kyle had left it every other day of the semester.

"Ugh," Jake sighed, realizing he should probably strip the sheets. He walked over and started yanking them up into a big bundle. When he lifted the pillow, a folded slip of paper fluttered to the ground. Jake stooped down to pick it up and immediately recognized Amy's flowing script.

I love you, Jake Taylor!
xoxo

Jake gasped for breath, and an eerie moan escaped his throat. He crumpled the note in his aching clenched fist and collapsed onto the now-bare mattress. His eyes scanned the various pictures of Amy scattered around the room, and he cringed to think of what her beautiful eyes had just witnessed. When they had broken up during their senior year of high school, Jake had left all of her pictures up in hopes that they would one day reunite. Tonight those hopes were all vanished, and he threw each of the frames one by one into the trash can by his door.

It was too late. There was no going back.

Their relationship was over.

Jake crashed onto his bed and pulled out his cell phone.

11:51pm | From: Jake | To: Chris
I really dont want to talk about it

7:14pm | From: Nicole | To: Jake
Good luck Jakey! Ill call u after the game

WHEN NOMIS—OTHERWISE KNOWN as Aaron Simon, the sophomore starting small forward last season—randomly invited Jake to play in a prominent street ball summer league in New York City, Jake accepted in a heartbeat, with one condition: Grant could come, too. Jake missed California, but there was no way he wanted to spend the summer at home, under the scrutiny of all his old friends. He was enjoying the freedom of being completely unattached, and he didn't have the slightest desire to give it up. Okay, that, and Nicole lived in upstate New York, and he definitely didn't mind having easy access to her.

They'd done plenty more "hanging out" since that accidental late night the weekend of the Amy breakup, but Jake had resisted jumping into another serious relationship. Nicole had been on-again, off-again with Nate for the rest of the semester, which had given Jake plenty of space to have his cake and eat it, too. Nate was home in Missouri for the whole summer, though, pursuing who knows how many other girls, so Jake finally felt free to go for something a little more consistent with Nicole. As "friends with benefits," they had all the makings of a dating relationship with none of the official commitment that made him feel tied down. It was perfect.

Even apart from Nicole, though, spending the summer in the Big Apple was totally surpassing Jake's dreams. He, Grant, and Nomis had all pitched in to get a cheap apartment in the neighborhood near where they would be playing. It was dirty, run down, hot, noisy, and different in a million ways from anything Jake had ever experienced in his nice little upper-class life. But he loved it.

Nomis had grown up in the area and served as an excellent tour guide, showing them parts of the city that most people would miss—parts they'd never dare to visit on their own. The nightlife, the ethnic flair, the hip-hop culture...every day was filled with new adventures that Jake couldn't wait to pursue.

Their apartment was right next to the elevated train line, which definitely had its perks—like having easy access to the rest of the city whenever they had a free day. And they ended up having quite a few of those. Jake's summer was a young man's paradise: hanging out with friends, playing lots of ball, and enjoying the spontaneity of a life without responsibility.

On top of all that, playing in this summer league was good for his skills. Street ball was a whole different game from the indoor polish of NCAA ball, but Jake had grown up learning the game on his own neighborhood concrete court. And even though his gated community at home was a far cry from this inner-city neighborhood, he'd always felt a little more at home on the pavement than on the hardwood. His present experience proved that hadn't changed. Here he was, competing alongside great athletes from all levels: from local neighborhood standouts to former college greats to rival competitors they'd face again in the regular season to even an NBA player or two. This was the perfect opportunity for Jake to push his game—to stretch himself out of his comfort zone and challenge himself with play on a different level.

But what a challenge! Jake and Grant were pretty much the only white guys on the court all summer, which virtually guaranteed that an invisible target hung over their heads during each and every game. They came into the league fully aware of their minority status but oblivious to the ramifications. Who would have guessed the extra intensity they would have to endure from their local opponents, the extra pushing and shoving and all-around roughness?

Jake still wasn't sure how he'd scored an invitation to be here in the first place. All Jake had known was that Nomis had a friend who knew somebody who knew somebody who knew somebody, and through that connection Jake had gained entry into the popular league. Sitting with a squad of unknowns, Nomis had wanted to try to add some "flavor" to their roster, and Jake and Grant became the spice for Team AnoNomis.

Yes, it was true: Nomis had persuaded the team to use the name as publicity for his newly self-released rap album. Jake had to admit that it was pretty catchy, and it fit their "anonymous" bunch of misfits all too well. Compared with the highly stacked rosters throughout the rest of the league, AnoNomis was outranked: Jake and Grant had only played in high school, Nomis was a college player who was better known in the 'hood for his rapping, two other guys were has-beens who hadn't seen their prime for at least a decade, and the other players on the team—well, Jake still didn't know their stories.

But even though AnoNomis started out unknown, by the halfway point in the season, in the sweltering heat of July, they had gained quite a following. AnoNomis was ranked fifth out of eight teams in the East Coast division—far from blowing the competition away, but fans still flocked to their games each night. Whether they came to razz them or cheer them on, Jake wasn't always sure, but he and Grant worked hard to give them a show. Jake got thrashed on the court more times than he could count, but he loved the challenge and after a while even began to hold his own pretty well.

Tonight's game was no exception. Seven minutes into the second half, AnoNomis was up by three, holding a steady lead against the top-ranked team, one that boasted several college stars, as well as the current NBA Defensive Player of the Year. Jake had unhappily sat out the entire first half, but when their other point guard—one of the "old" guys—complained of chest pain, the coach signaled Jake in.

Jake took the inbound pass from Nomis, who had been dazzling the rowdy crowd with fancy dunks and fierce blocked shots all evening. Jake shot a glance at the loose defensive setup and got ready to improvise. He crossed the midcourt line, flew by Mr. NBA with some fancy footwork, and immediately spotted Nomis flashing across the baseline to the right corner. Jake popped a hard chest pass to the corner just as Nomis turned to look. He caught it and in one single motion hurled up an uncontested three.

Swish.

There was nothing sweeter than that sound! Jake flipped onto defense and exchanged a cool smirk with his teammates as they loped down the court to guard the key on the opposite end.

On the subsequent trip up the court, Jake dumped the ball down low to Grant and then raced past his unsuspecting opponent directly to the hoop. Grant faked a jump shot and returned the ball to Jake in a picture-perfect bounce pass right under the basket. Jake softly laid the ball off the backboard for an uncontested layup and his first basket of the night.

Feeling his groove, Jake started to tune out the wild mob cheering and jeering his every move, and soon tunnel-vision took over. All he saw were the nine other guys on the spectator-lined asphalt court. This was the kind of basketball he lived for. Each play felt like slow-motion as the options unfolded before him, and each time down the court, he found a new way to connect with one of his teammates—ready or not. He crossed up his defender, dished some alley-oops, drove to the basket, and sank a few threes. He felt unstoppable...at least on offense. On defense, he was a little shakier, but just as in the NBA All-Star Game, who really cares about defense?

Jake stayed in for the remainder of the game, and by the time the final whistle blew, Team AnoNomis had emerged victorious, and Jake had tallied up twelve points with six assists. *Not bad for a little white boy.* He couldn't help congratulating himself.

✚ ✚ ✚

Back in their dingy little apartment, the three guys rehashed their glory moments from the game in excited play-by-play.

"We keep playing like today, studs, and we'll be a fearsome threesome next season," Nomis announced, shooting a fake jumper.

Grant pretended to pull down the rebound and then threw one of his pillows at Jake's head on the other side of the room. "Did you see that dunk I had in the first half?" Grant boasted, stopping to smooth a few hairs down as he looked at himself in the mirror on the door.

"No, I didn't notice, Mr. Humble," Jake lied. "I was too busy picking splinters out of my butt." Jake threw the pillow back, still a little annoyed that he hadn't been put in sooner. He could only imagine what he could have done if he hadn't sat the bench the whole first half.

Suddenly, Right Said Fred rhythmically growled about how sexy he was from Jake's cell phone. "Ohhhhh!" the other two guys yelped uproariously when they heard it.

Nicole had surreptitiously downloaded the ringtone onto Jake's phone and programmed it to play every time she called, which happened far more often than Jake's roommates would have liked. Jake could have changed it, but he secretly liked it.

"So sexy it hurts!" Nomis whined in a croaking voice.

"Speaking of humble!" Grant laughed. "Tell your girlfriend hi for us."

"Not my girlfriend," Jake reminded him for the thirty-seventh time as he picked up his phone and lay down on his bed. "Hey," he answered, knowing that every one of his words was being heard not only by Nicole.

"So, how'd it go tonight?" Nicole got straight to it in that cute little voice Jake had come to look forward to hearing.

"Oh, you know, twelve points, six assists," Jake yawned with feigned indifference, envisioning Nicole in the dangerously skimpy bikini she'd worn when they'd hung out at the beach last weekend.

"Jake, that's great!" she chirped, always positive. "How'd the fans like you?"

"Loved me, of course! What would you expect?"

"True, true. How could anyone *not* love Mr. Taylor? I wonder if we'll see any of these guys again when we're in the NBA a couple of years from now."

"Ha!" Jake laughed along, loving her confidence in him and her desire to stick around for the ride—unlike Amy, who had her own dreams to chase. "Hmmm...the NBA. Speaking of that, which team do you think I should sign with?" Jake continued their fanciful conversation, paying no attention to Grant's and Nomis's groans on the other side of the room.

"Obviously a team with red uniforms...you look really sexy in that color," Nicole shot back without hesitation, as if his question was something she had already given some thought to. "Maybe the Hawks...or what about the Rockets?" Nicole started giggling.

"What?" Jake questioned with a courtesy chuckle.

"Nothing. I was just picturing how they'd announce you at the beginning of games." Nicole's voice deepened to mimic that of a sportscaster. “Now starting at guard, Jake 'The Texas Tornado' Taylor!!!!”

“'The Texas Tornado?'” Jake wondered aloud. “Uh, I'm not from Texas. Where did that come from?”

“No, silly. You'd be playing in Texas, and you're like a whirlwind all over the court, taking down everything in your path,” she explained. “I wouldn't be surprised if they even change the mascot after a couple of years.”

“Are you auditioning for the job?” Jake teased.

“If it means we're together on road trips, then heck yeah.”

Jake never could tell when Nicole was being serious and when she was teasing. She was very good at keeping him on his toes. But while he loved her playfulness, the ramifications of what she was saying—if she was serious—kind of freaked him out. He'd had talks about marriage with one girl already, and look how that relationship had ended up.

“Jake, I'm just kidding,” Nicole broke into his thoughts, obviously reading into his awkward silence. “Besides, who wants to live in Houston, anyway? Hey, my parents are both out of town on business next week, so if you want to come up for a day or two, I'm all yours,” she offered flirtatiously.

Jake hated to compare the two girls, but that comment reflected one more way Nicole was easier to be with than Amy. Like Amy, she was gorgeous and fun, and she loved to take the initiative. Unlike Amy, she never forced the serious talk, and she was more than happy to follow him wherever he wanted to go—especially to bed.

24

10:37am | From: Mom | To: Jake
Flight 1246 arrival 5pm

TWO WEEKS LATER, Jake stood at JFK airport waiting for his mother to come down to the baggage claim. He couldn't help but think back to just a few months earlier when he'd nervously held that glittery sign in anticipation of Amy's arrival. As usual, he felt a tinge of regret.

He hadn't talked to Amy since his spiteful last words the night of their breakup, but there had been plenty of times that he'd wanted to. Jake hated to admit it, but he'd been missing her a little lately. He'd even come close to calling her a couple of times but always put his phone back down. What would he say? "How've you been? I've been having a jolly ol' time with Nicole!"

Yeah, he was pretty sure that wouldn't fly.

Each time, he'd checked out her Facebook page instead, just to see what she was up to. Surprisingly, she'd never deleted him from her friends. Maybe she forgot. Or maybe she was checking in on him, too. He kind of hoped so. With that in mind, he had avoided posting anything about Nicole—no need to stir up problems. But after their beach trip last week, Nicole had tagged him in a bunch of pictures—some of them not so...appropriate—so Jake figured there was no use hiding anything anymore.

Anyway, I'm waiting for my mom. Jake shook his head, trying to get back to current reality. No sparkly sign this time, but he did get her a bunch of flowers for good measure.

Pam Taylor had been disappointed when Jake had told her he wasn't coming home for the summer because of basketball. But when she found out he was staying in New York, she insisted on coming out to visit him and immediately bought a ticket.

Jake was blown away by how much his mother had changed over the past year since his father had moved out. Caught up in his own trials at the time, Jake hadn't fully realized how much his dad's workaholism, outbursts, and affair had affected her. But now that Glen was mostly out of her life, it was no wonder she was flourishing. Whenever Jake talked with her on the phone, she sounded so joyful and confident and full of life.

Of course, she gave all the credit to following Jake to New Song. She had never been a churchgoer, but once she noticed all the changes in her son's life, she had decided to check out this crazy place that he couldn't stop talking about. At least, that's what she'd told Jake.

Her third week at New Song, she had been invited to a women's small group, and after running through a gamut of excuses, she had finally attended a month later. And she'd gotten hooked. For the first time since college, she said, she had real friends, and she couldn't stop talking about them. Neither could she stop talking about God. She was as bad as Amy or Andrea or Chris. But if that's what it took to get her to sound so full of life again, then who was Jake to complain? She was his mother, and he loved her. And if Jake was honest, he had to admit that he was actually looking forward to her five-day visit.

"Mom!" Jake called out to her the moment she came through the terminal tunnel. Even from a distance, he could tell she was sporting a much younger, cooler, blonder hairstyle.

Pam subtly waved back, obviously waiting to fully greet her son until they were at a distance where she wouldn't have to shout. When she finally came within reach, Jake hugged his mom tightly.

"Oh, Jake!" Pam nearly cried. "It's so good to see you! Look at the gorgeous daisies! And oh, look! My baby's hair is so short!" she gushed, rubbing her hand over the crew cut he'd adopted to survive the muggy East Coast summer.

"Mom, this isn't cool," Jake whispered, grabbing the handle of her jumbo carry-on bag and leading them toward the air train. "I like your hair, too, by the way."

Even with all his exploring of the city this summer, Jake still hadn't mastered the subway system—probably because Nomis was always boldly leading the way. But after only two mistakes, Jake and Pam arrived at the fancy W Hotel in Midtown and dropped her bags off there. It was a distance from Jake's neighborhood but close to Times Square, the theater district, Central Park, and all the other tourist attractions, and a seven-day Metro pass ensured they could get back and forth pretty easily. By this time, they were both starved, so they walked a couple of blocks until they found a chichi little bistro for dinner.

Despite all of Jake's "sightseeing" with the guys, he had yet to do any of the real touristy things. So after they ordered, he and his mother opened a map on the café table and worked out a plan. They scheduled in a visit to the Empire State Building, the Statue of Liberty, and the World Trade Center Memorial. Pam said she wanted to take Jake—and his friends, if they wanted to join them—to see a play on Broadway, to eat a hot dog in Central Park, and to look around in FAO Schwarz, the famous toy store. She also wanted to spend an afternoon shopping, but she agreed that she might enjoy it more on her own. And of course, she wanted to meet Jake's friends and watch them play a game. They only had one game scheduled during the time she would be there—tomorrow. After that, Jake's schedule was wide open.

Their meals came, so they put her maps and brochures away and began eating and chatting. Jake had wondered how he would ever find enough to talk about with his mother for five whole days, but after several hours there still hadn't yet been a lull, and Jake realized it probably wouldn't be an issue.

"Oh, your friend Jonny told me to tell you hi. That kid totally cracks me up," Pam laughed, stabbing a tomato in her salad and popping it in her mouth.

Jake felt a knot tighten in his stomach, guilting him for not talking to his friend in several months. "When did you talk to him?" he asked. Wasn't Jonny supposed to be in Japan?

"Oh, we're friends on Facebook," Pam giggled, adding, "I just joined a few weeks ago. Do you realize how easy it is to keep in touch with old friends with that thing? By the way, what's the deal with you not letting me be your friend yet?"

"Oh, uh, I guess I just haven't been getting on there much lately," Jake lied, knowing full well that he checked in almost as often as he ate. Now he remembered with shame that he had never accepted his mother's request, reluctant to give her access to some of the pictures others had posted of him doing things she wouldn't exactly be proud of.

"Well, next time you do, make sure you add your old mother, kiddo! Anyway, Jonny was so cute. Before he left for Japan, he stopped by the house to give me a picture of a Ninja he'd drawn, so I could put it on the fridge to remember him." Pam burst out laughing.

"Did you hang it up?" Jake smiled, taking a juicy bite of his humongous hamburger—not exactly the thing most people would order in an expensive restaurant, but Jake didn't care.

"Of course, since my own son stopped giving me artwork back in third grade." Pam reached her fork over to Jake's plate and stabbed at a couple of French fries.

They sat in silence, slowly chewing their food.

"So I talked to Amy last Sunday at church," she said casually, as if Jake and Amy hadn't broken up almost four months ago.

Here we go again, Jake grimaced. After the breakup, he had eventually spent a good hour talking with his mom about it. He'd generally avoided conversations like that with her over the years, for fear of judgment or her disappointment or even just a boring lecture. But this time, she had graciously listened to Jake's side of the story and didn't even try to share her opinion until he'd asked. Given the opportunity, she had told him that she thought he was the stupidest man on the planet to let a girl like Amy go, but she reassured him that she'd love him no matter what. And that was that.

"How's she doing?" Jake questioned, trying not to sound too interested. The truth was that he was dying to hear all about her. A big chunk of him hoped she was miserable without him, but a smaller part genuinely wanted her to be doing well.

"She's doing so great, Jake!" Pam replied enthusiastically. "She gave me a big hug and told me all about getting ready to leave. I guess she's already got her class schedule for Stanford and a few churches she's looking forward to checking out."

How ironic, Jake mused, taking a long sip of water. He was the reason Amy had come into a relationship with God in the first place. But she had obviously long since passed him on their faith journeys.

"That's great," he faked, wondering how intentional his mom's bump-in with his ex-girlfriend had truly been. It would be just like his mother to orchestrate a "chance meeting" precisely for the sake of this current conversation. He also wondered how much else Amy had shared with her—either this Sunday or previously.

"Any new girls I should know about?" Pam looked over at him with a smile, as if she already knew something.

Jake had intentionally avoided any mention of Nicole in past conversations, because he knew exactly what his mom's response would be: *You're moving too fast.* But she had asked, so he decided he might as well be honest.

"Ahhh, well, there is kind of this girl," Jake mumbled, taking another large bite of what was left of his burger. "She's back home for the summer."

"Does she have a name?"

Jake chewed his food, reluctant to spit out the name. He finally gulped and said, "Nicole."

A look of horror appeared on Pam's face. "Not the same Nicole that Amy stayed with while she visited you?" She leaned forward, resting her arms on the table.

Jake said nothing, realizing his mother and ex-girlfriend were way too close to each other. *When did my mom become a professional interrogator?* he scowled inwardly. "It's not like that. It started after Amy left," Jake tried to explain. "You can't tell Amy."

Pam shook her head and looked at her son with disappointment. "You sleeping with her?"

When had this sort of thing ever been something he and his mom talked about? "What? Mom! What is this, a cross-examination?" Jake said defensively. "I already told you, she's home for the summer. And we're taking things slow," he emphasized, rationalizing that none of this was actually a lie. "She came to church with me, and we've been friends ever since." It sounded so much more holy and righteous when he explained it like that. "She's really a great girl," Jake stressed.

Pam leaned back against the cushioned seat of their booth and exhaled. "Sorry, honey. I'm sure she's a great girl. I just don't want you making any of the same mistakes you made with Amy."

The two sat in silence for a while, focusing on their meals, which were starting to get cold. Finally, Pam pulled out a piece of paper from her purse and flipped it on the table.

"What's that?" Jake asked, still mildly irritated by the whole Nicole conversation.

"Address for the Brooklyn Tabernacle. I hear they have an awesome Tuesday night prayer meeting, and I want to go check it out while I'm here." Pam nodded for a refill on her iced tea as the waitress walked by.

"Oh...um, I think I have practice that night," Jake made an excuse. "But I bet Nomis can tell you exactly what to do to get there," he offered, as if that made it any better. In one sense, he felt guilty about letting his mother trek around Brooklyn by herself, but he had absolutely no interest in going to a big prayer service with her.

"Oh, okay," she nodded, definitely looking disappointed.

Jake smiled as he reached across the table to steal back a bite from Pam's plate, so that once again things would be even in the world.

✚ ✚ ✚

"Grant, Nomis, this is my mom," Jake made the introduction after their game. Pam had stuck out in the raucous urban crowd, but it hadn't fazed her. She cheered with all her might, even when the spectators were decidedly antagonistic toward the crazy out-of-town threesome on the court. It was fun hearing his mom screaming from the sidelines every time he did anything remotely positive, something she hadn't been around to do much while he was growing up.

"Nice job on the boards," Pam warmly greeted the much-bigger forwards with a handshake.

"Thanks, Mrs. Taylor," the guys responded in unison.

"Oooh, you've got soft hands!" Pam grinned to Grant, rubbing the skin on his palm.

"Mom!" Jake groaned.

Grant smiled, slapping Jake playfully on the back. "Jake, your mom's got good taste. I don't know why *you've* never noticed."

"But those hands obviously didn't help you win the game tonight. What's up with that?" She raised her eyebrows, pointing to the scoreboard.

"Oooohhhh!" all three guys groaned together.

"Did your mom just dis us like that?" Grant laughed, while Nomis turned to give her a high-five.

"Dude, yo' momma's got spunk!" Nomis grinned.

Jake nodded his head and gave his mom a wink.

"I'm sorry. How about I make it up to you guys by taking you out to dinner?" she offered.

The boys all exchanged triumphant looks and then voted in unison: "Buffet Town!"

It wasn't that the food at the all-you-can-eat restaurant was all that great, but after a tough-fought game, quantity trumped quality. The boys immediately bypassed the salad bar to pile their plates with roast beef, ham, fried chicken, and a few slices of pizza, all stacked on top of each other. By the time they returned to the table, Pam was waiting for them with a small salad in front of her. She held her cell phone to her ear.

"Dude, your mom's getting worked by the system," Grant commented on the nearly empty plate that had cost her almost $15.

"You should have seen how much she paid for her rabbit food on her first night in town," Jake ridiculed under his breath.

"Okay, Glen, I'll tell him." Pam hung up the phone and smiled at the boys' heaping mounds of food. "You know, you *can* go back for seconds..."

"Was that Dad?" Jake interrupted.

"Yeah, he says hello," Pam replied, as if it wasn't that big a deal. "I pay, you pray." She nodded to Jake as she caught Grant with a drumstick in midair. Grant gingerly put it down and waited awkwardly.

"Wait, are you and dad getting back together?" Jake asked.

"We'll see," Pam smiled. "Let's talk about it later. I'm sooo hungry."

"I can tell, Mrs. T," Nomis piped up, surveying her mostly empty plate.

"You can call me Pam." She smiled, turning again to Jake. "How about you pray before your food gets cold?"

Jake wanted to talk about his parents, but stares from both of his dinner guests prompted him to utter the shortest prayer he could think of. "Rub-a-dub-dub, thanks for the grub. Amen."

Grant and Nomis tore into their food like hungry wolves as Pam stared across the table, annoyed at her son.

"What?" Jake asked.

"If you ask me, that's a pretty pathetic prayer for *that* much food." Pam scowled as she jabbed her fork into a slice of cucumber.

Grant laughed, sending a chunk of chicken flying across the table. It landed right between Jake and Nomis.

"Sorry about that," Grant muttered. "But I don't even pray, and I knew that was lame."

Jake rolled his eyes and sank his teeth into a slice of pizza. "I want to talk about Dad later."

That "later" may have never come had Jake not insisted on escorting his mother back to her hotel after dinner. Pam seemed anxious to drop the conversation, but Jake kept pressing, and finally in her room she admitted that they *had* been going to counseling together once a week for the past three months, but she had recently decided to end their sessions.

"Your father needs to make a decision about what he really wants," she explained, as they lounged in the modern but cramped space.

"Wait. Did Dad cheat on you again?" Jake barked. He could already feel the muscles throughout his body start to tense up. He flashed on that road-trip to Louisville, when he had started to trust his dad again, and his stomach rolled.

"No, no, no. It's nothing like that," Pam reassured Jake in a much more hushed tone, reminding him to keep his voice down, as well. "Your father and I had problems in our marriage long before I walked in on him and his secretary."

Pam's voice cracked a bit, and Jake stared at her awkwardly, trying to decide whether to hug her or give her space.

"I'm sorry, Mom. You don't have to talk about it if you don't—"

"I've told your dad that it's either me or his job," she continued resolutely. "We've always had our problems, as you might have been aware of growing up. I always thought I could hide it from you, but now I guess I was just fooling myself. But our marriage really started to crumble when your father started getting all those promotions, which is when he started going on all the business trips—and doing who knows what else."

"You mean Dad cheated on you a bunch of times?"

"Your father is a hard-working, dedicated, driven man. But there are plenty of women out there who know just how to get inside a man's head enough to make him lose focus on what's really important."

An image of Nicole shot through Jake's mind, and he cringed. "So you told Dad to just quit his job? Is that really fair? You know how much he loves it." Jake surprised even himself when he realized he was taking his father's side.

"I'm not willing to share him anymore. Not even if it's with a job," Pam shrugged but spoke with confidence as she stared directly at her son. "When you really love someone, you'll do whatever it takes to get them back."

"And Dad's not willing to give it up," Jake guessed out loud. He couldn't blame his father. Even to him, it seemed a little extreme to pull that kind of ultimatum on your spouse.

Pam shook her head. "Not yet, but I pray for him every day."

"Do you really think you could forgive him?" Jake asked quietly. "I mean, for the women?"

"I already have," she said simply, although a few tears trickled down her cheeks.

Jake shook his head, amazed at the woman sitting before him. He got up from the desk chair and sat next to her on the bed so he could give her a long, strong hug. "Are you going to be okay?"

Pam turned so she could place her hands on Jake's shoulders and look him squarely in the eyes. "Oh, honey. I'm going to be fine. I really am. The one I'm worried about is *you*."

Jake looked at her blankly. "Don't worry about me, Mom."

"I can't help it. I'm your mother."

✚ ✚ ✚

After several more days of tours and talks, Jake dropped Pam off at the airport. He sighed wearily. As much as he had enjoyed his mother's visit, it had been quite exhausting trying to balance his new lifestyle choices with her interrogations. Pam had managed to make it to Brooklyn and back safely on her own, and besides her pointed reminders that she would spend a lot of time praying for him, she let his lame excuses slide. But Jake felt her disapproval. He knew he should have accompanied her to the church, but two hours of prayer was definitely not his idea of fun—especially when the other guys were going out to one of Nomis's club shows.

Fortunately, Nicole had seemed to understand that she wasn't the kind of girl Jake wanted to introduce to his mom, and she had graciously stayed out of the picture for the week. But now that his mother was gone, Jake was only too ready to get back to her. It had been almost two weeks since he'd spent the night at her place, more than enough time to let absence make the heart grow fonder.

When his subway emerged from a tunnel, two new texts awaited him.

1:12pm | From: Mom | To: Jake
I love you kiddo. Thanks for a great week.

1:14pm | From: Nicole | To: Jake
Is she gone yet? How 'bout you ride that train right up to my house and we spend some time getting reacquainted...Parents are gone til 2morrow

25

8:32am | From: Cari | To: Amy
Can you stop by my house on your way out? I have something for you.

AMY HAD HOPED to get on the road by 9 a.m. for her eight-hour drive up to Stanford, but it was almost ten by the time she finally reversed the jam-packed minivan out of her driveway. Her mom had officially given her the car as a going-away present. It wasn't a Ferrari, but Amy was more than grateful for it.

Amy's mom Sherry now stood dutifully on the sidewalk in her bathrobe and slippers, watching her only child drive away, barely kept awake by the steaming mug of coffee in her hand. She had asked if Amy wanted her to come along for the long drive, but Amy could tell she really didn't want to invest the time or money into the trip, so she let her stay at home. In fact, Amy was pretty sure her mom was looking forward to Amy leaving—to being single and unhindered by a child again—not that she had let having a "child" actually hinder her much over the last few years.

Amy knew that, throughout most of her twenties, Sherry had struggled as a single parent. Once Amy had been old enough to be semi-independent, Sherry had seemed to go crazy trying to regain those "fun" younger years that she'd missed out on by getting pregnant and married at seventeen—and then divorced five years later. She stayed out partying on the weekends—getting home even later than her teenage daughter—and had so many boyfriends that Amy had stopped trying to get to know them. But all of her mom's wild living, Amy knew, did nothing to heal the bitter heart she nursed, and Amy wondered if living without a child at home would be detrimental to her mom. But no matter how many mistakes her mom had made, at least she hadn't just ditched her, the way Amy's father had.

"Don't forget to stop by Cari's," her mom groggily reminded her for the third time as Amy started to pull away.

"Thanks, Mom. Love you," Amy called out the open window and slowly pulled away from her house. Luckily, the Vaughns didn't live too far out of the way, and since they'd done all their goodbye hugs at church the day before, it could be a quick in-and-out visit.

Amy couldn't help but remember—and feel a little jealous about—Jake's departure to college some nine months earlier. His driveway had been lined with friends who had come to see him off.

Well, her driveway might not be packed with friendly faces at this moment, but she knew she was leaving behind plenty of people who really cared about her. When she thought about it, it was actually kind of funny, because even though she had been the epitome of popularity in high school, it wasn't until after graduation that she'd really learned what true friendship was. She had said her goodbyes to all those true friends this past week—from a last run with Andrea on the beach, to a last talk with Cari at Starbucks, to a last trip to Costco with the entire Vaughn family, to a ton of last hugs at church with people she had grown to love over the last year or so. In Jake's absence, Amy had been surrounded by more than enough love and support, and she was truly grateful for it.

Amy arrived at the house that had almost become her second home over the past six months and pulled her old minivan into the driveway next to Chris's Corolla. She jumped out of the car and jogged over to the door, knocking twice.

"Come on in!" she heard Cari's voice shout from inside.

Amy pushed the door open, and before she could even register that the room was packed with people, a massive shout greeted her: "HAP-PY BIRTHDAY!!!"

"Um, it's not my birthday," she stuttered, realizing that this surprise must be for her. Although completely confused, she was overjoyed to see all these people that she cared about standing around the room with birthday hats and party blowers.

Cari stepped forward to give the first hug. "We know, but you'll be gone in October, so we thought we'd celebrate early."

Never in Amy's previous 18 birthdays had anyone thrown her a surprise party, and her heart leapt as she smiled awkwardly at the dozens of eyes that were watching her every move. As she scanned the crowd, all of a sudden she saw her mother standing in the back, fully dressed, hair tied back into a ponytail.

"Mom?" Amy puzzled, glancing back at the driveway.

"I drive fast and know a few shortcuts," Shelly grinned sheepishly. "Do you know how hard this was to keep a secret?"

Caleb wriggled his way out from the crowd and threw his arms around Amy's legs, slightly crumpling the piece of paper in his hand. He reached up eagerly and announced, "I drew you a picture!"

"Yeah? Can I see it?" Amy reached down and picked up her little friend.

Caleb shoved the drawing into her face and pointed another pudgy finger toward the refrigerator, where a mostly matching picture was posted with four ladybug magnets. Both pictures depicted colorful stick figures, labeled "Amy" and "Caleb" in five-year-old scrawl, holding hands in a sandbox.

"Mommy said that was the day you became my big sister." Caleb smiled from ear to ear.

Amy hugged the cute boy tightly and took the crayon drawing from his dimpled hand before setting him back down on the floor. "Thanks, buddy." She grinned and held the picture to her heart.

Immediately, another hand tapped her on the shoulder. Amy turned to see Melia standing there with tears in her eyes.

"I miss you already!" the now eighth-grader cried, attacking Amy with a giant hug.

Amy embraced the crazy redhead, fighting the tears that were rushing to her eyes. She thought of her friendship with this precious girl and realized that Melia had truly become the little sister that Amy had always wanted.

"I'm already missing you, too," Amy whispered in her ear.

"I made us something." Melia pulled two identical beaded friendship bracelets out of her pocket. The flashy little fluorescent pink, orange, yellow, and green beads were interrupted by three white beads imprinted with the letters "B F F."

"Promise you'll never take it off," Melia commanded, tying one of the bracelets around Amy's wrist and then holding out her own wrist for Amy to tie the other one on.

"Promise," Amy assured her. And even though the gaudy color scheme wouldn't match anything in her wardrobe, she meant it.

Next in line stood Andrea, who in just a short time had become the best girlfriend Amy had ever had. Andrea handed Amy a little tissue paper-wrapped package. "So you can still feel kinda like you're running with me," she explained.

Amy ripped the thin paper off to find a pair of tall tube socks with green stripes at the top.

"These are awesome!" Amy grinned and embraced Andrea in another hug. "Remember, you're visiting me at least once a year!" she reminded her.

Andrea pulled an envelope out of her back pocket and waved it in the air. "Already got the tickets."

Amy shook her head in amazement, feeling overwhelmed at how blessed she was. If wealth was measured by the quality of friends a person had, she was full-on rich!

Over the next forty-five minutes, Amy received a series of tiny little mementos from tons of people from her New Song Church family, who just wanted her to know that they loved her. Frank and Jan gave her a recent picture of her holding Emily. Jake's mom gave her a beachy picture frame with the words "Oceanside: Home Sweet Home" written on a large shell glued to the corner. A number of girls from the college-aged group at church gave her a bag of quarters tied to a bottle of laundry detergent, and the parents of Gabbi and Alyx in her middle school small group pitched in to give her a variety of gift cards to different restaurants and stores. She got a gas card, some other picture frames, a few CDs burned with music favorites to keep her company on the long drive, a few packs of chewing gum, and a basket full of snacks she could munch on in the car. Finally, she got to Cari and Chris. "We got you one serious gift and one necessary one,"

Cari announced, handing her a rectangular box wrapped in shiny pink paper and a big silver bow.

"What did you get? What did you get?" Caleb asked eagerly, jumping up and down in excitement.

Amy delicately tore the pretty wrapping paper off to find the perfect going-away presents: a Bible with her name engraved on the pink and brown cover, and a refillable Starbucks cup with a gift card inside. Seeing as the Bible she'd been reading was an old paperback that had been mended with duct tape one too many times—and she was leaving her weekly Starbucks partner behind—this was just what she needed. Too moved to speak, Amy reached out and gave the Vaughn family a group hug.

Trapped in the middle, Caleb wiggled around, calling out, "I'm stuck! I'm stuck!"

They let him worm his way free. "If you ever need a little Starbucks lovin', we can always set up a Skype chat, and it will be almost as good as hanging out in person," Cari said.

Almost, Amy thought, knowing it wouldn't come even close without Cari's tight, reassuring hugs. But it was a thoughtful idea.

After an hour of hugs, tears, gifts, and farewells, the crowd spilled out onto the driveway to send Amy off with streamers and a sea of waves goodbye. Amy sighed with contentment, brushed away some tears, and summoned all her resolve to drive away from it all.

✚ ✚ ✚

Over four hundred miles and several bathroom stops later, Amy pulled her weary minivan onto the Stanford University campus just before 8 p.m. Move-in day had technically ended hours ago, which made every wrong turn even more frustrating. After the fifth exasperating U-turn, she finally found Sterling Quadrangle and Adams, a dorm residence specifically for freshmen and sophomores—and more importantly, Amy's new home.

Since Amy had deferred enrollment for a year, she was more or less a freshman, but thanks to passing six AP tests in high school and her community college courses, she'd transferred enough credits to be a sophomore. So the Freshman/Sophomore College—casually referred to as FroSoCo—seemed like the perfect blend for her. She couldn't wait to immerse herself in the academic and social activities she had craved for so long.

Although it seemed that no one was still moving in, seemingly happy people were everywhere, chatting it up with friends, and all-too-familiar insecurities slowly began to creep into Amy's mind: *Will I fit in? What if they don't like me? Will I be able to keep up after this past year?* She nervously wound the minivan through the well-lit parking lot, trying to not hit anybody while finding the ideal place to unload. She finally settled on a curb near the front, hoping it wasn't a no-parking zone with a hidden sign.

"Here we go," she exhaled out loud, as she popped the back lift-gate open and got out.

"Need a hand?" asked a cute guy walking by with a friend.

Amy looked back at the overwhelming piles of stuff in her van and turned to the boys with a smile. "Absolutely."

Each boy grabbed two boxes and headed toward the dorm entrance.

"Where are we taking these?" the cute one asked over his shoulder.

Amy fished through her shorts pockets and pulled out a scrap of paper. "212!" she yelled, hoping that this was not the last she saw of her luggage—and the guys. She quickly grabbed a duffel bag and a box of school supplies and hurried after the speedy helpers.

Holding the front door open for them with a smile was a college girl with a clipboard.

"Welcome to Adams. Are you with those boxes that just came through?" the girl asked cheerfully.

"Yeah," Amy laughed nervously.

"I'm Roxy, one of Adams' resident assistants. What room are you in?"

"I think I'm in room 212." Amy glanced down at her little piece of paper again.

"Shut up!" Roxy shot back with a huge grin on her face. "You're on my floor. We're like three doors down from each other." Roxy quickly glanced at her clipboard. "Let me guess—you're Amy Briggs?"

"That's me," Amy responded with a smile.

Roxy reached out her hand for a shake and then turned to a couple of athletic-looking guys playing cards at a nearby table. "My new friend Amy needs your muscles," she commanded more than asked.

The boys immediately jumped up and approached them. Amy was pretty sure that either of them could have worn a shirt a size or two bigger, but she had to admit that their bulging biceps were quite impressive.

Amy tried not to blush as they looked at her for instructions. "Uh, it's the blue minivan parked by the curb."

Before she could even say thank you, they jogged barefoot out the door toward her car.

"Don't worry about the rest of your stuff...they'll take it up to your room," Roxy explained. "I'll be up there in a couple of minutes. My shift is almost over."

"Thank you," Amy sighed with a smile. She had barely stepped into the dorm lobby, and already she felt welcome. As she made her way up the first flight of stairs with her meager load, her first helpers flew past on their way back down. "Thanks, guys! I really appreciate it," Amy yelled once again at their backs.

"We'll get the rest!" the cute one assured her without slowing down.

Amy didn't have the heart to tell them they had already been replaced. *Boys already fighting over me!* Amy laughed to herself.

The door to the second floor girls' side was partially propped open, and loud music blared down the hall. Amy zigzagged between a half-dozen smiling faces and warm welcomes until she found her boxes stacked up against the wall by her door. As Amy raised her hand to knock, the door flung open on its own. Standing in the doorway was a slightly plump African -American girl with a fresh weave and a gigantic smile.

"Oh my gosh! You're Amy!" her roommate shrieked, reaching out to give her a hug. "I'm Renee, your amazing roommate," she laughed, opening the door wide open for Amy to come in.

Remembering how Jake had to room with a guy who wasn't clean enough to work at the city dump, Amy had been apprehensive about her living situation all summer. When she found out she was assigned to a one-room double—instead of the two-room double that added a wall with a doorway between roommates—her worries had increased. But one glance inside the nearly immaculate room, and Amy was already breathing a silent sigh of relief.

"Hey, I'll totally help you bring all this stuff in," Renee bubbled, "but I've totally got to go pee. I was just heading out when you popped up." She did a funny little hopping dance from one foot to the other until Amy stepped aside, and she waddled down the hall.

I can't believe I'm actually here! Amy giggled inwardly as another load of her stuff was delivered by the buff barefoot guys. She set her box and duffel bag down inside the room and followed the boys back down to her car. With only one more load from everyone, her car was emptied, and she found a longer-term parking spot before returning to her room.

Back upstairs with all of her stuff piled inside the room, Amy stepped back to survey her surroundings. From the looks of things, Renee was nearly finished with her unpacking, and everything on her side looked neat and tidy and minimal. She had very little in the way of décor, save for a few scattered pictures of what appeared to be family and friends. Amy's eyes suddenly locked on a worn-out black Bible sitting proudly on Renee's desk.

"Uh, I don't mean to pry, but is that your Bible?" Amy asked nervously when Renee returned, not wanting to jump to any conclusions.

"Nah, the girl across the hall just asked me to store it for her." Renee shrugged, then broke into a huge smile. "Of course it's my Bible! I read it every day. My daddy's a preacher."

An overwhelming sense of joy flooded over Amy. "I try to read mine every day, too." She smiled.

Renee grabbed Amy's arm with both hands and looked straight in her eyes. "Wait! Are you a sistah from anotha' mistah?" Her roommate held tightly to her arm.

"Am I a what?" Amy laughed.

"Are you a Christ-ian?" Renee pronounced it slowly for her.

"Oh. Well, yeah." Amy nodded.

Renee looked up to the ceiling and shouted loudly, "Thank You, Jesus!" and broke into her funny little hopping dance again.

Ten minutes in and Amy still didn't know much about this girl she would be sharing a room with for the next year, but already she was confident that this was a match made, literally, in heaven.

9:13pm | From: Amy | To: Cari
Can't wait to tell you all about my new roommate. God is sooooooo cool!

12:41pm | From: Andrea | To: Amy
How was your second week?

12:43pm | From: Amy | To: Andrea
Ahhhhhhhwesome!

OVER AN HOUR LATER, Amy hung up the phone, fully content with life after a thoroughly satisfying conversation with her best friend back home.

Andrea was doing great, still loving the beginning of her senior year. She was running cross-country, writing for the school newspaper, and leading her girls' small group at church, enjoying every minute of it all. Her enthusiasm and joy in life was infectious, and Amy felt happier just talking to her—not that Amy wasn't already happy. Her positive first impressions of the university hadn't stopped with the helpful hotties, the friendly RA, and the perfect roommate that she met her first night on campus. No, they kept on coming, and Amy was daily falling in love with another aspect of her new school.

The entire first week on campus was Orientation Week, full of tons of fun and informative activities for the new students. That first night, she'd been whisked away on a midnight ice cream run—dorkiest pajamas required. Amy was actually glad she had packed the Curious

George footy-PJs she'd won in a Christmas gift exchange two years earlier. Who would've guessed that they would be voted first prize and score her a free ice cream? The next night they'd had a late-night dance party, and the night after that a campfire complete with s'mores. During the days, she had participated in meetings and introductory seminars and team-building activities and lots of food-centered socializing.

It was weird, Amy thought, because she'd assumed that people go away to college in order to grow up and move into adulthood, but the longer she was on campus, the more she felt the freeing joy of actually being a kid again—something she hadn't felt for a long time. The emotional weights she'd been carrying around all last year had somehow been left at home, and she didn't miss them one bit.

More than anything, and especially now that classes had started, Amy loved being part of FroSoCo. When she had looked into her housing options last spring, not only had the blend of freshmen and sophomores caught her attention, but she had heard that the special community had a slightly more academic focus and less pressure to conform to the typical college party lifestyle. Even so, she had also heard that the acceptance rate was only about 25 percent, and she figured she didn't have a chance. Now that she was here, she was blown away by it all.

In high school, she'd always felt that her intelligence had intimidated some of the guys, so she got good at playing the role of a dumb blonde while secretly bringing in the straight-A report card. But here, she could finally be herself. Intellectual discussions popped up everywhere, and people weren't embarrassed to take time to study. People weren't just taking classes because they didn't know what else to do with their lives—they *wanted* to be there. It was so refreshing!

More than three hundred students assembled in the lecture hall for her first class, Introduction to Statistical Methods. While that didn't sound particularly fascinating, Amy enjoyed math, and five minutes into class she fell in love with Professor Geradeaux when he explained the entire first page of the syllabus in a corny rap. After Stats, Amy had an afternoon Intro to Humanities class called The Art of Living. It met every other day, with a mandatory discussion hour on Tuesdays and Thursdays. Tuesdays and Thursdays ended up being her busy days, starting with an Intro to Brain and Behavior class in the mornings—a class she was excited about—followed by an Art Appreciation class, which she hadn't been so thrilled over. She'd hated art ever since third grade when she'd overheard her mom complain to a boyfriend about how tacky her daughter's artwork looked on the fridge. Amy hadn't drawn another picture for her mom since then. But eleven years later, Amy sat riveted as her flamboyant professor projected random pieces of art up on the screen and opened the class for discussion.

The second Thursday of the quarter, Amy walked home with a backpack full of books and a head full of knowledge after spending an exhausting afternoon studying in the library. She felt a rock or something in her sandal and leaned against a light pole to shake it out. When she looked up, Amy couldn't help but chuckle at what seemed to be divine intervention. Both Chris and Cari had encouraged her to check out the InterVarsity Christian Fellowship group on campus, describing it as a giant youth group for college students. But Amy had yet to find any information about it...until now.

Underneath her hand was a neon orange flyer that read:

InterVarsity Christian Fellowship's Intersect presents

WELCOME-BACK-TO-SCHOOL

Root Beer Kegger

Thursday • 8pm

at the Clubhouse

Amy beamed with delight and rushed back to her room to tell Renee.

Three hours later, the two of them walked into a packed courtyard with music thumping and people everywhere holding those all-too-familiar red plastic cups. A barbecue smoked in the far right corner, and a DJ went to town on his turntables to their left. In front of them, a limbo contest was going strong. Amy's memory flashed back with discomfort to the countless high school parties she had indulged in. The only difference here was that everyone appeared to be pleasantly sober. And at the kegs, a few students dropped ice cream scoops into the fuzzy liquid being pumped out to create perfect root beer floats.

"Welcome to Intersect! You ladies want a beer?" an extremely attractive male grinned as he approached Amy and Renee with a float in each hand. His trendy, orange-plaid, western-style button-down shirt contrasted nicely with his spiky blond hair and the little soul patch on his chin. He most definitely looked like an upperclassman.

"You know it!" Renee grabbed one from his hand. Amy timidly followed suit.

"My name's Steven. I'm one of the leaders here." He held out his hand to welcome them both, his eyes fixated on Amy.

"I'm Renee," Amy's roommate belted out over the loud music. "And this is my sistah from anotha' mistah, Amy." She just loved that line.

Steven smiled—*oh, what a smile!*—and Amy felt her cheeks flushing.

Renee continued, unfazed. "So, tell me, where all da black folk be? Don't you tell me it's just me an' those other two gals I saw walkin' by earlier. We 'bout to do something to make this here right, yessir." She waved her finger up in the air to emphasize her point.

Steven flashed his pearly whites again, and Amy just shrugged at her roommate's spunk and sudden Ebonics blend.

"What about those guys over there?" Steven asked. "And Stacy over there?" he pointed in another direction.

Renee winked at him with a grin. "Now that's what I'm talkin' 'bout! But we're definitely gonna have to do us some outreachin'," she continued with less of an accent.

Steven nodded in approval and was about to say something else when the music faded away and a girl's voice crackled through the sound system.

"Welcome to our first annual Fall Root Beer Kegger!" a perky Asian girl announced into a mic by the DJ booth. "We're mostly here to hang out and have fun tonight, but we're about to kick the real par-tay off right now with the worship band. So find your way into the clubhouse here, and we'll get started in five."

"That's my cue. I gotta go," Steven reported hesitantly. "I'm glad you guys came, and I really hope you get involved. Same time, same place every week."

"Sounds good," Renee replied, and Amy found herself simply nodding in agreement as she watched Steven make his way through the crowd into the building.

Amy and Renee finished their floats and followed not too far behind Steven, merging with the rest of the sixty-some students trying to squish through the doors. Once inside, Amy was surprised to see Steven at the front of the worship band behind the center mic. He strapped a guitar over his shoulder and plugged it in before looking out into the audience. Amy couldn't be sure, but it seemed for a moment that he was staring right at her.

"Are you people ready to sing loud?" Steven shouted into the microphone, as the band jumped into an upbeat song she'd learned back at New Song. The group spontaneously broke into a unified clap, and Amy immediately joined in.

"Mmmmm girl!" Renee crooned into Amy's ear.

"What?" Amy asked innocently, trying to keep rhythm with the drummer.

"Mmmhmm. He's got the hots for you."

Amy quickly turned to face Renee, who reaffirmed her opinion with pursed lips and an exaggerated wiggle of the eyebrows. Amy glanced back at Steven, strumming his acoustic guitar with fervor as he led the group in praising God. His voice reverberated through the room, and his eyes closed as he lifted his face toward heaven. For the first time since being with Jake, Amy felt her heart skip a beat. *This is stupid: He probably has a girlfriend,* she reasoned. *And why are you thinking about boys when you're supposed to be singing about God?*

But she was still thinking about him as she dropped to sleep that night.

The next night, Amy called Cari, not really sure if she wanted to confess her quick interest in a Stanford boy...but if the topic came up, she definitely didn't mind talking about the handsome worship leader. She'd spent the past six months single, which was a new personal record for her since her first official boyfriend in seventh grade. Jake was still the last thing she thought about before falling asleep each night and the first thing on her mind each morning, but as the months had passed, the hurt was slowly going away, and she was finding it easier and easier to move ahead. She hadn't even checked his Facebook page since early summer. And last night, Steven's brilliant smile and soothing voice had competed for the final spot in Amy's conscious thoughts.

"Hi, Amy," Cari responded cordially on the third ring. Her subdued voice was a far cry from her usual bubbly personality.

"Cari, are you okay?" Amy snapped to alertness. In all their talks together over the past few months, she'd never known Cari to sound less than cheerful—even on her bad days.

"You know, today's not been my best day," her mentor confessed. "But what's up with you?" she asked, changing the subject.

"Wait, wait, wait..." Amy refused to move on. "What's wrong?"

"Really, it's nothing."

"Cari."

"It's no big deal. Let's start this conversation over again." Cari paused then chirped in a much brighter tone, "Hi Amy! How's it going?"

"Cari! Seriously, I'm not telling you anything about me until you tell me something about you. What made today not so good? Is Chris too busy? Are the middle-schoolers giving you problems? How about this: How can I *pray* for you?" Amy persisted.

Cari sighed. "I just got some bad news from the doctor this afternoon, that's all," she finally admitted.

Amy shook her head to get rid of horrible possibilities flashing through her mind. "What happened? Is everyone okay? Did Caleb get hurt?"

A silence met her questions.

Finally, Cari answered softly, "It's nothing serious, sweetie. It's just...it looks like I'm not going to be able to have any more kids. I've got some medical complications, and—"

"But you already had Caleb, so can't they—"

"I know. The doctor said we should treat him as our little miracle," Cari interrupted. "There are some expensive procedures we could test out, but I just don't think it's worth it..."

"Worth it!" Amy protested. "Cari, you guys are like the best parents in the world. Anything it takes for you to be able to raise another kid is definitely worth it. *You're* worth it."

Cari chuckled softly. "Well, thanks for your vote of confidence, Amy. But how can I justify spending thousands of dollars on experimental solutions that may not even work in my case, when there are so many kids around the world dying from preventable causes that that same amount of money could help fix? I just don't know..." Her voice trailed off again.

"Oh, Cari." Amy searched for words that could be of comfort, but the only thing that came to mind were cliché phrases that were wholly insufficient. "I'm so sorry."

"It's okay. Really, I'll be fine. I guess this is just the final death of a dream," she sighed. But as always she ended with a positive spin: "I'm confident God has a plan in all this, and somewhere down the line, I'll be able to look back to this time and smile. It's all about just holding on until I get to that point, right?"

Amy sure knew that. How many times had Cari encouraged her with that same thought?

"Hey, Amy, I'm really sorry, but Chris and I need to get to a school concert for some of the kids," she jumped in suddenly, as if having just glanced at the clock. "Perfect timing, huh?" she joked. "Life of a youth pastor's wife!"

"Cari!" Amy protested. "Put Chris on the line. I'll tell him that you can't go," she argued in all seriousness.

Cari chuckled softly. "Just promise you'll pray for me."

"Of course I will," Amy answered helplessly.

"Thanks. I want to hear about you. Sorry for hogging the conversation. I'll call you later, okay?"

"No worries," Amy assured her, and they both hung up.

Amy's heart broke as she processed the news from her friend. Cari and Chris were the perfect parents, not to mention nearly perfect Christians. They of all people didn't deserve to get such horrible news. Amy recalled their conversation months earlier when Cari had first confessed her jealousy over Amy's pregnancy. Cari had obviously been hurting then, but Amy had never brought up the topic again. Amy felt a sting of guilt, thinking of how many trivial problems Cari had comforted her through in the past few months, all while Cari was struggling through her own, much more serious issue. *How self-centered have I been?* But while she could have been more supportive, Cari's problem wasn't Amy's fault. There was only one other person she could think of to blame.

Amy found her guilt morphing into anger. She got down on her knees next to her bed and started praying, "God, I'm ticked off at You right now..."

11:46am | From: Nicole | To: Jake
Sorority house party 2nite. Ur my date.

11:49am | From: Nicole | To: Jake
Meet me at 7 in front of the house. Wear that hot striped black shirt. Ooh!

11:57am | From: Nicole | To: Jake
Remember to use some of the cologne I gave u

JAKE KNEW THAT TONIGHT was a big night for Nicole. She'd spent the first six weeks of school pledging to become a sister in the most sought-after sorority on campus, and this party was it—the official welcome. But Jake didn't feel like being bossed around…so he didn't text her back. He couldn't deny that he felt a touch of pride knowing that she wanted him, but he wanted to make it clear who was in control here. *Nobody tells me what to wear!* he thought proudly.

The summer had been ideal: She'd been distant enough to leave him always wanting more, but close enough for him to get his fill when the desire got too strong. But since coming back to school, their relationship was definitely changing. They had yet to have the conversation making them official girlfriend/boyfriend, but Nicole was acting as if she had Jake wrapped around her little finger. What Jake had first considered to be attractive assertiveness, he now saw as annoying clinginess, and he was bugged that she wouldn't give him more space.

Originally, Jake had been drawn to that aggression, and if it hadn't been for Nicole pursuing him, they likely would never have met at all... or at least not have grown so "close." But now, like a hunter on the chase, Jake felt almost cheated. Nicole was like a deer that just fell into his lap, and while she was a nice trophy to show off, there was no thrill, no adventure to accompany the hunt.

Jake glanced at her barrage of texts again. They weren't even requests—just bullet-point commands. *Ugh!* Jake thought as he threw on the black pinstriped button-up shirt and squirted on two puffs of Ralph Lauren cologne. *I was going to wear this anyway,* he tried to comfort himself.

He walked into the kitchen of the on-campus apartment he now shared with Grant, who was making some nachos.

"Nice shirt, dude," Grant grinned.

"Whatever. Tonight's the night. I'm finally going to lay down the rules. I just didn't feel like dealing with it over the phone."

"Sure. I believe you. Why don't you practice on me?"

"No way, dude. This is between me and her."

"Whatever. You're going to melt like putty and come whining back to me tomorrow."

"Well," Jake protested. "Maybe tonight's not the best night, anyway. It *is* her big night, you know."

"Dude!" Grant scoffed. "You're going to have an excuse every single time. It's been like over a month already. Why don't you just man up and talk to her...unless you *like* being on her leash..." He threw a chip at Jake and grinned. "Seriously, pretend I'm Nicole." Grant pretended to flip his hair, stuck his chest out, and batted his eyes. "Hey, Jakey!" he warbled in a high falsetto.

"Ugh!" Jake complained and threw the chip back at his friend. Something about Grant's masculine physique made it a little difficult to imagine his hot female friend. "Now listen, Nicole. We really need to talk," Jake began.

Grant laughed. "Great start, Taylor...Okay, okay...about what, Jakey?" he resumed in the falsetto voice.

"Knock it off with the Jakey, bro. You're weirding me out. Um...I don't want you to take this the wrong way..." Jake continued.

"She will," Grant slipped in.

"...but if this thing's gonna work, then you need to chill out," Jake said, trying to muster up the intensity he would need. "With basketball season starting up and all, you know I don't have time for a serious relationship."

"Oooooh, yeah. That's gonna sting," Grant chuckled. "There's no way you're saying that to Nicole Baker."

Not appreciating Grant's pessimistic commentary, Jake threw up his hands and walked over to the door. "Watch me."

Fifteen minutes later, Jake met Nicole in front of her new sorority house. She wore a deep purple dress that fit her body like a glove, and immediately Jake's resolve—and the speech he had worked out on the way over—dissolved like sugar in water.

"You're late," she blurted out, before he could even give her a hug. Nicole went right to work straightening out his shirt and fixing his hair. "I just want my new sisters to love you like I do," she informed him and patted his cheek. "They're gonna be so jealous!" She grabbed his hand and tickled the inside of his palm.

Jake licked his now-dry lips, already wishing this stupid party was over so he could find out what was going on *underneath* Nicole's sexy outfit.

"Ready?" Nicole asked, pulling him toward the huge house before he could answer.

A tall, slender, and equally attractive dark-haired sorority girl guarded the front door with a clipboard. "This one's cute," she remarked casually to Nicole, as if Jake wasn't even there.

This one*? What's that supposed to mean?*

"Stacy, this is my *boyfriend,* Jake Taylor. He's on the basketball team," Nicole introduced him proudly, clutching tightly to his arm.

Whoa! Did she just introduce me as her boyfriend*?*

"Nice to meet you, Jake. Welcome to our house." Stacy gave a half smile and nodded them in.

Nicole leaned into Jake's ear and whispered, "Stacy is sorority president...I'm going to be her someday."

Jake nodded unenthusiastically as they entered the large living room packed with all the best-looking students Louisville had to offer. While there was probably no written rule in the sorority bylaws that all members must be thin and gorgeous, by the looks of every girl there, it was certainly an expectation.

A couple of other hot new pledges raced over to Nicole, and after a few minutes of their squealing conversation, Jake was ready to do something desperate. *Where are their dates?* Jake wondered, as he scanned the crowd for other solitary males to bond with.

"Can you get us some beers?" Nicole ordered more than asked Jake, pointing to the kitchen. And while Jake hated to be bossed around, he was grateful for the escape.

He squeezed his way through the throngs of students to the kitchen.

"Taylor! What up, dawg?" The greeting came from Jamal, who was obviously a bit inebriated already. He handed Jake a beer, and Jake gulped it down with appreciation. They both poured a refill from the nearest keg.

"Morning practice at 8 a.m." Jake grinned, toasting his cup.

Jamal tapped it with his own cup and laughed. "I play my best ball on a hangover." They pounded back a swig and sat in contemplative silence.

Over the next half-hour or so, they continued their meaningless small talk, their brains getting soggier with every refill. They watched with appreciation as the attractive sorority sisters filed in and out, greeting with approval the ladies' dates as they joined them at the watering hole.

"You with that Nicole-chick tonight?" Jamal suddenly questioned Jake.

Jake nodded half-heartedly.

"Watch out. Nate's here, and he's more drunk than I am," Jamal warned.

Jake hadn't considered Nate much of a threat when it came to Nicole since coming back to school after the summer. She was around Jake so much that there was no way she had time for his rival, too. Basketball, though, was a whole different story. By the end of summer, Jake was feeling pumped up and ready to take Nate on. He'd averaged just over eleven points and five assists throughout the summer league, and his level of toughness had increased exponentially. Unfortunately, in their first unofficial practice, Jake immediately realized that so had Nate's. Something must have been in the water back home in Missouri, because Nate came back looking bigger, stronger, and meaner, and his shot had improved, too. It was going to be interesting to see how playing time worked out at the point guard position this season. But suddenly, Jake was more concerned about who was currently getting playing time with his girl.

He knocked back the rest of his drink, picked up two more to take to where he had left Nicole, and pushed his way back toward the entrance. Two of the same girls stood talking airily, but Nicole was conspicuously absent.

"Hey, where's Nicole?" Jake asked them.

The subtle look they exchanged confirmed his fear.

"Uh, I think she went looking for you," one of them shrugged.

"Thanks," Jake scowled, shoving the two cups into their hands. He walked past them toward a dark hallway and started opening and closing random doors. It was still pretty early, so most rooms were empty, but the sixth one he tried rang in the jackpot. He twisted the brass doorknob, pushed the large mahogany door open, and saw movement in the shadows. Once his eyes adjusted to the dim light, he immediately recognized Nate's hulking, shirtless frame hovering over Nicole's barely clothed body on the bed.

Jake reached inside the doorway and flipped on the lights, anger seething through his veins. The hot and heavy couple winced at the bright light and quickly turned toward the intruder. Their reactions were completely opposite. A cocky smile spread over Nate's face, while Nicole looked at Jake in horror.

"Jake?" Nicole shrieked, pushing Nate away from her.

Without saying a word, Jake slammed the door shut and made a beeline toward the front door. *How could I be so stupid?* Jake asked himself, amid contrasting emotions of anger and hurt. Never had he felt more like a joke. He wanted to pummel Nate and his stupid smirk to the ground.

Just as he reached the front entrance, he heard Nicole's annoying voice shout out his name again. He just kept walking. If there's anything he didn't want, it was to make a scene in front of all those perfect, shallow sorority girls.

"Jake!" Nicole yelled again, and he turned around to see her chasing him down the walkway, her dress skewed, her high heels barely hanging on to her feet.

"What do you want, Nicole? It's over," Jake seethed, as she ran up to him and grabbed his arm.

"Jake, I'm sooooo sorry," she pleaded quietly, obviously just as concerned about the girls within earshot. "Can we at least talk about it?"

Jake shook his hand free and stepped back in disgust. "What's there to talk about, Nicole? I just found you in bed with Nate."

"Jakey, I was trying to tell Nate that it was over, because you and I are together now...and then...and then it just kind of happened..." Nicole begged, as if that explanation was a legitimate excuse.

"Look, Nicole, you're not my type. I'm not into cheaters," Jake found himself saying. *Where had that come from?* "I'm not gonna be another guy in your stupid game."

"You've got to be kidding me!" Nicole's voice rose a little, obviously forgetting about her current surroundings. "You're such a hypocrite!"

"Excuse me?" Jake shot back. "You get with another guy, and somehow *I'm* the one to blame?" He turned to walk away.

"Oh, you had no problem with me cheating when you were the one getting the action, huh? And what about you and Amy? You knew you weren't coming up to read the Bible that night," Nicole spewed.

Jake wanted to keep walking, but he had to defend himself. "You're the one who kept coming on to me! You wouldn't leave me alone."

Nicole laughed out loud. "Oh, poor baby! As if you minded. But you sure weren't going to initiate anything. You and your fake little Christian name-tag. You want to talk about playing games?"

Jake looked for something to shout back so he could regain the upper hand, but nothing came to his mind. "I'm out of here," was all he could think of. He glanced up at the porch where a half-dozen girls were watching.

"Yeah, walk away, Jake. I guess Amy got it right, knowing you weren't man enough to keep her satisfied. No wonder she dumped your sorry ass," Nicole sneered.

Jake's face burned hot, but he kept on walking. He walked all around campus for about an hour, finally arriving at Minardi Hall just after 10 p.m., still fuming. He slammed the apartment door and looked up to see that Grant had company. His roommate and a guy Jake hadn't met were sitting in the dark watching a movie.

"She didn't take it too well?" Grant guessed, his silhouette framed by the flickering blue light of the TV.

"Long story, but it's over," Jake mumbled, not wanting to embarrass himself in front of a complete stranger.

"Jake, this is Peter," Grant introduced his friend. "You want to talk about it?"

"Nah, it's cool. You guys enjoy whatever you're watching." Jake sulked to his room, closed the door, and flipped open his computer. He guided the mouse to the Internet Explorer icon, bypassed the latest scores on ESPN.com, and went directly to his Facebook page. A quick perusal of the updates showed that no one had done anything remotely interesting in the last three hours, unless he counted "Taking a nap then going to dinner," or "Just picked a booger the size of Texas. Too bad these guys aren't edible." He found his fingers typing in a name he hadn't thought about too much lately, and promptly the picture of a smiling Amy, standing next to a large African-American girl, stared back at him. For the first time since their breakup, he felt truly sorry for how he had treated her.

9:43pm | From: 16505559732 | To: Amy
Look bhind u

AMY FELT HER PHONE BUZZ in her pocket as she stood socializing after another amazing week of Intersect. Amidst crazy amounts of homework, not getting enough sleep from staying up too late talking with her roommate, and still struggling with some of her issues from back home, Amy had found InterVarsity's weekly large-group gathering to be a much-looked-forward-to refuge in her busy life. This evening, one of the graduate school professors spoke on the sin of stressing out. These days, she had plenty to stress about—but she'd never thought about it as micromanaging God. It made perfect sense, though. The speaker said that stress was proof that we really didn't trust God with everything in our life and our small way of trying to take back some control. Ironically, halfway through the talk, Amy caught herself actually stressing out about being stressed out so much.

With her mind whirling, Amy glanced down at the mystery number and spun around to find Steven, the cute worship leader. He was wearing a V-neck sweater sporting a faux hawk and several-days-old beard. Amy's stomach dropped down to her weak knees.

She and Steven had talked a few minutes here and there at Intersect over the past few weeks, and they'd bumped into each other around campus a few times, but never enough to validate Renee's earlier claim that he had "the hots" for her...unfortunately. "Hi!" Amy grinned, trying not to sound too excited. "How'd you get my number?"

She was certain she'd never given it to him—not that she wouldn't have gladly exchanged digits with the guy who made it hard for her to worship God each week. Not only was he distractingly attractive, but the more she studied him, the more she was drawn to the spiritual depth he exuded.

"One of the perks of being an Intersect leader is that you get a copy of the roster," he confessed, his lips forming a cute smile.

"Stalker!" Amy teased, observant that a bead of sweat was beginning to form at the top of her forehead. "You know, I could report you."

"To whom?" Steven asked in a playful taunt. "I'm friends with all the other leaders." Undistracted by the people pressing all around them, his eyes focused on hers.

"Hmmm...maybe to God," Amy shot back, her eyes glancing upward to indicate her direct line to the Big Guy in the sky. "I don't think He looks too fondly on leaders taking advantage of innocent sheep," she said with a straight face.

Steven's whole face broke into the wide smile that she had caught herself daydreaming about far too many times. "But what if He's the one who told me to call you?"

Amy laughed out loud. "God *told* you to call me?" Amy probed, shaking her head to indicate that she wasn't buying it. *Is this really happening?*

"Actually, He just told me to ask you out. The texting thing was kind of my idea."

Amy's insides flip-flopped around wildly. Of all the girls who came to Intersect, of all the many more girls on campus, was Steven-the-hot-guitar-player actually asking *her* on a date? "Well, then, how can I argue with God's will?" Amy replied, as if she had no choice and jammed her sweaty hands into the front pockets of her jeans. She caught herself staring at the sexy V in his sweater and quickly raised her eyes to meet his.

Steven had his phone perched and ready. "Say cheese!" He laughed and clicked a picture. "I just want to remember the look on your face the first time I asked you out." He glanced down at the screen. "Oh, shoot! I can't believe I didn't notice the booger before I took it."

"What?" Amy choked, quickly wiping at her nose.

"Just playing. You're hanger-free...and the picture's perfect." Steven grinned. "So, do you like Italian food?"

Amy nodded, wiping her arm over her nose one more time, just in case. "*Mangia, mangia,*" she replied, complete with hand motions, for some reason tapping into a distant memory of her great-grandfather from Italy.

"*Tu sei una stella,*" Steven responded without skipping a beat.

"What does that mean?" Amy questioned. "I don't really speak—"

"I said, 'I know the perfect pizza place,'" Steven interrupted. "It's called Do-mi-nos. How about tomorrow night at seven?"

Amy laughed again as the reality of what was happening sank in. She felt her face flush hot. "I'd love to," she whispered.

"Great! I'll come by your room." Steven beamed confidently, glancing behind his shoulder at a line of people waiting to talk to him.

Amy leaned in. "Wait. How do you know where I live?"

Steven smiled and winked before turning his back to talk to someone else.

"Oooh girl, we got something to talk about tonight," Renee's voice piped up right next to her.

"Whatever..." Amy unsuccessfully tried to shrug it off, but a huge grin overtook her glowing face.

"You want to know what he really said to you in Italian?" Renee chided with an elbow to her ribs.

"Yeah," Amy shot back, surprised once again at the wealth of her roommate's knowledge.

"Me too! Let's go Google it," Renee laughed. "I told you that boy's in love with you!"

Twenty-one and a half hours later, Amy mindlessly thumbed through one of her textbooks, nervously watching the minute-hand slowly work its way toward the top of the clock. She had already changed outfits five times, finally just settling on jeans and an olive-green jacket over a simple white shirt. Her cell phone vibrated, and she jumped in anticipation, assuming that Steven was just letting her know that he was on his way. Instead, the message she read filled her with dread.

6:52pm | From: Melia | To: Amy
Remember that promise you made me make? I'm scared.

Amy instantly recalled her conversation with Melia from their babysitting incident months ago, and then just as suddenly, another horrible memory from the past flickered through Amy's mind.

Her uncle refastens his belt buckle and looks at her coldly. "This will be our little secret, baby girl, our own little secret."

Five-year-old Amy curls up on her bed in the dark, all the blankets pushed roughly to the side. Terrified tears squeeze out of her tightly shut eyes.

Shaking her head violently to escape her hideous past, Amy immediately clicked to call Melia back. Was Melia finally admitting to being abused? Was she in trouble right then? Amy didn't trust Melia's parents.

Melia's phone kept ringing, but she didn't pick up. The thoughts in Amy's head grew more and more worrisome. Why wasn't she answering? She had obviously *just* used her phone. Was she in danger at this very moment? Melia's familiar voicemail message picked up, and a horrible sense of powerlessness overwhelmed Amy. What had happened in the last thirty seconds that now made her little "sis" unavailable to answer the phone? Amy hung up and dialed again. Again, the phone just rang until it went to voicemail. Amy tried again and again and again.

God, what do I do? Amy pleaded in desperation. Suddenly, Cari's face flitted across her brain. With now-trembling hands, Amy scrolled down to her mentor's number.

After two rings, Chris's voice answered. "Cari's phone."

"Chris, this is Amy. I really need to talk to Cari," Amy spewed anxiously, never even saying hello.

"Uh...Cari can't really come to the phone right now. Can I have her call you back?" Chris half-chuckled.

"Where is she?" Amy shot back, in no mood for Chris's humor. A girl's life could be at stake.

"Well, if you gotta know, she's dropping some kids off at the pool," Chris replied with the same annoying snigger.

"What kids? Isn't it a little late to be swimming?" Amy frantically reasoned.

"Uh, okay...um, my wife is going to the bathroom," Chris finally explained directly. "Amy, what's wrong?"

"Can't you just bring her the phone?" Amy groaned. "It's Melia. I think she's in trouble. I just got a text—"

A knock at her door interrupted her thoughts. Amy glanced one last time at the previously slow-moving clock on her wall: 7:00 p.m.—Steven was right on time. *Perfect!* Amy groaned.

"One second, Chris." Amy propped the phone on her shoulder and hurriedly opened the door.

Standing in the hallway, Steven stood with a long-stemmed red rose and a giddy smile. "You ready to—"

"Hey, Steven." Amy tried to sound somewhat undistracted. "Actually, would you mind waiting a few minutes? It's a long story, and I'll explain later. Come on in." A confused Steven nodded and handed her the rose. She mouthed the words "thank you" as she returned to her phone call. "Chris, you still there?"

"Yeah, what's wrong with Melia?" Chris questioned, the humor gone.

Amy pulled out her desk chair for Steven to sit down and proceeded to pace back and forth. "I just got a text from her. She said she was scared. I tried calling her, but she's not responding. I'm freaking out that something is happening to her right now." Amy's nerves finally exploded. "I'm really scared! What if she is...?" Her voice broke, and she couldn't go on. She collapsed onto the edge of her bed, tears starting to leak uncontrollably from her eyes.

"Amy, Amy..." Chris tried to soothe her. "I'll tell you what. Cari and I will call her, and if she doesn't answer, we'll head over to her house."

Amy was so intent on hearing Chris's solution for Melia that she didn't even notice that Steven had stood up until she felt his arm wrap tenderly around her shoulder.

"Chris, what if she's not home? What if by then it's too late?" Amy spewed her thoughts out loud. Steven's strong arm held her tighter, and she noticed out of the corner of her eye that his eyes were closed; he apparently was praying.

"Let's not worry about stuff we can't control, Amy," Chris reassured her. "I'll call you as soon as I know anything...Are *you* going to be all right?"

"Yeah, I think so," Amy sighed.

"Good. Now who's Steven?" Chris asked with a hint of a smile.

"Uh, that's another story," Amy answered, shaking her head. "Now go help Melia."

Amy hung up and dropped her phone to her lap, wiping her wet cheeks and knowing her little bit of makeup was probably now completely ruined. She inhaled and exhaled trying to control her still turbulent emotions. Steven sat in silence, comforting her with a gentle squeeze. "Sorry about that," Amy finally mumbled, looking up into his warm—*green!*—eyes.

"Are you kidding me? Don't be ridiculous!" he consoled her. "Do you want to talk about it?" he whispered after a pause, his left arm still holding her tight.

Normally she would have felt awkward sitting on her bed so close to a guy she barely knew, but with Steven she felt comforted and safe.

"Back home, I led a small group of seventh-grade girls at my church," she began. "One of them, Melia, I got really close with...and something's fishy about her parents...I think they might be abusing her," Amy whispered, her throat constricting once again. She started bobbing her right knee up and down, trying to distract her tears. "A couple of minutes ago, while I was waiting for you, she texted me saying she was scared. But then when I tried to find out why, I couldn't get hold of her...She trusted me, and I can't protect her!" Amy broke down again, letting her head fall against Steven's strong shoulder. His left arm continued to support her as his right hand gently stroked her hair.

"You can't protect her. But God can," Steven replied, once Amy's tears subsided. "How about we ask for His help on this one?"

Amy nodded her head from his shoulder. Steven dove right in. With his limited knowledge of the situation, he prayed that God's hand of protection would surround Melia, that anything or anyone who tried to harm her or make her fearful would be stopped. He prayed that Melia would feel strong and sense God's loving presence all around her, no matter what. He prayed that Melia would be wise and find an escape if she was in harm's way, and that she would get back to Amy soon with a positive report. He thanked God for Chris and Cari and prayed that they would be able to find Melia quickly and resolve the situation, pulling her out of danger if need be. He prayed for Amy and her ability to trust God with the situation. He even prayed for Melia's parents, whatever the issue was with them.

Amy didn't know how long he prayed, but by the time he said "Amen," a refreshing calm had washed over her, and the tension had disappeared.

"Sorry I'm such a lousy date," she grimaced, wondering if she had blown her one chance with him.

"Yeah, I'm thinking pizza is probably not the first thing on your mind right now...and that you might want to wait around for an update?" Steven said. Amy couldn't quite pinpoint if it was a tone of disappointment or relief in his voice.

"Maybe I could get a rain check?" she offered, suddenly cringing at how forward that sounded. *What am I doing?* her brain complained silently, hoping Steven didn't take it the wrong way.

"Definitely." Steven interrupted her concerns with a smile.

He moved to leave, but seemed reluctant to end the night so quickly. He sat back down on the edge of her desk and started making small talk. He asked how Amy liked Stanford so far, asked about her classes and Intersect, her roommate, and any other friends she had made. They were great questions, but Amy was having a hard time being a good conversationalist and offered little more than brief answers. Her mind was just too distracted. After at least a half-hour of this, Steven finally stood up to leave with a promise that he'd call her tomorrow. Amy relished one last hug from his reassuring arms and walked him to her door.

Just then, her cell phone started to ring. She jerked it to her ear, praying for good news. "Hello?"

Steven paused, his hand on the knob.

"Amy, we're just leaving Melia's house right now." It was Cari.

"Did you find her?"

"Yeah, she was at home. We talked to her parents for a while and even looked at the text," Cari explained calmly. "She said she was only joking with you."

"What? No! Then why didn't she call me back when I called her?" Amy challenged. She desperately wanted this all to be a misunderstanding, but something just didn't sit right with her.

"Melia claimed her phone didn't ring. She never even noticed your calls 'til we pointed them out to her."

"No. Don't believe her! Can't you just see she's just covering up so she won't make her parents even madder? You need to go back and—"

Cari's calm voice interrupted her. "Or maybe Melia was just desperately searching for attention. Amy, I could be wrong, but her parents seem really nice. We always take these things seriously, but remember, things aren't always what they seem."

Amy wanted to keep on defending her case, but Cari's argument rendered her speechless. The thought that Melia's peculiar descriptions of her relationship with her parents might just be a way to get more attention had never even crossed Amy's mind. Had she been worried sick—and cut short her date!—over an eighth-grader's lie? "I need to talk to Melia," Amy finally mumbled.

"I think that would be a good idea. But remember: She's in eighth grade. Sometimes things feel more dramatic to them at that age."

"Thanks, Cari. For everything. I'll call you later." Cari said goodbye, and Amy threw her phone on her bed. "Ugh! I'm so confused right now," she complained, grabbing the top of her head. She collapsed into her desk chair and explained the conversation to Steven. "If all this has been a lie...ugh!"

"What does your gut say?" Steven asked softly.

"I'm really not sure," Amy whispered back. But deep down, she knew she was. "Steven, I'm sorry. I just need some time to think. I'll talk to you tomorrow, okay?"

Steven squeezed her shoulder and walked out, and Amy closed the door softly behind him. *Melia! What's going on with you?*

12:25pm | From: Steven | To: Amy
Any drama I should be aware of before I come up?

12:25pm | From: Amy | To: Steven
Haha. You're safe.

A WEEK HAD FLOWN BY since the Melia incident, and while Amy had talked to her several times, she still didn't feel satisfied with the answers Melia was giving her. But what could she do?

She waited eagerly for Steven's arrival. Finally, they had found a time to reschedule the rain-check date, after eight days of conflicting schedules and pre-arranged responsibilities. In the meantime, though, Amy had noticed a distinct increase in the attention Steven was giving her, especially at Intersect last Thursday night. Rather than giving the usual short greeting and long looks from a distance, Steven had greeted her with a friendly hug within moments of her arrival and had engaged her in playful conversation until it was time for him to open the meeting with a song. Afterward, he had sought her out again, and they'd chatted for almost twenty minutes before Renee finally dragged Amy away. The butterflies in Amy's stomach were definitely multiplying. She couldn't help but smile every time she thought of him.

A knock on the door brought Amy back to the present, and she skipped to open it.

"Take two!" Steven grinned, as he offered her another beautiful rose.

"Oh! Thank you so much!" Amy rubbed the soft petals against her cheek and took the flower over to the windowsill, where a vase still sat from the last rose he brought.

"Hey, do you have a bike here?"

"No," she admitted. That was the one thing she wished she had brought from home. She hadn't used a bike in years, but here, everyone did. Getting a bike was definitely on her to-do list for Christmas vacation.

"I didn't think so," Steven announced, unfazed. "So I borrowed one for you. I thought we could go to a park down the road and enjoy our delicious Do-mi-nos with a little picnic."

That sounded great to Amy. Once she got used to riding a bike again, they pedaled off to their destination, the pizza box tethered precariously to the basket on the front of Steven's bike. It was a warm Indian-summer Saturday, perfect for an outing. At the park, Steven pulled a blanket, two sodas, and some napkins out of his backpack, and they feasted on pizza while watching five-year-olds play soccer. As delightful as it all was, Amy couldn't help but remember some of the romantic picnics she and Jake had shared in the back of his truck, overlooking the ocean. As much as she liked Steven, in her heart she really missed Jake. But Jake was uninterested and gone, so Amy tried to focus on this new guy God had brought into her life.

Amy was surprised at how easy it was to talk to Steven. He was a great question-asker and an even greater listener, and before she knew it, she had told him all about her wild senior year and all the changes and struggles she had experienced since. Steven paid attention without passing judgment and asked for details with genuine interest.

His story was, by contrast, much simpler, as Amy finally found out. Steven told her he had grown up in a Christian home back East. His parents were loving, supportive, and close. He had never walked away from his relationship with God, even for a little while, and had never found the party lifestyle the least bit appealing—although he had many friends who did. They respected his convictions, and he kept praying for theirs. He'd had one serious girlfriend in high school, but they had broken up when they went off to college on different sides of the country, and although he'd dated a little at Stanford, he just hadn't found many good-enough options. He was graduating this spring and wanted to pursue a career in music while doing ministry on the side.

He was, in Amy's humble opinion, perfect.

"Oh, and I'm totally stuck on you," he added with that irresistible grin, and he poked her in the stomach. "From the moment I spotted you at the Root Beer Kegger, I knew there was something special about you...a sensitivity of your spirit. I knew you were worth pursuing and that I needed to ask you out...It just took a few weeks for me to work up the nerve." He smiled.

Amy melted. How could someone so perfect be so interested in her, especially now that she'd shared all her deep, dark flaws? The butterflies were spinning somersaults inside, and she couldn't help but giggle.

"Can I ask you a personal question?" Steven abruptly asked in all seriousness.

Amy nodded, breathlessly wondering what his next words might be. Even if they were "Will you marry me?" she was pretty sure her answer would be "Yes."

"Do you think you were so quick to react to Melia's story because maybe it's so much like your own?"

A wave of chills shot through Amy's body as she stared back at Steven's inquisitive gaze. Unconsciously, she leaned the slightest bit away from him.

"I'm sorry. I didn't mean to pry," he whispered.

Amy had never told anyone other than her parents about the abuse. *And look how that turned out!* her subconscious reminded her. She'd never told Cari...or even Jake. But before she knew what she was doing, she found a word already spewing out, a filthy secret she had bottled up for too long. "Yes," she mumbled, folding her knees up to her chest and wrapping her arms tightly around her legs. She rested her chin on her knees and stared at the tiny soccer players without really seeing them.

"What happened?" She heard Steven's voice breaking into her horrible nightmare. His hand rested gently on her back, and she didn't want him to move it.

"My uncle molested me until I was in kindergarten. I don't know how old I was when he started." Amy sucked in a deep, ragged breath, trying to still the sobs that threatened to erupt. She knew that none of it was her fault, but she felt dirty sharing the secret that she'd held onto for so long. Steven's fingers gently rubbed her shoulders and neck, giving her the strength to continue. "When I finally told my parents, my dad didn't believe me. He told my mom that I was making it up to get attention. Seriously? I mean, how does a five-year-old make up something like that? I'm not sure if my mom really believed me at first, but she ended up taking my side. She told my dad that she couldn't believe he trusted his brother more than his own daughter. Dad ditched us, my uncle disappeared to who knows where, and I haven't talked to my father since." Amy finished softly, unsure whether it felt better or worse to get it off her chest.

Steven covered her hand with his. "Wow," he whispered. "I can understand why you think you should believe Melia."

They sat in silence as Amy grappled with how complicated yet freeing it felt to have someone know her so well and accept her so completely. While it couldn't wipe away the horror of her past, it sure made her future seem brighter.

"I don't want to sound like I understand even a fraction of what you've gone through," Steven finally said. "But it sounds like you're still harboring a lot of bitterness against your dad. And I know it sounds like he deserves it, but..." Steven hesitated before speaking again. "I wonder if you'd find it easier to move on if you found it in your heart to forgive him. If you don't, he's going to just keep on hurting you, without even knowing it."

What! Where did that come from? Amy was blindsided, and she felt herself getting upset. "Excuse me?" she erupted unexpectedly. "What can you possibly know about moving on? What can you possibly know about harboring bitterness? What can you possibly know about forgiveness? You're right! You can't come even close to understanding. I don't know why I even confided in you." Her brief tirade was interrupted when her throat constricted and shut down to keep the sobs from exploding out of the depths of her soul.

"Amy, I'm sorry. I didn't mean to upset you. You're right...It's none of my business," Steven quickly recanted, moving once more to calmly rub her back.

His stable voice and soothing touch gradually mellowed Amy, and she hid her face behind her knees, ashamed of her outburst. *Well, if I didn't scare him away last time, I've definitely done it now!* she figured, as he pulled away from her and sat staring into his own little world.

"Look, I'm sorry," Amy began, faltering for the right words. "I don't know what got into me. I'm not usually this emotional." She chuckled half-heartedly, expecting her date to get up to leave at any moment.

When Steven finally looked over at her, his eyes were glistening. "Amy, I admire you *so* much for the amazing woman you are in spite of your past," he managed to get out, after some hesitation.

What? Amy was blindsided yet again. Was this some kind of joke? "I'm sorry I wasn't more sensitive," he continued, then stammered, "I hope you'll give me another chance."

"Are you crazy?" Amy practically yelled. "I thought you'd be running away from this psycho woman by now."

"Is that a yes, then?" One side of Steven's gorgeous mouth turned up into a shy smile.

"How can I say no?" Amy laughed, feeling the need to pinch herself. "But maybe next time, let's stay away from the deep, personal questions."

1:03pm | From: Grant | To: Jake
We're ranked 21 in the preseason poll

THE BUZZING OF HIS CELL PHONE jerked Jake alert in his afternoon physiology class, and he discreetly read the text. *Whosoever's idea it was to schedule a class right after lunch should have been fired,* Jake complained to himself. Every day, the struggle to keep his eyes open was brutal, and his steadily dropping grade was evidence of the losing battle. It would have been bad enough to sit through the dry lecture on a full stomach in a hall that was always a little too warm, but trying to do it when he was already exhausted from early-morning workouts and grueling afternoon practices and more homework than he knew how to handle meant only one thing: Jake was dying.

As he tried to refocus on the lecture about plasma membranes or something like that, the message of the text slowly registered in his brain. They were ranked 21st! Out of hundreds of men's college basketball programs in the country...after such a dismal season last year...in spite of Tony Anderson being picked up at the end of the first round of the NBA draft...somehow, Louisville had broken into the top 25! *Wow!* If physiology was cancelled for the rest of the semester and Jake received an automatic A, he still didn't think he'd be more excited.

And not only was the team ranked 21st, but Jake was poised to be a valuable contributing member to this top-ranked group of players. Opening game was less than a week away, and finally—*finally!*—he would get his chance to prove himself on the court.

Last week, the school newspaper had interviewed several of the younger members of the team, and Jake had been included in the front page picture under the title, "The Future Is Here." Of course, he was standing right next to Nate in the picture, which was annoying, but hey, Jake would take what he could get. Since the article came out, everywhere Jake walked on campus it seemed as if people were waving to him and smiling at him and treating him differently, special somehow. Jake loved it—especially since Nicole was now officially out of the picture.

For the first couple of weeks after their blow-up, Nicole had used all her charm to try to win Jake back. But Jake's anger didn't cool off enough to be affected until after she had grown tired of trying and moved on. She was still all over Nate—something that Nate seemed to exploit with enjoyment whenever Jake was around—but Jake also noticed her cozying up to one of the new freshmen on the team, a towering oaf from Alabama who talked bigger than he could back up on the court. Feeling a little used and even a little lonely, Jake knew he had to shake it off and save his game for the court. Besides, he'd already noticed a few hotties in some of his classes and—thanks to that newspaper article—they were definitely noticing him. Life was starting to feel like high school again—in all the old ways.

Jake's professor continued to drone on about the regulation and function of plasma membrane channels, and Jake glanced at his watch, hoping that the hands had crawled closer to the 1:30 release time. He noticed the date, and suddenly his brain transported him back to this time last year—when he was standing in a hospital room holding Amy's hand as she delivered their child. Something like a twinge of sadness pierced his subconscious. Today, he had a one-year-old daughter. *Crazy!*

Jake wondered what Emily was doing, what she looked like, and if her parents were going to have a party for her. He wondered if she even knew who he was. *Probably not, huh?* He hadn't seen her since she was only six weeks old. That was a sad realization. But then Jake thought about how far he'd come in the past year. After rearranging all his plans, he was back to living out his dreams, and in only three days, he'd get the chance to deliver as the backup point guard for the twenty-first best men's basketball team in the nation! Jake sat up a little taller in his seat, and an absent-minded smile played across his face.

Fifteen minutes later, the mind-numbing lecture was finally over, and Jake bounded up the stairs to his apartment to check out the online pre-season poll before racing off to practice. His and Grant's schedules ended up perfectly mismatched, so besides weekends and late nights, they were rarely home at the same time these days. Jake dumped his books on the coffee table next to his laptop and quickly flipped it open to turn it on. What seemed like an eternity passed, and it still hadn't booted up yet. Impatient and running late, Jake noticed the bouncing ball of Grant's screensaver on the desktop computer in his bedroom. Jake hurried into the perfectly clean room and immediately jumped onto ESPN.com. He clicked on the college basketball icon at the top of the page.

The preseason rankings were the lead article, and even though Jake already knew where his team stood, he found his heart begin to race as he scanned the page. He envisioned the jerseys of every team ranked before them and fantasized about opportunities to play against some of them.

AP Top 25			
RK	TEAM	RECORD	PTS
1	Kansas (65)	0-0	1,625
2	Kentucky	0-0	1,559
3	Duke	0-0	1,427
4	Syracuse	0-0	1,412
5	Ohio State	0-0	1,377
6	West Virginia	0-0	1,365
7	Kansas State	0-0	1,209
8	New Mexico	0-0	1,043
9	Villanova	0-0	961
10	Purdue	0-0	915
11	Butler	0-0	903
12	Temple	0-0	843
13	Michigan State	0-0	836
14	Georgetown	0-0	788
15	Tennessee	0-0	616
16	Wisconsin	0-0	603
17	Brigham Young	0-0	600
18	Pittsburgh	0-0	566
19	Baylor	0-0	550
20	Maryland	0-0	394
21	Louisville	0-0	382
22	Gonzaga	0-0	359
23	Texas A&M	0-0	290
24	Richmond	0-0	141
25	Xavier	0-0	106

For the moment, each team in the country was tied; but soon those 0s would be replaced with actual wins and losses, and the true contenders would rise to the top. Jake found himself visualizing what could happen to Louisville's ranking after they blasted through its first three lowly opponents over the next ten days. Arkansas, East Tennessee State, and Morgan State were guaranteed numbers in the win column, which would certainly move Louisville up. *Right?* Although the Louisville Cardinals were young, Jake had already started to drink Coach's Kool-Aid, believing their team was a team of destiny.

A full-screen ad suddenly popped up out of nowhere, shocking Jake out of his basketball revelries. Staring straight at him was a tanned, muscular man wearing a tight leopard-print Speedo. Above his chiseled face, the words "Looking for something a little...exotic?" attempted to entice Jake to click on the ad.

"Ugh!" Jake objected loudly, shutting off the monitor as quickly as he could. Still, the disturbing image lingered in his brain. *That's something I could have lived without ever seeing!* Jake nervously laughed out loud as if to defend his honor, even though no one else was around. He grabbed his gym bag and headed out for practice, determining that next time he'd be patient and wait for his own computer—it didn't have pop-up problems.

At the practice gym, Jake hustled onto the court where Grant was already pounding down jump shots. They had made a pact to come to practice fifteen minutes early each day, in hopes that the extra work might help them see a little extra playing time this season. Before even saying hi, Grant zinged a chest pass to Jake, who caught it and nonchalantly knocked down the seventeen-foot jumper.

"Sorry I'm late," Jake apologized, rotating three feet to his right to collect another pass from Grant. His second jumper went long off the iron.

"Did you see the poll?" Grant asked, leaping up to grab the rebound.

"Yeah, I saw it all right," Jake laughed.

Grant dribbled the ball out to the free-throw line, spun around, and put up a fade-away. *Swish.* "What's so funny?"

Jake grabbed the ball and popped it out to Grant two feet farther back. "You got some crazy gay pop-ups on your computer, dude," Jake smiled.

Mid-release, Grant's expression suddenly turned serious. His shot banked hard off the backboard. "What were you doing on my computer?" He sounded annoyed and fully ignored the ball that bounced right past him.

Jake pointed at the escaping ball, but he forgot about the rebound as soon as his eyes met Grant's piercing stare. "Sorry, man," Jake quickly backpedaled. "My computer was too slow, so I just jumped on yours. No big deal," Jake reasoned, flashing a friendly smile. He'd never seen this side of the guy before.

Something seemed to click in Grant's mind, and he shrugged and ran after the errant ball. "It's cool, man. I guess I just get possessive of my stuff," he yelled over his shoulder. He grabbed the ball from half court and threw a perfect outlet pass to Jake in the right corner. Jake faked a three and raced toward the basket, leaping just barely high enough to dunk.

"If only Mr. Exotic could see me now!" Jake boasted.

"Who?"

"Oh. You'll see," Jake chuckled, picturing his unassuming roommate's face when he turned his computer monitor back on.

✚ ✚ ✚

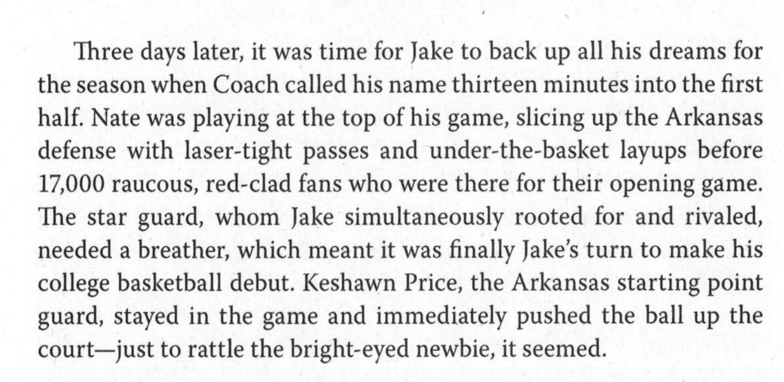

Three days later, it was time for Jake to back up all his dreams for the season when Coach called his name thirteen minutes into the first half. Nate was playing at the top of his game, slicing up the Arkansas defense with laser-tight passes and under-the-basket layups before 17,000 raucous, red-clad fans who were there for their opening game. The star guard, whom Jake simultaneously rooted for and rivaled, needed a breather, which meant it was finally Jake's turn to make his college basketball debut. Keshawn Price, the Arkansas starting point guard, stayed in the game and immediately pushed the ball up the court—just to rattle the bright-eyed newbie, it seemed.

"Hands up!" Coach hollered at Jake, as Keshawn picked up his dribble at the top of the key.

Jake's hands shot in the air, intently focused on stopping the ball. But with a three-inch height advantage, his opponent quickly lobbed a picture-perfect alley-oop to a leaping teammate, who slammed the ball hard down into the basket.

Crap. Jake grimaced, punishing himself for such a lame start. Jake ran to the baseline to collect the inbound pass, and Keshawn followed hard with a full-court press before Jake could even get in a dribble. Undeterred, Jake juked right and then jolted forward left, flying by Keshawn toward the weak side of the basket. Nomis posted at the top of the key, and Jake shot him a hard chest-pass and continued sprinting right toward the basket as Keshawn lagged a step and a half behind. With precise timing, Nomis tossed the ball back to Jake, who went up for an uncontested layup. *Swish.* A shot of adrenaline surged through Jake's body as he tried to just play basketball and not celebrate his first official college basket. But he couldn't stifle the smile that crept to his face.

The smile was short-lived, though, as the Arkansas inbounder turned and lobbed the ball effortlessly back to the other side of the court. *Where's my guy?* Jake panicked, just in time to watch the ball land perfectly in Keshawn's hands for a free layup right back in his face. Jake hustled down the court to retrieve his own inbound pass, but he could see Coach holding up his hands on the sideline to call a time-out. Before Jake even made it off the court, one of the assistants patted him on the butt and let him know Nate was going back in. Disgusted, Jake glanced at the game clock. He'd been in for less than sixty seconds.

Obviously, regular season ball was a whole different game than summer league.

In the second half, Jake and Grant both got in for the garbage minutes. With Louisville up 20 with only three minutes left, both coaches emptied their benches to play out the end of the game. As Jake jogged past Nate to relieve the star, his teammate flashed him an arrogant smirk and winked. Instantly, Jake felt his blood begin to boil. At some point during the offseason, Jake had resolved that he would be okay with just being the backup. But in that moment, he swore to do whatever it took to earn the starting spot in the lineup. Although they wore the same uniform, Nate was now an enemy.

Later that night, Jake tossed and turned in bed. Here he was, living out his childhood dreams, playing his first basketball game for the Louisville Cardinals, and they'd won. He'd even scored seven points and dished out two assists in his measly four minutes. But the victory felt hollow and unsatisfying. Nate's cocky wink replayed in his brain over and over, merging with that horrible smirk he'd given when Jake had caught him in bed with Nicole.

"I hate Nate Williams," Jake growled aloud to his empty room. Grant was out with his new friend Peter, so there was no one there to hear him. Just saying it out loud helped for a moment, but all too soon the images once again flickered across Jake's brain, bringing him right back to square one.

In frustration, Jake kicked off his sheets and plopped himself down at his desk, where he flipped open his sleeping computer. For the third time in not even two weeks, he found himself wondering what Amy was doing and typed her name in the Facebook search box. *How pathetic have I become?* he chided himself, as he waited for her page to load. He wasn't sure if he sincerely missed her or if he just missed having *someone*, but both felt about the same at the moment.

Her profile popped up, and his heart sank. Staring back at Jake was some guy in a V-neck sweater holding a guitar. Amy's radiant face rested on his shoulder as she hugged him from behind. Jake scrolled down her profile.

Relationship Status:
In a Relationship

Feeling like an icicle had just stabbed his heart, Jake slammed shut the cover of his laptop and collapsed back into bed. *Perfect.*

7:43am | From: Cari | To: Amy
Drive safely. Can't wait to see you this weekend at church!

BEFORE AMY KNEW IT, the fall quarter was over, and it was time for Christmas break. She couldn't have been more relieved. Finals week in high school was nothing compared to the past week of torture at Stanford. By the end of her last exam yesterday afternoon, her head hurt so badly from cramming so much information into her brain that she thought it might explode. Of course, she knew from her Brain and Behavior class that *that* was physically impossible, but you never know. That class had provided her with some pretty useful information, which she had started to put into practice in her conversations with Melia. Amy still wasn't satisfied with Melia's excuses about that weird night almost two months ago, but in other areas, Melia was maturing and outgrowing her quirks. Amy was proud of her.

Amy unplugged her microwave and newly defrosted refrigerator, gave one last pass to straightening up her room, and packed her toiletries in her suitcase. Renee had left for home last night, and now Amy was finally following suit. *Finally!*

The last few weeks since Thanksgiving, Amy had been growing more and more homesick. She'd spent the holiday with Renee's family, only thirty minutes away in Oakland. It had been wonderful…but it wasn't home. Nevertheless, Amy had been blessed by Renee's family's hospitality and warmth, and she absolutely loved the Sunday service at Renee's church. It was like nothing Amy had ever experienced before. By the end of the service, Amy was confidently joining the rest of the congregation in yelling out "Preach it!" or "Testify!" or "Mmmmhm-mm!" after every other sentence of Renee's father's lively sermon.

But in two days I get to go to New Song! Amy reminded herself. She couldn't wait to see her "family" there again. She locked up her room and lugged her stuff downstairs, eager to get in the car and start the long drive back to Southern California. But there, sitting on the front bumper of her minivan, Steven was waiting for her with a smile and his guitar.

"I thought you'd already left," Amy laughed, leaving her suitcase by the van door to give him a hug. They had said their goodbyes the night before, knowing that they both had early mornings today—Amy to get on the road and Steven to catch a flight.

"I couldn't sleep last night, so I just started writing down lyrics. But there's no way I could wait two weeks to play my new song for you," Steven explained as he started to strum. "It's called 'Amy'."

Thrilled goose bumps popped up all over Amy's body as Steven locked eyes with her and proceeded to sing the song:

She's leaving today, won't see her for a while
But just one thought of her and I can't help but smile.
Maybe I'll call her every day she's gone.
Maybe I'll just write her a goodbye song.

She stands out in a crowd, like the sun in the sky.
Her heart's a mile deep, her smile a mile wide.
Maybe one day I'll get to meet her mom.
Maybe I'll just write her a goodbye song.

She inspires me every day without even trying
I'm the luckiest guy alive, there's just no denying.
Maybe I'll call her every day she's gone.
Maybe I'll just write her a goodbye song.

Without even thinking, Amy planted her lips on Steven's unsuspecting mouth. She didn't care if there was a fourth verse, and she didn't care if their first kiss was in the middle of a dirty parking lot. Nobody had ever written a song for her. "That was so cheesy," she laughed. "I loved it!"

Steven leaned his guitar against the car and wrapped his arms around her waist. "I should write you cheesy songs more often."

"Well, you've set the bar pretty high now. That's what it takes to get a kiss," Amy joked, patting him on the chest.

When she finally drove away twenty minutes later, she couldn't wipe the smile off her face. She rolled her windows down, turned the stereo up full-blast, and joyfully sang along at the top of her lungs to the CD of worship songs Steven had given her. *Life after Jake Taylor,* she couldn't help thinking, *it's not so bad.*

✚ ✚ ✚

Once she arrived home ten hours later—the traffic had been gruesome—Amy was immediately confronted with the only part of her two weeks back in Oceanside that she wasn't excited about: living under the same roof as her mom. Amy had assumed she'd be out doing her thing, but surprisingly, Sherry had made it a point to be home to greet her daughter. She'd made a special dinner and cleaned the house, and for the first five minutes after Amy's arrival, she was all smiles and hugs.

But no sooner had Amy's stuff been brought in and the two of them sat down to the meal than her mother tore into one of her diatribes about the injustice of being a single woman in today's world. It apparently seemed to Sherry that the world had organized a meeting without her in order to plan all the ways to make her life a living hell. Bosses were unfair, coworkers were nasty bad words, and men were scum. Amy was supposed to appreciate how lucky she was that she'd been able to escape Oceanside and experience the good life before succumbing to all this. Sherry lamented that she'd never had that chance.

The complaining went on and on, without even a single question about anything in Amy's life. Sherry didn't know—and obviously didn't care—about Amy's classes, her roommate, her *boyfriend*. Amy tried to listen, but several hours into the conversation, the past week of finals and the ten-hour drive began to take its toll on her eyelids, and she struggled half-heartedly to stay engaged.

"Did you hear what I just said?" her mother questioned from across the couch, which they had moved to at some point in the evening.

"Maybe I'll just write her a goodbye song," Amy mumbled dreamily under her breath.

✦ ✦ ✦

"Good morning! Good morning! Good morning! It's time to rise and shine!" A familiar voice broke into Amy's deep sleep the next morning.

Groggily, Amy opened her eyes to see Andrea's smiling face leaning over her.

"You *are* awake!" Andrea cheered.

"I am now," Amy groaned. "What time is it?"

"Just after ten." Her spirited friend flopped down next to her on the bed. "So are you going to sleep your vacation away or go running with me?"

Amy glanced over at her bedside clock to make sure she wasn't getting pranked. "Unhhhh," Amy grunted. "I've missed you, Andrea, but I'm glad we're not roommates."

Unfazed, Andrea sprang back off the bed and danced around, ready to go. She was wearing a long-sleeve camouflage shirt over black running shorts with matching camo headband and wrist sweatbands.

Amy propped herself up and shook her head. "What are you wearing?"

"Oceanside's become a dangerous place since you left," Andrea replied with a straight face. "You gotta blend in, or those snipers will get you. Pichew! Pichew!" She shot at the invisible enemy with her fingers.

Amy laughed and held out her hand for Andrea to pull her to her feet. "You better go easy on me. I'm not a high school cross-country star."

"Whatever, Miss Five-Miles-a-Day-and-Six-on-Saturday! I bet you'd whup my butt if we raced."

"Well, let's not put it to a test, okay?" Amy smiled.

Although they had talked at least once a week on Facebook or by phone, Amy had forgotten how much she enjoyed Andrea's company. Andrea's planned visit in the fall had been delayed due to a last-minute emergency with her grandmother, and three months had been far too long to be apart. Andrea's exuberance and optimism were infectious, reminding Amy to suck every last drop out of her one and only life.

The two of them caught up with all the "latest," from the latest race times Andrea had posted, to their latest workouts, to the latest cool things they'd been learning in their classes, to the latest on what it was like to be Christians on their very secular campuses. Oh, and of course, Amy filled Andrea in on all the latest Steven developments. Andrea was giddy with excitement and said she couldn't wait to meet him when she came up for her rescheduled visit in February.

"Oh, hey, did you hear that Jake broke up with that girl?" Andrea asked out of nowhere.

The goose bumps that rose on Amy's skin with that four-letter word surprised her—*What's your problem, Amy? You've moved past him.* "No." She tried to sound uninterested as they approached an intersection and waited for the light to turn green. "I didn't even know he was dating someone."

"Well, he's not anymore," Andrea cheerfully reported, still jogging in place as Amy bent over to stretch her hamstrings.

"How often do you and Jake talk?" Amy asked as casually as she could manage. She'd forgotten that even though *her* relationship with Jake had ended so abruptly, that didn't mean it had for everyone else. Then Amy had a suspicious thought: *Is Andrea angling to see if it would be all right to pursue a relationship with Jake?*

"Never," Andrea sighed. "That dork doesn't keep in contact with anyone...I just read that on his Facebook page a while ago."

Amy breathed a little easier as the light turned green and they made their way back along the beach. The Jake conversation passed, but Amy found that her brain kept wandering to questions about him...and especially this rebound relationship. She had a distinct feeling she knew who it was with.

After stretching and talking for another forty-five minutes, Amy and Andrea hugged goodbye and made plans to hang out several more times before Amy headed back to Stanford.

Back at home, Amy enjoyed a giant bowl of Cheerios and the luxurious feeling of not having to rush anywhere. For the rest of the day, she was absolutely free. She thought about how nice it would feel to curl up with a good book and wondered if Steven would make good on his promise to call her every day. She stretched her arms out wide and sighed with contentment. Life was good.

After putting her dirty dishes into the dishwasher, she headed back to her room, where one of her mother's infamous Post-It notes awaited her.

Hey Ames!

Since you've got nothing better to do today, how about cleaning out your closet? I'm making a trip to Goodwill this weekend and would love to donate some of your things so your room will be a little more presentable when you go back to school.

Thanks!

Mom

"Hmph!" Amy protested, watching her plans to relax fly out the window. She sulked all through her lengthy shower, but in the end she buckled down and begrudgingly went to work on her mom's assignment.

She'd had no idea how many clothes she had accumulated over the years! Even though most of her wardrobe was in Stanford, the closet still had eight pairs of her jeans and pants, over twenty shirts, and more shoes than she could count, not to mention all the maternity clothes and other random clothing stuffed into her tiny closet. In the past, she could have convinced herself that she needed seven different pairs of black shoes, but today she easily parted with stuff, feeling good that it could help others. It was almost therapeutic to watch her closet chaos simplify down into a nicely folded, generous pile of giveaways.

Four hours later, Amy wearily hung up the last few things she was still keeping, like her old cheer uniforms, a couple of her favorite formal dresses, and some outfits she could still wear when she was at home on breaks. Her clean, organized closet was so inspiring that she decided to move on to her dresser, which was nearly empty and only took about a half-hour to sort through. Then it was on to her desk. She purged tons of old schoolwork and useless souvenirs, keeping only the best and most memorable pieces.

She was on such a roll that she enthusiastically pulled out the bottom drawer without even thinking...and that's when she saw it. There, peeking out from under an unused spiral notebook, lay a raggedy cardboard box that she'd intentionally hidden there several years ago. She gasped and felt the blood drain out of her face.

Amy shoved the drawer closed and leaned back against her bed. Her head fell back, and she stared up at the ceiling. *Why did I have to open that drawer?* Amy thought angrily, debating what to do.

Her cell phone rang on her bedside table, and she reached over to get it. She read the screen: *Steven.* Ten minutes ago, she would have been thrilled to talk to him, but suddenly it was the last thing she wanted to do. She tossed the phone onto her bed and sat moping.

But even after the phone stopped ringing, Steven's past encouragement started coursing through her veins, and Amy reached over to grab the box out of the drawer. Her hands trembled as she held it in her lap, and finally she lifted the lid. Inside, almost two dozen unopened envelopes addressed to her from her father sat begging for her attention. Another desperate urge to throw the box away and never think about it again flashed through her, but Amy resisted the urge and did the opposite.

With shaky fingers, she dug to the bottom of the pile and pulled out the oldest letter, postmarked three days before her sixth birthday. Inside was a corny card, a five-dollar bill, and the simple note, "Happy Birthday, Ames! I love you. Dad."

Hmph! Amy thought. *Not even an "I miss you." Typical!* She ripped into the second one, dated just before Christmas. Again, a cheesy card, five bucks, and a lame note. She tore through the next seven or eight, which were all the same. Every birthday and Christmas, he'd fulfilled his fatherly duty by sending her a few bucks and a stupid card. As if that really counted toward being a father. *No wonder Mom hates him so much!* Amy started to wonder if that's how Jake would have ended up if they had kept Emily. Judging by this past year, it didn't seem so far-fetched. And for the first time, she was actually grateful that she'd given her daughter the chance to have both a mom *and* a dad. An unsettling wave of emotion rolled over her, and she paused for a few minutes to pull herself together.

Amy continued carelessly opening each envelope, more for the money than anything else. At what must have been her tenth birthday, her dad increased his gift to ten dollars, and for Christmas that year, he included a twenty. She noticed a change of address on the return label. He must have gotten a new job or something, she figured. And then his stupid notes started getting a little longer...and not as stupid. He started asking her questions and telling her about his life. It still wasn't much, but at least it showed effort.

And then, there was an envelope that didn't correspond to any holiday, postmarked March 23, almost seven years ago. Amy had to admit she was a little curious, and she slit the envelope open. Rather than a card, the envelope simply contained a piece of notebook paper wrapped around a newspaper clipping. Amy unfolded the newsprint first, suddenly horrified to find herself looking into the icy eyes of the man who had molested her so many times. Amy was shocked to realize how much this man resembled the memory she had of her father; if it hadn't been for the man's mustache, it could have *been* her father. *Could that have something to do with why I hate my dad so much, too?* she wondered. In the yellowing photo, her uncle stood in handcuffs and a prison jumpsuit. The headline above the picture read, "Man Accused of Raping Girl, 9, Sentenced to Twenty Years to Life." Stuck to the article was a sticky note with one simple word:

JUSTICE?

Amy gingerly held the article, unsure of what to think or do. So her uncle was now behind bars. And her father knew the truth. The two things she had wanted most for so many years had just dropped into her lap. *So why don't I feel any better?*

She realized she was still holding the piece of notebook paper in her hand, so she looked at her father's neat, all-caps handwriting. Desperate to see what he had to say, yet fearful at the same time, she slowly let her eyes scan the page.

DEAR AMY,

I TOTALLY UNDERSTAND WHY YOU WANT NOTHING TO DO WITH ME, SO DON'T FEEL LIKE YOU HAVE TO RESPOND. I JUST NEED TO SAY WHOLE-HEARTEDLY: I'M SO, SO SORRY THAT I DIDN'T BELIEVE YOU. I'M SO SORRY THAT IT TOOK ME THIS LONG. I JUST COULDN'T BELIEVE THAT MY OWN BROTHER WAS CAPABLE OF SUCH EVIL, BUT NOW I REALIZE THAT

MY DOUBT HAS CAUSED ANOTHER INNOCENT CHILD TO BE HURT, AS WELL. HOW DID I NOT BELIEVE MY OWN DAUGHTER? I KNOW THIS IS NO EXCUSE, BUT I WAS YOUNG, SELFISH, AND STUPID. AND IF YOU CAN EVER FIND IT IN YOUR HEART TO FORGIVE ME, I'D LOVE TO TRY TO MAKE IT UP TO YOU.

LOVE,
DAD

(408) 555-7689
RAYMUNDBRIGGS@EMAIL.COM

A million thoughts and questions ran through Amy's mind all at once as the letter fluttered from her limp fingers into her lap. Did her mother know? What if Amy had read this seven years ago…how different would everything have been? Should she contact him?

With renewed interest, she dove into the remaining unopened envelopes of different shapes and sizes. The next one told her he had moved again. The next card told her he had gotten remarried. The next one talked about him going back to church, and from there, each letter got even better, sharing Bible verses that he'd picked out for her and prayers he'd prayed for her. All of the letters ended with apologies and the plea that someday she'd give him a second chance.

Amy hesitated at the final envelope, the one he had sent for her eighteenth birthday. She slowly slid her finger under the flap of the envelope, releasing the old glue from its grip, not sure if she wanted this experience to end. She pulled out the card, and fifty dollars fell out. But what struck her most was the sad tone of her father's words.

DEAR AMY,

THIS IS GOING TO BE MY LAST LETTER I WRITE FOR A WHILE UNLESS I HEAR SOMETHING BACK. YOU'RE AN ADULT NOW—THE SAME AGE I WAS WHEN YOU WERE BORN. WHAT AN AMAZING DAY THAT WAS! THE MOMENT I SAW YOU, IT WAS LOVE AT FIRST SIGHT. I KNOW I'VE SCREWED UP AS YOUR FATHER IN SO MANY WAYS, BUT I'VE NEVER STOPPED LOVING YOU. I'VE PRAYED A THOUSAND TIMES THAT GOD WOULD SOMEHOW LET ME GO BACK IN TIME

AND DO THINGS DIFFERENTLY, BUT I GUESS THAT'S IMPOSSIBLE. JUST KNOW THAT I PRAY FOR YOU EVERY SINGLE DAY, AND I HOPE THAT ONE DAY I CAN APOLOGIZE TO YOU IN PERSON. I'M STILL LIVING UP IN NORTHERN CALIFORNIA WITH MY WIFE, OLIVIA. PLEASE FEEL FREE TO CALL OR WRITE ANYTIME.

LOVE,
DAD

(408) 555-7689
RAYMUNDBRIGGS@EMAIL.COM

Tears oozed from Amy's eyes as she read and reread the desperate words of the man she had despised for so long. While hurt and regret still weighed heavily on her heart, she couldn't hate him anymore. She looked at the return address in the top-left corner of the envelope. His address was in Sunnyvale, which Amy was pretty sure she had seen on a freeway sign somewhere on the way to Stanford.

"Honey, are you home?" her mother's grating voice called from the living room as the front door slammed shut.

Amy took several deep breaths as she tried to compose herself and figure out how to respond. The sound of her mother's footsteps creaked down the hallway, and Amy felt her heartbeat quicken.

"Oh, there you are." Sherry nonchalantly stood in the doorway.

"Why didn't you tell me Uncle Harold was in prison?" Amy spewed from her seat on the floor.

Sherry looked stunned. She grabbed the door frame. "I see you finally read your father's letters," she replied, without answering the question. Just the way she spit out the words "your father's" reminded Amy how much her mother loathed him. No wonder Amy had grown up feeling the same way.

"You should have told me!" Amy rephrased her complaint, clutching the newspaper article in her hand.

"Well, Amy..." Sherry was obviously still taken aback by the question. "I didn't want to make you relive any horrible moments if you didn't have to."

"Mom, do you know how many times I've questioned if maybe the whole thing was just a repeating nightmare? If you and daddy got divorced over something that didn't even—"

"Amy, I never questioned you for a second," her mom interrupted. "It was your father who doubted you—and it's better that he left us."

"But now he believes me, Mom. He's believed me for seven years!" Amy held up the article and its accompanying letter.

"Hey, you're the one who chose not to read his letters!" Sherry bit back. "I was simply doing my duty as a *mother* to protect you…something your *father* knows nothing about!"

"Don't you get it, Mom? After all these years…" Amy's voice trailed off as she processed the reality of the situation. "I have to contact him."

Sherry's eyes darkened. "No. I don't get it, Amy." Her voice was cold. "What difference does it make whether he believes you *now* or not? The fact is he *never* wanted to be your father, and he sure doesn't know how to be one now. We're both better off without him."

Silence filled the room for a good thirty seconds as they stared at each other. Finally, Sherry turned and walked away. Amy's head sank between her knees, and tears flowed down unabated. She didn't know what to think and knew even less what she should do. Maybe her mother was right. But it couldn't hurt to find out for herself, right? Amy resolved to hold off on making a decision until she got back to school. Until then, she would simply pray about it.

7:13pm | From: Amy | To: Steven
I read my dad's letters today.

6:36pm | From: Dad | To: Jake
Vegas baby Vegas

6:36pm | From: Mom | To: Jake
Can't wait to see you honey

FOUR WEEKS AND SIX WINS into the season, Jake exited the airport terminal and boarded a hotel shuttle in the glamorous city of Las Vegas. The Cardinals' road game at the University of Nevada at Las Vegas was the closest Jake had been to the West Coast in almost a year, and he breathed in the warm, dry air appreciatively.

Jake read his parents' texts with mixed thoughts. He missed both of them and was glad they were coming to his game. But their attempts at reconciliation had deteriorated since Glen had accepted a promotion at work two months ago, and Jake wasn't sure if he wanted to get in the middle of that tension. Besides, this was *Las Vegas,* and even though most of the guys on the team weren't even old enough to gamble, they were all looking forward to a good time—one that wouldn't be nearly as fun with parents around. But after dropping the bomb that he wasn't coming home for Christmas thanks to basketball games two days on either side of the big holiday, Jake knew he had to concede to letting them meet him in Las Vegas—especially since his parents were willing to make the five-hour drive. Jake couldn't help but find that a little ironic, since they couldn't seem to make it to most of his *home* games in high school!

As the shuttle pulled up to their hotel on the Strip, Jake saw his parents standing out front. In spite of their smiles, there were several obvious feet of awkward space between them as they waited with their arms crossed, mouths unmoving. A single glance at Glen and Pam Taylor made it evident that spending time together was not one of their favorite pastimes.

"There they are," Jake muttered loud enough for only Grant, who was sitting next to him, to hear.

"Dude, your mom is even hotter than she was last summer!" Grant joked in a much louder voice, drawing most of the team into Jake's personal observation.

Heads turned and eyes peered out the window in search of this hot Mrs. Taylor. When they found her, a string of whistles and catcalls sprang out from all over the van.

"Gentlemen," Coach prompted as he stood. He was so universally respected by the team that it usually only took a glance from the future Hall-of-Famer for the guys to be on their best behavior, so everyone immediately piped down. "Now let's let Taylor off first so he can go hug his mommy." He winked at Jake, and the team erupted in laughter.

Jake rolled his eyes and smiled. When the shuttle pulled to a stop, he grabbed his carry-on and suitcase and took advantage of Coach's instructions. By this time, his mother was eagerly standing at the exit door, and Jake stepped off the bus directly into her excited embrace.

"Oh! It's so good to see you!" Pam gushed, holding her son's face in her hands to look at him more closely.

Jake wiggled free and stooped to give her a hug. "Good to see you too, Mom."

"Oh, how *cute*," Nate Williams mocked as he walked by, leading the rest of the pack.

If anyone else had said that, Jake would have laughed it off, but coming from Nate, it made Jake want to slug him in the face.

"What a jerk. Don't I get a hug, too?" His father's deep, matter-of-fact voice snapped Jake out of his momentary brooding.

Jake stepped a few feet over to his dad, who was already decked out in a bright-red Louisville basketball T-shirt. "Good to see you too, Dad." Jake patted his old man on the back.

Coach was the last to get off the bus, and he approached the Taylor reunion. "Mr. and Mrs. Taylor, I just want to say that you should be proud of your son. It's an honor to coach him." He extended his hand to Glen, who shook it enthusiastically.

"The honor's all mine. I've been watching you coach since—"

"Thanks for taking care of our son," Pam interrupted, reaching out to give the coach a hug. "Do you mind if we take Jake out to dinner?"

"Not at all. Team meeting in fifteen minutes, and then he's all yours until curfew."

They followed the rest of the team into the hotel lobby.

An hour later, after being warned to represent the team well, not to do anything stupid, and to get a good night's sleep for the next day's battle on the court, Jake sat across from his parents at an In-N-Out Burger, both hands gripped ravenously around a Double-Double, animal-style. Pam had anticipated her son's craving for his beloved In-N-Out and had mapped out directions to the nearest fast-food treasure of the West.

"Did you guys travel here together?" Jake asked, mouth full, trying to start up a conversation at the otherwise silent table. They had driven to the restaurant in his dad's new BMW, and the tension between his parents was so thick he would have needed a chainsaw to cut through it. Jake couldn't imagine them making the five-hour drive together.

Dipping a few French fries into his chocolate shake, Glen quickly replied, "Nah, I'm driving directly to a business meeting tomorrow right after the game. Your mother flew."

Jake couldn't help but wonder if his father had planned the business meeting after deciding to come out, or if he was coming to Vegas anyway and the game just happened to fit into his schedule. Stuffing the negativity down, Jake focused on enjoying his burger while Pam talked on about flying back right after the game to get home in time for a women's event she was coordinating at church.

For the next thirty minutes, the conversation stayed shallow and sluggish. His dad asked him how his grades were. Jake lied and said they were fine. His mom asked if he was still dating Nicole. He told the truth and said no. His dad asked if he was having fun. Mostly true:

Yes. His mom asked if he was drinking too much. Relatively true: No. His dad asked if he'd been putting in extra practice time. Yes. His mom asked if he'd checked out any other churches. No. The barrage of questions seemed endless until Jake turned the interrogation around on them and asked how marriage counseling was going. Silence...and irritated glares between them.

Jake took a long sip of soda and nearly laughed out loud at how ridiculous this family "reunion" really was. He wondered how long it would take before one of them got remarried and even *this* kind of reunion would be impossible. And then a faint realization flickered across his mind: Even if it all *was* just a façade, it was oddly refreshing for the three of them to be together as a family. As Nicole had said that one fateful night, *It's comforting in a weird way.* Her tempting voice echoed through his head, and images from that first kiss unexpectedly sprang to life. Jake's mind drifted away until his mother's voice piped in, competing with Nicole's body for center stage in his head.

"Amy's coming home for Christmas," Pam dropped the weighted observation.

Jake focused on the ketchup dripping from one of his last French fries onto his tray.

"Aw, would you cut that out?" his dad protested. "Who cares?"

For once, Jake was grateful for his father's outburst. While part of Jake would love to see Amy, that all-too-happy picture of her with Guitar Guy kept playing through his mind, and he knew that seeing her now would be worse than having a jackhammer rip through his brain.

"I was just thinking that it might have been nice for the two of them to sit and talk," Pam persisted. "That is, if Jake would have been willing to squeeze in a visit home, finall—"

"Pam, didn't you hear him? He's got a busy schedule," Glen interrupted, ignoring his soon-to-be ex-wife's exasperated glare.

Jake knew that avoiding home was a pathetic decision and that he'd have to return to California sooner or later, but basketball was a great excuse for now. Jake easily preferred relegating a trip back to his former life to the "later" category.

Pam went back to picking at her lettuce-wrapped burger while Jake and Glen wolfed down the rest of their Double-Doubles in silence.

On the drive back to the hotel, insignificant small talk resumed, and Jake was only too glad to be dropped off and watch them drive away to their own rooms at the timeshare they'd purchased several years earlier. Jake walked back into the lobby, the unsettled gnawing at his soul feeling raw. When he got back up to his room, Grant was gone, as were all the other guys. Whatever Jake was missing, he didn't mind. He flopped onto his bed and turned on the TV.

2:04pm | From: Chris | To: Jake
Got a whole crowd here at the house to cheer ya on to a win!

JAKE COULDN'T HELP BUT SMILE thinking about Chris's text as he warmed up with his teammates before the game. He hadn't talked to his former youth pastor in months, but Chris still texted him and left him messages periodically. And as much as Jake tried to maintain a separation from home, he had to admit that it was nice to know that people out there cared. Jake stretched his leg and looked up in the stands behind the Louisville bench, where his parents sat watching. In spite of their stiff interactions, he caught a smile between them every once in a while, and both seemed eager to cheer him on. Jake stepped up for his turn in a give-and-go drill, finishing it off with an easy pass to Grant for a ten-foot jumper. Let the game begin.

The Thomas & Mack Center just off the UNLV campus was filled with a sea of loud Rebel fans in red and white, ready to cheer their team on to victory. As the students began to stomp their feet, Jake actually could feel the court shake. Starting off strong with a 6-1 record, the Runnin' Rebels were now knocking on the top-25 ranking as the season rolled into the holidays. Paired with Louisville's perfect six-game start to the season, this was expected to be a pretty fierce matchup. ESPN had set up a full crew to televise the game nationally, and all the local sports shows were talking about the game. After Jake's shaky debut, he had averaged about ten minutes per game with just shy of seven points and three assists, which was nothing to be ashamed of. If Nate Williams wasn't averaging 17 points with eight assists and sitting as an early favorite to make the all-Big East squad, Jake would have been perfectly content.

From the moment UNLV gained possession of the jump ball, it was clear why they were nicknamed the *Runnin'* Rebels. The action felt more like a track meet than a basketball game, and with every possession they pushed the ball up the court. Within the first minute and a half, they had scored four quick breakaway baskets, and it wasn't until three minutes in that the Cardinals started to find their own rhythm. Louisville's first string clawed their way back, however, and by six minutes they brought the game to within two points. Back and forth, back and forth the game pressed on, with scoring as well as steals and turnovers in much higher numbers than usual. Calling a quick timeout, Coach turned to the bench three minutes earlier than normal, sending in fresh legs to relieve some of the winded starters.

Ready for his moment, Jake made an immediate impact, diving for a loose ball and hurling it in the direction of Nomis before sliding out of bounds. Nomis hurled it down to Grant, who converted for a quick two points. *Tie game*. Jake stuck to his man on defense like skinny jeans, and the shot clock almost expired before the Rebels threw up a lucky shot that just barely tipped into the basket. *Down two*. Jake grabbed the inbound pass and slowed the pace to give his teammates a chance to set up the offense.

"Take three!" he yelled, holding three fingers up into the air.

The play unfolded, and Jake blew by his man into the paint, dishing the ball out to a wide-open Jamal in the corner for a three-pointer. *Up by one*. A rush of adrenaline pulsed through his body as he sprinted back to play defense. He was in the zone. Five minutes later, Coach slapped him on the butt for his great hustle, as Nate went back on the court to finish out the first half. They were up by four.

With the score tied 58-58 and twelve minutes left in the game, Jake got the call again. He had to admit, although he still felt compelled to dethrone Nate from his starting position by the end of the season, Jake loved the rush of Coach sending him in off the bench with only a second's notice.

Jake didn't waste this opportunity either, singlehandedly breaking through the full court press and holding on to the ball from coast to coast. He leaped up, reaching beyond the outstretched fingers of the Rebel 6'10" center for a nice layup high off the glass. The whistle blew as the ball left Jake's hand, giving him two points and a foul shot. Two possessions later, Jake no-looked a pass to Grant as he had done thousands of times in their pre-practice shoot-arounds, and Jake couldn't help throwing his hands up in the air as his roommate's jump shot swished through the net.

Down the stretch, Coach put Nate back in, but Jake couldn't be too disappointed with his thirteen points and five assists. The Cardinals pulled off a two-point victory, and Jake celebrated with his teammates. Their win-streak would continue.

After shaking hands with his opponents and jumping up and down in a team huddle, Jake looked up to see his parents making their way onto the court.

"Congratulations, honey!" Pam threw her arms around her son in celebration. "You were by far the best player out there!"

"Thanks, Mom." Jake grinned, wondering how many of the other players she had been actually watching.

"I'm proud of you, son," Glen said nonchalantly, extending a handshake.

In spite of his father's stoic face, Jake felt a tingle down his spine. For so many years he had longed to hear those words, but instead he'd only received criticism or unhelpful advice. Now those words seemed so monumental, yet so oddly complacent. "Thanks, Dad," Jake muttered back unsteadily.

"Taylor, you comin'?" Grant's familiar voice called from a few feet back.

Jake had to rush to the postgame team meeting, but he was reluctant to hurry the moment with his dad. "Yeah, man, be right there," he answered. "Can you guys stick around a few minutes until our meeting's done?" he asked his parents.

"Jake, you know I'd love to," his mom said regretfully, her eyes glistening with what looked like tears.

"I've gotta get your mom to the airport," his dad explained, "and then I've gotta get on the road myself. You go out and have some fun with your friends." Glen smiled and reached out to shake his son's hand once more, winking knowingly as he pulled him into a man-hug. Jake felt him slip some money into his palm.

Jake reached out for both his parents and awkwardly pulled them into a group hug. "I gotta run," he apologized. "But it really means a lot that you came. I promise I'm coming home for at least part of the summer."

After another kiss on the cheek from his mom and a slap on the back from his dad, Jake waved goodbye and ran after Grant and the rest of the team, who were heading toward the locker room. Jake did a double-take when he noticed his roommate's friend Peter hanging back by the bleachers. *What's he doing in Vegas?* Jake thought to himself, but he didn't have the chance to ask Grant.

After several praises, a few comments about what the team needed to work on before conference play began next week, and some warnings about misrepresenting the university in downtown Las Vegas, the team was finally free to shower up.

"So, your parents came all this way, and you're ditching them, huh?" Grant asked, squirting a couple of puffs of cologne before he buttoned up his perfectly pressed dress shirt.

Jake pulled his favorite striped polo over his head and smiled at himself in the mirror. "They needed to hit the road." Jake shrugged, still a little in shock over his father's encouraging words. "Dude, did I see Peter out there waiting for you? Does he live in Vegas?" Jake asked.

Grant slammed his locker and glared at Jake. "He finished his finals early and was already home in Flagstaff. It's pretty close."

"Flagstaff? That's like in Arizona," Jake puzzled.

"Yeah, but it's only like three hours away," Grant defended, sounding irritated.

"Three hours! If I didn't know better, I'd swear that dude has a crush on you!" Jake laughed just as Jamal and Nate turned the corner with towels wrapped around their wet bodies. The two starters stood still for a moment as if they had just walked in on something they weren't supposed to hear.

"What?" Grant challenged more than asked.

The guys burst into laughter. "I don't know, man, but all I heard were the words, *dude* and *crush*." Jamal raised his eyebrows. "You boys have something you want to share?"

Jake grabbed his crumpled-up towel and threw it at the team captain's head. "Hey now!" Jake laughed. "I was just joking about one of his friends."

"Wait, is it that dude that's always waiting for you after practice?" Nate questioned. "I thought I saw him here today."

"His name's Peter. He drove three hours to see our boy here." Jake slapped Grant playfully on the back, ignoring the growing discomfort on his roommate's face.

"Wow!" Jamal affirmed, as a couple of other guys from the team stopped to see what was going on.

"Are you talking about that queer dude with the pinstriped shirt?" one of them asked.

"Oh, he is *so* gay all the way," Nate decided for everyone. "If he asks to sleep over, I'd make a run for it."

The whole cluster of guys erupted, and even Grant chuckled a little. Jake hated to laugh with his rival, but it *was* kind of funny.

"Seriously, Grant," Jamal interrupted. "Do you think he might be putting from the rough?"

Laughter erupted again. Jake knew it was immature, but he found himself unable to stop. In his senior year of high school, he had sworn to never again be a guy who laughed at others' expense, but Grant was smiling too, so was it really that big of a deal?

Twenty minutes later, the team emerged from the locker room to walk through the mostly empty arena toward the rental van. Peter waited by the exit, a Louisville towel slung over the shoulder of his lavender pinstriped shirt.

"Homo," Nate sneered under his breath as he passed by. Several of the guys around him burst into laughter.

Peter's smile sank into a look of wounded disappointment, and Jake glanced over at Grant, who was definitely not laughing this time.

Squeezing every drop out of their midnight curfew, Jake and his teammates raced to their rooms at 11:58 p.m., just in time for the coaches' bed checks. Sometime during the last few hours, the team had splintered into several different groups, and thanks to tagging along with Nomis, Jake had found himself in the company of Jamal and Nate all night—his dream come true. Grant had disappeared hours ago after their under-aged cluster nearly got caught at some blackjack tables and had to make a mad dash to evade security. Jake assumed he was with Peter, away from the annoying razzing of the rest of his teammates.

Sliding the key card into their hotel room door and shoving it open, Jake was immediately greeted by a hard pillow to the face.

"What the—"

The same pillow whirled toward his face again. Jake blocked most of the impact from the second blow with his arms and twisted the weapon from his roommate's grip. "Dude, what's wrong with you?"

"You suck, man." Grant threw a towel at Jake and went into the bathroom to brush his teeth.

Jake tried to keep a straight face. He hadn't been in a pillow fight since seventh grade. "You're really pissed, aren't you?" he asked, watching Grant's ferocious scrubbing in the mirror.

Grant spat his toothpaste into the sink, rinsed out his mouth, and shoved past Jake, their shoulders knocking on his way out of the bathroom. Jake sat on his bed and silently watched his angry roommate.

"Peter travels out of his way to root us on, and you…all you could do is laugh in his face?" Grant practically shouted. "You are such a jerk, you know that?"

Jake sat speechless. Grant was his best friend at Louisville, and Jake was distressed that he had let him down. He thought back to that party in high school when Jonny had showed up in a Wizard Wars costume. Everyone had taunted and jeered at him, and even though Jake hadn't even met Jonny yet, he knew it didn't feel right. After that night, he had promised himself never to be like that again. So what had happened earlier?

Grant was right. Peter didn't deserve it, and Jake knew he was the one who had started it all. "I…I'm sorry man. I just—"

"Just wouldn't stop," Grant shot back venomously. "You know, now I get why your 'friend' in high school shot himself! Some *friend* you are."

Jake sagged as if he'd just been socked in the gut. When Amy had thrown that same indictment at him months earlier, Jake had nearly hit her. Now a new flood of emotions raced through him as he glanced at his reflection in the mirrored closet door, and he had the sudden urge to shatter the image staring accusatorily back at him. Had he somehow become everything he'd sworn to never become again? He slowly turned back to Grant. "Dude, I'm so, so sorry. I don't know. I guess I just got carried away."

"Too bad Peter's not here to hear that," Grant snorted.

"Well, I'll tell him next time we see him, okay? Look, I know you're not gay and all. I mean, I've only lived with you for, like, how long now? But seriously, you've gotta admit that Peter's a little...you know..."

"A little what?" Grant wasn't giving Jake any slack.

"Okay, I'm not making fun of him or anything, but come on, don't you think it's kind of weird that another dude would drive so far—"

"Dude, don't you get it?"

"Get what?"

"Peter's my *friend*, Jake."

"And...?"

"Are you seriously going to make me say it?" Grant shook his head.

"Say what?"

"Jake...I'm gay."

12:17pm | From: Cari | To: Amy
You should come to the middle school Christmas party tonight 630

WITH ALL THE KIDS OUT OF SCHOOL and on vacation, the New Song lobby was already a buzz of activity when Amy showed up just after six. While she had dreaded walking into her own home, walking into her church home overwhelmed her with a sense of warmth and welcome, as she hugged her way through all the overjoyed students and volunteers. So many people were glad to see her. Just as Amy spotted Cari talking to a couple of students on the other side of the lobby, Amy was clobbered by a bunch of arms that hugged her and hands that covered up her eyes.

"Guess who?" a sweet voice giggled.

Just as Amy was about to name the girls in her small group, other fingers started tickling her, and Amy could only manage a squeal as she tried to wriggle away. Once free, she gathered the three girls in a tight group hug.

"Alyx! Gabbi! Lindsey! It's so good to see you guys!"

Immediately, the three girls started babbling about everything that had transpired since Amy had left them three months earlier, and Amy could barely keep up. She smiled and tried to follow their rapid-fire chatter as she realized how much she had missed her girls. But one of them was glaringly absent. "Hey, where's Melia?" she interrupted.

"In there," Gabbi shrugged and pointed toward the youth room, and then continued on with her story.

Amy tried to lead her girls in that direction as she listened, but before long, a cluster of eighth-grade boys walked by, and suddenly Amy was no longer the center of their attention. As the girls ran off after the boys, Amy reveled in the moment of silence they left behind.

"Oh my gosh, Amy Briggs!" Cari screamed enthusiastically and ran up to her in much the same way that the three girls had just run off. Amy embraced Cari as she said, "You've got a pretty big fan club, even if you can't compete with the boys!"

"It's nice to be back." Amy couldn't wipe the grin off her face.

Chris finally broke away from a conversation with one of the parents and came over to give Amy a warm hug. "I can't tell you how many girls said they were coming just to see you. You were our top advertising strategy!" he said, before turning to welcome a group of rambunctious sixth-grade boys. "High-Five Tuesday!" Chris shouted to the group, holding up his hands to slap some skin.

Amy turned back to her mentor. "If only that was true about Melia," she sighed. "She hasn't returned any of my texts or calls since I've been back. I wanted to hang out with her."

"Go talk to her," Cari said with a hint of concern. "She's already back in the youth room."

Amy chided herself for feeling nervous. What if Melia didn't want to talk to her? Turning the corner, Amy spotted her in the youth lobby engrossed in a game of foosball with a tall, gangly boy. *Well, maybe that explains it,* Amy figured, thinking Melia had been bitten by the boy-bug the way her other girls had. Amy waved hello to a number of other students but made a beeline to the girl she'd taken under her wing ten months ago.

She took a deep breath. "Hey, Melia."

Melia looked up, and her face instantly turned white. Something like fear flickered through her eyes, and then she quickly returned to her game. "Hey," Melia finally responded, focusing her attention on spinning the tiny plastic men.

The tall boy took advantage of her brief distraction and pounded a shot through her goal. "Oh!" he shouted triumphantly.

Melia scowled.

"Can we talk?" Amy prodded gently.

"I'm busy," Melia shot back, spinning her players so violently that the whole table shook.

Amy stood in silence, watching the ball jerk around the little soccer field as she searched for a suitable response. The longer Amy watched, the more flustered Melia seemed to get. The boy scored again and did a funny little victory dance.

"Whatever." Melia abruptly shoved the handles and walked away from the game toward a table in an isolated corner.

Amy followed her, and they both sat down. Melia crossed her arms tightly across her chest and tilted her chin slightly up in the air.

Lord, help me out here, Amy pleaded in her mind. "So, what's up?" she started simply.

"Nothing."

"Are you having a good vacation so far?"

"Sure."

"Look, I still have on the bracelet you made me." Amy smiled, showing Melia the fading but still colorful BFF beaded bracelet she hadn't taken off since Melia had tied it on her three months earlier.

"Great."

It wasn't much, but Amy thought she detected a hint of a smile tickle the corners of Melia's mouth. "So, you got any fun plans for your time off? Are you going anywhere for Christmas?"

"No."

Amy sighed, realizing that small talk wasn't going to get her very far. "Well, why haven't you responded to any of my texts or calls?" she finally blurted.

At this, Melia looked down and clenched her fists so tightly that her knuckles turned white. A teardrop splashed on her arm, and finally she mumbled under her breath. "My parents don't want me to talk to you anymore."

"What? Why?" Amy questioned, not sure what to believe from Melia any longer.

In the background, Chris's unmistakable shout informed the students that the party was about to start, but both girls sat motionless as students raced by. After the stragglers had emptied out of the game area and into the youth room, Melia finally spoke up. "They took my phone away," she faltered, and a few more fat teardrops fell to her arms. In between breaths, she muttered, "If they catch me talking to you, they'll hit me."

"They'll hit you?" Amy repeated, not sure how to respond.

"See! You don't believe me. I knew you wouldn't!" Melia hissed under her breath. "You're no different than—" Melia burst into tears before even finishing the sentence.

Amy reached out to wipe the tears off Melia's arm, but the eighth-grader jerked away. "Melia, it's not that I don't believe you." Amy whispered, inching closer. "It's just last time you shared something like that, you then said you were joking."

"But I wasn't," Melia whispered back in such a hushed voice Amy almost missed it.

"But...? Then...? Why...?" Amy stammered, unable to formulate a complete thought.

"I—I don't know. I had to lie," Melia sobbed.

"Why? What happened?" Amy asked, aware that she was in way over her head. She reached out her hand and brushed it through Melia's red hair. This time she didn't flinch.

"Sometimes I come home and my parents are..." Melia faltered. "You know..." She made a hand gesture that looked as if she was tilting back a can.

"They're drunk?" Amy tried to help her out, picturing all-too-clear memories from her own past.

"Yeah...something like that. Well, that time they were really bad...and I kind of got scared. But by the time Cari and Chris came over, my mom had somehow pulled herself together, and she got to the door first and..." Melia paused, seeming to search for the right words. "It just didn't seem worth it." She shrugged.

"Well, did they hit you? Threaten you? Hurt you?" Amy asked, her voice getting tight.

Melia simply nodded, her eyes boring holes into the tabletop.

"Melia! That's not okay," Amy protested, fighting back her own tears. "Has it happened again since then?"

Melia shook her head no, then subtly nodded yes and raised her eyes to see if anybody else was in the room. "Not until they saw how excited I was that you were coming back," she said. She slowly raised the sleeve on her right arm to reveal three fresh cigarette burns on the soft flesh of her forearm. "They're afraid you're onto them," Melia explained.

Amy watched in horror, realizing that her worst fears were indeed a reality. "I need to tell Cari," she said.

Melia shook her head as her eyes bugged out, and she yanked the sleeve of her baggy green Christmas sweater back down over the injury. "No, you can't! That would ruin everything!"

"Melia, it's only to protect you."

"No! Don't you get it? It doesn't happen very often. As long as I stay out of their way, they usually don't bother me. But if you tell Cari, then they'll never let me come to church ever again," Melia said.

Amy sat back and tried to figure out what she was supposed to do. "Melia, I'm your friend." She cradled Melia's wrist in her hands and pressed her beaded bracelet next to Melia's matching one.

"Amy, you have to promise that you won't tell anyone." Melia yanked her hand away and rose to her feet. "Otherwise, I'll just deny it. I'll tell everyone that I just did it to myself."

"But what if something even worse happens?"

"It won't," Melia assured her.

"But what if it does?"

"Okay," Melia conceded. "If *anything* else happens, I promise I'll call you right away, and I'll do whatever you tell me to do. Just don't make me break up my family."

Her last words hit too close to home. Amy knew all too well what it felt like to carry around the weight of thinking you broke up your family. And she wasn't sure it was worth it. Amy sighed and looked into

Melia's eyes. "Fine. But if *anything* happens, you'd better call me!"

Melia reached out and hugged her. "I promise!" She smiled, as if relieved of a heavy burden. As the two stood up from the table to join the party inside the youth room, Melia abruptly turned to Amy with a grin. "Sooooo, can I see a picture of your new boyfriend?"

"What? How did you know that I have a new boyfriend?" Amy shot back, wondering why Cari had spilled the beans. *I'm going to have to talk to her about confidentiality!*

"I didn't." Melia smiled deviously. "What's his name? Is he cute?"

"Ah!" Amy couldn't believe that she had been outsmarted by an eighth-grader. She pulled out her cell phone and showed her cunning little friend a picture she had taken of Steven after Intersect one night, the one she'd made her Facebook profile picture. "His name's Steven. Pretty cute, huh?" Amy finally broke out in a grin. "And you should hear him sing!"

"Can I be the flower girl?" Melia looked up from the picture hopefully.

✚ ✚ ✚

Nearly three hours later, Amy stumbled into her bedroom and sank onto her bed. In spite of the festive spirit she had managed to exhibit throughout the rest of the party, no amount of Christmas cheer could snap her out of the deep sadness she felt for her young friend. The worst part was that she'd promised not to tell anyone. *Was that really the right thing to do?* Amy debated for the umpteenth time in her head.

Suddenly, Amy felt a deep longing to know more about her own father. *At least* he *never laid a finger on me!* She heaved herself up from her bed, sat down at her desk, and pulled the box of now-opened letters out of the bottom drawer. She leafed through them and re-read the final letter several times. *I wonder what he's doing for Christmas?* She'd decided not to contact him until she returned to school out of respect for her mother, but she couldn't help but wonder what he looked like, how much he'd changed, and if he was really as nice as his letters made him seem to be.

Amy opened up her computer on a whim, and her hand directed the mouse toward her favorite distraction: Facebook. Although she assumed this would be a futile search, Amy typed the name "Ray

Briggs" into the Search box. When the screen loaded the sixth photo at the bottom of the page, an unmistakable face stared back as if it knew her. She hadn't seen her father in over a decade, and his curly dark brown hair was now mixed with gray, but his sparkling blue eyes were unmistakable.

Amy gazed intently at that bottom box, but it wasn't actually her father that she couldn't take her eyes off of. Instead, she was fixated by a young boy that her father was holding tightly in his arms. Dressed in an all-yellow soccer uniform, the tanned boy beamed with a happy smile.

"I have a brother," Amy whispered, goose bumps prickling over her arms.

8:02pm | From: Chris | To: Jake
I thought you barely touched him ☺

SHOWERED AND DRESSED in his street clothes, Jake sat alone in the bleachers of the downtown Yum! Center arena long after the Georgetown Hoyas had escaped with a four-point victory on Louisville's home court. Jake flipped his cell phone around in his hands, battling the agitation that gripped his heart like an iron fist. Although this had been the worst game of Jake's short college basketball career, it was far from the only thing on his mind.

What is my problem? Jake groaned, staring blankly at the hardwood court in front of him. The custodians clattered around in the empty stands cleaning up after the game, but Jake was no more interested in them than he was in the lone ant crawling toward popcorn crumbs five feet away.

Jake felt more lost than he had since the week after Roger died. He glanced back down at Chris's text message. Jake hadn't talked to him in months, but lately he'd been longing to reconnect, especially since Grant's Las Vegas confession three weeks ago.

In some ways, nothing had changed since his closest friend and roommate'd admitted that he was gay. But in other ways, *everything* was different. After an initial thirty seconds of stunned silence in that

Las Vegas hotel room, Jake had finally blundered through a panicked list of questions that had surfaced in his mind.

"Are you sure?"

"Yeah."

"For how long?"

"I don't know... maybe all my life?"

"Who else knows?"

"Nobody...just you and Peter."

"Not even your parents?"

"Hell no!"

"But you don't look gay..."

"What does gay look like?"

"I don't know, but ummmmm..." Jake hesitated, wondering how he would phrase the next question.

"No, Jake, I don't find you attractive."

It was definitely reassuring, but Jake had still slept in a T-shirt and gym shorts that night. And since then, he couldn't help but feel self-conscious around Grant. Jake now found himself constantly glancing over in his roommate's direction before stripping down, and he never walked around their apartment in just his boxers anymore. He made sure to lock the door when he showered, and he cringed whenever Grant walked out less than fully dressed.

Jake felt guilty even thinking this way. He would have never considered himself a homophobe in the past—but he'd never been in a situation that was quite so personal. Jake didn't find every girl attractive, so it made sense that Grant wouldn't find every guy attractive. But then again, even an unattractive girl waltzing around half-naked in their apartment could tempt him over time. Thoughts like those totally weirded Jake out.

And what about the locker room before and after practice? The crowded, steamy room full of muscular men showering together definitely didn't seem harmless anymore. Again, Jake imagined the heterosexual equivalent: showering with girls. Just thinking about it raised his internal thermometer. Of course, Grant's situation wasn't exactly the same—Jake pictured sharing a locker room with the groupies that surrounded the team at all the parties, or the hotties in some of his classes, or even the tall blondes on the volleyball team. That would be pretty awesome! But no, the comparable situation would have to be the women's basketball team. Jake started picturing some of them. Sure, they might not be bad-looking, but whew, they were tough. Jake considered how intimidating it would feel to be surrounded by girls who had absolutely no interest in him whatsoever—while he was in such a vulnerable state of nakedness. Then he thought about getting caught looking at them, and he shuddered. They'd kick his butt.

Suddenly, Jake felt a new compassion for Grant. *Is this why he was usually so reserved?* Jake wondered how his teammates would respond if they found out that one of the guys they showered with didn't have the same fascination with women that they did, and he didn't want to even think about what guys like Jamal and Nate might do. The burden of Grant's secret felt like a hand grenade with the pin dropped out. He'd kept secrets for people before, but this one felt so ominous and heavy.

Although neither mentioned it, the stress was taking its toll on Jake's relationship with Grant. Jake could feel them drifting apart—like a rubber band slowly being stretched past its elasticity. They still showed up to practice fifteen minutes early for their extra shooting practice together, but their conversation had shrunk to surface-level questions and unintelligible grunts. Even their unspoken habit of sitting next to each other on road trips had been broken when Jake grabbed a seat next to Nomis on the way to their game against Seton Hall. When Grant had boarded a few minutes later, Jake thought he had detected a hurt expression across his face, but Grant simply smiled and nodded as if everything was fine and slipped into an open seat a few rows back.

Back at the apartment, they tried to carry on the way they normally did, but they were no longer alone. Jake could almost see the giant elephant that now crouched in the corner as they talked about almost every topic except the one that was really on their minds. In an already stressful life of basketball and school, this mess was the last thing Jake needed.

So tonight, all the anxiety Jake had been carrying finally crossed over to his performance on the court in their conference game against Georgetown. After erratic play throughout the first half, Jake was unhappily relegated to the bench for most of the second half. The score was closer than they'd expected, and Coach probably didn't want to risk it while Nate was playing solid. But with five minutes to go in the game, Nate needed a breather, and Jake was finally called back in. An intentional hard shoulder bump from his teammate started Jake off with a sour attitude, and it only got worse from there.

Jake's defender stole a pass the first time down. The second time, he blocked what Jake thought was an open shot. The Hoyas converted both turnovers into points on the other end. Jake kept struggling to find his open man, and the Louisville lead slipped to a one-point deficit. Playing down low, Grant just didn't seem to be working hard enough to get open. And no one else was coming to Jake's rescue, either. Jake felt his irritation growing.

Back on defense, Jake raced around the front court to keep up with the speedy Georgetown point guard, when suddenly he ran head-on into a hard pick that leveled him to the ground. The "no call" by the referee enraged Jake, and he reacted without thinking, pushing his opponent in the back as he blocked out for an offensive rebound. The ref saw Jake's shove, and Jake was immediately called with the technical.

"What!" he exploded, walking toward the ref.

Grant and Nomis ran over and pulled him away before he did anything else stupid, but that was the end of Jake's playing time for that game. Coach had no patience for a player who couldn't keep himself under control.

With Georgetown's last basket and two made free throws, the Cardinals sank to five points behind, and not even Nate was able to dig them out of the hole. They added a fifth defeat to their loss column, and no one was happy with that. Jake couldn't help but feel the weight of responsibility, which wasn't helped by the fact that none of the guys, including Grant, spoke to him in the locker room afterward.

So here Jake sat alone in the stands, wondering what his life had come to. The weight on his shoulders felt unbearable, but he had no one to talk to, no one who cared...except Chris. And while Jake had done everything he could to avoid his old friend up until now, he suddenly found himself scrolling down the cell phone's screen to call him.

Jake paused, his finger poised to press the Talk button, deliberating the ramifications of his next movement. He glanced around nervously. The nearest custodian was three sections away, bopping away to the beat in his headphones. Jake let his finger push down and silently pleaded for voice mail. On the third ring, Chris picked up.

"Jake!" the familiar voice greeted him excitedly.

"Hey, Chris." Jake did his best to attempt enthusiasm. "How did you know about the game?"

"It's a little thing I invented a few years back called the World Wide Web," Chris joked. "Seriously, I've seen better refs in a Foot Locker."

Jake leaned back in his fourth-row seat and smiled. He had missed Chris's dorky sense of humor. "How often do you watch my games?"

"Let's just say I've used you as an excuse to spend a little extra time checking scores and stats online this past year. Don't tell Cari, okay? This was like the third or fourth game I've actually been able to watch."

"Great," Jake groaned. Of all the games to stumble upon, Chris had definitely scored a doozy tonight. "Sorry I played so crappy."

"Are you kidding me?" Chris shot back. "You should have heard me cheering at my computer screen when you first got in the game. Cari and Caleb ran in from outside, and we all watched the rest of it. When that guy screened you, man, we were all yelling at the refs."

Jake imagined the Vaughn family hunched over Chris's laptop in their dining room. "How's Caleb?" Jake broke into a smile just thinking about the little guy who used to latch onto his leg whenever they saw each other.

"Now that's where I have a little beef with you." Chris sounded a bit more serious. "After the game, Caleb went outside and found one of his little neighbor friends to play ball with. Next thing I knew, Caleb just pushed him hard to the ground and said, 'I'm Jake Taylor. You better watch yo'self.'"

Jake sat up in his seat. "What? Are you serious? I'm so sor—"

Chris's laughter interrupted Jake mid-sentence. "Jake, I'm just messing with you, man. Caleb would never hurt a flea, unless you count his smothering hugs. He does have a pretty solid drive to the hoop, though, I must say."

Jake chuckled softly. He missed those guys.

"But seriously, Jake," Chris broke in. "I'm really glad you called. How are you doing?"

That's what Jake loved about this guy. After months of silence and unreturned texts and calls, a "Where have you been?" would definitely be in order. But Chris was never one to live in the past, and his genuine concern set Jake at ease. Jake knew there were multiple ways he could answer the question, but he was tired of pretending.

"Well," he began. "The past few weeks have been…interesting." Jake paused, the issue that was really bothering him feeling a little too awkward to just blurt out. But when Chris didn't reply with a question, Jake continued on. "You're not gonna believe it…but my roommate just told me he's gay." Again, Jake waited for a response, but Chris remained silent on the other end. "Nobody else knows but me…the whole thing is kind of freakin' me out."

"Why?" Chris finally commented, apparently unfazed by the new information.

"Why?!" Jake protested. "Did you hear what I just said? The guy I share a room with likes *guys*."

"Does he like *you*?"

"No. I mean, we're friends, but he doesn't *like*—like me in that way," Jake clarified. "But things have changed between us. I feel so uncomfortable now, so self-conscious. And now *I* have to keep this big awkward secret."

Jake heard Chris sigh heavily. "Have you put yourself in his shoes, Jake?" he asked.

"Yeah…at least, I've tried." The custodian with the headphones was making his way to Jake's section, so Jake stood up and climbed the steps to the upper deck.

"Well, maybe I'm way off, but can you imagine how scary it would be the first time *you* came out? Especially in a setting like a college basketball team. It seems like that would be a secret you would guard with your life, until something happened to make you want to—or *need* to—let someone else in on it."

Jake was listening.

"You wouldn't tell just anyone," Chris continued. "It would have to be someone you absolutely, completely trusted, someone you knew would have your back no matter what, someone you could count on to be your ally if things went bad…And he chose you! What a compliment."

Jake snorted. *A compliment?*

"Jake, you have a huge responsibility here."

Several silent seconds lingered as Chris's words sank to the pit of Jake's stomach. Jake knew he'd dropped the ball the past few weeks. But he wasn't sure that he wanted to pick it back up. Beside, Chris was a pastor. Wasn't it his job to tell Jake what the Bible said about homosexuality?

"So, are you saying that it's okay to be gay?" Jake skirted Chris's challenge.

Chris chuckled, surprising Jake. "Jake, I'm saying that's not the real issue here."

"Then what is?"

Chris took a moment to mull over his words. "The real issue is how you can best love your friend and show him Jesus. Jake, that's your responsibility."

A pang of guilt stabbed Jake's conscience. As if Jesus had been a priority in his life lately. Even before this whole gay thing, Jake hadn't done anything close to showing Grant—or any of his other teammates, for that matter—Jesus. Probably none of them would even consider Jake a Christian. He sure hadn't given them any evidence of it.

"Uh, Chris," Jake responded hesitantly. "I haven't exactly been the greatest Christian here." That's an understatement!

"Good thing there's grace, huh?" Chris said without a hint of a guilt trip.

"Yeah," Jake found himself agreeing. "Good thing."

9:07pm | From: Grant | To: Jake
Where r u

9:11pm | From: Grant | To: Jake
Seriously dude

9:13pm | From: Grant | To: Jake
We need to talk

IMMEDIATELY AFTER HANGING UP with Chris, Jake was barraged by Grant's annoying messages. Jake sighed, not quite ready to face the music, but knowing he couldn't hide out in the gym forever. Chris's insights had helped a little, but Jake still wasn't sure he felt like talking about it with Grant. He trudged stiffly down the bleachers and out of the deserted gym across the parking lot to his lonely truck.

As Jake drove back to campus, Chris's words rattled around in his head. *You have a huge responsibility...What a compliment...How can you best love him?* But what if Jake didn't want the responsibility?

What if he didn't know how to love him? Life was going just fine until Grant came out with this bombshell...at least, kind of. Immediately, one of Chris's questions from a year ago popped into Jake's mind: *What if God wants more from your life than 'just fine'?*

Again, Jake sighed. He parked his truck and plodded up to his room. Opening the door, he was shocked to find Nate, Jamal, Bojan, Nomis, and a few other guys from the team, all waiting for him with crossed arms and angry looks. Grant stood with them.

'We need to talk,' huh? "Hey, guys." Jake faked a smile to try to cut through the layers of awkwardness hovering in the room. Nobody smiled back. If anything, his teammates seemed irritated by his casual greeting.

Nate stepped up. Just watching Nate strut forward as if he was in charge made Jake want to turn around and walk right back out the front door.

"You lost it today, Taylor," Nate said, his eyes glaring at Jake as if he were a little kid. What made it worse was the other guys all nodding their heads in agreement. Even Grant.

"Look, I'm sorry." Jake tried not to sound defensive. "I know I let the team down."

"'I'm sorry' is just not gonna cut it." Nate's husky growl reminded Jake of Clint Eastwood about ready to draw his gun.

Is this really happening? They were talking about one technical foul. It's not as if he was the first to ever get one called. Sure, it had contributed to the loss, but they were struggling before Jake's errors. There was no way he was going to take the brunt of this. "What else do you guys want from me?" Jake crossed his arms and widened his stance, his eyes throwing daggers back at Nate.

Nate took a threatening step closer to Jake, breathing arrogantly in his face. An urge to slap the punk coursed through Jake's veins, but he resisted and merely clenched his fists.

Jamal stepped forward, his body forcing Nate aside. His hand rested on Jake's shoulder. "Look, man, it's obvious that something has been bothering you the last couple of weeks, not just tonight. Whatever it is, you need to deal with it."

Out of the corner of his eye, Jake saw Grant tense up. "It's nothing. I'm fine." Jake ignored his roommate and focused on Jamal. "I was just playing crappy, and I let that Georgetown guy get under my skin. It won't happen again."

Nate piped up. "Look, if you're still pissed off about Nicole, you can have her. I got plenty of other women—"

Jake laughed out loud at Nate's generosity. "I don't want the tramp," he sneered.

Nate stepped back into Jake's face, but Jamal and another teammate held him back.

"Don't talk about my girlfriend like that!" Nate snarled.

Jake couldn't help but enjoy the stifled snickers around the room.

"Look," Jamal cut in. "If you say it's nothing, then fine. Prove it. But if you ever pull another stunt like today and cost us a game..."

"OK, fine." Jake shrugged, holding up his hands in surrender, even though he still thought they were nitpicking over an incident that wasn't entirely his fault. He turned and brushed by Nate on his way to his room, bumping his shoulder.

"Dude!" Nate grumbled, but Jamal must have shut him down, because nothing followed.

Jake slammed his door shut and flopped onto his bed, listening to the muffled conversations and shuffled departures. After a few minutes, complete silence enveloped the apartment. Jake assumed it was just a matter of time until Grant ruined that, and he wasn't disappointed. A quiet tap on his door signaled Grant's intrusion.

"'We need to talk,' huh? Thanks a lot, bro," Jake said icily.

Grant pulled out Jake's desk chair and sat on it backwards. "I appreciate you not telling the guys, you know," he mumbled, boring a hole in the rug with his stare. His fingers traced the curve at the top of the chair.

Jake just huffed.

"Well, don't pat yourself on the back too much," Grant looked up, his eyebrows furrowed.

"Excuse me?"

Grant rolled his eyes. "Look, we both know what's been really bothering you. Sure, you didn't rat me out to the guys, but maybe that's just because you're too afraid to face it yourself."

"Face what?"

"Jake! I don't care about your stupid technical! I don't even care so much that we lost the game," Grant seethed. "What does piss me off is that you can't just be a man and come out and deal with it."

"Be a *man*, huh?"

"See, there you go again, taking your little pot shots while avoiding the real issue."

"Avoiding the real issue? Hey, I'm not the one who lured my roommate into a blindside attack!"

"Well, I'm not the one who can't keep my head in the game!"

"Oh, so this is *my* fault?"

"It's not mine!"

"Then whose is it?"

Their escalating shouts died out into a heavy silence. Their locked glares gave way to averted gazes. Thirty seconds ticked by. The only thing that moved was a spider crawling up the windowsill.

"Why did you have to tell me?" Jake finally broke the silence with the quiet question that had plagued him countless times since Las Vegas.

Grant's scowl vanished, and the eyes staring back at Jake held a look of insecurity. "I don't know, man," he stammered. "I guess I just thought you would understand."

"Did you think I was gay?" Jake shuddered.

Grant smiled faintly, shaking his head. "No, dude. You are as straight as a board." He rested his arms on the chair back. "I guess I've just heard you talk about your friend Roger, and I kind of thought…"

An image of Roger walking all alone down the road with a few cruel classmates making fun of his limp flashed across Jake's mind. He stood up and paced to the other side of the room. He needed some space to process it all out. "No, no, no. You were captain of your basketball team. You said they voted you homecoming king. Roger was different. He was—"

"Alone." Grant finished the sentence for him. "Jake, that's how I've felt my whole life."

Jake stopped his pacing and turned to face his friend. "Whatever. Everyone likes you. You have more friends than I do."

"They're friends with someone that doesn't exist. Sure, I can play the part, but sometimes..." Grant's voice faded. "Jake, you've had a hard time carrying around this secret for three weeks. I've been carrying it around for almost two years."

Jake walked over to sit on the edge of his bed, his head feeling like it wanted to explode. He cradled it in his palms and stared at the floor.

"You're the first straight person I've ever told. Do you know how terrifying that was for me?"

"Yeah, yeah," Jake sighed. "That's what my youth pastor was just saying. But—"

"You told your pastor about me?" Grant interjected.

"No. I mean, yeah. But I didn't say your name."

"Oh, so maybe you could have been referring to your other roommate."

Jake shook his head to try and reason. "Grant, he lives in California. It's not like he's gonna tell anybody."

"That's not the point. I know how preachers feel about homosexuals. No wonder you've been acting like such a jerk. That's the last thing I need—another bigoted preacher wagging his finger at me."

"You don't even know Chris. He's different," Jake tried to explain.

Grant shook his head and laughed sarcastically. "Yeah, different like that preacher you dragged me to with Nicole?"

The only thing Jake remembered from that morning—besides Nicole's revealing dress—was Grant's bobbing head from almost the moment they sat down. "What are you talking about? You slept through the whole thing!"

"God made Adam and Eve, not Adam and *Steve*," Grant mocked the preacher's joke.

"Oh, please!" Jake argued. "It was just a joke."

"Yeah, make fun of the gay guy. Sounds funny to me...You're all the same! Intolerant and hypocritical. And you know what, Jake? You're the worst."

"Oh, really?" Jake exploded. "Explain that to me."

"Your friend commits suicide, and I don't see you doing a damn thing about it. You obviously didn't learn anything from that whole situation, based on the way you've been avoiding me these last few weeks! You're all uncomfortable with my choice of partners, but look at you, hooking up with Nicole before Amy's spot was even cold—and while Nicole was still entertaining Nate on the side. Yeah, there's a good choice! You make me sick," Grant spat.

Jake stood silent. He wanted to fight back, but no words came to his mind. And then Grant struck with his final blow.

"I totally get Roger now...You were too much of a coward to say it to his face, so you simply started acting as if he didn't exist. That's one thing you're really good at."

The pulse pounding at Jake's temples begged for relief. Everything his roommate said was absolutely true, but Jake just couldn't swallow the accusations.

"You wrecked it, not me!" Jake vented, knowing his words were completely opposite from what they should be.

"Well, sorry for wrecking your perfect little world," Grant shot back and stormed out the door.

That night, Jake awoke in the middle of a vivid nightmare. He was back in Pacific High's Senior Hall, reliving every last detail from that tragic morning. Three gun shots shattered normalcy, and the screams of terrified students racing down the hallway, away from the kid with the gun, echoed violently. Jake's heart pounded as he stood up from behind a table and slowly inched toward his old friend. The shooter's head was turned as Jake pleaded with him to put the gun down...but it was as if the shooter couldn't hear him speak. He pulled the gun up to his chin and looked back squarely at Jake before pulling the trigger.

The boy holding the gun was Grant.

4:22pm | From: Steven | To: Amy
What r u doing

almost always skipped a beat whenever Steven's sexy voice sang "You're beautiful!" from her phone. He had recorded the song and programmed Amy's phone to play it every time he either called or texted—which was often. But right now, Amy had bigger things on her mind.

4:23pm | From: Amy | To: Steven
Can't talk right now. Call u in an hour

Amy stared at her computer screen, her mind beating itself against the brick wall that wouldn't stop taunting. After seeing that captivating picture of her father and the little boy several weeks ago, she had intentionally put off sending him a message until she had the freedom to pursue him far away from her mother's disapproval. But two weeks into the new quarter, Amy was no closer than before. *What do I say to a man I haven't talked to for fifteen years?* She agonized as her fingers hovered over her keyboard. From the looks of her first few classes, this quarter appeared to be even more strenuous than her first, but she was pretty sure no term paper would be as difficult as this short email she had been working up the nerve to write all day.

"You're beautiful!" Steven's voice chimed from her phone.

Ugh! Amy groaned silently. Normally she would have seen this persistence as adorable, but she needed to get this message to her dad over with.

4:30pm | From: Amy | To: Steven
I'm writing my dad. I need to concentrate

This should buy me some time. Amy had told Steven about the letters she'd finally opened and her desire to get in touch with her father. Steven had listened attentively, as usual, and had supported her and encouraged her in this new pursuit. In fact, he was the one asking her every day if she'd written to him yet. So he'd better understand right now.

Amy typed the words "Dear Dad," but suddenly writing a direct email felt way too scary, and she got skittish. She clicked her email closed, plunged her hands under her legs, and sat nervously bobbing her knees up and down. *What is wrong with me?* she cringed.

After staring out her window for who knows how long, she logged onto Facebook, skipped past several new messages and friend requests, and typed her dad's name into the search box as she had done at least a dozen times already. And just like the previous eleven times, she found herself more and more fascinated with the little boy in her dad's arms. What was his name? Was he as clueless about her as she had been about him? He looked to be about the same age Amy was when her dad had left her. Would this little boy ever know what that was like? Overcome by ragged emotions, Amy was about to click this screen closed as well when the little "+1" icon silently begged her to add her father as a friend. *My dad...a friend?* she squirmed. But she knew she needed to do it.

With eyes almost shut, Amy nervously clicked on the button and then clicked on the option to add a message with her request. She took a deep breath and started typing the words she had already rehearsed dozens of times in her mind. "Dear Dad, I know it's been a really long time, but I finally just read your letters. I'm a student at Stanford and wanted to see if you would like to meet for coffee someti—"

"You're beautiful!"—from her phone yet again.

Text: 5:00pm | From: Steven | To: Amy
Done yet?

Amy angrily turned off her phone and threw it on the bed without responding. Steven of all people had to know how important this note was to her. *Why can't he just leave me alone?* There were so many qualities about Steven that she loved, but his clinginess definitely wasn't one of them. *At least Jake didn't have to be around me 24-7,* her mind wandered. *Why am I even thinking about him?* She frowned, the empty spot Jake had left in her heart feeling suddenly raw.

Trying to stifle her rising irritation, Amy looked back at her letter in progress. This was not the state of mind she wanted to be in as she sent out maybe the most important message of her current life. She inhaled and exhaled slowly, willing herself to calm down, and finished the word "sometime." After she skimmed the brief note once again, she decided to add one more line: "BTW, is that my brother?" Amy wrestled with how to end the message. "Love" was definitely too much, but "From" sounded so sterile. Were there any other options? Finally she settled on a simple dash: "—Amy Briggs (your daughter)." *As if he's not going to figure that out on his own!* She almost erased it, but then decided she liked the little sting that it might carry with it. Kind of like saying "in case you forgot about me!" Sure, the letters her dad had sent had been a nice gesture, but what else had he done to try to show her how sorry he was? She wasn't going to let him off the hook *that* easily!

Amy leaned back in her desk chair and read over the message one last time.

New Message

To: Raymund Briggs x

Subject:

Message

Dear Dad,

I know it's been a really long time but I finally just read your letters. I'm a student at Stanford and wanted to see if you'd like to meet for coffee sometime. BTW, is that my brother?

—Amy Briggs (your daughter)

Attach: Send Cancel

This was it. Amy held her breath—and quickly pushed the send button. She exhaled long and slow, and stared motionless at the screen as if waiting for an immediate response. Her eyes glazed over, half blurred by tears and half by exhausted relief, when suddenly the strum of a familiar guitar reverberated on the other side of her door.

Ugh! Amy sighed again but found it impossible to be angry as Steven's smooth voice broke into the chorus of a John Mayer song.

Amy slowly opened the door just as Steven broke into one of the verses.

His eyes gazed deeply into Amy's as he took off into the repetitive chorus again.

Doors opened up and down the hall as girls rushed to hear Steven singing at the top of his lungs. Amy could feel the frustration draining out of her body as she leaned against her doorframe watching her crazy boyfriend. "I'd like to say something," Amy tried to speak up over the music.

Steven nodded his head, indicating that he heard her, but he continued to play. Amy playfully began to shut her door, and Steven wedged his foot in front of it as he brought his song to a close. "—to sa-a-a-a-ay."

Applause echoed throughout the hallway as Steven finally put the guitar down. Amy's dorm mates flashed her smiles and grins as they returned to their less-interesting lives of homework, no doubt dreaming of the day when their own guy would serenade them. Amy turned and walked back to her desk.

"Okay, okay, I'm *sorry!*" Steven laughed, following Amy into her room.

"You are so annoying. I was trying to write my dad." Amy stated her case as simply as possible. It was hard for her to stay mad at him when he looked so cute, but she was giving it her best effort.

Steven pouted. "I know," he sighed. "I tried to give you time, but I have these, and I couldn't wait any longer." With that, he flourished two tickets from his back pocket and waved them in front of Amy's face.

"What are they?"

"My apology?"

Amy grabbed them out of his hand to look more closely. "You got us Lakers tickets?" she looked up with bulging eyes.

Steven smiled. "Well, I got us Warriors tickets...when they just so happen to be playing your Lakers."

"Shut up!" Amy yelled back in excitement. "How did you get these?"

"Friend of a friend...long story. But we need to leave now if we're going to make opening tipoff." Steven winked at her.

All her lingering annoyance was instantly wiped away as Amy clicked her laptop shut and grabbed a jacket. Maybe the clinginess wasn't quite so bad after all.

Their seats at the Oakland Coliseum were even better than Steven had described. From six rows up at center court, they could hear every grunt, complaint, and cuss word that flew out of the players' mouths. It was almost as good as being a cheerleader on the sideline.

Over the course of Amy's high school cheerleading and Jake-Taylor-dating career, she had watched hundreds of basketball games, but this was the first one with Steven. He was a sweetie for getting the tickets, but she could tell he wasn't really enjoying himself. He kept fiddling with his phone—playing games, searching the Internet, texting friends, taking pictures of her. Amy could imagine how he felt, because she knew how annoyed she used to get at Jake for wasting so much time watching the games on TV. But since they broke up, she had found herself watching the Lakers more and more. She wasn't sure if it was because she actually missed the games...or just that she missed Jake. Either way, the Lakers had become a sort of mini -obsession for her, so much so that Steven had obviously known how much she'd appreciate these tickets.

But despite the fact that Steven was sitting next to her, his hand resting cozily on her knee, Amy found her mind thinking about Jake. Was he truly living out his dream at Louisville? Was he happy? She chuckled. *Will I ever get to see him play an NBA game?* That would be crazy.

"What's up?" Steven turned to her, a cute little-boy grin on his face.

"Oh, nothing." Amy quickly regained her focus and leaned her head on his shoulder. "I was just thinking about my high school cheerleading days."

"I bet you were the hottest cheerleader out there." Steven smiled, reached his arm around her shoulders, and softly kissed the top of her head.

"Yeah, I was." Amy replied super-sweetly, then giggled.

"Oooh, and modest, too, I see!" Steven laughed.

"You know it." The ref called a blocking foul on the Lakers, and Amy yelled from her seat, "Are you blind? That was a charge!" She settled back and looked over at her boyfriend, whose eyes—fixed on her, of course—glowed with fascination. A familiar tingle raced through her insides. She interlocked her fingers through his and squeezed his hand.

Five hours later, after a Lakers' blowout and a second thrilling parking lot kiss—which came after Steven bashfully reminded her about his hallway serenade—Amy finally floated into her dorm room. It was almost midnight, and Renee was already asleep. Amy had neither the mental energy nor the desire to finish the reading for her Ethical Reasoning class and decided to get ready for bed.

After quickly washing her face, brushing her teeth, and changing into her sweats, Amy sank into bed, still smiling from her night with Steven. But as her eyes fluttered to a close, one final thought jolted her awake.

She nervously flipped open her computer, its cool blue light illuminating her side of the room. She refreshed her Facebook page to see if there just *happened* to be any new messages. Her heart leaped. There was one from Ray Briggs.

Amy clicked to open it with trembling fingers, her heart beating rapidly. Her eyes scanned the brief, five-line message before her brain could comprehend its meaning. It was so short.

◂Back to Messages

Between **You** and **Raymund Briggs**

Reply

Amy,

You have no idea how excited I was to get your message. I'll meet you anywhere, anytime. My schedule is wide open. Call me: (408)555-7689.

Love, Dad

PS Yes, he is your brother. His name is Ramon.

Attach:

Reply

Amy leapt from her chair and yelped in celebration. "Woohoo!"

Renee groaned from across the room and sleepily murmured, "What's going on?"

Amy pounced on her bed and hugged her roommate tightly. "I'm meeting my dad!" She ran over and reread the message. He'd even signed it *Love*!

3:49pm | From: Amy | To: Cari
Pray for me...I'm about to go hang out with my dad.

AFTER MORE THAN TWO WEEKS of sending messages back and forth, Amy and her dad were finally meeting. Amy was so excited she could hardly concentrate on anything else. Her dad had sent her his phone number several times, but Amy hadn't felt comfortable enough to talk to him on the phone. So they messaged back and forth until her dad had finally identified a Starbucks just off campus where he promised to meet her after her Monday afternoon Ethical Reasoning class got out at four o'clock.

Amy glanced down at her watch. *3:52.* This was proving to be the slowest class she had ever endured, not so much because of the lecture itself, but because of the never-ending nerve-racking questions rattling around in her brain like a pinball machine gone wild. How should she introduce herself? Should she hug him? What would they talk about? Were there certain topics that should be kept in the past—or was everything fair game? When would Amy get to meet his wife? What if his wife didn't want to meet her? What if her dad was as much of a jerk as her mom assured her he was? And how do you make up for nearly fifteen years over a cup of coffee?

The professor ended the lecture a minute before four, and the shuffle of students packing up shook Amy back into awareness. She stuffed her laptop into her bag, slung the bag over her shoulder, and joined the mass exodus out of the big hall, rehearsing her opening speech. The only part she was having trouble with was the greeting. *Hi, I'm Amy...your daughter.* Somehow the "daughter" part felt really weird. *Hi, I'm Amy Briggs...* No, the Briggs part was completely unnecessary. *Hi, Dad. Remember me?* Nothing sounded quite right as she weaved in and out of students hustling their own separate ways. Amy wondered if any of them were headed toward appointments anywhere near as significant as her own.

In spite of the chilly winter air, Amy had to wipe the sweat from her hands onto her jeans for the third time. *Why am I so nervous?* It would have been nice to have Steven by her side, but he couldn't get out of his vocal performance class. He'd promised to meet her at Starbucks as soon as he was done, though, and she couldn't wait for that. Crossing the street into the shopping plaza, Amy glanced down at her watch again. *4:13.* Her father should definitely be there by now. She walked through the parking lot to the Starbucks she'd been to at least a dozen times over the last few months. But this time, every step toward that familiar green sign brought her closer to a meeting that could change her life forever.

Amy pulled open the heavy glass door and peered inside the café. Her eyes slowly adjusted to the darker environment as she scanned the handful of faces seated around the room. And then almost before she knew it, there he was. Walking toward her. His face an undecipherable mix of emotions. It had been a decade and a half since they'd been in a room together, but pictures of a younger version of him swinging her around in his arms instantly flashed to the forefront of her brain.

"Hi, Dad," Amy nervously croaked out, trying to remember at least part of the opening speech she had rehearsed so many times.

From ten feet away, she noticed her father's wet eyes, and his wide smile spoke volumes. Amy lost it. Without saying another word, the two lunged into an awkward but adoring embrace, tears of joy running down freely. Amy hadn't yet asked a single question, but the only one that really mattered had been answered in an instant: Her father loved her.

"I can't believe it's really you," he finally spoke, wiping his sleeve across his wet cheeks. "Amy Grace Briggs," he enunciated with a grin.

"I haven't heard anyone say my middle name for years," she chuckled. It was weird to hear a near-stranger reciting an intimate detail about her that few others even knew.

"I remember the day when your mother and I chose it." His eyes got foggy again, and his gaze drifted off to a past Amy couldn't see. Then he abruptly stepped back. "How 'bout I get us something to drink?" he suggested, stepping over to the counter to order.

Amy followed him over and ordered a hot peppermint green tea after he asked for his plain black coffee. This was all so surreal. As they stood awkwardly waiting for their drinks, Amy fidgeted with her sweatshirt zipper, unable to voice any of the questions that had plagued her for years. So instead she turned to the one that her father had just instigated. "Is there a story behind my middle name?" she asked shyly.

"Hasn't your mother ever told you?" Ray looked surprised.

Amy shook her head.

"You were born almost two months early, you know," her father began, "and spent the first six weeks of your life in the hospital. At first that was kind of a relief, because we didn't have to take responsibility for you yet. I was only 18, and I had other priorities, other plans. But during that time, I started visiting you more and more often in the hospital. You were so tiny and fragile and...beautiful. And that's when I came to realize how much I loved you—I didn't know I could love something so much! And I knew I wanted to be part of your life...I didn't want to be like some of my buddies, just moving on without taking responsibility. And so that's when I proposed to your mom, and we decided to try to make it as a family. I went back to church and dragged her along with me, and the first sermon we heard together was about God's grace, and I turned to your mom, and it just clicked: Amy Grace. You were the grace that turned my life around."

Watching her father soften as he told the story filled Amy with warm longing. "I've never heard that before," she said softly, wondering how many other little-known facts her dad had to offer.

Ray squeezed her to him once more and inhaled deeply, as if trying to soak up as much of her as he could. "Enough of my blabbering. I want to hear all about you."

They picked up their drinks from the counter and found a cozy little cluster of chairs in the front corner of the store. For the next thirty minutes or so, her dad asked continuous questions about Amy's current life: her classes, her roommate, her boyfriend, her involvement with InterVarsity Christian Fellowship and her new church, her interest in psychology, and her possible career goals. Like a man emerging from days abandoned in the desert, he seemed to eat up every detail from her life and just kept responding, "Wow."

This was so unlike her recent visit home with her mom that Amy just kept talking. It felt so good to have a parent actually interested in her—even if he hadn't really been a parent for most of her life. But that got Amy thinking. She felt a bug of resentment toward her mother gnawing away at her heart a little, but then again, where had her dad been all these years? Sure, it was easy for him to just waltz in right now, but if he had never left, Amy wouldn't need to be filling him in on all these details. If Amy *Grace*'s birth had been so life-changing for him, then why did he leave so easily, so quickly, never to be seen again, until now?

During a brief lull in the conversation, Amy considered how to bring this up. It was great sitting here and catching up with her dad, but the glaring reality that it had been almost fifteen years since they had last talked seemed like a four-hundred-pound gorilla sitting next to them sipping a latte. Sooner or later, that gorilla was going to want more. *Why did you never visit? Why no phone calls?* Or the biggest question of all: *Why didn't you believe me so many years ago?* These questions fluttered around in Amy's brain, begging for escape but afraid to come out.

"Dad." Amy's voice finally shifted into a more serious tone. The look on her father's face suggested he knew what was coming. "Can we talk about...the letters?"

The smile that had taken up residence in her dad's eyes contorted into a wince, but he nodded his head and whispered back, "Ask me anything."

With such an open-ended invitation, Amy wasn't sure how to start. "Um, why did you leave us in the first place?" She hadn't meant to be so blunt, but the question flew out of her mouth before she had time to be more diplomatic.

But her father didn't seem bothered by the brashness at all, almost as if he'd been preparing an answer for years. He placed his drink on the table and looked at Amy. "Amy, let me start by saying that you're not going to be fully satisfied with my answer, nor do I expect you to understand everything that happened." He hesitated and broke eye contact before continuing. "My older brother—your Uncle Harold—practically raised me. Our mother died when we were young, and after that, our father couldn't cope with his grief and turned to the bottle for comfort. Over the years, it got worse and worse, and that's all we knew of our father. He would either come home drunk out of his mind or not come home at all for days. Harold was four years older than me, so he stepped up and took charge. He made our meals, he helped me with my homework, he walked me to school in the morning...he was the only parent figure I had. As we got older, Dad started blaming his crappy life on us. The only thing he loved more than his beer was coming home to beat Harold just for the fun of it." His voice cracked, and his gaze drifted toward the window.

Amy sat silently, waiting for the rest of a story she had never heard before. Why hadn't her mother ever told her this side of things? And then when she least expected it, Melia's sullen face at the Christmas party flashed through Amy's mind. Why was this story of abuse becoming so frequent in her life? That thought was cut short by her dad's voice.

"Amy, in my almost ten years of living in that house, Harold never allowed my father to hit me even once. My big brother took every punch and crack of the belt. He would hide me in the closet, push me under the bed, even run in front of me and shield me with his own body while he got beaten bloody." Again, Ray's voice cracked, and he struggled to maintain composure. "When he turned eighteen, he left home and took me with him. I had just turned fourteen, and Harold got a job and supported me through high school. I don't know what I would have done without him."

Amy found her own eyes moist with tears, as she actually agonized for the man who had brutalized her all those years ago. She saw him as a little boy, and Melia's sweet, hurting face covered up the wild eyes and rough whiskers that usually haunted her dreams.

"After all those years of toughening up with Dad," Ray continued, "I'll admit, Harold wasn't a happy person. He had an ornery side and was crude and rude and sometimes downright mean...So from the beginning, your mother didn't like him. And Harold didn't think she was such a winner, either. When she got pregnant with you, he cussed me out for ruining my life—a life he had worked so hard to make good—and told me to run and go make something of myself. Well, of course, you surprised us early, and I fell in love and settled down with your mom. Harold and I, we stayed close, but something changed. At the same time, neither of us was ready to grow up...we didn't know how, I guess. You'd think we would have learned from Dad's mistakes, but we were young and stupid, and before we knew it we were all into the drugs and drinking and partying all weekend—basically living a life of no responsibility while you sat watching us from the sidelines. Your mom tried to clean up a few times, but we'd always just drag her back down again with us. I think she always blamed Harold for his bad influence on me...So, that day...when you—"

Her dad cleared his throat and took a long sip from his drink. Amy sat on the edge of her seat, knowing what was coming. Her own eyes were now welling up. As painful as this was, she hung on his every word as if watching a suspense thriller in which she was one of the main characters.

"When we figured out what you were saying that your Uncle Harold was doing to you, I felt like I was being ripped in half. Deep down, I knew you must be telling the truth, but at the same time I just couldn't believe that the brother who had done so much to protect me all those years could then turn around and hurt you, and me, in this horrible way. And in some sick, twisted way, I thought that protecting him could maybe repay him for everything he'd done for me."

Amy nodded, surprised that she could actually understand this unthinkable decision through her father's eyes.

"For your mom, this was just the final straw—understandably. She kicked me out and told me not to bother trying to ruin either of your lives ever again. And so I left. But I can tell you, Amy, not a day has gone by—even before Harold's arrest—that I haven't regretted my decision." A lone tear dropped from her dad's face onto the table, and he grabbed Amy's hands and looked her straight in the eye. "What kind of dad lets that happen to his little girl? I am so, so sorry."

In what felt like an out-of-body experience, Amy heard herself saying, "I forgive you, Dad." The man she had grown up resenting sat here broken before her. What else could she do? Steven was right. It felt better to forgive. A weight tumbled off her back, and she squeezed her father's hands. "Dad, it's okay. I forgive you."

Her dad stared back at her, a mixture of disbelief and relief radiating from his moist eyes. Amy smiled back at him. She still had a long list of questions to resolve, but for now, they all seemed unimportant. Maybe she'd revisit some of them in the future, but she was satisfied for the time being.

"What do you say we move on for a while? Tell me about my brother." She couldn't tell if he wanted to move on or not, but after a few seconds of hesitation, he sat back in his chair. A warm smile crept across his face.

"Well," he began tentatively. "He's five years old...and he and his twin sister couldn't be more opposite."

"Wait a minute!" Amy interrupted. "I have a *sister?*" Her exuberance triggered curious looks from several of the patrons sitting around them.

Amy's dad nodded eagerly, fishing around in his back pocket for his wallet. He pulled out a plastic sleeve containing several pictures of Amy's siblings. "This is Marissa, and this is Ramon," he explained.

With one glance, Amy was in love. Besides their slightly darker skin tone, she could see a little bit of her father—and herself—in each of their faces. "Oh, they are so beautiful!" she squealed.

Her dad flipped over the next pocket to reveal a portrait of him and his new wife, a gorgeous Latina woman who looked at least ten years younger than him. They looked so happy and so in love that Amy couldn't help but feel a little jealous.

She glanced up at her dad. "When do I get to meet them?"

"Well, let me talk about it with Olivia. She would love to meet you, but we wanted to see your response before telling the kids and getting them all excited."

A shadow appeared over the table. Amy and her dad glanced up to see Steven standing over them.

"Steven, I have a sister!" Amy yelled out again, quickly covering her mouth as stares turned back in her direction. She jumped up and wrapped her arms around his neck.

"That's great, babe." Steven returned her hug and rubbed her back. "I thought you said you had a brother."

"She has both, actually." Ray stood to shake Steven's hand. "Steven, it's been so great to hear a little about you today. I'm Ray, Amy's dad." He pulled an extra chair over to their table.

They all settled back down, and Steven looked at both of them expectantly. "So...what did I miss?"

✚ ✚ ✚

Several hours later, Amy hugged her dad goodbye, lingering in the tight embrace she had missed for most of her life. He promised to call her to let her know when she could meet the rest of the family. Amy practically skipped all the way back to her dorm, pulling Steven along with one hand as she chattered on and on, rehashing all the glorious details. Steven simply held on tight and bobbed along on the rushing current, smiling at the new joy Amy couldn't contain.

Just outside her dorm, Steven grabbed her free hand and swung her body around to face him. "I love you, Amy Briggs," he said softly, looking into her eyes.

Completely caught off guard, Amy stood in silence for a moment trying to catch up with the gravity of the moment.

"I love you...too?" she giggled back, but with not nearly the same confidence.

Apparently Steven didn't care about the not-so-subtle difference. He pulled her close, enfolding her body in his strong arms, and kissed her. This kiss lasted a lot longer than the others, and Amy finally pulled away.

"You owe me a song," Amy said, poking her boyfriend in the chest.

Undeterred, Steven's smile just got wider. "I'm gonna write you a hundred songs, just to have some on layaway."

Amy squeezed him tightly and then turned to skip away. Her dad loved her. Steven loved her. And she had a little sister.

9:14pm | From: Amy | To: Cari
What a day! I'll call you tomorrow

12:52pm | From: Dad | To: Jake
Saw the standings. You guys just can't shake em, huh? You'd better step it up.

Big East Men's Basketball Standings	
Team	**Conference Record**
Syracuse	11-2
West Virginia	9-4
Louisville	9-4
Pittsburgh	9-4
Villanova	9-4
Marquette	8-5
Georgetown	8-5
Seton Hall	7-6

Jake stared at the top half of the conference standings for at least the fiftieth time in the past month, his dad's text bothering him like a piece of apple skin stuck between his teeth. *He always finds something to be critical of!* Jake scowled. But his dad was right. With every game, the numbers moved closer and closer together, and Louisville stayed stuck in the mix, unable to move ahead. At least they hadn't dropped down a spot. But with only five games left in the regular season before the Big East tournament, they were running out of time.

Unfortunately, three of those five remaining games pitted them against the very teams they were battling it out with, and two of those were on the road. Tomorrow they faced the Marquette Golden Eagles, a team that was on a seven-game win streak after their sketchy start. Next week, Louisville traveled to bottom-ranked DePaul and top-ranked Syracuse before heading home to finish up their season against Villanova and under-.500 Providence. If they could win at least three of the games, Louisville was all but assured a place in the NCAA tournament. But if they weren't able to pull it off, they could be looking at another trip to the NIT—a disappointing end to a season that started out with such promise.

Jake glanced at the time at the bottom of his computer screen. *Crap!* Having stayed online a few minutes too long, he would have to hustle if he was going to make it to practice on time. He clicked his laptop shut, grabbed his duffel bag, and rushed out the door. Good thing he wasn't meeting Grant early to shoot around. Of course, if he had been, then he wouldn't have wasted so much time on his computer, and he wouldn't have to worry about being late now.

Ever since their argument over a month ago, neither he nor Grant had talked much, besides strained hi's and bye's in passing, and their extra practice together had simply stopped. Jake showed up early the first day after the argument, but after fifteen minutes of shooting around solo and then Grant ignoring him the rest of practice, Jake didn't even bother. He knew he should do something, but he just didn't feel like it. And so they just kept coexisting—miserably. Fortunately, Jake had managed to not let it get to his performance on the court again, so the other guys didn't really seem to notice the tension. But Jake definitely missed the days when he and Grant were such good buddies.

Jake flung open the glass door to the practice center and hustled to the locker room. Most of the guys were already done and had gone to the gym. Jake hurriedly dressed out and laced up his shoes, running onto the court with a minute to spare.

Practice was relatively light today in preparation for tomorrow's game, and after a couple of hours of shooting, drilling, and running through plays, Jake walked back toward the locker room with Nomis and Bojan. Grant walked alone a few yards in front of them. As the threesome bantered back and forth, an older man sitting a few rows up and to the right caught Jake's attention. Jake recognized the guy, but he could not figure out where they'd met. Then, the man caught Jake's eye and smiled.

"Hey, Jake!" he said jovially. "Did you ever get that ice cream?" He stood up slowly.

Jake stopped. *Buddy!* It was that usher from that first church Jake had checked out over a year ago. Jake nodded to his friends as they kept heading toward the locker room and walked over to the old man dressed in black polyester pants and a grey Louisville sweatshirt. "Hey, Buddy!" Jake smiled back.

"You remembered!"

"How could I forget you?" Jake hopped up to the second row and reached his hand out to greet him. "What are you doing here?"

"I met up with some old college buddies on campus and thought I'd check out the new practice facilities. This place is huge!" Buddy said in a loud voice as he looked up into the rafters. It was as if he was hoping to get an echo. "A lot bigger than where we used to practice."

"You used to play basketball for Louisville?"

"What? Don't I look like a baller to you?"

Jake laughed at his use of slang.

"I averaged almost twenty points a game my junior year," Buddy continued, beaming. "And then I met Yvonne and gave it all up to marry her. Sixty-three years later and I still think I made the right choice." Buddy's voice trailed off, and his eyes got misty as Jake silently watched the endearing man. "Hey, you got plans for dinner?" Buddy snapped back to his energetic self.

Jake looked at him, perplexed by what he assumed to be an invitation. They had met one time a year ago and had only talked for a few minutes. It wasn't as if they had any catching up to do. But something inside Jake was intrigued by the man standing in front of him who was so full of life. "Uh, not yet," he hesitated.

"Let me buy you dinner, then." Buddy grinned.

Wavering and reluctant, Jake tried to think of a plausible excuse to say no. He liked Buddy, but having dinner with him seemed like such a commitment.

"Come on, Jake. I know a great place!" Buddy pressed good-naturedly.

Jake thought about his other options: end-of-the-week cafeteria food, making something back at the apartment while trying to avoid Grant, or going out with the guys, which would probably lead to him getting wasted the night before the game. None of those options sounded appealing. And so before Jake knew what he was doing, he found his mouth saying, "Sure. Why not? Let me go get my stuff."

Fifteen minutes later, Jake walked back into the gym full of second thoughts. What was he doing? What if any of the guys found out? Fortunately, none of them had asked about his dinner plans—he could just imagine how awkward that might have been: "Sorry, I'm going out with an old man." In the midst of his qualms, an abrupt snort startled him.

There was Buddy sitting straight up, arms crossed, chin resting on his chest, and snoring away without a care. Jake immediately saw his opportunity for escape but let it pass. His new problem was how to wake Buddy up. Jake intentionally squeaked his shoes against the waxed hardwood flooring in hopes that the noise would rouse him, but it didn't. Jake loudly cleared his throat, but Buddy was still out cold. Jake tried whistling. No movement. *Classic.* Jake chuckled. With no other ideas, Jake approached with a direct line of attack.

"Buddy," he said, lightly shaking his shoulder.

Buddy's eyes popped open. "Jake! I guess I must have dozed off there for a minute." He grinned as if he had been wide awake the entire time. He gingerly pushed himself up from his seat and gave Jake a firm handshake. "You ready to go?"

Jake soon learned that the one catch to the free dinner was that Buddy needed a ride. He had driven over with his friends but chose to stay behind to talk to Jake when they headed back home. Jake wondered what would have happened if he'd declined the invitation or even outright ignored the guy he'd only met once before. Considering the snail's crawl with which they trekked across campus to Jake's truck, Jake couldn't picture Buddy walking home on his own.

But in spite of his slow pace, Buddy was an animated dynamo—and an exuberant conversationalist. Jake could barely keep up with all the friendly questions he kept asking. From the moment they started walking, Buddy hit him with a barrage of questions about what California was like, his family, why he chose to attend Louisville, even his dating life. If anyone else had pried that much, Jake would have felt uncomfortable. But the genuine interest Buddy showed was refreshing, and the more questions he asked, the more Jake liked him.

They finally made it to Jake's truck and got in. Jake started the ignition. "Where to, boss?"

"You like pizza?" A smile played on Buddy's face.

"Sure." Jake nodded.

"Ever hear of a place called Chuck E. Cheese?"

Jake had to laugh. *Are you serious*? He wasn't sure the greasy cardboard they served could actually be called pizza, but Buddy looked so excited that Jake couldn't turn him down. "Sure. I think I know where it is."

They drove off campus and into town, and with Buddy's guidance pulled into a parking spot in front of the brightly lit restaurant with a giant mouse out front. Jake chuckled to himself, realizing that at least the risk of meeting some of his teammates here was nonexistent. He held the front door open for Buddy, and they walked into the unruly Friday night environment of screeching kids and blaring video games. A birthday party was in full swing to their left, and a kid shrieked to his mom about wanting more coins to their right. Jake shot a sideways glance at Buddy, wondering if this was really just a joke. But his bright smile was ample evidence that this was exactly where he wanted to be.

"What do you want on your pie?" Buddy asked, making his way to the lady behind the cash register.

"Uh, pepperoni." Jake shook his head as the shrieking next to them turned into wailing and stomping.

"Okay, I'll order the food, you grab us a table," Buddy said over his shoulder.

Jake glanced around at the crowded restaurant, filled with parents and their little kids. *What am I doing here?* he wondered. He liked Buddy, but he was starting to feel like this was a bit creepy. *What's he going to want to do next? Play games?* Jake walked through the hordes of kids and finally located a booth in the corner, away from the loud gaming area. He scooted in and checked out the activity all around him, trying to recall when he had had as much fun as some of these kids seemed to be having.

"The meal came with ten tokens!" Buddy gleefully broke into Jake's thoughts. "How about a little skee ball tournament?" He placed a stack of five tokens on the table in front of Jake and gave a little wink. "Unless you're chicken."

Jake chuckled and stuffed the coins in his pocket. "You're going down, old man."

Not surprisingly, Buddy was much better at trash talking than at the actual game. But his hilariously exaggerated windup and release soon attracted a crowd of laughing kids who rooted him on. Buddy high-fived his faithful fans after every roll and listened attentively as they gave him their expert advice. And even though Jake was clearly not the crowd favorite, Buddy's joy was contagious, and Jake found himself having a blast.

After three rounds, Buddy suggested they each team up with a child for the next game. A dozen hands sprang up, their owners jumping up and down, pleading to be picked as a partner. Buddy ignored all the wiggling fingers, though, and picked a little girl who sat watching quietly from her wheelchair in the back. Following suit, Jake noticed a chubby little boy standing by himself over to one side and asked if he would help him out. The smile on the boy's face burned itself in Jake's memory. A chorus of bummed "Awwwws" made its way around the circle, but the unpicked kids quickly got over their disappointment and crowded around anyway.

As the reigning victor, Jake went first, debuting a new and entertaining release inspired by Buddy. He wound up like a baseball pitcher, pretended to throw the ball, then spun around three times before releasing it down the runway. The ball bounced and wobbled and somehow found itself falling into the hole marked 30. Buddy took a turn with some crazy antics of his own, scoring a 30 as well. Then it was Jake's chubby teammate's turn. Concentrating seriously, he sank a ringer in the 50-point pocket. Jake gave him a high five, and they did a silly celebration dance together. Buddy's partner heaved the ball with all her might, and even though it barely made it into the 10-point zone, Buddy celebrated as if it had found the 100-point pocket.

They continued going back and forth, and before long, everyone was practically oblivious to the scores. The new object of the game became how creative the release could be. The young spectators got involved by giving suggestions, and Jake and Buddy and their teammates did their best to imitate the recommended moves. Somewhere in the midst of it all, Jake's problems and frustrations with basketball and his roommate were completely forgotten...and for the first time in a while, Jake felt truly happy.

They were so engrossed in the fifth game that they were startled when a restaurant employee interrupted them to let them know their order had been waiting on their table for the past ten minutes. Jake and Buddy let their new partners each finish off the round, then divvied up the tickets that had accumulated on the floor. The kids ran off, and Jake and Buddy made their way back to the corner table.

"I wonder what kind of junk they'll get with those tickets," Jake said with a smile as he slid into the booth.

"I always thought those bouncy balls were pretty cool." Buddy slowly lowered himself down onto the vinyl bench seat. "Hey, will you say the blessing?"

Jake had just pulled a flimsy piece of pizza from the round tray. He quickly dropped it onto his plate and folded his hands in his lap. "Um, dear God, thanks for this food we're about to eat. Somehow take out all the grease and bless it to our bodies. Amen."

Buddy echoed an amen and pulled his own slice of lukewarm pizza off the pan. Jake could have sworn Buddy wrinkled his nose a little. *Why'd he bring me here if he doesn't even like pizza?* As if reading his mind, Buddy piped up as Jake took his first bite.

"Do you know why I brought you to this place, Jake?" Buddy sipped his glass of water.

Jake swallowed his mouthful. "You thought kids my age like to hang out here?"

Buddy snickered. "You're a sophomore in college, not a seven-year-old. Is that what you really thought?"

Jake shrugged, curious about Buddy's ulterior motives.

"Jake, you want to know the secret to a good life?"

Jake placed the rest of the slice of pizza back on the plate and leaned his elbows on the table. "Sure."

"Glow."

And that was it. Buddy bit off a large mouthful and chewed contentedly, leaving Jake to ponder the cryptic advice. Jake took a fork and played with his food, trying to figure out what he had missed. He took another bite and stared back at the game area.

Finally, Buddy grinned and explained. "Have you ever noticed how many light bulbs they use in this place?"

Jake glanced around. There were lights everywhere, flashing and blinking and brightening what would otherwise be a dark room.

"We both know kids don't come here for the food," Buddy continued, holding up a forkful of soggy pizza. "They come here for the glow. You saw it, there at the games. The glow was infectious, unstoppable. In Matthew 5, Jesus tells us that *we* are the light of the world. He says, 'Let your light shine before men, that they may see your good deeds and praise your Father in heaven.' Jake, He wants *us* to glow, wherever we are. And when we glow, that's when we find true happiness."

Jake slowly chewed his second slice of pizza.

"I don't know what's been going on in your life since we last met, Jake. It sure seems like you've lost your glow. But there are a lot of hurting people there at the University of Louisville. And God needs you to bring the glow to their lives." Buddy looked at Jake with kindness in his eyes.

A couple of giggling kids ran by wearing glow-in-the-dark necklaces, probably prizes "bought" with game tickets. Jake's eyes followed them as he wrestled with Buddy's words. "It's just not that easy," he mumbled.

"A little glow goes a long way," Buddy encouraged. "Keep your spark lit, Jake, and open your eyes. God will show you what to do."

What Buddy said made so much sense. Jake knew he wanted what Buddy had just described. But he also knew what happened to him when he was back at school. Keeping that spark lit was tough.

They picked at the rest of their meal, and then on the way out, Buddy stopped at the prize counter. It turned out that he had pocketed a wad of tickets for himself. He selected a greenish bouncy ball from a plastic jar and paid the 25 tickets. He handed his remaining few tickets to a little boy looking at some rubbery spiders. The boy beamed.

Outside on the sidewalk, Buddy bounced the ball to Jake. "Catch!"

Jake barely grabbed the ball before it would have bounced into a planter.

"You can't tell so much right now," Buddy said, "but when you get back to your room, try holding that ball to the light. Then turn off the switch and watch how it glows in the dark. Its light will shine throughout the room. Now the glow won't last forever, but when it runs out, all you have to do is hold it back up to the light source. That's like you, Jake."

Jake examined the little object lesson, rolling it around in his fingers. "Would it be all right if we hung out again sometime...maybe over some better food?" he asked.

Buddy smiled. "I'd love that."

After dropping Buddy off at his duplex, Jake drove back to campus with plenty on his mind. Grant still wasn't home, so Jake wandered aimlessly into his room. He found his Bible under a stack of books and old papers, and opened it to Matthew 5. As he read Jesus' words from the Sermon on the Mount, pangs of guilt shot through his conscience. *Blessed are the merciful...Blessed are the peacemakers...Blessed are those who are persecuted because of righteousness...*Jake thought of how he'd been treating Grant lately. He got ready for bed and flipped off the lights. The room was dark, but a green light emanated from the little ball sitting next to his wallet on his dresser. *Glow.*

10:37pm | From: Jake | To: Grant
Sorry...for everything. It's gonna take me time, but I don't want to lose our friendship.

2:04pm | From: Dad | To: Jake
Destroy them! No excuses!

1:17pm | From: Mom | To: Jake
Have a great game honey!

THE KFC YUM! CENTER ARENA was packed with a sea of red and white, the rally towels given to fans at the entrance waving unceasingly. In the student section, bare-chested frat guys spelled out GO CARDINALS! on their bellies, and red and white face paint was everywhere. The cheer squad led the mob in a foot-stomping cheer that made the entire building feel as if it were shaking. And in addition to the twenty-two thousand cheering fans, the ESPN crew was on hand to broadcast this contest to the world. The atmosphere was electric.

Unable to resist the pandemonium, Jake cheered loudly as the announcer introduced the Cardinal starters. Although he wouldn't join the action for a while yet, Jake could still feel the hairs on the back of his neck stand straight up in anticipation. He stood holding his breath as the referee tossed up the ball for the opening tipoff. Bojan outreached the Marquette center and slapped the ball right to Nate, who charged down the court, passed off to Nomis, and received the assist for Nomis's short jumper. Louisville was on the board, 2-0.

Whether Jake liked to admit it or not, Nate Williams was and would be the starting point guard for the rest of the season. Accepting that reality had actually helped Jake to embrace his role off the bench. He liked to think of himself as an instant spark of energy that his teammates could depend on every time his number got called. Except in that disastrous game against Georgetown, Jake had proven his reliability, and he knew that his teammates and coaches appreciated his consistency—as long as he didn't do anything stupid like that again.

Feeding off the adrenaline pulsing through the entire arena, Louisville burst out of the gates with their A game and didn't let up. Jamal was relentless from beyond the arc, and Bojan was making the Marquette big men look like a high school junior varsity team. Nate orchestrated the attack like a seasoned field general, calling the perfect plays each time down the court. By the time it was Jake's turn, Louisville was already cruising to a sixteen-point advantage. But as Jake and Grant crouched on the sideline waiting to get in, Coach warned them not to take their foot off the gas for one second or else they'd be watching the rest of the game from the bench. The Cardinals weren't safe until that final buzzer sounded.

Jake promptly acted on that warning, stealing the opening inbound pass and charging down the court for an open layup. The raucous roar from the packed house reverberated through Jake's whole body like a steroid, and he rode the swell the next few trips down the court. After a picture-perfect alley-oop to Grant, his roommate returned the favor, popping the ball out to Jake in the corner for an uncontested three-pointer. Swish! Although they still hadn't talked, none of their personal struggles mattered for now. This 94-by-50 foot stretch of hardwood was neutral territory.

At halftime, Louisville led by twenty-one, and Coach's pep talk was the shortest Jake had ever heard: Stay focused. By ten minutes into the second half, it seemed that not even a colossal meltdown could prevent a Louisville victory. It was easy to read the defeated body language of the Marquette Eagles. Their slumped shoulders, lack of hustle, and despondent faces said it all—they had already lost the will to fight.

The ESPN crew must be kicking themselves for picking a blowout, Jake thought to himself as the teams walked to their respective benches for the last television timeout. Normally, Coach would give some last-second instructions to the players huddled around him, but the scoreboard made it clear that no speech was necessary. They tried not to celebrate prematurely, but smiles were all too evident on everyone's faces. When a few familiar cheerleaders raced to the center of the court, most of the team's attention shot to the hotties in the short skirts, probably hoping for one of their sexy dance routines. Instead, one of them grabbed a microphone and announced the name of the fortunate fan who would get a chance to win a car by making a half-court shot.

"Today's lucky contestant is Peter Swanson!" she yelled.

An excited holler rose from the student section as everyone craned to see who this Peter Swanson was. Everyone knew the odds were stacked against the shooter, but just the chance of going home with a new car was always entertaining. Jake's jaw dropped as a very familiar face walked to the center of the court: It was Peter...Grant's Peter. Jake glanced at his teammate sitting two seats down from him on the bench. His eyes were glued to the mid-court spectacle, but anticipation was definitely not what they revealed.

While Grant had gone out of his way to keep his homosexuality a secret, Peter was much more overt. His mannerisms were flamboyant, as was his wardrobe: tight-fitting red Louisville T-shirt tucked into a pair of dark skinny jeans, accessorized by a white belt with a bejeweled buckle, and crisp white loafers. Peter awkwardly dribbled the ball with both hands to the center of the court and flashed a smile to the crowd.

"Faggot!" Nate snarled with a smirk, causing several of the other guys to laugh.

Jake glared sharply at him, but Nate just ignored it. Jake glanced again over to Grant, who tightly clutched the towel hanging around his neck. The compassion he felt for Grant actually surprised Jake.

"I bet anybody twenty bucks he can't get the ball to the free-throw line," Nate sneered, garnering another chorus of jeers.

Jake could feel the blood start to pound in his ears. *Why don't you sit down and shut up?* he felt like saying. Out of the corner of his eye, he could see that Grant wasn't even watching. His head sank low, and his shoulders were hunched as if he was carrying the weight of a heavy load. For the first time since Grant's disturbing confession, Jake didn't see gay—he simply saw his friend. Jake wanted to scoot over and put his arm around his friend's shoulder, but that would only raise other questions that could only make things worse. The elation Jake had felt over the team's impending victory had given way to a horrible lump of dread in his stomach.

Peter moved back five steps behind the half-court line, and then, after a running head start, heaved the basketball with both hands in the direction of the basket. From the moment he released the ball, every spectator—even those up in the nosebleeds—knew that it didn't stand a chance of going in. The shot fell pathetically short of the hoop, and a ripple of boos and disappointed murmurs raced around the stands. Undaunted, Peter waved like a pageant queen to the crowd. His effeminate response prompted even louder laughter from Jake's teammates.

"I told you gay boy couldn't get it up," Nate taunted, turning to high-five a few teammates.

As Peter walked off the court, Jake detected a quick glance between him and Grant. Peter's smile seemed to plead for affirmation, but Grant simply looked away and laughed with the other guys. Suddenly, a hand reached out to Jake, and he looked up to see Nate waiting for a congratulatory slap. Instinctively, Jake pulled away and glared at him with irritation.

"What's your problem, Taylor?" Nate's demeanor instantly shifted from amusement to confrontation, which caused all the guys nearby to look at Jake.

Don't do anything stupid, Jake reminded himself. He ignored Nate's question and stared out to the court.

"I asked you a question, man," Nate growled, stepping close so the coaches wouldn't hear him.

Jake looked Nate squarely in the eyes and tried to sound calm. "I just don't think it's cool to be cracking jokes about someone just because he's different. What did he ever do to you?"

"Did you just try to lecture me?" Nate's voice shot up an incredulous octave.

The buzzer sounded the end of the timeout, and Jake tried to get up to make his way back to the court, but Nate pushed him back into his seat. Nomis sprang up and pulled Nate away before the coaches could see what he had done. Jake hurried out to the court and collected the inbound pass, trying to shake off what had just happened and focus on the play ahead of him. He had barely averted a confrontation, and he knew there would be repercussions. He started to chide himself for opening his big mouth, but then Buddy's words from the night before replayed in his head. As Jake dribbled down the court looking for the open pass, he kept hearing one word: *Glow!* He wasn't sure if he'd just done a very good job of glowing, but he felt that his feeble attempt at defending Peter was at least better than silence.

The tall freshman muscle-head that Nicole had been cozy with popped up to the post, and Jake snapped him the pass. The kid turned and scored a sweet swish. *Glow.*

"Good job, dude!" Jake called out to his teammate, as they spun around to defense.

The next time down, Jake purposely held on to the ball until Grant was open, weaving a bounce pass around his defender to give him the easy shot. A faint smile flickered across Grant's face. *Glow.* No longer thinking about himself, Jake looked for someone else he could assist on each trip down the court, and the last couple of minutes were the most fun he'd had all season.

As the final buzzer sounded, Louisville walked away with an 88-64 win. The guys all clustered around, congratulating each other on the twenty-two point spanking. After shaking their opponents' hands, they headed to the locker room. As Jake walked through the tunnel out of the gym with the rest of his teammates, he felt a firm hand on his shoulder. He spun around and found himself eye-to-eye with an unhappy Nate.

"Look, man, I'm sorry for whatever happened out there," Jake quickly apologized, not wanting their previous tension to dampen the celebratory mood.

Nate's grip squeezed tighter, and Jake winced. "You know," Nate seethed. "I spent the last few minutes trying to figure out why in the world someone like you would dare to challenge me over something so stupid. It just doesn't make sense."

Jake waited, wondering what point he was trying to make.

"And then it came to me." A sinister gleam glinted in Nate's eyes. "The only reason Jake Taylor would make a big deal about that faggot... is if Jake Taylor had something to hide."

Jake tried to follow his logic and came to a temporary impasse before Nate's insinuation dawned on him. "What?...Wait—"

"No, no. I get it, dude. You're gay."

"No!" Jake protested, his face starting to flush.

"Yes!" Nate jabbed his finger into Jake's chest. "The puzzle pieces fit together all too well. That's why your 'girlfriend' left you. That's why Nicole was so eager to come back to me. That's why I haven't seen you with any girls since then...And that's why you were so upset about poor little Peter. It all makes perfect sense, Jake. So who do you think the rest of the guys are going to believe?" Nate turned to walk away.

"Dude!" Jake yelled, completely taken aback by the turn this had taken.

Nate's laughter echoed off the concrete walls.

Jake stood speechless for a moment before realizing that he probably should get back to the rest of the team on the outside chance that he could defend himself. *How messed up is this?* Jake complained to himself. *So much for glowing!* He had kept his roommate's secret all this time; he had even stood up for Peter while Grant had remained silent. But now he was the one being forced out of the proverbial closet—a closet he'd never stepped into!

Jake made it into the locker room only a few steps behind Nate, where the rest of the team was still in celebration mode. *Please don't say anything. Please don't say anything,* Jake's brain repeated nervously. Down the row, Grant was laughing it up with a few guys in the corner. *He should be carrying this weight, not me!* But Jake's fears and complaints were temporarily silenced as the coaching staff walked in for the post-game debriefing. Coach kept it short.

"You guys played well out there tonight," he praised in typical minimalist fashion. "But don't lose focus. That's one game down, but four important ones to go. We can't let up for one second. So get some rest tonight and come back ready to practice hard and play hard. Everybody in!"

Everyone stood and stretched their arms out into the center for a team yell and then proceeded to jump around whooping and hollering for the next few minutes. Eventually, Coach and his assistants slapped the guys on the back and headed out the door, and the cheering dwindled as the guys headed to their lockers and the showers. Jake sighed with relief, hoping that maybe Nate had lost the opportunity for his announcement.

Jake peeled off his sweaty jersey and sat down next to his locker. He leaned back against the cold metal, closing his eyes and letting the chill reinvigorate his bare skin. After a few moments he bent forward to untie his shoes. As he fiddled with the knots, he slowly realized that, aside from the blaring music playing through the speakers, the normal locker room ruckus was strangely missing. He shed his sweaty socks and flung them to the floor, wondering what he had missed. When he looked up, Nate was whispering into Bojan's ear. They both looked over at Jake, and the naked Serbian quickly grabbed his towel and wrapped it around his waist. He stared at Jake in disgust. A couple of the freshmen who hadn't even played that day walked by and sneered. Everywhere Jake looked, his teammates averted their gaze and quickly dressed out of his sight. Except Grant. Grant just stared at him with his eyes wide open.

Immediately Jake understood. "Nate!" he yelled, rising from his seat in only his shorts.

Nate quickly threw his hands up as if to ward off Jake's advances. "Whoa! Back off, dude. I'm not your type."

Snickers echoed around the room.

"This isn't funny, dude." Jake stared Nate down, then turned to the rest of his teammates, pleading for support. "I don't know what he told you, but the joke's over—"

"This ain't no joke," Nate interrupted, looking innocently around the room. "I'm dead serious. We have a teammate that's been keeping a secret, and it's about time we all found out about it."

Jake stared back at his teammates in disbelief. "Are you serious?" Grant's stare was starting to get on his nerves. *I'm not the one with the secret!* Jake wanted to shout at everyone.

"Is that why you were so quick to defend that queer who air-balled the half-court shot?" Jamal asked quietly, obviously repulsed.

"He's a friend...of mine," Jake hesitated. "How would you feel if—"

"Yeah, what kind of friend?" Nate interrupted. More snickers.

Jake shook his head. Was this really happening? Never in his wildest imagination would he expect to be in a position like this. "I..." His voice trailed off, a reasonable explanation evading him.

"Jake's not gay," Grant's voice piped up from his seat in the corner.

All eyes turned toward the reserved backup forward, and Jake's flushed face gave way to icy chills. He knew what was coming next. The secret he had carried with resentment was now about to be spilled, and suddenly Jake desperately wanted his roommate to just keep his mouth shut. Jake could endure the teasing. The truth would eventually come out. But Grant's truth? Jake couldn't see any good in that.

"Oh, really?" Jamal took the lead this time.

Jake could see Grant's left leg shaking and the fear flickering through his eyes. But there was also something like determination in his face, and his jaw was set with resolution.

"I'm the one with the secret," Grant declared. "And Jake's been keeping it for me…I'm the one who's gay."

Silence fell thickly on everyone present, until Nate tried to regain center stage. "Wait. You guys are roommates." He grinned, but the joke fell lifelessly to the ground. This was far past the laughing stage.

Now it was Jake's turn to join everyone in staring. Somehow, this felt even worse. Grant had actually admitted it himself. There was no speculation, no debate. Grant had sealed his own fate.

Grant stood up and walked toward the exit. "So now y'all know." He shrugged and brushed by Jake without even a glance.

"Wait." Jake reached out his arm and grabbed Grant by the shoulder.

Grant hesitated and looked at Jake. The rest of the guys watched like dumbfounded spectators at a Ping-Pong match.

"How many points did you score today?" Jake asked with confidence.

"What are you talking about?" his roommate mumbled.

"Just answer the question," Jake pushed.

"I don't know."

Jake kept at it. His heart felt as if it was beating a million times a second. "How many rebounds?"

"I don't know," Grant snapped, obviously irritated by the seemingly irrelevant line of questions.

Nate protested, "This is ridiculous! Who cares?"

"You *should* care!" Jake said as he turned to face the team. "My *friend* here had twenty-two points and eleven rebounds today." His voice was rising in volume and intensity. "That's a career high for him in both. If that were me, or any of the rest of us, we would have already tweeted about it." A few of the guys smiled knowingly. "But Grant, he didn't even notice—because the only thing that matters to him is that we won as a team." Jake glanced around the room, hoping the guys would get his point. "There is not a more selfless or committed guy on this team, and *nothing* has changed. Do you hear me? Everyone loved Grant yesterday. Well, Grant is still that same great guy, even though now we all know his little secret. Let's not forget that." Jake knew he was preaching to himself as much as to any of the other guys.

The silence hung in the air like an impending storm cloud. No one acknowledged Jake's argument, but no one challenged it either—not even Nate. He just huffed away and finished getting ready. Within minutes, everyone had wandered back to their previous activities, but the conversation and laughter was decidedly more reserved. Grant and Jake exchanged a look of uncertain relief before Grant continued walking toward the door and Jake collapsed once more against his locker. *Thank You, God,* he prayed, not totally sure what he was thankful for. His situation still seemed pretty precarious, but something had just happened. He had no idea where his words had come from.

He let his eyelids hang closed for a while, not feeling the strength to deal with the covert glances and hushed laughter. When he finally lifted his head, he was alone. Jake trudged to the shower, overcome with emptiness as he stood under the hot water and let it wash the salty sweat off his body.

11:22pm | From: Jake | To: Grant
Dude where r u?

AFTER FIDGETING AND PACING in their apartment for several hours, Jake was officially worried. He wasn't surprised to find Grant gone at first; as it was, Jake took his own sweet time getting back to his room. But this late at night and still no sign of his roommate—something didn't seem right. Jake had even looked up Peter's number and given him a call. Peter sounded as if he had just woken up and groggily informed Jake that he didn't know and didn't care where Grant was. Then he hung up.

Where had his roommate gone after leaving the locker room? He'd never even dressed out of his uniform after the game. Jake didn't want to overreact, but he couldn't help but think back to Roger and Jonny. *Did I do the right thing?* Jake wondered, thinking back to how this whole mess started. Standing up for Peter had felt like the right thing to do at the time, but Jake couldn't help but think that if he'd kept his mouth shut then this whole ordeal would have never happened. *Great job glowing, dude,* Jake cringed. *You only made things worse.*

He fell back onto the couch and tried to focus on "Sports Center," but the latest scores and highlights blurred together. Who cared?

While Jake would have normally eaten up every last detail of the other college games around the country, waiting impatiently for how they impacted his own Louisville Cardinals, tonight was different. Their stats, their ranking, their competitors...none of it was nearly as important as what was really going on with their team. Jake couldn't stop seeing Grant's anguished face. The commentators' voices faded to the background as Jake stared blankly at the screen, silent words flooding through his mind.

God, I know we haven't spent a lot of time together lately. I'm sorry. But I just want to pray for my friend Grant. I don't know where he is, and I'm worried about him. Maybe he's just hanging out at a friend's and I'm stressing out about nothing, but please help him stay safe and help him know that he doesn't have to go through this whole thing alone...I know I've been a lousy friend lately, consumed with my own stupid stuff...But I'm done with that. I don't want to live like that anymore. I want to glow, like Buddy said...Please show me what to do. I really need Your help...I'm done ignoring You. You're the best thing that ever happened to me. I'm sorry for letting You down...

The words ebbed to a stop, and Jake sat motionless for a few minutes. He wasn't really sure what he was waiting for, but he didn't know what else to do. Chris always said that if he listened long enough, he always heard God speak. Well, that may have been easy for Chris, but Jake didn't have the patience. He did, however, have an overwhelming desire to go out and search for Grant.

He threw on a jacket and ran out the door, thinking through the most obvious places on campus where Grant might be. He ran by the main library, the practice gym, the weight room, the coffee shop, the student activities center, and even some of the frat houses. Nothing. The University of Louisville was spread out over 320 acres, and for the first time Jake really resented it. How was he supposed to find his roommate in all this space? He could be anywhere!

Walking dejectedly back toward their apartment, Jake started heading down Fourth Street and just kept going. Soon he realized he was heading toward the off-campus apartments where so many parties were held. There was probably one going on right now—one that he had conspicuously not been invited to. Could Grant be there? Jake broke into a run again, desperate to find out.

As he ran through the chilly night air, his thoughts returned to his first night at Louisville over a year earlier. He recalled the pressure he'd felt to fit in and shuddered when he remembered that initial challenge, that do-or-die three-pointer at the park basketball court on that frigid January night. What if he had missed that shot? Would it really have mattered? Would his life be any different from the life of ostracism he could be facing now? Or what if he had refused to play along with their game from the beginning? Jake slowed to a walk, trying to remember which street they had turned down to get to that court. He wandered down a side road that looked vaguely familiar and suddenly heard the rattling chains of a net and the thudding bounce of a ball. Jake peered down the street and saw the faint silhouette of a single shooter on the unlit court. Jake picked up his pace, suddenly hopeful that he had finally found his roommate.

"Grant?" Jake called out into the darkness, racing through the pools of eerie yellow light spilling onto the pavement from the overhead streetlights.

The basketball stopped its echoing bounce. "What do you want?" Without waiting for an answer, the shooter turned around to swish a seventeen-footer through the shredded rusty net.

Jake jogged onto the court to grab the rebound and pass it back to Grant. "I've been looking all over for you, man."

Grant dribbled the ball twice and threw up another shot. This time it clanged off the side of the rim. "Well, you found me. Congratulations."

Jake dribbled the ball out to the three-point line and tossed up the same shot he'd made that first night. *Brick.* "I know you're mad at me for getting you into this whole mess. I'm sorry. I should have just kept my mouth shut about Peter."

Grant grabbed the rebound and held the ball in his arms. He turned to face Jake squarely, as if to say something, then turned back to the basket and shot a perfect swish. He ran after the ball and grabbed it before Jake could.

Jake fumbled for words. "I know I've been a jerk lately. I've totally blown it..." Grant swished another shot. "But I want to change. I've been talking with Chris and this guy named Buddy, and they've given me a lot to think about. I started reading my Bible again—" Grant's shot banged against the backboard, but he retrieved it on his own and shot it right back up again. Swish. Again, he chased the ball down before Jake could get to it. "Grant, I know you have no reason to believe me, but just give me a chance. Give me another shot at being your friend."

Grant kept his back to Jake as he dribbled the ball methodically back and forth. Jake wasn't sure what to say—or do—next. Was Grant that mad? Was he just going to stonewall him? Just as Jake was wondering if he should simply turn around and head back home, Grant's voice rang out coolly.

"Was it worth it?"

"Uh..." Jake stammered, not completely sure what "it" Grant was referring to.

"That's what I've been doing out here this whole time. Asking myself that question."

"Look, I said I'm sorry," Jake repeated, starting to get a little annoyed. What more did Grant want from him? "But you didn't need to bail me out. I could've handled it on my own."

"No." Grant turned to face Jake. "What you did was cool, man. For Peter. For me. It was about time I just came out with it...But there's no going back now." He tossed Jake the ball, and Jake spun it around his fingers. "Peter called on my way back from the gym. He said he couldn't be with someone who hurt him like I did. So now, everyone knows I'm gay, but the one guy who pushed me to come out doesn't want anything to do with me. Perfect."

Jake stared at him, clueless about what his next move should be. What was he supposed to say? "I'm sorry"? Sure, Jake felt bad about the break-up because his friend was hurting, but he honestly preferred Grant to be single—it made the whole gay thing easier to forget. And what was he supposed to do? Give Grant a hug? As if that wasn't awkward. "Well, I still want to be your friend," Jake offered, with a shrug and a bounce pass.

"Don't you get it, Jake?" Grant glared at him. He caught the ball and looked as if he might pop it. "Everything's going to be different now. You saw how the guys responded to you—for like five minutes. That's going to be the rest of my life. And no one gets to back *me* up on this one. I am what I am, and there's no denying it now."

"*I've* got your back, bro," Jake assured. "I told you, *I'm* going to be different."

"Different!" Grant scoffed. "Great. Because obviously your little Christian thing did you *so* much good before!"

"You can criticize me as much as you want," Jake said, knowing that Grant had a point, based on his past behavior. "But I don't see any of the other guys walking around after midnight looking for you...Not even Peter." The moment he said that last line, Jake knew he had gone too far, and the pain that shot across Grant's face made Jake wish he had a rewind button. "Look, I'm sorry. I didn't mean—"

"Yeah, different," Grant whispered. "Jake, you're going to have some choices to make, so let me just spell them out for you. The guys on the team...or me. Your precious Bible...or me. Why don't you just go on home and make it easier on both of us." He dribbled the basketball and laid it up half-heartedly. It bounced off the underside of the rim. He caught it and dribbled it through his legs before exploding with a more powerful shot.

"No, Grant," Jake replied, surprising even himself with his boldness. "You're the one with the choice to make. I'm here, begging to be your friend. I'll admit, I'm far from perfect, and I'm going to screw up plenty more times. But with God's help, I'm going to love you and support you and make up for my lameness. So you can either take me with this new little Christian 'thing' or you can just go on home and do it on your own. But either way, I'm not giving up on you—because neither is God."

"God." Grant snorted. "Yeah, I've heard too much about what He thinks about people like me. No thanks."

"What do you think He thinks about the lifestyle *I've* been living this past year? C'mon! Don't be so judgmental." Jake ran up and stole the rebound and dribbled it out to the three-point line. "You know that old guy that I mentioned?" Jake shot the ball, missing badly to the right.

"Yeah," Grant grunted unenthusiastically, as he ran into the darkness to retrieve the ball.

"I think you would like him."

Grant returned, dribbling the ball effortlessly between his legs. "I'm not interested. As if I want to listen to you guys talk about your religion. I don't care how old he is."

"What do you got to lose?"

"What do I got to win? Jake, I've got enough of my own issues to deal with right now." "Okay. One game to eleven. I win, and we hang with Buddy. You win, and I'll never bring it up again."

Grant dribbled to the top of the key, shaking his head. When he turned around, Jake expected a flat-out refusal, but instead he detected a slight smirk. Grant's left eye winked.

"It's on."

42

10:44am | From: Amy | To: Cari
Eek! We're meeting my dad's family today! I'm so excited!

AMY WAS BOTH EXHILARATED AND EXHAUSTED as Steven finally drove them up the 880 freeway toward her dad's house. She hadn't slept more than a few hours last night in anticipation of this visit that had been almost a month in planning, and she tried to close her eyes right now. But her mind kept racing.

Since finally meeting her dad that wonderful Monday at the end of January, Amy had spoken with him almost daily. Sometimes their conversations were just brief greetings, and other times they talked for hours. Every time, Amy hung up loving her life more than ever. She was slowly getting to know her father again—and he was amazing. And now, she was going to get to know her brother and sister. *My brother and sister!* Just saying those words gave her giddy goose bumps.

Amy's dad had suggested that they take it slowly at first, letting the two of them reconnect for a while before throwing the rest of the family into the mix. This was also supposed to give Amy time to break the news to her mom—something she put off for as long as possible. For the last fifteen-plus years, Amy had heard nothing but negative things about her father, and she could only imagine the long, whining lecture she would receive when her mom found out that Amy was getting close to him. But Sherry was surprisingly cordial when Amy had finally told her last night.

"Just make sure you don't ever love him as much as you love me," she joked, with an edge that said she wasn't really kidding.

Amy hadn't promised her anything.

Thirty minutes into the drive, Steven switched the radio station to smooth jazz and mindlessly started playing an air saxophone with his right hand while his left hand drummed the rhythm on the steering wheel. Amy had to laugh.

"What?" His beautiful lips curled up into a shy smile.

"You're just so cute," Amy giggled and rubbed his arm. She had to admit, she was one lucky girl. Steven had been so supportive through the past month and a half, listening to her talk endlessly about her dad and her new family. He had given her so much encouragement and advice, and she loved him for it.

At the same time, she could tell it was taking a toll on him. Amy knew that if it were up to Steven, they'd be spending every spare moment together. He never seemed to get enough of her—which was totally sweet, but a little smothering. So rebuilding this relationship with her dad had come as a welcome excuse—she felt as if she now had a legitimate reason not to be thinking of Steven every waking minute of the day. And though she knew he didn't like it, Steven had given her the space. He was a great guy. She wished she could repay him for how great he'd been.

But as much as Amy cared about him, they hadn't even been dating for six months yet, and she still wanted to take things slow. Besides her new family, college offered so many other opportunities that were competing for her time right now, and she still wanted to fully enjoy them, too. She loved the weekly Friday barbecues that her dorm hosted and their special seminars on topics like How to Polka and Ice Cream Tasting 101. She'd almost missed the annual FroSoCo trip to Tahoe last month in order to make up for lost time with Steven, but Renee had persuaded her to go at the last minute, and Amy was so glad she did. Steven had been bummed, and at first Amy had felt guilty. But the bonding with her roommate and the other girls had been worth it.

The second night of the trip, a bunch of the girls had gotten into a conversation about sex, and Amy openly shared her story and why she was choosing to wait until she was married to have sex again. Most of the girls rolled their eyes and disagreed good-naturedly with her plan, but a few of them were genuinely intrigued, and they'd stayed up until the wee hours of the morning talking about it and other spiritual topics. Since then, two of the girls had regularly attended Intersect, as well as the weekly girls' small group that Amy and Renee were co-leading this semester. Amy couldn't have been more thrilled. She was nearly overwhelmed by all the blessings she was experiencing in her life, and while Steven was one of the major ones, she didn't want to miss out on the other blessings or take them for granted.

One of the biggest highlights from this past month was Andrea's visit over the Presidents' Day holiday. They ran for miles, talked for hours, and ate tons of chocolate over the four days she was there. Andrea and Renee immediately connected, and the three girls stayed up late every night talking about God, clothes, and boys. On the boy front, Andrea was still very much enjoying being single, although she was quite impressed by all the hot college guys. She gave Steven her immediate approval, but Amy couldn't help but notice that she brought Jake up quite a few times. Based on information she had gleaned from Facebook and Chris, Andrea informed Amy that Jake was apparently making a turn for the better. Amy wouldn't let herself think about him too much, but ever since hearing that, she'd let him occasionally slip into her prayers. She hoped Andrea was right…for Jake's own sake.

"What are you smiling about?" Steven interrupted her thinking, moving his hand from the stick shift to her leg.

"Uh, nothing," Amy responded, flushing a little. She interlaced her fingers with Steven's, hoping he wouldn't notice. "I guess I just can't stop thinking about meeting my brother and sister."

"Well, we're almost there," he grinned, as he steered his Mustang off the exit.

"Oh my gosh!" Amy gasped, covered by a new wave of goose bumps. After so many years of wishing, hoping, pleading for a sibling, here she was, about to meet two! "What if they don't like me?" she worried as he slowed the car at the first stop sign. "Or what if my stepmom is like psycho? Or what if—"

"Or what if they love you, like I know they will," Steven interjected, squeezing her knee. "Doooooh doo doo do-da-doodadoo," he started singing. "Don't worry...be happy."

His smooth voice tickled her ears, even on a silly song like this, and she giggled, leaning over to give him the kiss he had earned. He was so good at getting her to stop stressing.

As they passed an upscale strip mall on the left, Steven's GPS instructed him to turn right, and they passed a well-maintained elementary school. Amy wondered if that was the one Ramon and Marissa attended. They drove by an ice cream shop where Amy imagined the family walking to get ice cream together and a park where Amy imagined the kids playing. Fascinated by every little detail of what her brother's and sister's life might be like in this neighborhood, Amy caught herself wondering how different her own life might have been if she'd only read those letters sooner. So many things—both good and bad—could have changed had she lived with her dad instead of her mom. Caught up in her own wistful thoughts, Amy didn't notice the gigantic sign up ahead until they were only a few houses away. Suddenly she realized that the butcher paper stretching across the entire front of the white house to her right was for her. It boldly proclaimed "WELCOME HOME AMY!!!" in big, black, block letters. Clusters of tiny red, blue, green, and yellow hands decorated the border.

"Oh my gosh," she whispered, dabbing at her eyes with her fingers as Steven pulled up alongside the curb.

Before they could get out of the car, a little boy exploded out of the house like a cannon ball. "Amy!" Ramon yelled, racing toward her. Amy emerged from the car just in time to hug her cute little brother.

"You must be Ramon," Amy smiled and bent down to his level.

"Are you really my sissy?" he asked, gazing at her with his rich brown eyes.

"Well, is that your dad?" Amy pointed to her father who was walking out the front door, holding the shyer Marissa in his arms.

"Yeah," Ramon whispered, his large eyes growing even bigger.

"Well, he's my dad, too, so I guess that makes me your big sis...and you're my little bro."

"Whoa!" His whole face lit up as he placed his chubby little hands on his cheeks.

Steven came up behind Amy and placed his hand on the small of her back. Together, they made their way up the sidewalk to meet the rest of her new family.

"Marissa, this is your big sister, Amy," Ray spoke softly to his timid daughter as they approached.

Marissa looked over at Amy and Steven and promptly dug her head back into her father's shoulder.

"Hi, Marissa. It's nice to meet you." Amy gently rubbed her back. "I heard you like to play with dolls."

Her five-year-old sister peeked at Amy through her burrow in her dad's neck.

"I was hoping we could play together sometime," Amy continued.

Marissa smiled shyly.

Olivia came out and joined the cluster on her front porch, wiping her hands on a dish towel. Amy noticed how much more stunning she was in person than in the pocket-sized picture her dad had shown her. Her long brown hair flowed over her petite frame, and her warm toffee-colored complexion glowed with radiance.

"Hi, Amy. I'm Olivia," she greeted with a slight accent, pulling Amy into a warm embrace. "It's so wonderful to finally meet you. We've been praying for this moment for such a long time."

Amy could only smile, limited by the lump forming at the back of her throat. Everything seemed just too good to be true.

"Welcome home, honey." Her dad grinned, pulling her into his own hug. As they pulled apart, Marissa whispered in Amy's ear.

"Do you want to play with my dolls right now?"

"Ay, *mija*, how about after lunch, okay? It's already on the table," Olivia interjected, kissing her little girl on the cheek and hoisting her to her hip.

"Okay, but can I sit next to Amy?" Marissa asked.

"Why don't you ask your sister?"

Marissa looked down bashfully. "Can I sit next to you, Amy?"

"I would love that." Amy ran her fingers through Marissa's silky brown hair.

Marissa smiled and pointed to the door. "That's my house."

"Do you want to show her inside, *mija*?" Olivia asked, lowering Marissa to the ground. Marissa grabbed Amy's hand and walked her inside. She pointed out the living room and the bathroom and her brother's camouflage-themed bedroom before finally leading Amy to her pink, princess-themed room. Amy smiled and followed her through the doorway, where she was given a tour of her dolls and stuffed animals and dress-up clothes and bookshelf and pretty much everything else.

"*Mija*, you can play later," Olivia's voice called from the front of the house. "Bring Amy back so we can eat, *por favor*."

Amy suddenly realized she'd left Steven alone and wondered what he was doing. When they rounded the corner into the kitchen, there he was engaged in a game of thumb wrestling with Ramon.

"I got you!" Amy's little brother cried, holding Steven's thumb down with both of his hands.

Steven pretended to struggle before accepting defeat. "You got me," he groaned and tousled the little kid's hair. He caught Amy's eye, and they smiled at each other. Amy's heart flip-flopped.

Over the next few hours, Amy stuffed herself full of love, laughter, and homemade tortillas, salsa, and carne asada. After a long lunch around the much-used dining room table, Steven volunteered to help with the cleanup while Amy went to the back to play with her adorable siblings. She quickly discovered that simultaneously engaging both five-year-olds was a potentially chaotic situation. Ramon's main goal seemed to be to knock the heads off of his sister's dolls with his Transformers, which made Marissa's tea party a bit of an adventure. But somehow Amy managed to avoid any tragedies, and before she knew it, an hour had flown by, and Olivia was popping her head in to tell the kids it was nap time.

"Can Amy read us the story?" Ramon clamored, and Amy was only too happy to oblige. He picked a G.I. Joe story, and Amy couldn't help thinking that he'd get along great with Caleb back at home.

When Amy was done with Ramon's story, he obediently closed his eyes and tried to doze off. Amy kissed his forehead and crossed the hall to Marissa's room. She was eagerly waiting with, of course, a princess story. By the time Amy flipped to the final page with the traditional "happily ever after" ending, Marissa's breathing had softened into a regular rhythm and her hand rested limply on Amy's leg. Amy looked down at the sleeping beauty and couldn't help but marvel at her own "happily ever after." While she hoped this was far from the ending, she was perfectly content with all the happiness overflowing in her life right now.

Amy softly lifted Marissa's head from her lap and placed it on her pillow, and then tiptoed out of her room to join the rest of the adults. During what Olivia liked to call "the peaceful hour," the adults gathered in the living room sipping a fresh brew of gourmet coffee.

"They're beautiful," Amy sighed to her dad and Olivia, who sat hand in hand on the love seat across from her.

"Just like you, honey," her dad replied.

"So, what have you guys been talking about this whole time?" Amy asked.

Steven and her father exchanged a funny glance. "Oh, you know. Sports, classes, things like that," Steven answered.

Amy looked at Steven curiously, then sipped at her coffee. She had started to drink it again this semester, thanks to so many late nights, and she relished the rich liquid. Her dad made it strong! *Maybe that's where I get the addiction from,* she thought. Steven wrapped his arm around her shoulder, and Amy wondered if he understood how much this whole afternoon meant to her. From what she could tell, his family seemed almost perfect. Again, she couldn't help but wonder how different her life might have been if she'd grown up with her dad instead of her mom. "So," Amy broke the lull in the conversation, "tell me how you guys met." The look that passed between her father and his wife piqued her interest.

"Well, it's interesting that you should ask," her father started quietly, then hesitated.

Amy watched him, waiting for him to continue.

"It was seven years ago last October...We met at Disneyland."

"Disneyland, huh? How did that happen?" Amy probed. It didn't seem like a likely place for an older couple to meet. Again Ray and Olivia looked at each other with what seemed to be uncertainty. Amy wondered what kind of scandal they might be hiding.

"I worked there on the weekends for a year to make some extra cash," Olivia admitted.

"She was Princess Jasmine," Ray interjected.

Olivia smiled and slapped him playfully. "As if that matters, *chismoso*," she chided. "Anyway, one day I saw Ray just looking so sad sitting all alone. I had to go talk to him."

"What were you doing at the happiest place on earth alone?" Amy wrinkled her nose.

"Pretty pathetic, huh?" Ray admitted. "Someone I knew was coming, and I was waiting to see her."

"Really? Was it another girlfriend?"

"Oh, no, no." Ray chuckled. "Let's just say she was someone very special to me, that I hadn't seen in a very long time..."

The way his voice trailed off and his eyes got misty as he stared straight at her gave Amy the chills. A mental picture of her and her friends racing through the theme park on her thirteenth birthday flickered across her brain. "Wait." Amy's tone turned serious, and she did the math in her head. "I went to Disneyland around that time..."

Her dad nodded slowly. "I know."

Amy sat there trying to process what this meant.

"After your uncle was sentenced, Amy," her father explained softly, "the full realization of what I'd done, what I'd left behind, hit me almost harder than I could handle. I knew I'd made the biggest mistake of my life when I left you behind. And I didn't know how to make it right. You clearly weren't interested in responding to my letters, so I started calling—"

"What? You called me?"

"Your mother tried to protect you, Amy, and told me to leave both of you guys alone. I can understand. Why should she—or you—trust me, after what I'd done?"

Amy felt her heart tightening inside her chest. "But—"

"But, anyway," her father hurried on. "That year for your birthday, I called and asked if there was anything you particularly wanted, and your mom told me about your wish to go to Disneyland."

"I always wondered how she afforded that!" Amy interjected.

"So we agreed that I'd buy the tickets if she told me exactly what day you were going."

"And you just sat there watching me." Amy put the pieces together. "How come you didn't come talk to me, though? Don't you know how much that would have meant to me?"

"You really think you would have wanted to talk to me then?"

"Well...maybe not...But it would have been better than you just stalking me. If you weren't my dad, I'd say that was pretty creepy."

Her dad grinned sheepishly. "You have no idea, Amy."

"What?" she asked. "Do you mean you did it other times, too?"

His head nodded almost imperceptibly, and his eyes grew moist. "I didn't want to miss out on the significant events of my oldest daughter's life. So I tried to be there...I saw your sweet sixteen, your cheer championships, your graduation..."

Amy's hand instinctively clutched her stomach. "So you saw...?" Somehow in all their conversations, she had never managed to bring up the fact that she'd had a baby. But if her father had been at her graduation, then he had surely noticed her pregnancy.

"Amy," Olivia pitched in. "We sat in the hospital parking lot here praying our knuckles white the day you gave birth, and we drove down and watched from *your* hospital lot as you said goodbye to your baby."

"We've tried to pray for you through every step of your life, and honey, I just have to say, I'm so, *so* proud of you and the woman you've become." Her father got up and sat down on the other side of Amy to hug her.

"I had no idea." Amy shook her head, feelings of resentment toward her mom shifting into unexpected gratitude at this new connection she had with her father. "It's like you've been my guardian angel," she whispered.

With her father on her right and Steven on her left, Amy basked in the feeling of being completely loved and thoroughly happy.

43

4:03pm | From: Steven | To: Amy
Great news!

AMY GLANCED DOWN at the text as she exited her two-hour Ethical Reasoning class, her head throbbing from a discussion on the ethics of euthanasia, not only for humans but also for pets. She scrolled through a mental list of what Steven's big news might be... besides, of course, that this was their six-month anniversary. But he'd already greeted her this morning with a serenade and six white roses, so that wasn't anything new.

One thing she loved about Steven, though: He was an eternal optimist. He didn't just make lemons into lemonade; he threw in strawberries and yogurt and crushed ice and called it a smoothie. For Steven, great news could simply be that he'd found his car keys—that she never even knew were lost. Or that he'd bought her a drink from Starbucks—which was always welcome. Or that he was just thinking about her—which was sweet, and how could she complain?

Curious to find out how excited she should be about this great news, Amy called her sweet boyfriend. After four rings, it went to voicemail.

"Can't wait to find out the great news! See you soon," she cheerily told the recording as she walked into her dorm room.

To celebrate their special day, they were going on a double date with his parents, who were in town from Virginia and were taking the two of them out to a fancy restaurant in downtown San Francisco. Amy was excited about their choice of venue, but she couldn't help thinking she would probably enjoy the special occasion with Steven a little more without the pressure of meeting his parents for the first time.

Amy *was* pretty excited, however, about the opportunity to dress up. After a quick shower, she pulled her classic little black dress out of her closet and slipped it on. With a straight strapless neckline, the bodice fit snugly through her waist where it flared into a flowing knee-length skirt, flattering her figure without being inappropriate or risqué. Renee insisted that Amy wear the necklace she was always ogling, a gauzy deep-blue flower hanging from a delicate silver thread. Amy paired it with the diamond pendant earrings Steven had given her for Valentine's Day—an exquisite gift that had made Amy's thought-filled coupon book seem paltry. But they looked beautiful tonight. Renee helped her curl her hair in loose, hanging ringlets pinned in place by a few strategic rhinestone-edged hairpins. After doing Amy's make-up in dramatic fashion, Renee spritzed on a few squirts of perfume and then spun Amy around in view of the full-length mirror on the back of their door.

"Ohhhhh!" Renee squealed, dancing up and down. "You look beautiful, Amy." She hugged her roommate carefully to avoid messing anything up.

Amy grinned and blushed and slipped on her black heels a minute before six, when Steven was coming to pick her up. He was promptly heard singing down the hallway. "Well, I can't wait to see what his good news is." She flung the door open before he could even knock.

"Whoa, dang!" he blurted mid-lyric as his jaw dropped. Looking quite dashing himself in a black suit, he stepped back to admire his girlfriend. "Uh, Amy, uh...wow!"

"Sp-sp-spit it out, junior. Just say it. She's smoking hot!" Renee piped up from where she was sitting on the edge of her bed.

Steven's speechless nod made Amy blush again. She hugged Renee goodbye and accepted Steven's outstretched arm. "See you later, sistah!" She grinned back to her roommate as the door swung shut behind them. Then she turned to her attractive date. "So what's the good news, hot stuff?"

It started as a cute little smirk at the corners of his mouth and then blossomed into his full-blown irresistible grin. But he just kept walking without saying a word.

"What?" Amy stopped in her tracks and grabbed his suit jacket to pull him back to her.

"You really want to know?" Steven whispered, nuzzling his face against hers.

"Yes!"

"Well..." He paused for effect, then swooped down and kissed her lips. "That was for my song in the hallway, by the way."

"Steven!"

"Well, you're just going to have to wait until we meet my parents at the restaurant," he grinned impishly. He delicately raised her fingers to his lips and gave her a flirtatious wink. "I promise you, it's worth the wait."

"Ugh!" Amy pretended to pout and playfully pushed him as they resumed walking hand in hand to his Mustang.

Their drive into the city was delightful, Steven serenading Amy with love songs and getting his fill of little kisses in exchange. He was always a romantic, but Amy couldn't help thinking that even this was a little extreme for him. *Oh well,* she figured. *Better he gets it out of his system now before we're with his parents!* She traced his fingertips and basked in the thrill of his love.

They pulled up to the restaurant, where Steven gave his keys to the valet and escorted her inside. Amy had been to what she would have considered a fancy restaurant once before, with Jake before their senior prom. But one step through this doorway and she knew this was a whole new type of fancy. The swanky lounge paired modern furnishings and ambient lighting with extravagant crystal chandeliers. Lavish draperies hung from the walls, adding an elegant warmth to the atmosphere. Amy breathed in the impressive air, and smiled. *Wow!*

Steven wrapped his arm around her waist and looked down proudly. "Nothing but the best for my girl." He kissed her forehead then bent over to whisper something to the host, who led them to one of several tables on raised platforms along the back wall. Fringed by elaborate velvet tapestries, each table was curtained in intimacy.

At the second table from the left sat an attractive couple that shared a striking resemblance to Amy's boyfriend. Amy felt a chill go down her spine as she approached. *What if they don't think I'm good enough for their son?* Her fingers instinctively brushed her hair off her shoulder as the couple rose from their seats.

"Mom and Dad...this is Amy," Steven introduced, pushing her gently forward.

"Mr. Jensen, Mrs. Jensen." Amy shook their hands cordially, but Steven's mom pulled her into a warm hug and gave her a quick peck on the cheek.

"Please, call us Mitch and Barbara," Mitch said, with a smile identical to the one Amy loved so much on Steven.

Always the perfect gentleman, Steven pulled out Amy's chair before seating himself, and everyone took their seats around the cozy table.

"It's so great to finally meet you, Amy," Barbara gushed, grabbing Amy's hand. "Steven has told us so many wonderful things about you."

"Thank you," Amy responded, suddenly wishing Steven had done a better job informing her about them. She realized that pretty much all she knew was that Mitch owned his own business back in Virginia and Barbara sang each week in the church choir. "So, what's the choir going to do without you this Sunday?" Amy grinned lamely.

The look Barbara exchanged with her husband seemed to indicate that she approved, though. Her eyes sparkled. "I'm sure they'll survive."

"Barb's got a beautiful voice," Mitch asserted, rubbing her hand. "And the choir never sounds quite as good without her. Steven was fortunate enough to get her genes there." He chuckled. "Me, on the other hand, I'm a jailhouse singer."

Amy looked at him, puzzled.

"I'm always behind a few bars, and I can't find the key!"

"Ha ha, dad," Steven groaned, while the others laughed.

A crisply dressed waiter appeared at their table. His gregarious smile made it seem as if they were the only people he wanted to serve. "My name's Benji, and I'll be your server this evening. May I take an order for your drinks while you have a little more time to look over the menu?"

Not sure if a restaurant like this served regular water but feeling pressured by everyone's stares in her direction, Amy quickly asked for sparkling water, hoping that was reasonable enough. Apparently it was, because Steven's mom followed suit. Steven ordered a Coke and his father picked a bottle of wine from an extensive list. The light banter resumed as soon as the server left the table, and laughter flowed freely.

Amy decided she liked Steven's family. *No wonder he turned out so good!* she smiled. His father was an expert at self-deprecating humor, while Barbara was the perfect wife, rolling her eyes on cue with her husband's corny punchlines. It was obvious that they were still in love, even after twenty-plus years of marriage. And they were proud of their son. Slowly, Amy's nerves began to relax, and she started to enjoy herself more than she had expected.

Before long, Benji returned with their drinks and proceeded with their order. "Have you decided on any appetizers you would like me to bring for your first course?"

Mitch took charge after only momentarily glancing down at the menu. "I'll start with the seared sonoma foie gras with the caramelized red onions."

"And I'll take the lobster bisque with saffron-orange rémoulade," Barbara smiled eagerly.

Steven, too, seemed quite at home in this chichi atmosphere and confidently ordered an asparagus salad with zucchini pearls. All this seemed so far beyond Amy's comprehension, and she struggled to find something she recognized. She had to admit, Steven's initial date of a pizza picnic was much more up her alley. Her eyes frantically scanned the page for something familiar, landing on a salad with words she'd actually used before.

"Um, I'll take the arugula salad with cranberry vinaigrette," she ordered hurriedly.

Mitch and Barbara seemed to exchange looks, and Amy wondered if her choice was too simple. But before she could worry too much, Steven reassuringly squeezed her knee under the table.

"Still eating that foie gras, Pops, what with all the controversy surrounding animal rights and all?" he prodded.

"Ah, but it's so velvety and delectable," his father countered.

"Whatever. So, what did you guys end up doing today?"

"Oh! We went for a delightful bike tour from Fisherman's Wharf to the Golden Gate Bridge, and then had lunch at a little bistro with an enchanting view of the bay. It was just lovely! You two should definitely do it sometime," Barbara chirped.

Their server returned with their appetizers, a basket of mini baguettes, and a bottle of wine that Amy was pretty sure cost more than her minivan. He then proceeded to take their meal orders. Steven must have interpreted Amy's subtle look of despair, because he promptly but casually recommended the roasted stuffed quail with orzo and some other things that Amy couldn't remember. She smiled gratefully and said, "That sounds great. I'll take it."

As they dined on their appetizers, the conversation traveled quickly and lightly. Amy discovered that the Jensens were great at asking questions, inquiring insightfully about many aspects of Steven's and Amy's lives while Benji continued to bring out more food and drink.

Some time after the main course was served and everyone was relishing their mouth-watering meals, Steven lightly tapped his knife against his wine glass. "I believe I shared with each of you that I received some great news today," he said, a mysterious smile playing at his lips.

By this time, Amy had all but forgotten about Steven's "great news," but suddenly her interest was on high alert. She placed her fork down on her plate and gave her boyfriend her undivided attention. Steven's parents did likewise.

"Well...as you all know, I will be graduating in three short months. With only one more quarter to go, and only two classes to take this quarter, I've been giving a lot of thought to what I'm going to do next. This chapter of my life at Stanford has been amazing, among other reasons because of this fascinating, beautiful woman sitting here at my side. But this chapter is coming to a close, and it's time I make some decisions about where the next chapter will lead me..."

The tiny bite of stuffed quail still in Amy's mouth suddenly felt extremely dry and impossible to swallow. Her mind panicked, wondering what his last statement could mean. They had talked a few times about the future, but Amy was loving her present so much that she always tried to change the subject. She didn't want to think about what was next. It had taken her long enough to get to Stanford in the first place, and as much as she didn't want to imagine being there without Steven, she also didn't want to picture not being there. Steven's voice hadn't stopped talking, and Amy snapped herself back to attention.

"I didn't want to get anybody's hopes up, so I never told any of you that I even applied, but..." Steven waited just one more moment. "I got into the Manhattan School of Music!"

The Jensens burst out in celebration at their son's exciting news. Barbara stood up and reached from her seat to give him a hug and a kiss while Mitch grabbed his hand and patted him on the back.

"Steven, that's great," Amy smiled, but inside she was feeling like her heart was ripping apart. He was the most gifted musician she'd ever heard, so it was no surprise that he'd want to study at some place prestigious like New York. But New York was so far away. And she'd already seen how the long-distance thing worked. In her mind, Steven's great news rang the death knell of their relationship.

"It's an incredible school," Steven rambled on zealously. "I got accepted into their contemporary performance program, which is just amazing...And it's New York! I mean, how cool is that?" He looked to Amy for confirmation, seemingly oblivious to her reservations.

Amy nodded numbly, trying to show him the enthusiasm he deserved.

"Which brings me to my next great news!" Steven's smile grew even wider and he turned to face Amy directly. "I've been at Stanford for almost four years, but it wasn't until a few months ago that I fully understood why God brought me all the way to California to go to school." He reached out and grabbed Amy's clammy fingers.

Instantly, the questions in Amy's mind shifted into overdrive. *What is going on here? What great news could come out of this?* Steven started fishing around in his pants pocket and then slid off his chair to kneel on one knee. *What is he doing?* Amy's brain protested as her heart pounded violently inside of her chest.

"You are the true music in my life, Amy Briggs." Steven gazed into her eyes. "And as great as the Manhattan School of Music is, it would be horrible if I didn't have you there with me." His left hand pulled out a little black box, and he flipped it open to reveal a stunning engagement ring. "Amy Briggs...Will you marry me?"

Amy wasn't sure if the entire restaurant had grown silent waiting for her response or if it was just her imagination, but suddenly the weight of the world climbed upon her shoulders. She had dreamed of a moment like this since she was a little girl, and really, it was perfect. The diamond was huge and sparkled brilliantly. Steven looked so handsome as he eagerly awaited the expected response out of her mouth. And it was an easy answer, of course. Why wouldn't she marry him?

Steven was everything she could ever hope for in a husband. He was gorgeous, smart, funny, and kind. His voice could melt mountains. And he had seen her in her best and worst times—and loved her for them. So why was the "yes" sticking in her throat?

Amy quickly glanced around the table and the room, where it seemed as if every eye was impatiently waiting for her answer. But she just couldn't get it out. This was just a little too fast. She was only twenty years old, and they'd only been dating for six months. They'd never even talked about marriage until now. A slight feeling of annoyance started to creep into her mind. Why had he put her in this situation?

Steven continued to look at her, his eyes pleading for acceptance. And Amy so desperately wanted to say that one simple word she knew everyone was dying to hear. But there were so many questions she wanted to ask him first. *Is the proposal and moving to New York a combo deal? What if I want to stay at Stanford? Would we have to get married right away?...Why now?... Are you sure?*

"I know this is a little unexpected, honey," Steven broke into the ever-increasing silence. "But I love you, and I know that I want to spend the rest of my life with you...I even asked your dad, and he was thrilled."

A picture of her brand-new family flashed across Amy's brain. "What? When?" she gasped.

"Uh, I can tell you all about it later. Right now is kind of the time you're just supposed to say yes," Steven whispered.

But she was just getting to know her family. *How can he expect me to just leave them?* Did he know what he was asking? "Do I have to leave Stanford?" Amy mumbled, wishing only Steven could hear her. The last thing she wanted to do was embarrass him, but this was her whole life they were talking about.

Steven stared back, seemingly in disbelief. "Uh, I don't know, Amy, but isn't that something we could talk about tomorrow?" He sounded agitated.

"Well, it kind of affects my answer, Steven." Amy's voice warbled unreliably and she choked back tears. "I'm sorry," she pleaded. "But—"

"Forget it." Steven shifted his weight and slid back into his chair, stuffing the ring box into his pocket. His head hung down, and Amy could see his knee trembling.

Amy glanced over at Mitch and Barbara on the other side of the table. They obviously didn't look very excited about the fact that she was turning down their beloved son. "Can't we just talk about it first?" she begged quietly, leaning forward to talk only to her boyfriend. "This is all just happening so fast."

"Never mind, Amy," Steven practically growled.

"But Steven!" The tears now rolled freely down Amy's cheeks.

"I guess I thought I knew you better than this." He still refused to make eye contact. "Just forget about it."

The silence was deafening around their little table as the clinking of silverware awkwardly resumed around the restaurant.

Mitch cleared his throat and clumsily attempted to lighten the mood. "Well, who wants dessert?" The only response he received was a fierce look from his wife.

Amy looked down at her half-eaten plate of stuffed quail, momentarily wishing she could exchange places with her meal. At least the bird had been put out of its misery. *What did I just do?* Amy thought, stabbing the stupid quail with her fork.

6:58am | From: Cari | To: Amy
We need to talk

DO WE EVER! Amy thought to herself as she glanced down at her phone and burrowed back into her blankets. Although it wasn't even seven yet, she had been awake for at least the past hour, replaying last night's horrifically awkward proposal over and over and over again, desperately trying to figure out how she should have handled the situation differently. But her mind remained mute.

Amy hadn't slept much at all. After a painfully silent drive home, Steven had dropped her off at her dorm around eleven and then raced away without a word. Amy couldn't blame him for feeling hurt, but she wanted to talk to someone about it. Unfortunately, Renee was already asleep when she got to her room, and it was way too late to call the Vaughns. So Amy changed into sweats and jogged over to the little pond by her dorm for a late-night chat with God. And while He didn't give her any answers, He sure was a good listener. Five miles or so later, she trudged back to her room still cringing at what had happened, but much more at peace that she had done the right thing.

Amy looked at her phone again and pulled her comforter off the bed as she got up to go to the lobby, which would no doubt be vacant at this time on a Saturday morning. Once there, she snuggled down into a comfy couch by the window and dialed Cari's number.

"Hello?" Caleb's distinctive voice answered, reminding Amy so much of her brother, Ramon.

"Hi Caleb! It's your best friend, Amy." She tried to sound upbeat.

"I'm sorry, Amy, but G.I. Joe is my best friend. But you can be second," Caleb replied.

"Okay, well, can I talk to your mom for a minute?" Amy chuckled to herself, remembering his parachute man.

"Mommmmm!" Caleb shouted. Footsteps hustled in the background.

"Caleb, what did I tell you about yelling in the house?" his mother's voice scolded softly. "Hello?"

"Hey, Cari. It's me." Again, Amy tried to sound cheerful. "I got your text."

"Amy, I'm so glad you called. It's early! How are you?" Cari asked genuinely.

Amy loved that she didn't have to pretend with Cari. They had already been through so much together that small talk seemed like a waste of time. "I'm not doing very well, Cari. I need some advice."

"Uh-oh. What's going on?"

Amy recounted the previous night in detail, concluding with a desperate plea. "What should I do?"

"Do you love him?" Cari finally responded after a thoughtful pause.

"Yes!" Amy cried. "But I'm just not ready—"

"Do you love him as much as you love Jake?" Cari clarified without missing a beat.

"I've been over Jake for awhile, Cari," Amy defended. They hadn't spoken in almost a year. *Almost a year exactly!* Amy suddenly realized with a shudder, remembering her agonizing experience that Friday night fifty-some weeks ago. Her heart started burning with the tingling ache that she hadn't felt...since Steven had told her he loved her.

"You sure about that?" Cari questioned.

Amy sighed, hating how well Cari knew her. It was so annoying. "I don't know. Maybe not," she conceded. "I thought I was, but..."

"Well, it seems like you might want to be careful committing the rest of your life to someone when you still have even a hint of feelings for someone else."

"But Steven's the one who proposed to me...not Jake. Jake got over me a long time ago."

"That may be true, but you don't want to do anything on a rebound. Take your time to figure this out, sweetie."

"I know! I was trying to," Amy groaned. "But then Steven had to mess it all up and rush me...in front of his parents! Oh, Cari, it was so embarrassing!"

"Amy, I can't make your decisions for you, and it seems like Steven is a great guy who really cares about you deeply...so much that he's ready to roll right now. But don't forget that he's a few years down the road from you. He has a clearer idea of what he wants. But that doesn't mean you have to hurry to catch up with him and trust him that that's what you want, too. Wasn't that the whole reason you chose Stanford over Louisville? It was about you figuring out your own dreams instead of following someone else's." Cari paused while her words sank in. "Now, a year later another great guy is offering you the same deal Jake did...What's changed?"

"Ugh! Men!" Amy sighed. "Just when you think they're perfect, they go and ruin everything."

Cari chuckled. "You've just got to be patient with them. They're like bananas: They take a while to mature, but once they do... MmMmMmmm."

"Cari Vaughn! I can't believe you just said that," Amy laughed for the first time.

"What?" Cari played innocent. "I'm just sayin'."

"So you think Steven's just green?" Amy asked wistfully.

"I think Steven just needs to hold his horses and hang out on his own tree for a little while longer," Cari said bluntly.

They both laughed quietly. While Cari hadn't exactly solved Amy's dilemma, she had given her plenty to think about.

"So, have you spoken to Melia recently?" Cari gently changed the subject.

Amy quickly remembered that Cari was the one who had initiated this call. "We talked about a week ago. Why? Is something wrong?" Amy replied, picturing those horrible cigarette burns on her little friend's arm at Christmas time and wincing at the secret she'd been carrying around since then.

"Well, she showed up on our doorstep late last night"—Cari wavered—"after walking here from her house. She wouldn't say much, but I noticed bruises around her wrists. We let her sleep in the guest bedroom, but I have to call child protective services this morning."

"I knew it!" Amy exploded.

"That's why I wanted to talk to you. If she won't tell me anything, I need to know what you know...That time she texted you and we stopped by her house, did something really happen?"

Amy squirmed, not eager to respond. Her promise to Melia to not tell anyone had been on the condition that nothing like this would happen again. But something *had* happened...and Amy knew she should have never made that promise to begin with. Still, she wanted to give Melia at least a little warning. "Uh, do you think I could talk to her first, Cari?"

"Okay. Let me go see if she's awake yet."

Amy heard footsteps, a door opening, and rustling noises. Then Melia's voice was on the other end.

"Hi, Amy." She sounded like she'd been crying.

"Hey, Melia," Amy replied softly. "Sounds like you had a rough night." When Melia didn't respond, Amy pressed on, trying to figure out how to get the girl to talk. Amy closed her eyes and breathed a quick prayer. "Melia, I don't know what happened, but obviously something did. Cari saw bruises on your arms last night." Amy heard Melia catch her breath. "And she has to call CPS this morning. I know you don't want to break up your family or get in trouble again, but enough is enough. You can't keep living this way." Amy paused to see if Melia would say anything, but she didn't. "Melia, I need you to tell Cari everything. You can trust her. She'll help you...Please, Melia. Do it for me."

The breathing on the other end grew louder and more ragged until it dissolved into sobs.

"Okay, Amy," Melia whimpered, and Amy could hear Cari comforting her.

After a few moments of listening to muffled noises, Amy spoke up. "I'm going to get off the phone now so you can talk to Cari, Melia. But you can call me at any time. I love you, and I'll be praying for you."

"Okay."

"And Melia...No matter what happens—to you, to your parents, whatever. Remember, none of this is your fault. Okay?"

"Okay."

The phone clicked, and Amy sat there staring out the window. The morning sky was dreary and gray, fitting her mood perfectly. *God, why?* she asked, too weary to give her complaints any more words. Something tickled her face, and she brushed it away only to discover that her cheeks were wet with tears.

Amy curled her knees up to her chest and rested her forehead against them. Her heart hurt with her own burdens from last night and even from last year, but all of that paled in comparison with what was going on with the special friend that God had brought into her life. She prayed for Melia's difficult conversation with Cari, that she would have no fear of being completely honest. She prayed that Cari would have just the words Melia needed to bring peace to her unpleasant world. She prayed for Cari's difficult conversation with CPS and prayed that they would handle the situation in a way that would help and not hurt Melia. She prayed for Melia's future; it looked so dim and troubled right now, but Amy begged God to protect her and bless her and give her a life full of happiness that she'd never known before.

After she had exhausted all thoughts for Melia, Amy also prayed for her relationship with Steven and for wisdom about what they should do now. She prayed that Steven would forgive her and understand that her hesitation wasn't a rejection. She prayed that they would figure out what was best for *both* of them. She prayed that his parents would be a source of support for him right now...and that they wouldn't hate her forever. And she prayed that she and Steven would be able to talk through all this...hopefully sooner rather than later. She thought of how unsettling her lack of closure with Jake had been and prayed that that wouldn't be a recurring theme in her life. Gradually, she found herself praying for Jake, too. Wherever his life had taken him, she prayed that God would keep pursuing him, that Jake would be overwhelmed with God's love for him, and that he would then be passionate about spreading that love to everyone around him at Louisville.

She had no idea how much time had passed, but when she next looked up, the sun had pierced through clouds in front of her, and a slender beam of light warmed her toes. She smiled and stretched and...was abruptly startled by her buzzing phone.

"Hello?" she answered without even looking at who was calling. While she hoped it was Steven, Cari's soothing voice was almost as nice.

"I just wanted you to know that we filed a formal report with CPS, and they supported our request to keep Melia with us. We don't know how long it will take for them to act on it, but Melia will be safe here."

"Thanks," Amy replied.

"No, thank you. You've done a lot for this girl, Amy, and we all appreciate it...God's got a great plan for your life, sweetie...Don't sell yourself short."

Amy hung up from their brief conversation feeling once again at peace with her actions the night before. Now, if she could only get Steven to understand.

4:38pm | From: Jake | To: Dad
We're going to the big dance!

ALTHOUGH IT WAS NEVER GOOD PRACTICE to celebrate after a defeat, Louisville's near victory over Syracuse in the final game of the Big East tournament did more than enough to ensure their spot in the NCAA tournament, and they just couldn't help it. The day following their three-point loss, the whole team gathered together in the coaches' office to watch the selection show on ESPN to see where they would end up in the sixty-five-team tournament. When Chris Berman announced that Louisville had earned the number six seed in the South bracket, the team roared in unison. Their opponent next Friday would be the eleventh-seeded Oregon Ducks, who had barely squeaked in from their fourth place finish in the Pac-10.

Jake breathed a sigh of relief as teammates high-fived all around him. *We did it!* But while their berth in the NCAA tournament was as much as he could hope for, life off the court could have definitely been better. As Grant had predicted that chilly night on the lonely basketball court a month ago, things had changed. Although none of the guys ever said anything aloud, they didn't have to—their actions spoke much louder than words. No one, not even Jake and Grant's summer roommate Nomis, acted normal around Grant anymore, and since Jake had allied himself with the pariah, they were weird around Jake, too.

As a result, Jake and Grant often found themselves on the outside of team activities, from pre-practice banter to post-practice dinners and hanging out and pretty much every other aspect of their former social lives. Even on the court things had changed—not enough for Coach to notice, but enough that they now had to work a lot harder just to get the ball. If any other guy was remotely open, their teammates naturally looked to the other guy first. Jake had called Nomis and Jamal on their behavior, but they just stared back at him and denied it.

The silent exclusion seemed to be taking its toll on Grant, but Jake was actually starting to appreciate it. Now that he was trying to get his life back on track the way he knew it should be, it helped to be free from all the distractions the basketball team had offered. Not partying with the guys left him more time—to do things like sleep, study, and read his Bible and pray. He'd even gone back to Buddy's church the last three Sundays. It wasn't anything like New Song, but Buddy was hard to beat. Jake loved being around him and hoped that maybe some of his infectious enthusiasm for life and God would rub off.

Tonight, Jake overheard most of the guys talking about heading downtown to continue their celebration. It stung that he and Grant were clearly not invited, but they had other plans anyway. Thanks to Jake's narrow victory in the park, Grant had reluctantly kept his end of the bargain, and tonight they were hanging out with Buddy. Grant had only two conditions: Jake had to buy his meal, and there was to be no talk about God. Grant may have hoped these were deal breakers, but Jake agreed without hesitation. He'd warned Buddy about the "rules" last Sunday, and Buddy's eyes had twinkled. Jake wondered if he had something up his sleeve.

"It's nice to meet you, Grant!" Buddy extended his hand as he slowly stood up from his seat in the waiting area of a local buffet. "I went and scouted out the salad bar for us. Wowee! It's going to be good tonight."

"It's nice to meet you, sir." Grant shook his hand, unable to keep up the scowl he had been wearing the entire drive over.

Buddy laughed and patted Grant on the back. "Call me Buddy. It's not like you're my limo driver." Buddy reached out and gave Jake a hug. "How are you, Jake?"

"We got great news today. We're officially in the NCAA tournament!"

A waitress approached to lead them to a table.

"Hi, sweetie!" Buddy greeted her. "I hope you're having a great day today! Do you have any crayons we could use?"

She looked back at him, not exactly thrilled by his enthusiasm or his juvenile request.

"My boys here just found out they're going to the NCAA tournament," he continued, giving her a little wink. "Maybe they could autograph their placemats if you'd like?"

The waitress gave Buddy and the boys an awkward smile. "Congratulations. I'll see what I can do."

Jake and Grant both turned red, and Grant's glance at Jake made it clear that he was regretting coming.

"Buddy, I'm pretty sure she doesn't care about our autographs," Jake whispered across the table after the waitress had left.

"Oh, I know." Buddy grinned. "They're really for one of the guys in my pinochle club. He's a diehard Cardinal fan, and I know he'll just be tickled pink! Well, I'd love to sit and chat, but that buffet is calling my name." Buddy scooted to the edge of his bench and waddled over to the food without wasting another moment.

Jake and Grant followed suit. They quickly filled their plates from the wide variety of steaming trays and returned to the table where a four-pack of waxy crayons awaited them. Buddy was nowhere to be seen. Jake looked around the restaurant, finally spotting him shaking hands with one of the employees and smiling gregariously. As Jake and Grant watched, Buddy proceeded to personally introduce himself to each of the servers and thank them for making supper. Some of them seemed taken aback by this guy encroaching into their personal space, but most lit up with a cheery smile.

"This guy is crazy," Grant chuckled, throwing a crouton in his mouth. "Have you told him...anything about me?"

"Oh, you mean like you're gay?" Jake bit off the top of a french fry and smiled. "Nah, he just knows that you're my roommate."

"Wow! Look at all this food!" Buddy hobbled up and set his half-filled plate of salad down on the table. "We've sure got a lot to be thankful for...Thank you, God!" he prayed with his eyes wide open, and then promptly took a bite of lettuce.

"You're pretty friendly out there," Jake ribbed him, stuffing his mouth with fried chicken.

"You know, I learned a long time ago that it doesn't take much to make someone's day." Buddy took another bite from his salad. "It's kind of like a glow ball, huh, Jake?"

Grant looked confused, so Jake jumped at the opportunity to explain. "That's Buddy's translation of a Bible verse we'd studied a few weeks ago."

"Oh," Grant cut him short. "Well, did you see you got your crayons?" He held up the box the waitress had left.

"Oh, wonderful!" Buddy gleamed, quickly rearranging their table to make a clearing for the extra paper placemat. "Could I get your John Hancock right here? Sign it to Bob. You too, Jake." Grant scrawled his signature and then passed the crayons to Jake. "So, tell me about yourself, Grant," Buddy asked, taking a big bite of beets.

Grant popped a meatball into his mouth and shot a quick glance at Jake. "I don't know. There's not much to say. I'm from a small town in South Texas, and I love to play basketball, I guess." Buddy reached across the table and stole a meatball off his plate. Grant cleared his throat accusatorily and watched the meatball make its way to Buddy's mouth.

"That's great, great..." Buddy nodded, chewing thoughtfully. "So, now I know where you're from and what you like to do. But I want to know who you *are*," he pressed, giving Grant a wink.

"Okay, uh..." Grant faltered, resting his fork on his plate. "I'm an art major...and I want to coach high school basketball someday."

"Wonderful. What else?"

Grant laid his fork down and folded his hands in front of him. After a few seconds of thought, he continued, "I'm the youngest of three brothers—a late surprise—and my dad left just after I was born. I guess I was the final straw." He chuckled under his breath. "My older brothers were always in trouble, constantly in and out of juvie. They never even finished high school. So my mom, she was always pretty hard on me growing up. She knew she couldn't control them, so I guess she just took it out on me. I love my mom, but I can't stand her either, you know?"

Buddy nodded as if he understood perfectly. Jake just listened quietly as he discovered a whole new side to his friend. They'd talked briefly about their parents, but neither of them had ever elaborated on their challenges with them. Now Jake realized that he'd never really cared or stopped to listen.

"That's tough," Buddy said softly, his eyes full of compassion. He hadn't taken a bite of food since Grant started opening up. "So what drew you to basketball?"

Grant chuckled. "In middle school, I had an early growth spurt. And what else is the tallest kid in school going to do? The more I played, the more I loved it. And it suddenly made me cool."

Now they were getting into familiar territory. Jake and Grant had talked plenty about how much they enjoyed escaping on the basketball court, and together they had done it plenty, too. Anticipating the conversation turning toward basketball topics, Jake was about to spit out Grant's impressive stats from their Cincinnati game four nights earlier when Grant came out with a shocker.

"I know you're like an elder in your church or something, but I guess I should just come out and say it. I'm also gay." Grant's eyes squinted as he waited for a response.

Jake held back a gasp. *Where did that come from?* He fidgeted, trying to figure out how to fix this quickly derailing dinner conversation. *Did they turn up the heat in here?* Jake felt drenched with sweat. He looked at Buddy, silently pleading with him not to say anything offensive. But Buddy didn't say anything at all. He simply nodded his head, just as he'd done throughout the entire conversation so far. He continued to fix his eyes on Grant.

"It's like I've been living two lives," Grant went on when nobody else did. "I was the homecoming king in high school. I had tons of friends. Girls were always flirting with me. But I don't know. I just wasn't interested. I felt...*different* inside, but I didn't know why, and I sure didn't want anyone to find out. So I put up this cocky, life-of-the-party front, but inside, I felt inadequate...never good enough...and completely alone, because I figured that if anyone ever found out the real me, then it would all come crashing down." Grant picked up his fork and pierced it through his last meatball. "Sorry to talk so much. I don't know what got into me."

"No. Don't be sorry. I appreciate you sharing all that with us," Buddy reassured him. His smile was warm and inviting. "I spent a lot of my life trying to be someone that everybody would like. It's a rough road to walk!" Buddy leaned back in his chair. "Can you relate to that at all, Jake?"

Jake nodded, still stunned at the direction this dinner had taken.

"But one day," Buddy shook his head, "after a really miserable week, I realized I couldn't live like that anymore. My marriage was suffering, I hated my job, and no matter how hard I tried, I couldn't get *everyone* to like me. So that day, I just stopped trying."

Grant and Jake had both leaned forward in their seats.

"What did you do?" Grant asked.

Buddy laughed, his eyes twinkling. "I could tell you, but I promised Jake I wouldn't." Instead, he opened up the box of crayons, wrote something on his placemat, and pushed it over to the guys.

Grant read it out loud. "Galatians 1:10? I don't get it."

"I think Jake's got a Bible that's been starting to get some exercise again." Buddy winked. "If you really want to know, why don't you guys read it together later tonight? The first sentence is the question that changed my life."

Jake glanced over to Grant, surprised to find him nodding along.

"How about we all meet up here again after you guys win the national championship and talk about this stuff some more?" Buddy asked.

Jake waited for his friend's response.

"I'd like that," Grant replied.

"Wonderful!" Buddy grinned and then glanced over at the buffet stations. "I only grabbed a salad to start, so I've gotta go get my money's worth, if you don't mind."

Three more platefuls and an hour later, Jake and Grant finally bid goodbye to their dinner date and returned to their apartment with stuffed stomachs and a Bible verse to look up. Jake grabbed his Bible and flipped to Galatians, then handed it off to Grant to read.

"Am I now trying to win the approval of men, or of God?" Grant read. He paused and looked up at Jake. "Jake…I can see how something like this could be inspiring to someone like you or Buddy…But what does this mean for a guy like me?"

Jake looked back at him, searching for an answer. *God?* he pleaded silently. "I don't know, man. But you've got to admit that trying to win the approval of man sure hasn't been working very well."

They both laughed softly at the grand understatement there.

“Every Christian I’ve ever known has made me feel bad about myself,” Grant said quietly. “Why would God be any different?”

“God tends to do things a lot better than the rest of us,” Jake shrugged. “It can’t hurt to give—”

“I’m not sure if I’m there yet, bro,” Grant interrupted. “But let’s just say I’ll give *you* a chance.” He smiled, stood up, and stretched.

Still weirded out a little by the whole gay thing, Jake was ready to simply shake hands and call it a deal. But something inside him practically shouted that he needed to do something more. Before he knew what he was doing, Jake jumped up and tackled his friend in a huge bear hug. “I hope I don’t let you down,” he mumbled.

1:37pm | From: Grant | To: Jake
Let's get ready to rumbllllle!

ALTHOUGH HIS ROOMMATE was sitting right next to him during the entire flight to Houston, as soon as the stewardess announced it was okay to use cellular devices, Jake's phone buzzed the incoming message.

"Dude, you excited or something?" Jake nudged Grant with his elbow.

"What do you think?" Grant grinned.

Jake had to admit that he too could already feel the adrenaline of excitement pumping through his veins. Ever since he could remember, he had dreamed of playing in the NCAA March Madness tournament. He used to lie on his living room floor watching all the games, picturing himself in the shoes of the players on TV. And now here he was, less than forty-eight hours away from living out that dream. It was exhilarating.

True to its name, March Madness was a little crazy. Unless you were a basketball lover—and then it was paradise. Sixty-five teams fought ruthlessly for the esteemed grand prize: the national championship. Each round was single elimination, meaning that when a team lost, they were done for good. Every game was go hard or go home, and no one wanted to go home. Yet even the lowest-ranked team was a mere six wins away from the title, and Cinderella stories cropped up everywhere. Louisville was ranked right in the middle of all the hype: As a middle seed, no one expected them to do much, but they had a good chance of sticking around for a while.

The first round of the tournament was non-stop action: thirty-two games played in eight different cities in just two days. Louisville had drawn game two on day two in Houston—which meant that Jake and his teammates had plenty of time to scout out their possible future opponents. But Jake would have much rather just gotten it over with. He watched each game with increasing agitation, the butterflies in his stomach multiplying with every other team's win or loss. He knew his team had put in hundreds of hours of practice this season, and he was ready to see whether or not that would be enough.

After a restless night's sleep, Jake couldn't stop fidgeting while watching ESPN the next morning in the hotel room. He tried to read his Bible but couldn't concentrate much on that either. When the team met for a late brunch, he could barely swallow down a protein bar, and he waited with jitters until they finally arrived on the court to warm up. The game before theirs went into overtime. Jake sat on the sidelines as the rest of the guys joked around, staring up at the nearly full stands, twirling a ball in his fingers. The feel of the bumpy leather in his palm, the power with which it recoiled from the glossy wood flooring into his hand, the whooshing sound it made as he snapped a pass to Grant...the comforting familiarity of this one consistent thing in his life set Jake at ease again. He inhaled the dry air of the gym and focused on the task at hand. Although he knew he wouldn't enter the action for a while, he was ready to go when his team needed him.

From the moment the ref tossed up the opening tipoff, the game was off and running. Oregon was a scrappy team that focused on offense and loved to push the ball up the court in a hurry. What they lacked in size, they more than made up for with speed. And although Louisville was the easy favorite in this opening-round matchup, Coach had warned his reserves that they might see action earlier in the game if the pace was as quick as anticipated. Five minutes in and the Ducks showed no sign of slacking. Nate tried to slow down the pace every time he got the ball, but Oregon's full-court press and long outlet passes up the court carried them to an early seven-point lead. And sure enough, Grant was sent in at an early timeout to relieve Bojan, who complained of a muscle cramp. Less than a minute later, Jake was directed to give Nate a breather.

The two roommates immediately set to work to make their presence felt. Jake loved the fast-paced play—it reminded him of his summer in New York—and he used his fresh legs to put the pressure on his Oregon opponent. In the next five minutes of play, Jake had two steals, three baskets, and a handful of assists. When Nate was finally sent back in, the Oregon lead had been cut to one.

Jake continued his fervor from the bench, cheering loudly as Nomis skied high to break up a full-court pass to a streaking Oregon guard. He immediately flung the ball down to Nate on the other side of the court, who charged the basket fearlessly. Two Oregon big men jumped up to meet him in the air, swatting the ball away and knocking Nate hard to the floor. The referee blew his whistle for the foul, earning Nate two free throws, but when the star point guard heaved himself up to his feet, his left ankle buckled, and he toppled to the floor again. While the trainer ran out to assist the injured player, Coach looked at Jake and signaled him to check in.

This is it. Jake breathed in sharply. *God, help me not to screw up.*

5:32pm | From: Cari | To: Amy
Turn on CBS right now!!!

Amy looked at her phone buzzing on her desk and ignored it. She already had a billion things on her to-do list, not the least of which included studying for her quarter finals. This term's exams were going to seriously kick her butt if she didn't figure out how to concentrate quickly. But that focus kept eluding her.

In the week since her dinner debacle with Steven, they still hadn't talked except for a few brief, strained phone calls that *she* had initiated. And while Steven had yet to officially break up with her, his lack of interest or response sure seemed to indicate that they were headed in that direction—which was a horrible position to be in while attempting to study for difficult tests! Even now, Amy caught herself on the verge of tears. *Why couldn't you just have said yes?* she berated herself. *Would it have been so hard to just enjoy the moment and discuss the details later?* In spite of Cari's encouragement, this was the line of thought she found herself traveling down lately. *I mean, what are the chances I'll ever find another guy like him? God dropped him into my lap, and I just took him for granted and tossed him away.*

Amy gazed out into the darkness beyond her window, her heart aching with rejection and regret. *Ah! Amy, you can't do this to yourself!* Willing herself to focus, she swatted at the teardrops resting on her cheeks and stared down at the textbook sitting unread underneath her elbows. But no matter how forcefully her eyes bored into the words on the page, all she could see was Steven's disappointed face when she couldn't give him the answer that he expected. Then, the hurt in his eyes morphed into memories of times when his smile lit up the room. He was such a great guy. *So why won't he call me back?* Her fingers twiddled with her cell phone, pleading with the screen to light up and announce that he wanted to talk to her. But it remained blank.

As Amy picked up the silent phone for the umpteenth time, she read Cari's text again. What could be that important on TV? *It couldn't hurt to just check it out for a few minutes,* she rationalized. It wasn't as if she was getting anything done just staring at her book. And Renee was studying in the library, so it wasn't as if Amy would be distracting anyone else.

Before she could convince herself not to, she stretched over to Renee's desk and grabbed the remote. She pressed the power button and scrolled through the channels until she found CBS, expecting Oprah or Dr. Phil or someone else to be talking about dealing with breakups or finding true love or something ridiculous like that. What she saw instead caused her heart to freeze: There on the screen in front of her was Jake Taylor's face, larger than life...and cuter than ever.

Amy quickly turned up the volume, just in time to hear the announcer rehash the injury to Louisville's starting point guard, Nate Williams, and the pressure that would fall on his backup, sophomore Jake Taylor. She gasped as the camera zoomed in on Jake walking onto the court as the trainer and assistant coaches helped his teammate to the sidelines. Jake jumped up and down, his face a stoic mask of extreme concentration. She had seen this look so many times before in high school, but it never seemed as serious as it did now on national television.

Although she and Jake hadn't talked for over a year, Amy's emotions immediately revved up at the sight of her ex-boyfriend. He was living out his dream, and she was proud of him. The players on the court lined up at the free-throw line, and Jake stepped up to shoot Nate's shots. *Oh my gosh, Jake, you can do this.* Amy's heart felt as if it had stopped beating as she watched him methodically bounce the ball three times, focus on the back of the rim, and fluidly bring the ball up to its release.

Swish.

Amy breathed again. Jake had just tied up the game. He stepped back from the line and then went into his routine for the second shot. Again, swish. Amy smiled—he was good. There was no chance she'd be able to focus on studying now, so Amy gave in and pulled her comforter and pillow off her bed and plopped down on the floor in front of the TV. "Let's go, Jake," she said, aloud this time, as he faded back to half court to pick up his man on defense.

She had seen him play more games than she could remember at Pacific High, but this was different; this was Division One basketball—and here Jake was, right in the middle of the action. It was amazing! Jake tipped a pass from the Oregon guard directly into the hands of the teammate who had hit on her at that fateful party—Amy thought she remembered his name being Jamal. Without hesitation, Jake sprinted down the middle of the court like a wide receiver. Jamal heaved the ball like a quarterback right into Jake's hands for a wide-open layup.

"Yes!" Amy screamed, not caring if anyone heard her.

Again, Jake spun around on defense, and the game went back and forth, back and forth, neither team able to pull ahead on the scoreboard. The first half wound down with Louisville up by a single basket. As halftime dragged on, Amy stood up and paced around her room, wishing they'd get back to the game. Her stomach was in knots with nerves for Jake. She couldn't wait to see him out there again.

Finally, the players stepped back onto the court, and Jake looked more determined than ever. A teammate inbounded the ball to him, and he brought it up the court. Amy watched, enthralled, as her former boyfriend of four years and the father of her child raced past his defender into the front court and darted straight to the basket. The defense converged on him, leaving one of his teammates wide open in the corner.

"Swish!" Amy cheered, throwing her arm into the air the way she did in her cheerleading days.

Amy remembered one of the times they were hanging out in the back of Jake's truck, and he explained to her what an amazing feeling it was to be in the zone—when all the distractions around you faded into an unimportant blur, when everyone else on the court seemed to be running in slow motion and the basket felt twice as big as normal, when you felt unstoppable. As Amy watched Jake tonight, she could tell—he was absolutely in his zone. The confidence in his eyes was unmistakable, and his reflexes were sharp. This was what Jake lived for.

"Yes!" Amy celebrated under her breath, as he knocked down a three-pointer at the top of the key. A minute later, he knocked down another three and then another one after that.

The commentators couldn't get enough of this on-fire guard from Oceanside, California, who was carrying his team on his back. They talked incessantly about the poise with which he'd taken over this game and the intensity with which he was leading the Cardinals on to victory. They joked that it was almost as if the rest of his teammates were waiting to see what Jake Taylor would do next. Amy listened to all this and swelled with pride. Not that she'd had any part in his life recently, but she couldn't help but be elated for him.

Jamal missed a wide-open jumper, but Jake leaped above the much taller defenders to put the rebound back in. *How many points is that now?* Twenty-one, the commentators answered her promptly. Back on the defensive end, Jake drew a charging foul, causing the Oregon coach to call a timeout. Before cutting to a commercial, the announcers posted the game clock. With six minutes left to play, Louisville held a fragile five-point lead.

"Come on, Jake," Amy whispered, closing her eyes and praying for him during the break.

The game came back on, and Jake kept going strong, but the rest of his team seemed to be fading. An Oregon player had just sunk a three, when a hand tapped Amy on the shoulder, startling her so much that she screamed. There behind her stood Steven, looking a bit worse for wear. His week-old beard looked far less stylish than normal, and his eyes were red and puffy.

"Oh, hey, Steven!" Amy gasped. Apparently, she'd been so wrapped up in the game that she'd never heard him calling or knocking on the door.

"What are you doing?" he asked, glancing at the open book on her desk and the basketball game on the TV.

"I'm, uh, just taking a short break," she faltered, obviously unable to explain that she was actually mesmerized by her ex-boyfriend's basketball skills—currently being broadcast across the nation—and she couldn't study if her life depended on it. "You want to watch with me?" Amy half-heartedly offered, patting the floor next to her. With less than five minutes to go, Jake and his teammates needed her full attention.

"Actually, I'd like to talk about our future," Steven replied, stepping in front of the screen to turn the volume all the way down just as Jake released another three-pointer from the corner.

"Ah!" The little yell escaped impulsively, as Amy dipped her head to see what had happened to her ex-boyfriend's shot. Through Steven's legs, she managed to see it fall perfectly through the net. "Yes!" she sighed, and tried to fix her attention on her current boyfriend.

"Amy, what's going on?" Steven looked down at her and crossed his arms. "You've been pestering me all week to talk, and now that I'm ready, you can't stop watching some stupid basketball game?"

He had a point. An hour earlier, this much-needed conversation was all that she could think about. But now, as she tried to recall her list of questions, her mind was completely blank. Steven had waited this long to talk. Couldn't he wait like fifteen more minutes? Amy opened her mouth, but no words came out. Finally she croaked out a quiet, "I'm sorry," and looked at Steven. He seemed so dejected and broken, and she wished she knew what to say to make things better.

"I'm sorry, too," he whispered. "I'm sorry I've been so...distant all week. It's just...Well, what did you expect when you rejected me?"

"Steven," Amy pleaded. "I didn't mean to reject you. Your proposal just took me off guard and—"

"But you know how much I love you, Amy. That shouldn't have come as a surprise." His voice barely hid his bitterness.

"I know," Amy groaned. "But loving me and expecting me to move all the way across the country are two very different things, Steven."

"But I just assumed you'd *want* to be with me...I mean, I can't imagine life without you...and I guess I thought you felt the same way about me."

He shifted his weight, giving Amy a clear view of the TV again, and she couldn't help but glance at the screen—just in time to see Oregon tie up the game with just over three minutes left to play. An involuntary gasp escaped her throat.

Irritated, Steven turned to see what was capturing his girlfriend's attention—just as the camera zoomed in on Jake as he walked to the sideline for a Louisville timeout. His name and stats appeared in a bar at the bottom of the screen. Steven's eyes shot open. "Amy! Is that *your* Jake Taylor?" he cried out.

Amy cringed and nodded her head.

"So, *I* asked you to marry me a week ago, but today you're more interested in a guy who dumped you and never looked back?...I think I'm starting to understand."

"Steven, I'm sorry," she whimpered and promptly shut the television off, but it was obviously too late.

"Maybe you're not the girl I thought you were," Steven muttered under his breath.

Amy felt the wind being knocked out of her, but something still gave her strength to fight back. "Who did you think I was, Steven?" she asked pointedly. "Did you think I was a girl without any ambitions of my own? A girl who wouldn't mind leaving my family behind—a family I'm just barely getting to know? Is that the kind of girl you want?"

Steven took a few steps over and sank to sit on her bed. He stared at the carpet underneath his feet. "I guess I just thought our relationship was worth it...But I guess I thought wrong."

"Ugh!" Amy exploded. "You men are all the same! Why is it always about you? Isn't our relationship worth you staying out here to wait for me to graduate?"

"Oh, don't lump me with that jerk!" Steven said, pointing toward the television. "I want to marry you, not just get you knocked up and leave! Don't you realize how great it would be for us to live in New York City? The Manhattan School of Music is one of the best programs in the country. It's my dream!"

"Well, Stanford is *my* dream," Amy countered, amazed by how similar this was to the conflict she'd had with Jake.

Steven stood up and wandered toward the door. "Then I guess we both need to figure out what we really want," he said quietly. He looked at her one last time and then turned and walked silently out the door.

Amy watched him go and said nothing. She wasn't sure if this was the end of their relationship or just the first major disagreement they'd have to work through. She hoped for the latter but didn't feel like dealing with the struggle. Emotionally exhausted, she collapsed onto the floor. *God, what are You doing right now? What do You want from me?*

Unsurprisingly, the heavens did not open up with an audible response. But Amy did start thinking about the game again. Although it seemed like the last thing she should be doing in her situation, she rolled over and flipped the television back on. She knew the game was obviously over by now, but at least she could find out who won.

As the screen came to life, who else should be standing there talking to a reporter but Jake? Amy's eyes were glued to his face, and she quickly bumped up the volume.

"You scored twenty-nine points and had eleven assists, almost all in the second half. And you pulled your team to a nail-biter two-point victory. America is asking, who is this Jake Taylor?" The female reporter smiled and tilted the microphone into his face.

Jake laughed, still panting and dripping with sweat. "I don't know what got into me today." He grinned. "But win or lose, I give God all the praise."

The reporter smiled curtly and asked Jake a few more questions before he ran off toward the locker room with the rest of his team. But Amy heard nothing else. That one line stuck in her head, and she stared at him, noticing a familiar spark in his eyes. An image of him holding her hand and praying her through Emily's delivery flashed into her mind. Her heart fluttered. She mechanically clicked the television off once again and closed her eyes. *Seriously, God?*

9:56pm | From: Mom | To: Jake
I'm soooooo proud of you honey!

9:56pm | From: Chris | To: Jake
Don't forget us little people when you go pro "J"

9:57pm | From: Nicole | To: Jake
I miss you. Wanna get coffee when you come back? You were soooo hot out there 2nite.

9:57pm | From: Dad | To: Jake
You think Nate's ankle will still be busted next game? Lucky for you.

9:59pm | From: Doug | To: Jake
Matt and I just saw you ballin. It's been a while. We should hang out over summer.

10:02pm | From: Andrea | To: Jake
My dad said you had a great game. Woohoo! Pichew pichew!

10:24pm | From: Amy | To: Jake
I watched your game. Just wanted to say congratulations Jake.

AFTER THE USUAL POST-GAME ROUTINE with his team—and then another bunch of interviews from newspapers he'd never even heard of—Jake finally made his way up to the hotel room just before midnight. Thanks to their win, Louisville had another game in two days, and he was wiped. He waited for the green light to blink on the door handle and then pushed it open to find Grant sprawled out on his bed watching ESPN highlights.

"You're all over the show tonight," Grant grinned, tossing an empty water bottle at Jake's head. "It's like you're famous, man."

"Whatever," Jake tried to downplay his success, but he couldn't hide his smile. The truth was, the whole game still felt surreal. Had that really been him out on the court, knocking down just about every shot he took...in front of millions of viewers? That was the kind of performance he'd fantasized about since childhood. Was it possible that he had actually done it in reality? Ridiculous! He couldn't wipe the giddy look off his face.

But he also understood the reality that by the next game, Nate's ankle would probably be healed enough to play. And then Jake would quickly go back to being the same old guy off the bench that no one really cared about. *Oh well!* he grinned. *Might as well just enjoy the moment.*

He dropped his duffel bag on the floor by his bed and pulled out his cell phone, flopping onto the soft mattress and scrolling through all the messages. He smiled at Chris's and his mom's, and scowled when he read Nicole's. *Typical!* Jake deleted it without a second thought. His dad's was...well, typical, too. Doug's was unexpected. But in spite of how their senior year had ended, he kind of looked forward to reconnecting with those guys. Andrea's made him chuckle...and then Jake saw the next one and froze.

His hands started to tremble as he read and reread and then reread again the short message from Amy.

"You okay, man?" Grant's voice invaded his thoughts from the other side of the room.

Jake laid his phone down to stop his hand from shaking and looked over at his roommate. "Uh, yeah. I'm cool." But the truth was he was anything *but* cool. He suddenly felt feverish, and sweat oozed out of his pores. He had just maintained composure in the biggest basketball game of his life, and yet this simple little text message had him spinning.

Jake immediately hit "reply" to Amy's text. But when the blank screen popped up, he stared, paralyzed, searching his brain for the perfect words to say in 160 characters or less. *What do you say to someone you haven't talked to in over a year?* And not just someone...

Amy was the mother of his child, the only girl he had ever loved, the brightest thing in his life. And he hadn't just *not* talked to her...His last words to her had been cruel and spiteful, he'd left her to fend for herself while he got high, and then he'd immediately fallen prey to that slut Nicole. What *could* he say in a short text message that could even come close to making up for all the ways he had let her down?

Jake canceled the text and dropped his phone at his side. He heaved himself up off the bed and walked toward the door.

"Hey. Wait. Where are you going?" Grant called after him.

"I need some fresh air," Jake muttered and rushed out of the room.

His head was spinning mercilessly, all the wrongs he'd done over the past year surfacing to the front of his memory. *God,* he cried silently as he crashed through double doors into the cool night air and jogged down the street. *I am so sorry! I have screwed up in so many ways, and I'm ready, really ready, to make it right. I don't want to mess around anymore...I don't know why Amy texted me. I'm sure it's no big deal. But if there is any hint of a spark left at all, God, then please help me to do what it takes to fan it back to life. I love her, God. I really love her. I don't deserve her, but I'd love another chance. Please help me...*

Out of sight of the hotel, Jake realized he should probably turn around and run back. The chilly air cleared his head, and he started to smile. He had just had the best game of his life...and Amy had texted him. What a great day! He started to compose a note to her in his head, and the words strung together like pearls. Jake raced up the stairs to his room and grabbed his phone, where several more text messages awaited him. Ignoring them, he immediately booted up his laptop, went to Facebook and searched for Amy's name. There shone her radiant face, next to guitar boy, of course. Maybe guitar boy was a great guy and deserved Amy more than he did. As long as Amy was happy, Jake knew that was enough. But that wasn't going to stop him from sharing his heart with her.

"You writing to your fan club?" Grant chuckled.

"Yeah, something like that," Jake laughed. He clicked on "Send Amy a Message" and just started writing.

New Message

To: Amy Briggs x

Subject: Thanks!

Message

Hi Amy, Thanks for the text.

This might not make a lot of sense but I just felt like I needed to write you tonight. I guess, as you know, today was a really good day for me. I've dreamed of moments like this forever, but I don't know. Now that I'm here, it feels a little empty. I'm surrounded by people who suddenly want to talk to me, but will these people even remember my name tomorrow?

But then I got your text, and I don't even know how to explain it. I guess I never imagined being here in this moment and not being able to celebrate it with you. It's like incomplete or something.

Attach: Send Cancel

Jake had never been that great at typing, but his fingers seemed to fly across the keyboard tonight as he tried to keep up with the tidal wave of thoughts surging to the front of his brain.

Message

I don't know how to say it any other way but I'm so sorry. I'm sorry for being a lousy boyfriend, and treating you so horribly. I'm sorry for not finding you a better place to stay, and for not taking you home, and for not giving you a ride back to the airport. I'm sorry for being all over you that week, and for pressuring you in ways that we both knew were wrong.

Jake leaned back against the headboard of his bed for a minute. He knew that this was bigger than just him being a lousy boyfriend. Somehow his relationship with God was right in the middle of it all. His fingers went back to work.

Message

I'm sorry I wasn't a better example of a Christian. To be honest, college hasn't been so good for me and God. I'm embarrassed to say that even after all that happened with Roger and Jonny, and with Chris's friendship, I somehow let it all slip away. But lately I've been hanging out with this really cool guy named Buddy and he's getting me back to where I was before. I remember I used to pray every night that you would accept God like I had, and now you could probably run spiritual circles around me. I'm really proud of you.

Jake paused again and read through what he'd written so far. He was pretty sure that this was the longest letter he'd ever written in his life, but he wasn't finished yet.

Message

I'm also really sorry for not supporting you in pursuing your dreams like you did for me. I don't know what happened. You bent over backwards to support me, but the moment you had a dream of your own, I freaked out. That's so lame! I'm sorry I expected you to go to Louisville just because that's what I wanted, and for not celebrating with you when you decided to go to Stanford. You are so awesome, and again, I'm so proud of you.

I guess the bottom line is I'm sorry for taking you for granted. I know it's probably too late, but I just wanted to get all this stuff off my chest.

I'm going to be home for most of the summer, and it would really be great to see you.

Love, Jake ☺

He debated ending with the "love," feeling a little like a third-grader anguishing over a silly note. But in the end he left it. She could think what she wanted. The truth was, he really did care about her, and it was about time that he let her know. He took a deep breath and clicked the "send" button before he could change his mind. What a day!

Jake set his phone on the end table and got ready for bed. Sinking his head down into the fluffy pillow, he yawned and ran through his list of evening prayers. After saying goodnight to God, he closed his eyes and drifted off to the most peaceful sleep he'd enjoyed for a while.

Two hours later, Amy closed her Ethics book and stood up to stretch, weary but well-studied. She opened up her Facebook account to quickly update her status: Amy Briggs is... "Ready to ace my finals." Somehow, she had managed to maintain super concentration despite all the earlier interruptions, and she smiled. Life was okay.

She had no intention of getting distracted, but Amy couldn't help but notice that she had one new message. She clicked on the icon and immediately got a chill up her spine: The message was from Jake. Her eyes scanned it slowly line by line and then went back up to the top to read it again. She tried to quell the ferocious beating of her heart, but it was useless. She felt as if she had just turned over a new chapter in her life—but the first page of that chapter was blank...and she held the pen.

Not wanting to sound desperate, she was tempted to shut the computer down before she had a chance to reply. But Jake had poured out his heart and Amy figured she owed him a response. She took a deep breath and clicked the "reply" button.

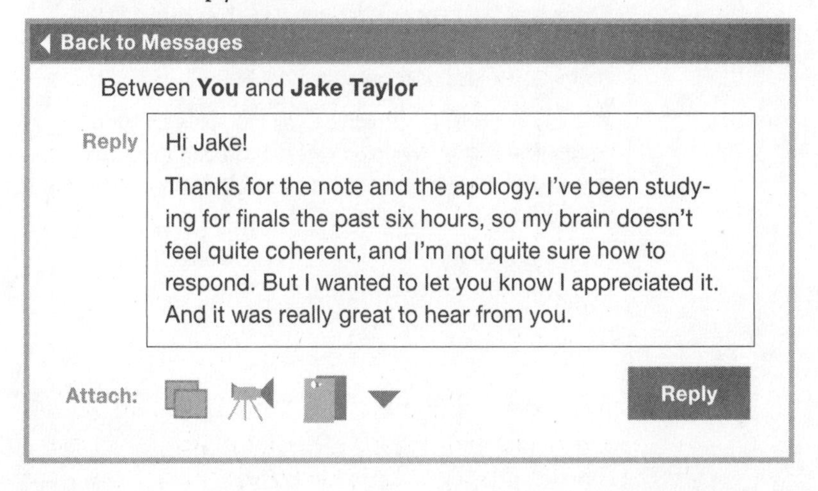
Back to Messages

Between **You** and **Jake Taylor**

Reply

Hi Jake!

Thanks for the note and the apology. I've been studying for finals the past six hours, so my brain doesn't feel quite coherent, and I'm not quite sure how to respond. But I wanted to let you know I appreciated it. And it was really great to hear from you.

Attach:

Reply

Amy reread her opening lines and took a deep breath, trying to figure out what to say next. As wonderful as it felt to finally communicate with Jake, she was practically engaged—or at least could have been. Her emotions battled within her mind. *What are you doing, Amy? What about Steven!...But...*She cut her thoughts short, not wanting to even entertain the idea that this ironic timing could be a second chance with Jake. *I don't know, God! What do You want me to do?* She allowed her fingers to start writing again, hoping they would not betray her.

◀Back to Messages

Between **You** and **Jake Taylor**

Reply

Your note comes at an interesting time for me, Jake. Let's just say, things are a bit complicated. So while I'm totally grateful for your kind words, and yes, I do forgive you—for everything—I'm not quite sure where to go from here.

This past year has been a crazy, amazing time of self-discovery for me. For the first time in my life, I think I'm starting to understand who I really am, and who God maybe made me to be. I'm learning that my past doesn't have to define who I am anymore, and even crazier, that God can redeem my junk to actually be a blessing to others. I don't know how to explain it, but it feels like the old, insecure, people-pleasing me has been shattered into like a bazillion pieces, and one by one—with the help of some amazing people around me—I'm getting to put myself together again. I guess this sounds kind of overly dramatic. But it's been soooooo good.

Anyway, I'm still in the middle of all that, plus an added twist just unfolded this past week. So I need to resolve some other things right now. But I would like to catch up with you.

I'm praying for you.

Amy

Attach: Reply

Amy sat back and sighed, her finger still hovering over the mouse. She thought of Steven and his proposal. *What would he say if he read this?* she worried. But then, almost unwillingly, Steven's face melted into Jake's, and Amy's heart skipped a little. *God, I don't even know what I want!*

She scanned back over the lines, carefully checking each sentence for the right words and tone. After reading it through three times, Amy stretched her back and neck and called it quits. *God, please, guide us both, and help us follow Your plan—not ours.*

She took a deep breath and hit "send."

Wait! No! She had forgotten the one thing she most wanted to say. *Just say it,* she thought.

She wrote a new message and hit "send" without hesitation:

New Message

To: Jake Taylor x

Subject:

Message

Oh, and yes, of course I'll see you in June ☺

Amy

Attach: Send Cancel

To Save A Life is available on DVD for home use.>>

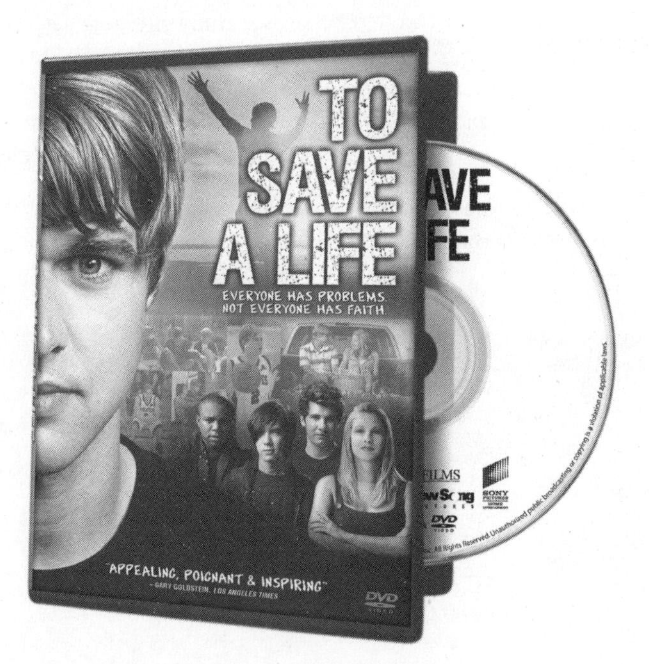

The home-use DVD includes these special features:

- Deleted Scenes
- Music Videos ("Bounce" by J-Rus & "Sunset Cliffs" by Paul Wright)
- Commentary
- Gag reel
- Behind the Scenes feature

NOTE: To Save A Life is rated PG-13 for realistic topics that may not be suitable for younger viewers.

Retail DVDs are only for use in your home–if you plan to show it in another location, you'll need a *To Save A Life* movie license. Visit OutreachFilms.com for details on showing it to your group.

Look for the these resources at your local Christian bookstore or visit **Outreach.com** for bulk quantities!

Through Jake's journey, readers are challenged to answer the question—what's your life going to be about?

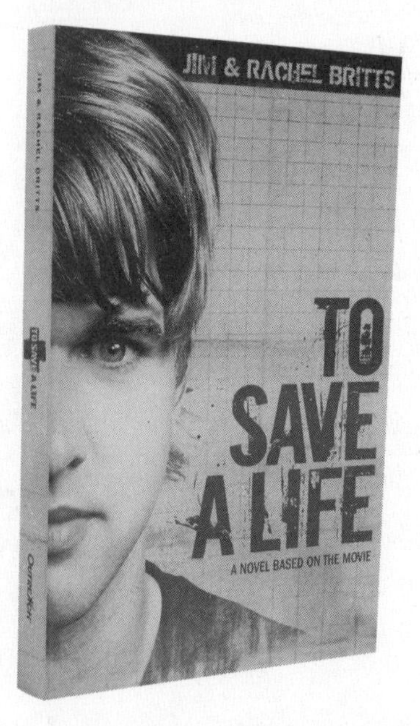

JAKE AND ROGER GREW UP AS BEST FRIENDS. Then, in high school, Jake becomes a star athlete who has it all: a college scholarship and the perfect girl, an ideal life that comes at the exclusion of his childhood friend. Roger, who no longer is in Jake's circle of friends, is tired of always being pushed aside and makes a tragic move, causing Jake's world to spin out of control. As Jake searches for answers, he begins a journey that will change his life forever.

To Save A Life is a story about real-life challenges and hard choices. For anyone who has struggled with regret, loneliness or pain, it is a story of hope. For all of us, *To Save A Life* is an inspirational story about living a life of significance.